MASTERPLAYER

Shakespeare & Elizabeth

Mathew Bridle

2021

Dedication

To anyone who loves history and does not object to
artistic licence

Acknowledgements

Thanks to everyone who helped in the shaping of this novel. To my friends in Horsham Writers Circle, Gaynor Hollis for multiple test reads, Lesley Hart of Author's Pen for copy and proof editing, and to Ginny Monroe for the original concept.

I would also like to thank the Globe Theatre, the Tower of London archives, and the researchers at Academy.edu for sharing their knowledge with me.

This is a work of fiction. Some events have been sequenced differently for storytelling purposes.

1588

THE BATTLE OF GRAVELINES

PLYMOUTH

Day One

'Mother of God.' The lookout stared ashen faced as a plague of sails spread along the horizon. An ill wind whipped his dark hair about his face, lashing him into action. Snatching up a stake, he thrust its linen wrapped head into a jar of flaming oil. With a glance toward the blistering sickness on the Channel, he lowered the dripping torch into the brazier and set the Lizard beacon ablaze. A second fire raged further along the coast, chased by a third and fourth, on and on until the warning came in sight of Plymouth.

A wan sun warmed the sea with a tepid hand reflecting the mood of the walled-up citizens. Church bells rang, not to call the faithful to heel but to summon the captain-at-arms. Cannons grated on iron wheels to peer out and espy the invading Spaniards.

'My lord, the beacons are ablaze to the south and west. Our enemy approaches,' Captain Hawkins stood with his helmet tucked beneath his arm, his back straight, awaiting instruction.

'So be it,' Sir Francis tugged at his beard, refining its point. 'We have yet time. We cannot force the tide to our favour,' Drake looked to the sky. 'No rush. With this wind they will be on us in a couple of hours. If Walsingham is right, and he usually is, they will pass us by. It is Parma they seek and his army. It will be our job to harry them and sink as many as we can.'

Captain Hawkins waited for Sir Francis to finish straightening his clothing before they walked out of the town into the sheltered anchorage of the Plym where the fleet awaited the embrace of the waves. With the sun on their backs, they boarded the launch and took up their seats as they were rowed across the estuary to the Swallow.

'Any plans forming in that dastardly mind of yours you'd care to share?' Hawkins looked up at his vessel. The Swallow rolled on the turning tide.

'Follow my lead and watch for signal,' Drake smiled. 'Trust me, we'll have fun.'

Richard Hawkins reached for the rope ladder and climbed aboard. He strode across the deck to the other side where Sir Francis' ship, Revenge, sat poised to strike.

'With the wind to our backs we will have them!' Hawkins cried to all who had an ear to hear. 'They shall rue the day they festered our waters.'

THE ARMADA

Day Two

The afternoon sun scurried behind darkening clouds as the war front scourged the English coast. The invincible Armada rolled on turgid seas, their guns belching fire and ruin at the coastal villages.

Aboard the San Martin the confident Duke of Medina Sidonia sat at his dining table sucking oysters from their shells as the guns fell silent. The song of the ocean against the hull took up the battle cry as the mighty Armada of one hundred and thirty ships rode the seas to war. Unmolested the Spaniards sailed forth into the night.

'My good men,' Sidonia raised a crystal glass. 'In a few days we will tear the barren whore from the throne and raise the flag of Spain on the bloody towers of London.' Wine sloshed from bottle to glass, marinating the captain's banquet. 'To Felipe, our King, and the victory of our God!'

'To Felipe and to God!' roared the officers as the miles cruised beneath their hulls.

The door to the captain's cabin burst open. 'The English are at our tails. The rear of the fleet is under fire.'

The messenger held the door as the officers threw the remains of their breakfast wine down their throats and surged onto the deck. The unmistakable sound of cannon fire sobered the Duke's mind.

'Fetch an eyeglass,' Sidonia stood at the poop rail with his hands folded behind his back, counting the shots of the English. 'Their guns,' Sidonia took the telescope from the captain, raising it to his eye. Through the curved ranks of the inner fleet where the supplies and settlers sat, encircled by the greatest warships the Spanish had ever constructed, the flash of cannon fire was closing in. 'Can you hear them? They sound different.'

'Our man in London reports the pirate Raleigh,' Mendoza spat on the deck, 'has refitted his ships, they are strong and swift. We too adapt the merchants. But unlike us, they have no God.'

'You speak the truth, my Captain. True and loyal, one in whom I can trust,' Sidonia hugged Mendoza with the strength of a younger man. 'Ensure the guns are primed and powder is kept dry. We cannot lose this war; the Holy Father has given us his blessing.'

The afternoon darkened into evening, bringing a strong wind to hurl the ocean at the Armada. Cannon fire continued into the dark hours, the bright thunder-flash marking the passage of their enemy.

'What losses?' Sidonia looked up from his map with a raised eyebrow.

'One: the San Salvador sank off Portland. Some of the smaller ships are damaged. The English shot passed right through a slave vessel; some cargo was lost but none of the men. One ship burns but will be out soon.'

Mendoza lifted a slice of salt beef from the platter waving it before his commander. Sidonia brushed it aside smiling as he swilled his wine around the glass.

'Makes me think,' Sidonia refilled his glass. 'The English pigs harass us all day and now leave us in this hole ...,' Sidonia blew out his cheeks. 'Gravelines ... who would name a place such? Why? We are going nowhere. Speaking of swine, where is Parma?'

Mendoza adjusted his ruff and coughed into the back of his hand. 'He gives apology. He says he only has twenty ships and none of them worthy enough to assist you.' The captain stood with his hands together as though cradling his stomach.

'Pompous mule!' Sidonia banged his fist on the table, upsetting his wine. 'The King's cousin thinks he is too good to serve me. He will see we do not need his ships. We will rout the English peasants ourselves. Come morning the seas will run red with the blood of the whore's men. I will press my foot to the neck of my enemy and gut their admiral myself.'

Sidonia unfurled a map of the channel before ramming a dagger through one corner to keep it open. An incandescent light flickered upon the name of Calais, scattered by candlelight from the jewelled gold handle of the dagger.

'Signal the fleet to hold fast. No one is to break formation. The pigs harass us all day on the right and left and still we prevail. We can ride out any storm that may assail us,' Sidonia tucked his hand behind his back and gave a nod toward the door. 'Make sure a watch is put on every ship; I do not want another Antwerp on my hands.'

'Very well, your grace,' Mendoza took up a lantern and returned to the deck leaving Sidonia to himself.

PLANS IN THE DARK

A heavy moon bled through blackened skies as the storm swept down the channel with a northerly bite. The weather had turned, no longer kicking a flamenco: the wind now favoured the British as they poured out of the Thames estuary to blockade the narrow sea to Europe. The Revenge sat heavy in the water, her forty-six guns primed and corked, ready to engage the enemy. Vice-Admiral Sir Frances Drake climbed the rope ladder amid the rolling waves to reach the deck of the Ark Royal.

'Admiral Howard,' Drake saluted his superior. 'Frobisher.' he added, shaking the hand of his counterpart.

'Time is critical, Francis, we must make haste. Despite the weather, the Spanish hold formation as tight as a Scotsman's purse strings,' Howard ushered his vice admirals through to his personal quarters.

'Have we any losses?' Frobisher lifted a port decanter from the table and, filling a glass he offered it to Thomas Howard. 'Drake?' He poured a second drink for himself, watching Drake and Howard arrange model ships on a table map. The ship rolled on an uneasy sea. Dark waters hissed along the length of seasoned timbers. A candle cast its flickering eye over the plan, its dim light cast much of the quarters in quivering shadows.

'No losses to report, a few peppered hulls and perforated sails. We made good use of the culverts and kept the Spanish at range. Most of their shot was pissed into the ocean,' Drake scoffed.

'Aye, was the same for us too. Their tiny weapons are no threat to our Virgin Queen.' The three commanders laughed at the Admiral's jibe. 'Jesting aside, men, what can we do to break their formation? Unless we can get to the heart of the fleet, we have no hope of preventing them from reaching London.'

'I'll not risk a full assault; they'd carve us up.'

A knock at the cabin door cut Martin Frobisher short.

Admiral Howard motioned toward the door. 'See who it is? I'm expecting John Young with his report. The door was opened to a man in his late thirties, his blonde hair tied back in a ponytail wet from the sea. Unlike most men of the day, he preferred a clean face to a fashionable beard. His emerald eyes caught the candlelight giving the impression of an inner fire. He stood with his hands straight at his sides, water dripping from his black jacket and trousers.

'Your report?'

Young straightened at the voice of the admiral.

'Parma is nowhere to be seen. Walsingham was right about him: he is refusing to come to the aid of Sidonia; there is no love lost between those two. There are patrol boats around the Spanish formation, they carry small signal lanterns. But the commanders are all surrounded. The seas are rough for small vessels, but our fleet sits sound,' Young stood at ease.

'We'll not be able to surprise them unless we can take out the patrols first,' Frobisher adjusted the position of his ships on the map. 'There is chance we could slip alongside them and rain havoc on their flank.'

Frobisher drew a line with a finger where he thought the action might take place.

'We'd have better hope of success in the early hours before light breaks: we'd have the sun to our backs,' Drake finished his port and placed his glass back on the silver tray with the emptied decanter.

'Either way we'd risk too many ships in such a manoeuvre. With so many of our hulls turned toward them we'd be impossible to miss. And should they run at us we would be food for fish,' Admiral Howard added his glass to the others.

'Three years ago, we broke the Spanish in Antwerp with fire. Why not this time?' Drake adjusted the ships on the table. 'We position ourselves thus, with the sacrifice between us, holding them until we have them aligned on our enemy. Then we peel off and wait here — and here. Admiral, you take the rear to prevent an easy escape.'

'My lords, if I may.' John Young took a step forward. 'The man you need is among us. Frederigo Giambelli is on this ship. With him, we can get started on the construction right away. The wind still favours us, and we can move into position as we prepare.'

'Make it so,' Admiral Howard set eight tokens on the map ahead of the fleet.

John Young left the Admiral's cabin with haste, running the length of the main deck before disappearing through the crew door at the prow. Below decks, lanterns swung with the heft of the sea, throwing portions of the hold in and out of shadow and back again. Men stood by their guns, adjusting the powder kegs and stacking cannonballs. All shutters were held fast to keep light from straying out into the night. John Young found his man working in the near dark in the bowels of the ship, ensuring the stack kept dry.

'Giambelli!' Young called out to the figure fastening a net over a pile of barrels.

'Sir.' Giambelli rubbed at the small of his back as he straightened up. His black hair hung in sweated clumps about his scarred face.

'Our services are required by the Admiral.'

'Oh aye,' Giambelli pulled a grimy hat back over his head, securing his hair beneath it.

'We are to repeat our exploits in Belgium upon this hellish armada.'

Giambelli smiled. 'It's going to be long night.' He looked around the stacked barrels and crates of produce. 'Gather all the kindling you can — and oil. We'll need plenty of oil.'

HELL BURNERS

Day Three

The English fleet moved under the shroud of night. The moonless sky held time at bay as Giambelli and John Young secured the hell burners between the supporting vessels. The British navy spread across the Channel, preparing to strike. Admiral Howard turned his ships toward the shore; Frobisher took the outer flank toward the home coast, while Drake held his crews mid-channel. Sir Francis stood at the helm of the Revenge, hands clasped tight behind his back, an eye to the ocean. 'Now, Mr Young,' John Young winched Giambelli back along the rope suspended between the two ships, his feet dipping in the swell of the sea.

'Are we ready?' Sir Frances called to Giambelli.

'Aye, sir.' Water poured from Giambelli's clothing. 'The sails and rudder are all set. You can cut them adrift whenever you wish.'

'How long before the lamps catch?' The Rear Admiral stared at the groaning lines as the ships strained at the ropes to be free.

'No more than a quarter-hour, before all hell breaks loose.' Giambelli smiled toward his creation.

Sir Francis drew his sword and severed the ties between the Revenge and its eight Trojans.

Dark clouds scudded across the black of night. The Spanish fleet rose and fell on the pistons of the ocean.

Pinpricks of lantern light peered into the inky void, trembling in the aftermath of the summer storm. Brave-hearted men rowed against the anger of the sea, patrolling the waters for assassins and blood-crazed Englishmen. The creaking hulls sang a weary lament in answer to the enquiring hiss of the waves as they swirled around them in search of ingress.

Pulling hard against the current, with their backs hunched to the spit of the sea, the oarsmen headed out on yet another patrol. With the Armada to their right, they began their arc around the fleet, away from the French coast.

Beneath the main deck, a purpling flame flashed into life in the darkness of the early morn. Candles guttered into pools of oil in a gasp of fiery rage. Tongues of fire licked along the boards tasting paper, cloth and bloodied rags. The fury of hell unleashed upon the tinderbox. Flames spread with ravenous haste, consuming everything in their wake. Nothing would escape their fury — not furnishing, not rope, nor sail.

The roar of flames called as a lion in the dark, a foreboding of the closing maw. Another roar raged into the night and another; three English lions calling to the pride. A breath later the remainder of the pack answered the call as eight raging galleons leaped out of the darkness seizing the weary Armada. The tiny patrol boat plunged its oars into the sea turning its prow back toward home, a home it would never reach as the paw of the lion clawed its fragile hide.

Bells rang out in harsh tones, an ominous call: death approaching. The Spanish crews erupted into life, the order to remain in formation disregarded. The Fleet scattered. Many turned tail and ran for home, glad of the ill wind and turgid seas. The Duke of Sidonia, strolled from stem to stern of the San Martin, his head high, his heart heavy, his fleet scattered leaves in an autumn storm.

'Never have I seen such madness!' Sidonia allowed a smile to brighten his mood, tucked his hands behind his back, and retired to his cabin.

The high winds carried the hell burners to the heart of the Armada. Slave ships lowered their oars into the sea and beat a rhythmic retreat, pursued by the Venetians whisking their treasures back to holy hands beyond the claws of the heretic Queen. She would wait for another day.

Panic swept across the Spanish fleet.

'Hell approaches!' A fevered sailor hacked the anchor line allowing his vessel to drift out of the demon's grasp as the fire ship raged by. Night terrors perforated the air, screams of the dying were hissed out by a hungry sea as it filled its deep belly with a platter of Mediterranean delicacies.

Blackest night turned to an angry dawn, red with blood and cindered ash. The beaches of Gravelines were littered, smouldering pyres where three burning hulls bled their cargo into a hungering tide. Three shattered vessels run aground, waiting for the looters to pick through their bones until only their carcasses remained. Hell had come and wreaked its fiery havoc upon a restless sea.

The San Martin with its five escort ships, were anchored off the Calais coast. But now they too must venture forth into the sights of the English Navy and the devil himself, Sir Frances 'El Draco' Drake.

EL SAGRADA

'Why do they not give chase?' Captain Mendoza stood beside his commander who held an eyeglass to his eye.

'The English are devils unlike any other.' Sidonia swept the horizon, searching for his adversary.

Bright sun paled the sea with a blue wash, an effulgence of halos spangling upon its surface. A brisk wind drew the ships along the English Channel, past the blockade at Flanders where the Duke of Parma rested with his surplus invasion force.

'Helmsman, steer out to deeper water. I do not wish to attract the attention of their fleet,' Sidonia turned his back on Flanders, fixing his gaze toward the north and the journey home.

Scattered remnants of the once invincible armada littered the Channel. Some fled to the south-west, opting for the shortest route home, while others were harried into the cold embrace of the Gaelic Catholics.

'Warship ahoy!' Sidonia glanced up to the herald, and out along his waving arm toward the open sea.

'El Draco,' Captain Mendoza breathed the name as though Death himself had come to claim his soul.

'He is nothing more than a pirate who will one day die in a festering hole,' The Duke lowered the eyeglass. 'Take the deck and bring us about. I want every breath of speed from these sails.'

'You wish us to flee?' Mendoza stood with his mouth agape.

'Do we have powder?' Sidonia paused, glancing back over his shoulder.

'No,' Mendoza sighed, his shoulders falling, loosening.

'So, we run,' The Duke returned to his cabin.

'Signal the fleet, we head for home,' Mendoza pondered the approaching devil. 'Helmsman, I want you to take us close enough to shave off El Draco's beard.'

'Yes, Captain.' The San Martin turned to face the English demons. Sails billowing in the summer's breath lifted the ship through the waves, carrying its Spanish masters toward the Revenge.

Mendoza strode from the upper deck. Taking the steps two at a time, he turned toward the door to the lower decks where the last of the gunpowder was being fed to the ravening guns. The men, blackened and filthy from three days of battle, were dauntless in their task. Bloody and blistered, the gun crews positioned their cannons one last time.

'Men, the Duke has set our course to charge down the bull: El Draco comes,' Mendoza waved for silence. 'Pray for our deliverance as we have only one shot. We are going to pass the monster as close as we can. The Revenge is a powerful ship with a thick hull. When we are alongside,' the Captain looked out of the open porthole, 'fire at will.'

'Mary, Mother of God, deliver us,' the crew crossed themselves as they turned in silence toward their enemy.

Mendoza stood at midships counting the waves as the sun climbed ever higher in the unsettled sky. The uneasy sea rose and fell, still drawn by the storm in its hunger for the moon. Gulls cried out with the promise of sanctuary and surefooted safety, but alas, it was a false hope, the nearest land now lay on the far side of the English fleet. Their only choice was to cut through the heart of Drake's men and run north to darker tides.

The cold rush of the English Channel hissed defiance at the Spanish invaders as they entered the final furlongs. Furlongs closed to chains until the last rod gave way to the starting gun.

Shouts of victory melded with cries of death as timbers shattered into splintered bones. Blood washed decks veiled with smoke, their wounds salved in the cleansing caress of the ocean. A single pass through the gauntlet, one chance for freedom, and the Spanish rat took its moment to limp a ragged mile beyond the scope of English eyes.

'We live to fight another day,' Mendoza plucked a splinter from his cheek, mopping the tide of blood with a soot-stained kerchief.

'Tis not us they seek but the Holy Sagrada. We have failed his Holiness and God in the one breath. Those swords were for Catholic hands, not filthy Protestant paws. Take us around this wretched isle … I long for home.'

The Duke of Sidonia dropped into his chair. With his face held in his hands, he wept bitter tears of defeat. Mendoza closed the cabin door in silence behind him and returned to his command. The invincible Armada was beaten. Only a remnant would pass beyond Scotland and survive unseasonable storms. Few would ever see the Mediterranean sun again. It would be many years before

King Philip would again turn his eyes toward the heretic lands and the Gloriana he so desired.

TILBURY

8TH AUGUST

'Now. Sir Martin,' The Queen held the Mayor in her gaze. 'My barge is ready?' She pointed toward The Thames.

'Your Highness,' The Lord Mayor of London doffed his hat as Elizabeth swept past. 'Yes, Majesty,' He cast his eyes to the ground, 'All of your entourage and consort await departure.' With a bow he stepped aside.

'Good,' Elizabeth continued down the ramp onto the barge. Through the corridor of oarsmen in their brilliant white jackets and bright red trousers, holding their oars at arms. She snatched up a cushion from a seat, turned and flung it at Leicester, who caught it, plumped it, and sat beside his Queen.

Leicester held his mirth, 'What has your goat now, my goodly Majesty?'

The Queen's eyes narrowed for a breath which she released in a huff of impatience. 'As if you have no idea.' She forced a smile.

The oarsmen took up their seats, nine to port and starboard with their oars high while the port side pushed the boat into the muddy waters of the Thames. Two Yeoman Warders stood at the entrance to the royal enclosure ensuring Her Majesty and the Earl of Leicester would not be disturbed: by anyone.

A string quartet of Black Moors began to play at the prow, filling the barge with soft melody. The gold roses on their red velvet jackets glittered in the sun, sending light dancing across the deck.

'Most pleasing, indeed,' Elizabeth waved a hand at the musicians who continued with their eyes lowered so as not to displease their monarch.

'Elizabeth, why do you tease?' Robert Dudley, Earl of Leicester, stroked his greying beard. 'Could any man be more loyal than I? And yet I was not to be yours,' he soughed.

'Perhaps, but your scurrilous Commonwealth—,' Elizabeth leaned across Leicester gesticulating at the southern bank of the river. '—Magnificent animals.' She clasped her gloved hands to her mouth. 'Who would keep such fine stock on the Marsh?'

'Are we going to discuss the matter at hand or talk horses?' The Earl straightened his hat.

Elizabeth slid her hands down her dress, drawing a long breath. She brought them to rest on her knees. She tapped her fingers twice, inspected the delicate stitching of her purple gloves, before snapping her head toward her good friend.

'I ... never ... wanted ... this, Leicester.' with a tilt of her head. 'I wanted Dover.' She pushed herself back into her seat, folded her hands in her lap with her nose toward the sky.

'God's strength,' the Earl muttered to the swirling eddies of the oars.

'Bridge approaching!' the Mayor barked.

Shadows played over the water, masking the excrement flowing on the river. Bobbing corpses of cats and dogs made edible rafts for sleek furred rats. The ebbing tide lacked the pull to drag the foul stench of yesterday's life out of the city. Buckets of filth poured from the triple-storied shops and tenements bordering the two lanes of traffic on London Bridge. Carts piled with goods from every country of the world vied for carriageway alongside the dung-carts of the street cleaners. Two hundred thousand beating hearts fought for space on the overcrowded streets.

'Gloriana, Gloriana.' the cheers of the peasantry hailed Queen and country as the Royal barge slipped beneath the bridge eastward toward Tilbury below the death-gaze from severed heads atop crude pikes.

'I shall be glad when we pass beyond the city limits with the Tower to our back and the green fields of England unroll before us.' Leicester winced as he adjusted the pillows in his ornate carved chair. 'Was this seat meant to be sat on by noble blood?'

'Are you going to gripe all the way, or must I issue a decree of silence?' Elizabeth scowled at her companion. Her eye was drawn to the plight of three men hanging from chains along the Southwark shore. 'A clear sign the Liberties come at a cost.' The Queen turned her attention to the opposite bank where the grey towers thrust up at the sky, warded by the dark stone bailey, a challenge to all would be invaders.

The Thames River meandered through the English countryside pulling the royal barge toward the sea. River traffic, traders and ferries dwindled as the city faded behind them. The sun slipped across the August sky, heading into the afternoon wastes as the royal party dined on hampers. 'Have you considered who might succeed you?' Leicester opened a hamper. Taking out a decanter of wine he poured them both a drink. Queen Elizabeth sipped from a golden goblet. 'Essex, if tutored, would make a worthy King, would he not? Right now, he is preparing your troops, is he not.'

'Tell me,' Elizabeth peered into the distance where small barges were aligning across the half-mile width of the Thames. 'What are they doing? Why are so many assembled?'

'Before I left Tilbury to collect you in person, I had them set a boom across the Thames. Should the vile Spanish make passage up the river, they will strike the anchored masts.'

'Will it work?' Elizabeth teased a smile, returning her goblet to the tray.

'I hope not to find out,' The Earl of Leicester rose to his feet as the barge nestled against the jetty. 'Take care, my Queen, the moorings are not fastened, and the lands here are soft underfoot.'

'I would like to inspect the troops before travelling to Saffron House,' Elizabeth strode from the boat toward the entrance.

'Essex will have everything ready for the morrow, Majesty, will it not wait another day?'

Elizabeth spun around, 'It may.' Glaring at Leicester, she snapped, 'I will not.'

'As you wish,' Leicester lowered his head one hand pressed to his brow, allowing Elizabeth to continue to the Blockhouse.

THE PAVILION

9ᵀᴴ AUGUST

'Are we prepared or not?' Elizabeth looked out of the Royal Pavilion, across the Thames to Gravesend, where the muzzles of a dozen lion-hearted culverts waited to roar.

'Essex has the men as ready as possible, given the shortness of time he has had to recruit and train,' Leicester checked the buttons of his collar giving them a deft twist of his thumb. 'For one so young he has proven himself beyond measure.'

'I do hope so. After yesterday's poor showing. Nothing more than a few armed peasants having a stab at each other,' Elizabeth waved a limp hand at Leicester.

'Essex assures me the men are ready to face any invader foolhardy enough to step foot on these shores,' The Earl of Leicester coughed into his hand, wiping the dark spots with a kerchief.

'I do hope you're not going to die on me, Leicester. It would be most inconsiderate of you on such a fine day in front of all the men.'

The clash of steel chimed on the breeze stirring the heart of The Queen. Three Man-of-war sat poised in the estuary, survivors of Flanders, elegant as swans with the breath of dragons. With their sails rolled and their anchors lodged in the bed of the Thames, they waited in solemn pride.

Elizabeth smiled.

'What now?' Leicester stood with one hand on the hilt of his sword, the other he ran through his dark grey hair. He eyed Elizabeth, taking in the full image of her glory. Her flame red hair tumbling over her shoulders onto her white and black satin dress. Only the sun outshone her radiance.

'Harness,' Elizabeth stabbed a long finger at the leather straps on the armour rack.

'Oh, seriously, your Majesty?' Leicester strode forward only to be stopped by the hand of The Queen.

'Today they will get more than a mere woman,' Elizabeth straightened her back as the harness was fastened about her. 'They will get a warrior.' Leicester stepped back with a polite bow observing his beloved as she was adorned in silver cuirass and spaulder over her right side.

'You win,' Leicester doffed his black velvet cap.

'Of course,' Elizabeth stood with her hands on her hips inspecting her image in a full-length bronzed mirror. 'The Yeoman and the garter are to remain in the pavilion. Fetch the Black Earl and Essex, together with the Master of Horse. And have my page bring the grey charger. I am ready to inspect the troops.'

AMONG THE MEN

The bright August sun cut through the fading clouds as Elizabeth stepped out of the royal enclosure with only a handful of her trusted consorts. Thomas, the Black Earl, bowed deep as he took the Sword of State from Elizabeth's hands and strapped it around his waist.

'And how fares my Black Earl this day?' Elizabeth blew a gentle kiss.

'I fair well as ever, my good cousin,' the Black Earl, smoothed his moustache into his beard.

'Let us walk among the men, show them we are not distant figures viewable only through an eyeglass but warriors on the same fields of blood,' Elizabeth removed her gloves and passed them to her page. She ran her hand along the back of her grey mare. 'Have the animal saddled. I shall need her when I address the men this afternoon.'

'Is this necessary?' Leicester huffed.

Elizabeth rounded on Leicester her eyes narrowed, lips drawn in a painted red line.

'Then we will commence the inspection at once, your Majesty.'

The Earl took his place two paces behind The Queen, to her right, while Essex fell in at his stepfather's left. None of the men spoke.

'Do lead Thomas; at least someone knows the protocol,' Elizabeth barked.

The small entourage wound its way down from the Pavilion through the ranks of Yeoman and the Royal Garter.

Surrounded by the clatter of ill-fitting armour and dulled blades, the Gloriana went among her people as one of them. Pikes wielded with the finesse of a clothes pole clashed with shields more used to being ploughshares as the soldiers were drilled beneath the bright sun.

'Again,' the captain barked at his men. A man of no more than eighteen, thick set with a tangle of reddish-brown hair and the beginnings of a beard, shook his aching arms as he raised his sword and took his stance.

'Move aside,' Essex bullied his way through the throng, drawing his thin-bladed cutlass. 'Copy me, boy.' Flourishing his sword, he struck at the young man's weapon. He thrust forward, swept right and left forcing the young man to guard and parry. 'We may make something of you yet,' Essex shoved the hilt of his sword into his opponent's face, leaving a stud mark from the jewelled hand guard, ending the spar. 'Who are you, boy? Do you even have a name?' He smiled at his own wit.

'Johnson, sir.' His fingers clasped the handle of his bastard blade, 'John Johnson.'

'Well, Johnson,' Essex thrust his sword into its sheath. 'Work hard, and you might make a soldier.'

Johnson glowered at Essex strutting along after his Queen, oblivious to the eyes upon him.

'Again,' The captain restored order.

At the end of the field stood the archers learning to tend their fletches. Elizabeth plucked an arrow from the dirt inspecting its shaft. She held her hand out to the master at arms. 'Knife, if you please.' With a practiced hand, she trimmed the fletch and returned the blade. Turning toward the row of dummies she lifted a longbow and knocked the arrow. Drawing it to her lips, she kissed it, and loosed it to its target, striking the gold centre. The men clapped and cheered.

'Care to challenge me, Essex?' Elizabeth coquetted.

'Perchance, under other circumstances, Majesty,' Essex puffed out his chest.

'Careful, Robert,' the soft tones of his stepfather cautioned. 'Always respect who she is.'

'Wise words indeed,' Elizabeth returned the bow to its owner with a courteous smile.

Rallying Cry

Sitting astride her grey mare. Elizabeth rode into the heart of her men. The Black Earl stepped aside, allowing her Majesty to pass. Leicester slowed his pace until he stood beside the Black Earl. Only Essex remained next to The Queen as though it were his birthright. The handsome dark-haired youth held the royal mount by the reins, turning it to face the amassed rank and file of twenty thousand soldiers and conscripts.

Elizabeth straightened in her saddle, pushing herself as upright as possible.

'My loving people.' She turned her head from left to right taking in the sea of faces staring back at her and smiled.

'We have been persuaded by those careful of our safety,' Elizabeth waved a hand as though batting a fly. 'To take heed how we commit ourselves to armed multitudes, for fear of treachery; be assured I have no desire to cause distrust.' Bolstering her tone, she continued. 'Let tyrants fear. I have always so behaved myself that under God, I have placed my utmost strength and safeguard in the loyal hearts and good-will of my subjects; and therefore, I am come amongst you, as you see.'

She paused for the cheering to abate. The grey mare pawed at the earth with a snort. 'At this time, not for my recreation and disport, but being resolved, in the midst and heat of the battle, to live and die amongst you all; to lay down for my God, and for my kingdom, and my people, my honour and my blood, even in the dust.'

Elizabeth turned her mount around, searching for more troops to inspire. 'I know I have the body of a feeble woman; but I have the heart and stomach of a king, a king of England, and think foul scorn should Parma or Spain,' she spat the name in the dirt, 'or any prince of Europe, dare invade the borders of my realm; to which rather than any dishonour shall grow by me, I myself will take up arms. I will be your general, judge, and rewarder of every one of your virtues in the field.'

The applause of sword on shield beat the air with iron-clad hands.

'I know already, for your forwardness you have deserved rewards and crowns; and we do assure you on the word of a prince, each will be paid their due. In the meantime, my lieutenant general shall be in my stead. Never has a prince commanded a more noble or worthy subject; and I know you will obey my general. By your concord in the camp, and your valour in the field, we will soon have a famous victory over these enemies of my God, of my kingdom, and of you, my people.'

The lion-hearted roar of England filled the air to cries of 'Gloriana, Gloriana! Long live our Queen.'

The grey mare reared in salutation to her mistress. Essex pulled hard on the reins, bringing the animal under his control. Elizabeth gasped, grasping the young master's shoulder with a firm grip. Essex, ever the hector, raised an eyebrow at his Queen with a playful smile. Elizabeth half-closed her eyes and turned her attention toward the accolade of her subjects.

1593

THE PLAYERS

Soft leather soles fell silent upon the royal chamber floor as the young dandy strolled up to the dais. Elizabeth's smile broadened with pleasure as the young Earls strutted about before her, each of them more handsome than the last until only Essex remained in her gaze. He lifted his cape from his shoulders as though he was about to issue a challenge to the royal throne and assert his Boleyn blood. Instead, he preened his immaculate beard and tweaked his waxed moustache while practicing his finest sycophantic smile. He winked at Her Majesty and strolled off to be admired by the gathered nobles.

'He's such a charmer, do you suppose he would make a good king?' Elizabeth stroked the fine stitching on her purple gloves, a gift from Stratford, marked with a delicate embossed quill. Her eyes followed the rear of the young Earl in his broad ruff and silver-black outfit, cinched at the waist and emphasising his fit young body.

Raleigh paused. Shaking his head as the young peacocks displayed their worth before the court ladies. 'Not my passion.' His words trailed to impatience. 'I prefer the fairer sex, ma'am, and there is none finer than she who sits upon the throne.'

'Persistence is one of the many things I admire about you Walter, you never give up.' Elizabeth tipped her head, casting an emerald eye over the gold-clad knight. 'Do continue the hunt, one does so enjoy the chase,' Elizabeth returned her attention to the exotic display of lords and their suitors. 'Well, who is this?'

The figure dressed from head to foot in black walked with a slight stoop, though his steps were well considered, each placed, with deliberate thought, where he wanted them. William Cecil, Lord Burghley, would not be hurried: he had served The Queen since she was a young princess and knew her better than any other in the entire realm. None could match her, or withstand her wrath, as he could. At his side walked a young man whose youthful looks were set upon a fine frame befitting any nobleman. His brown hair hung above his shoulders resting poignant over his narrow ruff. A white lace frill peeked from his deep green jacket sleeves as though it were unsure of its opulent surroundings.

'Majesty,' Cecil doffed his woollen cap with his right hand, ensuring it was folded in neat halves while he greeted his oldest friend. 'May I present, from the heart of the Sussex countryside, my young ward, Henry Wriothesley, Third Earl of Southampton.' Cecil straightened his aging back with a click.

'How do you do, young man. And where has my wizened fellow kept you secreted?' Elizabeth leaned forward in her throne, the pearls in her hair glittered in the shafts of light dancing upon her from the windows.

Southampton clasped his hands behind his back, 'At Cowdray, the family home.' He held The Queen's gaze.

'I hope to be seeing more of you,' Elizabeth turned her eye in question to Cecil. 'Is he to accompany the troops to Oxford?' Her tone conveyed her wishes.

'Indeed,' Cecil nodded his acquiescence.

'Please, do acquaint yourself with the rest of my stable,' Elizabeth waved a gloved hand in the general direction of the strutting nobles as they went about their courtship rituals. 'Some are runners, some riders.' Queen Elizabeth trailed her tongue across her smiling lips. 'I shall wait with bated breath to see which side of the stable you belong.' Southampton bowed, taking a step back before he raised his head and turned toward the strutting peacocks.

'My good ladies and gentlemen,' Cecil began. 'I should like to introduce my young ward.'

'Southampton, how wonderful to have you here,' Essex extolled, almost falling over his ego to be the first to greet the latest lamb to the fold. Essex inclined his head to Cecil's ear, 'Don't tire yourself with the introductions, I shall take it from here.' Cecil left his ward in the hands of Essex.

'I believe you had Earldom thrust upon you from a tender young age,' Essex smiled at the court harem, among them a young blond girl fresh from her patron's care. 'This — this is the exquisite Miss Marie. Do not be beguiled by her beauty, she is more cunning than a fox and deadlier than a viper,' Southampton gave the girl a less than subtle wink. Following a step behind the dandy Essex, he feigned his interest in the happenings of court.

'Tell me,' Southampton paused, tightening his hands behind his back. 'Essex, do you never tire of this?' He waved a hand at the gold gilded walls and the ornate plaster ceiling from which hung a glittering chandelier befit of the King of France. 'This is all so pleasant but scratch the surface and what lies beneath? How true are the hearts and how blue is the blood flowing within?'

Southampton strolled about the room, noting those who curtsied and those who straightened as though his mere presence was a threat to their social standing.

'What could be more thrilling than to stand among the kings,' Essex glanced across the room toward the dais, 'and queens of England? I, of course, am of royal descent,' Essex bowed toward The Queen as he continued his discourse. 'My gratitude goes to her father, King Henry, it is because of him I sit in line, not counting a Catholic uprising.'

'Why would that be?' Southampton raised a glass to his lips; the sweetness roused his nausea. He returned it to the table.

'Why, then James would be king, and his blood would surpass my own. I would be a mere shadow in the court,' Essex took the rejected tipple, swirled it around the glass, warming its red heart in his hand, 'A fine wine, almost as fine as the one who sells it.' He flicked a drip from his moustache at a lowly courtier.

'One of your wines,' Southampton laughed to himself. 'You should take to the stage. The Lord Chamberlain's Men could use a man of such fine breeding and manners.'

'One day, I will light up the boards with my Majesty and hold my sword on high,' Essex pulled his gold-handled rapier from its sheath, alarming the palace guards.

'My good Earl, that would not be wise in the presence of Her Majesty: one might be mistaken for a traitor,' Sir Walter took the rapier from Essex, turning it over in his hand. 'An interesting blade. Not one to be carried by the Master of the Horse?'

Raleigh allowed Essex to take it from his hands all the while reading every twitch in the young earl's face.

Raleigh leaned in, whispering, 'I should be more careful when unsheathing a weapon in future. It is not my desire to be the one to spill royal blood.'

'Mayhap it would not be mine that spills,' Essex brushed the annoying tick from his ear. Turning to his new conspirator he smiled, 'It is a marvel to me how commoners can pirate their way into royal hearts. But I suppose a lady is easy to charm with sparkling jewels and a sycophantic smile.' Southampton mimicked Essex.

The young guests continued to mingle and chatter. Essex, the choice of all the ladies, strutted his worth as a peacock displays the eyes of its tail to a prospective mate. Southampton practised his courtly smile under the all-seeing eye of Cecil, Elizabeth giggled and laughed her way through the afternoon, in an open display of enjoyment of her company. Sir Walter regaled her with tales of heroism and cunning while her champion, George Clifford, stood ever ready to lay down his life for his Queen.

'Majesty,' a footman bowed low before her. 'The royal entourage is assembled.' Bowing, he stepped back three paces before leaving.

The hubbub was silenced as Elizabeth, rose from her throne. She smiled at her fawns as they blinked their doe-like eyes, a hundred twinkling lights wishing to be noticed and selected for service in the royal household. Essex half-stifled a yawn. Placing his wine on the table he wandered out of the door trailing behind his distant cousin.

UNREST

Rain pelted the wet earth from a filthy sky. Dirty grey clouds broiled over a sullen landscape dappling the green hills a muddy black. With heads bowed, the horses dragged their loads through the highway of churned mud across the moors to Ulster. A cold wind bit at exposed flesh, driving the stinging rain deep into shivering bones. It was hard to believe it was still summer. The wagon train clattered to a halt behind the raised fist of Red Hugh O'Donnell. 'Hold.'

Water ran in rivulets from his ragged beard as he surveyed the empty world around him. Endless grey skies promised more misery on the road ahead; another day or two would make no difference to the preparations. The English were entrenched in The Pale, and nothing short of the entire might of Spain could remove them. Hugh knew the invaders well; he knew what war with them was like. He also knew if he was to lead his people as a real king, he must one day oust the beast from Ireland.

'We'll make camp in the woodland on the hill,' Red Hugh urged his horse through the wet mud. The animal turned its head toward him with a snort and stepped out as commanded.

The woods, though small, were a welcome shelter with their dense canopy of summer growth. The men knew the drill: raise the king's tent and muster food while the scouts skulked through the fading light to survey the land. Fires lit the gloom with a welcoming glow, and the aroma of a simple stew filled the air with the promise of a warm belly. Tarpaulins were erected on half-pikes giving the rain a drum-skin upon which to beat out its march. The gentle rhythm of the night stole the thunder of the darkness, allowing a reprieve from the drudgery of inclement weather.

'My lord.' The young officer stood with his helmet tucked beneath his arm, his back held straight to attention. 'The perimeter is sealed, and we cannot be seen from the road or the lower slopes.'

'All is well,' Red Hugh raised an eyebrow at the youngster. 'Aidan, you can relax when we are alone.'

'I wouldn't want the men to think I was favoured among them, uncle,' Aidan combed his wet hair with his fingers, his eyes fixed on the spread before him.

'Take, eat,' Red Hugh slid a plate across the rough table, which was the seat from the wagon he'd been driving 'The men all think you are a spoiled brat,' Hugh smiled, loading a plate with bread, cheese, and meat.

'Is there no ale to wash it down?' Aidan's eyes sparkled in the torchlight.

'You'd take the dying breath from me lungs,' Hugh laughed as he splashed ale from his horned cup into a battered pewter tankard.

'Much appreciated,' Aidan downed the ale in a single swallow with an exaggerated sigh. 'No?' He waggled the tankard at his uncle.

'No,' Hugh barked, harder than intended. 'Now get your skinny arse out there and see the men are fed. If they should ask, it'll be a slow start on the morrow. Tyrone will meet us at the Derg, where we'll be a good four days out of Belfast, far enough from English Eyes.'

Aidan flashed a smile at his uncle as he crammed his pockets with the bread and meat from his plate, 'I'll see you at the head in the morning.'

The tent flap waved the curly-haired youth farewell leaving Red Hugh to ponder the future alone.

Morning came with a brisk wind edged with the chill of wet earth. The odour of horses and urine musked the air as Red Hugh rubbed his face with water from a barrel. All around the camp, soldiers packed away their makeshift tents and cleaned their armour, such as it was: poor quality plate spaulders and tattered mail, swords as old as Ireland itself and shields fit only for wall hanging. Some had leathers hardened in boilers, older than those who wore them. It was a sad sight for a king to see his men so ill-equipped for the rebellion against the foreign crown. The thought of Elizabeth and her promises of riches bolstered his resolve: he was a determined man, determined to drive the Protestants into the sea back to whatever miserable hole had birthed them.

It was late morning by the time the wagons rolled out of the shelter toward the road, bumping their way across the hill beneath the line of sight of Dungannon to the north and Henry Bagenal with his English army to the east. It would be a long day under the pale sky where ravens laughed as they gathered for the coming feast.

Aidan trotted along the length of the train, inspecting the troops, giving encouragement where he felt the need. Summer meant long marches baked by sun, but not today. Merciful Mary had looked upon their plight and sent clouds across the endless green heart of Ireland, a land of peace: until the English came. The army marched, following the one man who could unite a nation divided by conquest.

Red Hugh viewed Aidan with fondness. He had seen the boy become a man and father a son of his own.

'How fare the men?' Red Hugh coughed, 'Cursed rain.'

'The weather will break by this eve, but the men, however, will not.' Aidan pulled a silver cannister from his vestment and tossed it to Red Hugh. 'Caitlin made it. It may not put hair on your chest, but it'll keep the blessed cold from it.'

Red Hugh caught the flask, opened it and took a swig. ''Tis good. Take care of the lass, she's a keeper.'

Aidan smiled as he turned his horse aside to cheer the men as they passed.

The sun crept across the sky, warming the sodden earth until it sank below the western horizon and cast red delight across the fading blue. Once more they detoured from the main track into nearby woodland and pitched their camp. The mood was lighter, brightened by a balmy night scattered with stars and dancing fireflies. The soft chatter of the troops broke the otherwise silent night as the campfires lowered their flames and sleep took all but the last watch.

One more day of infernal marching, and near one hundred miles of soaking in the summer rain would be done. Mile after mile of sweating filth and gnawing on stale crusts. Castlederg would be a welcome sight when its walled confines and high tower reared on the horizon. They passed to the north of Omagh. Hugh knew there would be no Englishmen to espy them this deep in his principality, nonetheless, he still wished to go unnoticed.

It was late when the caravan entered the grey maw of the castle. The blood-red sky was showing purple bruises as the last soldier was waved home. Red Hugh left his horse with his groom and the instruction to hand it to a stable lad to bed down. He wanted all the men to feast, they had earned it.

'Let's see what his lordship wants,' Red Hugh sighed. His boots scraped across the courtyard; pebbles rattled across the cobbles as he dragged himself into the castle. 'Aidan, would you get yourself settled in, I've got to find the ditch and relieve myself. 'Tis a pity to waste celebrations on such natural needs, but I fear if I do not go now, I shall go where I stand.' Aiden laughed as he walked away.

The sounds of merriment carried out across the yard as Red Hugh wandered into the hall. Sank into a chair and drank the nearest ale. Food was piled onto his plate, more than any man could eat alone. He scanned the room, content at last, his men were safe. Lasses danced and swerved aside from enquiring hands of soldiers in search of something more exotic than bread and ale.

'You have done well, my fine fellow. My gut was right about you,' O'Neil raised his cup for a refill. 'I knew any man who could who break out of Dublin Prison and survive winter in the Wicklow Mountains was one to rout the canker from our shores. I don't think there's a task too great for you, Red, you're an O'Donnell through and through. A true Irishman. I'll be honoured to have you at my side.'

'The honour is all mine, Tyrone. I name you thus as you are as much the land as you are our King. The quarrel between our people is ended, and now we must unite as many other clans as we can. If they are not for us, they are against,' Red Hugh raised his cup to his ally. The young man stood, lifted his tankard high, proclaiming, 'To our Lord and King, one people under one flag against one enemy. My good men, I give you our Lord Commander, Aodh Mór Néill, Hugh, The Great O'Neil, our one King.'

Red Hugh gave a courtly bow. The room erupted into rapturous applause.

1596

ALL AT SEA

STORMS

A warm June sun lit the Plym with yellow fire, as the turning tide lifted the flotilla high in the water. The soft lapping sea lulled the ships toward the open ocean and an adventure with the Dutch command.

Essex took the helm of the Duc Repulse, commanding his ship to the head of the fleet alongside Lord Admiral Howard aboard the Ark Royal.

Dismayed, Raleigh held his position among the body of the hundred strong vessels. 'It is a fine day to bloody the nose of a Spaniard, is it not?' Raleigh leaned on the handrail watching the ocean foam along the hull.

'Aye sir,' midshipman Wallace stood to attention. 'Revenge for Mousehole and Penzance. I lost family in Mousehole.' he stared out to the endless blue horizon.

Raleigh turned to face the officer, placing a hand upon his shoulder. 'You will have your vengeance. We all will.'

The coast of France slipped below the horizon as the war fleet moved out into the dark Atlantic waters. Grey clouds broiled over the ocean, twisting into anguished knots as though the heavens could not decide who to strike. Sharp winds cut heads from waves, throwing them against the hulls of the English ships. The ocean grew more restless as the sky and sea became one beast. Rain beat the decks in stiffened rods as sailor and soldier fought against the elements. The sails ran with rivers of water as the storm set the might of the ocean against the fleet. Before the first storm had abated, the fleet had broken into four squadrons. Essex and the others were nowhere to be seen.

A moonless night fell on the turbulent seas blotting the ocean from view. The second storm drove Raleigh's ships beyond the Bay of Biscay far from the shores of Spain.

Morning revealed the misty coast of an island, obscured by the remnant of the fading storm. Essex sailed into view, for once a welcome sight. By late morning, the two commanders were aboard the Duc Repulse.

'What the bloody hell are you doing in the Azores?' Essex strode toward the ladder where Raleigh was climbing aboard.

Sir Walter dusted himself down and straightened his clothes before he looked at the ship's commander. 'There was no way we could make safe landing, so we ran with the wind,' Raleigh squared up to Essex, thirteen years his junior, 'and here we are. What, pray tell, is the excuse for your command?'

'Trying to keep the fleet together,' Essex turned to follow Raleigh into his own quarters. 'Do not turn your back on me, I am— '

Raleigh spun around, clenching his jaw as he stood face to face with Essex, 'Cousin to The Queen. Look around you, man! What is that, here? Perhaps you should get a frock and call yourself queen. You have no idea how to command and even less respect for your men. Now, I will ask but will not care how *you* answer,' Raleigh inched forward, 'May I re-provision my ships? Your Highness.'

Essex's nostrils flared as he considered his answer. 'You may. Get to Cádiz with all haste.'

'Do not fear, we shall,' Raleigh closed the door behind him, leaving Essex stranded, his fingers clenched around the hilt of his sword.

Emerging with his beard waxed and his hair impeccable, Raleigh scrutinised Essex, his hair, beard and stance, he snorted and left for his own ship. Essex stormed into his cabin. The crashing of cutlery and servers could be heard on the main deck, peppered with profanity and cursing any sailor would have been proud of.

Essex turned his ships about and set sail toward Cádiz and a rendezvous with the rest of the fleet.

CÁDIZ

Spanish merchants turned in terror as the Warspite sailed into Cádiz. English flags rattled from masts lashed with salt spray as the grey skies cracked and split. There was nowhere to run except back into the affray. Sir Walter pressed his ships into the mouth of Cádiz, between Puntal and Matagorda, sealing everyone inside. Raleigh spread his fleet in a broadening arc, as a fisherman drags his net. Cádiz was now his, he could assault Puerto Real at leisure. Drawing the net tight, he teased the shoal of ships into a stone-walled corral where Admiral Howard and the flamboyant Essex were commanding their assault.

Sir Walter raised an eyeglass, 'What in hell's name are they doing?' He scanned the English ships. 'Bloody Essex. Ready a launch. Signal the fleet to blockade the exit, keep everyone inside, let no Spaniard reach open water,' Raleigh commanded Commander Fisher, 'You have the helm. Make the bastards pay.'

'Aye sir,' Fisher saluted. 'May one enquire as to the nature of your mission?'

'One may indeed enquire,' Raleigh allowed himself a tight smile. 'I'm going to rip a hole in Essex.'

Raleigh strode across the deck and climbed over the rail. With gloved hands, he grasped the rope and slid down into the launch. Thrusting the oars into the oarlocks, Raleigh set his back to the prow and rowed through the thick of the fighting. Pellets fizzed into the water around him; one clipped the gunwale and sent splinters into his hand. Undaunted Sir Walter pressed on, urging his tiring arms to pull him through the pending storm. The skies above blistered with the threat of rain, yet the clouds withheld their wrath upon the feuding warlords. The Spanish vessels, anchored to the ocean bed, caught unaware, waited for death to come from the raging lions.

Raleigh reached the Duc Repulse and climbed aboard as another boat of over-burdened troops was lowered to the sea and a watery grave.

'Where is the Admiral?' Raleigh stormed toward the aft of the ship.

'In his quarters, your lordship.' the soldier saluted.

Raleigh yanked the door open, leaving it to bang on its hinges.

'What is the meaning of this slaughter?' Raleigh thrust a shaking hand toward the door.

Essex laughed into his glass, 'We're killing Spaniards, Raleigh.'

'You surprise me!' Raleigh turned to look Essex in the eye. 'It looks more like a sacrifice to me. Boatloads of your men are sinking to the bottom of the sea.'

Raleigh held the taste of the ocean on his tongue as he stepped toward Essex.

'Sir Walter, why are you not at your command?' Admiral Howard placed his quill aside his logbook before reaching for his glass. 'Do have a seat.'

'I will not,' Raleigh gave a curt bow. 'Not while our men are sent to their deaths without so much as drawing a sword. Who is the idiot responsible for the current action? Who thought it wise to send boats filled with armoured men to clamber aboard the Spanish ships? Do tell.'

'How else would we take them?' Essex swirled his wine about his glass. 'What would you have us do?'

'Follow The Queen's orders and take Port Royal. Why do you think she gave you an army Essex ... to go fruit picking?' Raleigh snatched the glass from Essex's hand.

'Calm down Walter, they're only soldiers,' Essex sneered. 'Not important.'

'You're incompetent, Essex. You are sending men to their deaths,' Raleigh emptied the glass onto the floor.

'Our orders,' Admiral Howard steepled his hands.

'Our orders were to take Port Royal,' Raleigh kept his eyes on Essex. 'You have sixteen thousand troops to take a town one third the size. You should be able to manage that,' He looked Essex up and down. 'If you had half the courage you pretend to, you would have captured this area on arrival and have those galleons secured.'

'You're washed up, Raleigh,' Essex spat, hesitating as he retrieved his glass.

Raleigh tipped the glass toward Essex. 'I suggest you pull yourself away from the mirror and look around you. We're losing to ourselves. Your great reputation is at stake. What will they cry in the streets about the vainglorious now?' Raleigh let the glass drop from his fingers. 'Glory slips from your grasp.'

'Raleigh,' Howard's shout went unheard as Sir Walter walked from the room. The Admiral glanced at Essex and

Southampton, sitting in quiet contemplation with a book in his lap.

'I guess it would not hurt to see what has riled him so,' Howard ushered Essex from the cabin to the deck. Raleigh was back in his launch, powering through the sea toward the closing Warspite.

HEROES

Smoke poured from a burning galleon, tumbling over the ocean, consuming everything in its path. A launch filled with English soldiers lurched into the smokescreen where it vanished from sight. Men cried in gargled screams for mercy to the brass heavens. The tiny boat overturned, pouring the men out in a cascade of armour and flesh, another twenty souls sank to the harbour floor.

Raleigh rowed all the harder, his face set with rage. Tears stung his eyes and wet his cheeks as boat after boat of English soldiers succumbed to the same fate. Stabbing an oar into the ocean, Walter turned his launch hard to port as he came alongside the Warspite. Jumping to his feet, he leaped onto the ladder and clambered aboard his ship.

'Head straight for the harbour, sink anything in our way. Including Essex,' Sir Walter stood beside the helmsman, his sword at the ready. 'Take us in, we will show the admiral and his consort what should be done.'

The Warspite cut through the water, venting its fury on the Spanish. Its cannons roared in defiance at Medina Sidonia, as the rest of the English force hurled itself at Puerto Real. Spanish guns replied in anger at the invading privateer. Sidonia waved a fist amid the clamour, his rage turning to pure joy as the deck of the Warspite vomited splinters. Raleigh staggered through the smoke, dragging his sword toward the breach.

'Have this patched,' Raleigh waved his sword at the damage before stabbing it into the deck to prevent his collapse.

'Medic, a medic for the captain!' the helmsman called as he held his course. Another barrage tore through the Spanish ranks, sending good men to an early grave. 'Medic!' Cannon fire whistled across the deck; some embedded in the masts and railings, its power lost to the ever-increasing distance between them.

'Somebody stop the rider,' Raleigh forced himself to stand against the pain in his leg. He looked down at the ragged wooden fingers clawing at his thigh: blood ran down the heavy golden thread of his leggings. 'That is The King's messenger. Bugger it,' Raleigh bit his lip against the pain as the ship's doctor yanked out the largest splinters with black iron pliers. 'Just wrap it.'

The medic tied off the bandage, tucking the loose ends in over the top of the binding. 'Sir Walter,' he glanced toward the town where a gaggle of peasants were crying out for help from the local defence. 'You cannot ... '

'Lower the bridge,' Raleigh readied his sword with a grin. 'Thank you, you can finish when I am done gutting Spaniards.' Placing a firm hand on the doctor's shoulder he rallied his men to arms. 'For Queen and country.'

Sir Walter Raleigh held his sword high and, swinging it toward the harbour he led his men in the assault of Port Royal. A thousand English throats cried out for Spanish blood among the narrow streets and plazas of Puerto Real. Swords and shields clashed and swung in a song of iron and death.

'Well, well, what have we here?' A shadow stepped from the Church of Saint Sebastian. Dark robes lined with red swirled about the shaded figure. 'Sir Walter Raleigh, my king will honour me when I hand him your head.'

'That has been tried before.' Undaunted, Raleigh raised his sword to meet the gold-handled blade of his enemy. Together they danced upon the steps, the sun smiled on their flashing blades. Raleigh swept his arm high, fending off a daring lunge to his chest and he countered his foe. 'The Jesuits taught you well, though your stance is of an Englishman,' Raleigh parried another thrust, his blade slicing up across the top of his assailant's brow knocking his hat to the ground, revealing dark auburn hair beneath. 'Do you wish to retrieve it? We have the time,' Sir Walter turned his injured leg away from his assailant.

'I will fetch it when I have done with you,' the man spat, adjusting his grip on the sword.

'Then it shall be my prize,' Raleigh lunged forward, catching the man's wrist below the hilt of the sword. The attacker cried out as his sword fell to the ground. Raleigh struck again but was too slow. His strength waning, he managed only to slash across his opponent's arm.

'Another day, Sir Walter.' The assassin turned and ran clutching at his injury.

'Adieu,' Raleigh retrieved the fallen weapon and hat. He tried the hat and tossed it aside, its high towered centre was far from the fashion of court. Walter dropped himself into a pew where he examined the sword. Its plain blade belied its craftsmanship, beautiful, balanced with a golden handle formed into a Spanish cross, embedded with three small rubies. Sir Walter drew a long, weary breath, wincing as he rose to his feet, he walked out into the sun where the clamour of battle faded with the drifting smoke. A gentle breeze swirled through the streets where soldiers picked the corpses of their enemies clean of rings and trinkets: gifts for sweethearts back home. He struggled back to the harbour where Essex and Admiral Howard had gathered the survivors. They watched the smoke carry ash into the sky as their ships burned. Every vessel was ablaze. Explosions tore through the wooden hulls as powder kegs erupted, scuttling the fleet.

'Where is Sidonia?' Raleigh slid his prize sword into his belt aware, of Essex's hungry gaze upon it. 'I said, where is Sidonia? Have you checked the cellars for him?'

'There was no need, dear boy,' Essex smiled, tossing his head to one side, 'he got away on a horse.'

'Did you send anyone after him?' Raleigh stopped to adjust his bloody bandage.

'Are you hurt, Sir Walter?' Admiral Howard stepped out of Essex's shadow.

'Ah, the Warspite took a shot to the deck,' Raleigh waved a dismissive hand. 'A few splinters is all.'

Essex glared at Raleigh. Tucking his hands behind his back he stepped up to Sir Walter and tapped his injured leg with his gold-handled sword. Projecting his voice as though taking to the stage at the theatre, 'You are beyond doubt the true hero of the people.'

Sir Walter held Essex by the shoulder. 'And you, sir, are an absolute arse. You let the captain of the Spanish fleet walk away. I sometimes question your loyalties.'

Raleigh turned and left for the faithful companionship of his crew.

1598

London

Two Bards in the Hand

The city stank, a rancid perfume of horse shit, urine and unwashed bodies bathed only in evening sun. London was glorious. A mixture of people swirled in a miasma of culture and class. Where the rich fed upon the efforts of the poor, the poor fought for scraps from the master's table, while dogs licked up the vomit of the plagued. Dung men drove their spades through the foot-thick squelch, swinging up load after load until their carts bristled with stench and dripped effluent into the festering streets.

Old St Paul's stood as a stoic monolith brooding the loss of its magnificent spire and subsequent poor rebirth. Now a common place for discussion of commerce among the higher echelons of society, and a den of gossips and vice. Yet, it remained to cast its omnipotent eye over much of the city, including the meeting of bards on the corner of Bread Street and Friday Street on the run of Cheapside.

'How many deaths?' A wide-eyed gent in a crimson velvet jacket fingered the frills of his white shirt. 'What were you thinking, Will? If you were thinking at all?' Tying off the thong around the leather folder, Marlowe dropped the manuscript on the table with much theatrical aplomb. 'Buckets of blood for everyone, I love it!'

'Why thank you, my good man. Do come to the show, it should be on stage at The Theatre soon.' Will could not resist a smile.

Marlowe jumped to his feet and, snatching up the manuscript, he stepped up onto his chair and placed one foot upon the table, spilling stew from his bowl. 'Hear ye, hear ye,' he proclaimed, waving the bundle high above his head, and in so doing disturbing loose crumbs of plaster from the ceiling. 'Coming soon from The Lord Chamberlain's Men, with more blood and guts than a Smithfield slaughterhouse, Titus Andronicus, by Master Shakespeare. Come see, come see.'

'Sit down, you arse,' Shakespeare snatched the manuscript from Marlowe's hand, cuffing him about the ear with it. 'And tell me where you've been Kit, your absence has been noted.'

Marlowe flopped into his seat with a deflating sigh, as the chorus of cheers died down among the patrons. 'Traveling, France and the like. With Walsingham gone the Toad keeps me busy.'

'Conspiracies abound, as they always do,' William supped his ale wiping his mouth on his sleeve. 'Sagrada, that was one.'

Shakespeare pulled a silver dagger from inside his coat and proceeded to slice off a piece of beef from a platter of meats and cheese.

'Is one,' Marlowe corrected him and darted forward, snatching the meat from Will's knife. Swirling the meat beneath his nose he took in the bouquet. 'A fine animal, fed on grass.' Taking a bite, he rolled the morsel around in his mouth. 'Local, less than two years old, a vintage year for cattle.'

Shakespeare cut another piece for himself. Stuffing it straight into his mouth he narrowed his gazed at Marlowe. 'The place is full of vagabonds and thieves.'

Marlowe raised his tankard to a passing waitress, wending her way through the crowded tavern. 'Indeed,' His raised hand followed the sway of her curving backside. 'Where was I?' Kit's brow furrowed, he took up his bowl and scraped the spilt contents back into it.

'Sagrada,' William belched.

'I chanced to witness a most peculiar encounter. While in France, with the Huguenots, we were set upon by some Venetian Jesuits. One, a brute of a man with wild auburn hair and waxed beard, brandished a blade identical to those captured by Sir Francis from the Armada. Were it not for the timely intervention by young Essex, I am of mind I would have been skewered like this beef,' Marlowe stabbed the meat on the platter with a short sword pulled from under the table. The returning waitress screamed, almost dropping the tray of ales she was carrying. 'Fear not, good maiden, for this is not how I would spear one such as thee.'

He flashed her a smile. The waitress turned with a huff and went about her duties. Marlowe sighed with regret.

'Essex was there?' William reached for fresh ale. 'And Southampton?'

'As always, loitering in a shadow,' Marlowe peered over the top of his tankard at his downcast friend. 'Oh, I am most sorry, I forget your affections for your benefactor. I did not mean to cause offence.'

"Tis only my pride you wound. I often wonder how I came to be in the company of such illustrious people. Having spent much of my youth in slaughterhouses gathering hides with my father.'

'Not to mention buckets of piss,' Marlowe guffawed. 'I am sorry Will, but the image of you with a pail of piss in one hand and a quill in the other amuses me so.'

'Quite,' Shakespeare ran a hand through his thinning hair, where smears of grease stuck the last remnants to his scalp. 'Shoes for you, was it not?'

'Never put my foot in shit in all my life,' Marlowe chuckled to himself, peering into his half empty pot. 'Hmm, appears to be a hole in it.'

The evening plunged itself down a well of debauchery as the night-time clientele began to peruse the available offerings. Shakespeare and Marlowe had moved to as quiet a booth as was possible in such a popular part of town. Their conversation drifted in and out, secrets and scandal, returning after many digressions to the Sagrada.

'I tell you, it was so,' Marlowe jabbed his index finger on the table. 'Essex and this huge Jesuit were at each other like devils until they were face to face,' Kit put his fists together in front of him. 'This close, only the hilt of the swords kept their faces apart. I cannot tell what passed between them, but they parted company as acquaintances do. The Jesuit vanished in a blink.' Marlowe pushed himself back in his seat. 'You must never trust Essex. I think him a rebel and a cur. Like as not he would lift the crown of England upon his own scurvy head.'

'I would confess, I have a distrust of him, but Southampton is a good man. I think only well of him,' William stifled a yawn.

Marlowe rose from his seat, grasping at the table, 'Should you see such a weapon, gold hilt with a red gem set in it, get word to Cecil he must know.' He staggered into the table, 'Whole world's gone woozy.'

'Take care, Marlowe, we have work to complete,' Shakespeare leaned forward. 'I should hate for anything to happen to you. You are a gentle soul. Your writing is a gift for all the world.'

'You too, William. We have yet to see your best.' The two men embraced. 'Those who seek to rule through subterfuge will by themselves come undone.'

As the two friends parted, Marlowe pulled his jacket tight about his collar and stepped into the dark embrace of Bread Street. Shakespeare cleared the table of their platters and pots and took them to the bar, where the waitress smiled as she thrust out her bosom.

'Night good sir, any business for yer?' Shakespeare shook his head smiling back at the young girl, her dirty face a perfect picture of her thirteen years.

'Give my best regards to the Fraternity. I'll not be joining them as I have a date south of the river.' Shakespeare turned to leave.

'I bet you do, sir,' The waitress cleared the bar and went about her trade. The hour was late and there were customers waiting.

Shakespeare left The Mermaid and headed toward the Thames and a rendezvous with his benefactor.

Shrouded Moon

London was a different world by night. The bustling crowds were locked inside their homes; the markets had closed and dispersed to resupply for the morrow. The streets were clean enough to see the stone and pressed earth beneath, the dung men had done their job well: two tons of horse droppings is a lot of shovelling. Jackals stalked the city by night: thieves and cut-throats preying on the weak and foolhardy. The theatres were all closed, though some took in people for a price, keeping their inns busy and the landlord's purses full.

The streets were safe enough if you kept your wits about you and your eyes and ears open. Shakespeare had taken a waiting carriage. Southampton cared for those who cared for him, and dedicating your work to the earl was a guarantee of favour both in and out of court. Marlowe had no such luxury, although successful and respected, he had no friends at court; those he could do without.

Marlowe headed west toward St Paul's, taking a less salubrious route north, where his ride from the city was waiting. Accustomed as he was to the streets of London and its varied inhabitants, the ale was taking a heavy toll on his sharpness of mind. One dingy alley began to look and smell much like another. Marlowe rested one hand against a wall, his eyes drawn to the brightness of the waxing moon. 'What secrets you must know, and yet you cannot tell. How blessed be your confidence.'

He leaned back against the wall fighting rising nausea. The world around him skewed to one side, blood coursed his veins, swirled as oceans in his ears. His breath caught on the night air: it was cold for May. Swallowing his supper, he peeled himself from the building and staggered in what he hoped was the right direction.

Ever the gentleman, Christopher Marlowe was a polite drunk to all the aberrant passers-by he encountered. A strip of cloud wrapped itself around the throat of the moon, strangling out the light. Footsteps, echoes of trespass, became muddied by the fog in his mind, a deepening miasma of confusion.

'You all right guv'nor?'

Marlowe straightened his stance, tugging the hem of his jacket down to add to the appearance of sobriety, he turned to face his saviour.

'You left this in Flanders.'

Marlowe gasped, took one step back, before collapsing in a crumpled heap. The apparent saviour stood silhouetted by the moon; it now appeared to Kit, his saviour may not have come to his aid after all. The ribbon of cloud unfurled from the moon to coil itself around his own throat. The air was thinning, becoming more difficult to acquire and swallow. The night was growing cold about him, his stomach ached - no, it hurt. He put a hand to the wetness and named it blood. When he looked down through his failing vision, he saw only the red eye of the golden dagger staring back at him. The click of quality soles faded into the darkness as the curtain came down on the final act of Christopher Marlowe.

THE BISHOP'S CAP

Deep calls to deep, animals of the night. Dark shouts and muffled screams cried out from the maw of darker alleys. The black carriage sped along wider streets to the stone bridge spanning the Thames. With no regard to the comfort of its passenger, the carriage cut across the bridge swerving to avoid the deluge from chamber pots as it clattered along the dual carriageway of the bridge. Escaping the reach of the law into the stews of Southwark, the land of licentiousness and wanton lust: where the real people lived.

Here was a world where the city first breathed, where the Romans built their fort and brought with them sex slaves: London, the city of sin. Shakespeare breathed in the seedy air. Here darkness changed nothing: in truth, darkness was yet another light by which lonely housewives would flit between bars and stews to sell themselves for pleasure and money. Here the taverns and inns thrived and throbbed, life was lived to the full.

'We're here,' The driver hopped down from his seat, to find William Shakespeare out of the carriage taking note of old London.

William turned around, inhaling the toxic cocktail of filth and depravity. 'Where is here?'

'Beggin' your pardon, sir, I was unaware you had not been here before. The area often models itself on the finer parts of Bankside. This is Maiden Lane, where you can partake of many fine skirts, and that way is Cock's Lane,' the driver paused, 'if you prefer boys, men and the like.

And this alley,' he grimaced. 'well, you can cop a feel of something older, well used, possibly diseased,'

'I get the idea,' Shakespeare took out his purse.

The driver raised his hand. 'The master insists.'

'And where might he be?' William tucked his purse back in his jacket, fastening the top button against the cold.

'He'll be in the Bishop's Cap, the one with the sign,' the driver pointed to a wooden notice hanging from a wrought iron frame hung over a vulvic door.

'The one that looks like he's wearing a foreskin for a hat?' Will laughed. 'Oh, what a place this is!' Shaking the driver by the hand he bade him goodnight and strode to the inn.

Accustomed as he was to whores at the places he frequented, such as the theatre, taverns, inns and gossipy St Paul's, he was not ready for the bedlam of Southwark. Squeezing his way between drunken lords and gagging earls, brushing against plump backsides and rouge-nippled whores out for the kill, he made his way to the bar and the only vacant seat. The air hung with the scent of hot bodies sweating ale, hog roast and ripe women. An ale appeared before him in the hand of a smiling woman, her round emerald eyes gleamed from her lead-painted face. Her black hair hung in sweat-bound clots as she thrust her exposed breast upon the counter.

'The ale's on me, luv.' Though her words were common her accent was not.

'My thanks,' Shakespeare lifted the tankard to his lips. 'To your good health.'

The young woman leaned in closer until her bosom brushed his hand. 'The master would like to see you, through the back door. Wait a while before you go through, don't want you coming too soon,' she drew back and kissed his cheek.

'Right.' William drank from his pitcher. The dark ale, unlike his usual tipple, brought fire to his belly.

Raucous laughter burst from every corner, and wherever he tried to avert his eyes, more merriment would erupt. Peers and queers alike were rubbing shoulders with sewer rats and flunkies, whores and pretty boys. The division of class was forgotten: you could not tell where a person was from when in such a state of undress.

'Get yer filthy hands off me.' The barmaid slapped away a contender for her flesh as she shoehorned her bosom into her bustier. 'These ain't for the likes of you,' cupping her hands beneath her bosom, she chided, 'I've rested Lords on these.'

William could but smile: the place was full of charm and wit, an inspiration to his soul. Here were a people he could understand, a people quite capable of entertaining themselves. How much more could he and his men entertain them?

'Madam,' he called in his theatrical best. The young lady brushed herself down as she walked with intent toward him. 'May I inquire, is there a theatre or performance house nearby?'

'Not at present, sir, The Rose is shut on account of the plague.' Shaking her head in dismay, with a hand to her brow. 'It is with much regret; few have seen fit to come this side of the water. Perhaps the reputed lawlessness scares such investors. And the plague, well …' her sigh deflated her stature, she continued, 'Many of us run the gauntlet of the bridge of an afternoon. I, myself, have frequented many a playhouse and seen things of wonder. Though I must confess I am not one for clowns such as Will Kemp. He might have a talent or two but he do go on. Some say, by the time he's done they've all but forgotten the play. But you must know this, sir?'

'Indeed,' Shakespeare touched a finger to his lips. 'You have given me much food for thought.' Rising to his feet he returned the lady's favour with a peck to her cheek. 'It is always best to get it from the horse's mouth.'

'You best be going through to the Master. It's getting early and this place will empty, and the beds will fill quick.' with a nod, she returned to her duties.

William watched as she took a waistcoat from under the counter and slipped it about her person with a touch of elegance. There was romance in the way she walked, a lover taking a stroll, her eye catching every movement in the room. Shakespeare emptied his cup of ale, shuddering as the dark brew swirled in his belly. Clutching his manuscript to his chest he passed through the unstable patrons with the skill of a swordsman parrying a flashing blade. He stepped over one last recumbent reveller and out through the rear door.

The wood-panelled corridor was a gallery of the most pornographic art: etchings on brass and wood, framed drawings in charcoal and ink hung on every door with a price tag pinned beneath each one. Dim oil lanterns flickered as Shakespeare wend his way down the darkening depth until at last, he reached the end. A lone lantern hung from a hammock hook beside a crude carving of a cat.

'Do come in.' the voice commanded in a gentle, if not effeminate tone. William grasped the wrought iron handle and gave it a firm twist. The latch lifted, granting him access to the master's room.

'Henry!' Shakespeare walked with a brisk step across the tapestried floor to embrace his friend. 'Why all the mystery?'

'William — William, to what shall I compare thee?' The Earl of Southampton lifted a poker and rearranged the logs in the hearth, replacing it with a flourish. 'Now, do tell me, how was the meeting at The Mermaid? Were all the bards together?'

Henry lifted a small round table from beside the double bed and placed it between them, he sat in a plump upholstered chair beside the fire with his legs crossed at the ankle.

'I only spoke with Marlowe, the others were still gathering as I left to come here; some of them are shocking time-keepers,' William relaxed into a chair.

Henry brushed a finger across his right cheek, 'I see the barmaid has left her mark.' Taking a kerchief from his breast pocket he tossed it to Shakespeare. 'Marlowe was to have left the city.' Southampton drummed his fingers on the arm of the chair, pulling his feet in closer to it.

'Is there a threat to him? He spoke of the Sagrada, Essex and some Jesuit in Flanders.' Southampton raised an eyebrow, pursing his lips as though about to speak. 'Gold-handled blades.'

'With a ruby eye?' Henry stared at the flames imagining the flames of war on the horizon. 'I must inform my mentor; this is grave news.' Southampton put his hands together as though about to pray. 'You know of their history? The Sagrada,' Henry inclined his head towards William.

'Only that Sir Frances went after such a vessel when the Armada came. Did he not pursue some later, with Essex?' Shakespeare leaned forward rubbing his hands before the fire.

'I was with them, as I often am,' Southampton cleared his throat. 'We lost a lot of ships chasing treasure. Our own vengeful armada was pitiful. We did, however, capture a treasure ship running for Cádiz. Sir Frances is out there now, somewhere, but all is not well, I fear. This ship was laden with an impossible amount of Inca treasures, but it was not what brought us home early. In the captain's quarters, hidden beneath his bed was a cache of Sagrada, the Holy Sword, intended for these shores.'

'Why?' William leaned in closer, his voice a whisper of conspiracy.

'It is no secret in Court, the Spanish plan to invade. Walsingham believes it will be through Ireland, though the Spanish continue to raid the Cornish coast. Cecil is obliged to acquiesce. Essex is keen to gather ships and go to war on all fronts, but there are not the coffers for such recklessness. There are times when I would like to box his ears.'

'Your smile says everything, Henry. I see you are looking at this,' Shakespeare held out his manuscript. 'Titus Andronicus, but I might have overdone the slaughter,' William made a pinch gesture, 'a tad. This kind of carnage is all the rage, so I thought, why not?'

'I look forward to reading it.' Henry sat the manuscript on his lap. 'Her Majesty has seen fit to grant powers to Earl Tyrone in Ireland. To wit, he was quick to avail himself of our wagons. Loaded them with arms and vanished from The Pale. Keep an ear to the Irish; they love to get one over us. As for the Sagrada,' Southampton tossed another log onto the fire. 'We have no idea where they were destined for, Catholic sympathisers no doubt.' Southampton rubbed his face in his hands, masking a yawn. 'Will you want use of the ante chamber?' He gestured toward a small doorway nestled in the corner of the room.

'I think it best, it is too late to return to Shoreditch. The fewer eyes that see me the better,' Shakespeare stood up, stretched his arms and yawned. 'You have me at it now. I will bid you good night. Will you be here for breakfast in the morning?'

'I doubt so. I have to be seen in court: I have many arses to kiss, and none of them pretty.' Southampton handed Shakespeare a lantern and closed the bedroom door behind him.

Favourite things

'When will the old hag realise it is time for her to set her wig aside and give me the throne? Who else but me could take this nation of ours forward and conquer the new worlds?' Essex raged at the gilt-edged mirror. Tearing his ruff from his neck he threw it on the floor, grinding it beneath his boot. 'I conquer kingdoms in her name: France and the stupid Canaries, Cádiz, Flanders ... God alone knows how many times I've bloodied King Philip's nose. What do I get in return? A few favours and a sickly, yellow toothed smile every time she sees me.'

'Robert, my dearest kin, you should have more care of your words.' A dark-haired beauty caught his jacket as it was hurled across the room.

'What do you know of it? You're just a woman, as is she,' Essex turned in a sudden fury. 'Where is my bath? I asked for it to be ready for when I came home.'

Servants scurried around the house with extra pails of steaming water to ensure the copper tub remained hot. The dark-haired girl moved towards the bath.

'Penelope, have you lost leave of your senses? It is for servants to do.'

Penelope looked down her elegant nose at her brother and continued with what she was doing. 'Go on ... go. There is no pleasing the brat when he is like this. I will deal with him,' she shooed the servants from the room. Turning to face her brother, who stood, hands planted on his hips, his bare chest heaving, she continued, 'Bath time,' She stabbed a finger at the tub, her lips drawn to a tight line. 'Get in. Now.'

Essex straightened his back, tossing his long, dark brown hair over his shoulder with a flick of his head.

'Do you suppose to treat me as she does?' Essex pulled off his boots, throwing them to the floor.

'Yes, I do.'

'I am a grown man. I lead men into war. I will not be spoken to in such a manner by any woman,' Essex fought to control his trembling lower lip.

Penelope removed the purple glove from her left hand, taking a moment to examine the fine stitching. 'I wonder if I could make such fine leather from your skinny rear?' The copper bath made a dull gong sound as she kicked it. 'The bell tolls for you. So, either get in of your own accord, or I'll make you.' Penelope picked at her fingernails, Essex stropped across the room to the bath, thrust his trousers to the floor and stood as God intended.

'I thought you said you were a man?' She smiled. 'In. You smell like a horse.'

Essex thrust a foot into the water, splashing his other in next to it, he dropped into the bath sending a wash of hot water over the sides.

Steam filled the room as Penelope poured extra water into the tub, together with jasmine oil and dried rose petals. Taking a pot from a low table beside the bath she opened it and took out two scented balls of soap.

'This one is frankincense, and this is a mixture of herbs to help keep the plague at bay. Shall I scrub, or can you manage by yourself?'

'Must you always be so bloody belittling?' He looked his sister in her deep blue eyes. 'I did a good thing today. I saved the life of a common man.'

'Good for you,' Penelope lathered soap in a sponge, 'and what did this common man need saving from, other than himself, of course?'

'Prison, the gallows, I do not know what the punishment is for a rapist,' Essex took the sponge and began to caress his skin with it.

'Rapist?' Penelope crossed to the bath table and drank from the wine decanter. 'You spared a rapist? You disgust me at times.'

'He was caught in the act. We were disembarking at Whitehall when we heard the kerfuffle down a street. There was this fellow, Thomas Derek, helping himself to a woman's virtue in broad daylight. So, I dragged him to the training ground and gave him a beating to remember,' Essex threw the sponge at his sister. 'Are you listening to me?' Penelope looked at him and shrugged her shoulders. 'Charming, here I am pouring out my life and you're getting drunk,' Essex slapped his hands into the bathwater. With a shake of his head, he continued his discourse. 'So, there we were on the parade ground and I had the most merciful idea.' Pausing for effect he drew a breath, 'I gave him a job: he's to be the new executioner at the Tower — Brilliant.'

Penelope finished the wine and went looking for more. When she returned, Essex was out of his bath and wrapped in a linen robe, it clung to his wet skin.

'What am I to do when you go?' Penelope handed her brother a large glass and a jug of wine.

'I want you to entertain Mountjoy, it is important. And you get along with Lady Ormond so well. Perhaps you could all go shopping at Richmond,' Essex scoffed.

'Ah yes, I need a new dress for the ball. Such a good idea, why thank you, Robert,' Penelope Rich gave a most excellent curtsy. 'I do hope Marie is there, she is an absolute hoot. Have you invited any of the Irish harlots over?'

'Red Hugh's daughter is no harlot, so I'll not have you talk of her in such a manner. They are a vital part of our future. They have connections to James, so we cannot afford to war with them.'

'War with the Irish is inevitable. Elizabeth keeps awarding their land to her puppies as reward for gallantry and sucking up. How's your list of favours coming along? Knight of the Garter, Master of the Horse, King of the World? Oh no, Philip and the Infanta have that one ...or is it the Pope? I get so confused since I am, after all, only a woman. I'm going home to my husband; is your good lady not here?'

'No, you know well, she is out of the city,' Essex looked at the glass in his hand. 'This is my last chance, for a few weeks at least, to get blinding drunk.'

'Is Southampton going with you and Sir Walter?'

'Her Royal Majesty has forbidden it,' Essex emptied his glass and poured himself another one.

'So, he is going. If only to annoy her. How does Southampton get away with it all?' Penelope gathered up her cloak and swung it around her shoulders.

'When I find out I'll kill the bastard responsible. Until then I shall be only too glad to have him along if only to annoy Raleigh.' Essex drained his glass yet again. 'I have my own ship to command this time, so I won't have to listen to Sir Walter going on all bloody day. Such a hero.'

'Aw, I love it when the drink starts talking. First, you'll get sad, then angry until you become invincible,' Penelope opened the door to the entrance hall.

'You know me so well. Now get lost. I have a date with a fine-bodied wench,' Essex fell into a chair cradling the jug of wine. 'Have the servants come tidy this away.'

'Yes, master. Good night, do take care and don't do anything stupid or rash,' Penelope paused, 'Farewell Robert.'

'Farewell Lady Rich, see you whenever,' Essex saluted his sister, slopping his wine on the floor. 'Bollocks.'

BAD NEWS

Beneath the golden gaze of a thousand gilt stars Elizabeth sat upon her throne, listening to the ramblings of the Privy Council. Those chosen by The Queen to discuss all matters important to Her Majesty. Elizabeth's gaze wandered about the dark panelling draped with her associate heraldry, the dark blue ceiling littered with golden stars. The old wooden benches, upon which sat her most trusted and loyal supporters. One notable absence: Essex.

'Sir Walter,' Elizabeth bade her noble knight draw closer so she could have his ear. 'Has my good fellow the Earl of Essex given any just cause as to his absence?'

'None, your Majesty,' Raleigh glanced to the empty seat nearest to the royal platform. 'Though he may be preparing for the morning,' He straightened up.

'Ah, the voyage. Do remind me, I do love to hear your tales of the sea,' Elizabeth feigned interest in the grumbling of her private court.

'We will soon be departing from Plymouth. I have —' Raleigh mulled over the precise wording, '—as requested, given Essex charge of a secondary fleet. When we encounter the Spanish as they head north, we shall be able to take them on two flanks. We will then go on to bolster the treasury with any donations the Spanish might have secured in the southern islands.'

'Excellent. I believe it is about time he proved worth through his own command; do you not think?' Elizabeth cast a knowing eye at Raleigh who smiled as he doffed his cap. 'Walter, you are not in agreement?' She turned in her throne.

'Your Majesty knows well my thoughts on the Earl, so I would rather stay silent than utter anything defamatory,' Raleigh clasped his hands behind his back. 'You are being hailed from the floor, Majesty.'

Elizabeth blew out a testy sigh as she looked at each member of the Privy Council in turn until she found the supplicant. 'Sir Francis, what is it?'

Francis stood, 'Ireland,' Elizabeth's shoulder sagged. 'Tyrone has taken a large shipment of our arms and armour over to Castlederg,' Francis looked down his nose at Elizabeth.

'Tyrone? The young man I gave my trust to,' Her Majesty waved a hand for more. 'I assume it will only get worse from here on in?'

'Majesty,' Sir Francis drew a breath, before exhaling. 'Captain Willis, the crown-appointed sheriff, has been driven out of the region by Hugh O'Neill and a contingent of local clans. They now press against our forces south of Ulster. It is known he is displeased with his non-appointment as Lord President of Ulster. It is believed he will mount an offensive for the whole of Ireland.'

'The savages,' Elizabeth drummed her fingers on the arm of the throne. 'Send another two thousand troops to bolster the forces.'

'Your Majesty, I must obj …' The Earl of Sussex withered beneath the gaze of The Queen.

'It is apparent, at least to me, the Irish are about to rebel. We cannot afford to be caught unawares. Should they assail Sir Henry Bagenal in The Pale, all will be lost. I will not sit idle while my father's work is torn apart by warring Catholic tribes.'

Cecil struggled to his feet, 'One further notice, my Queen—'

'You may remain seated: some do not wait to be told,' The Queen glared at Essex.

'—Philip II, the Spanish King—' began Cecil.

'I am aware who he is,' Elizabeth raised a hand, taking the opportunity to inspect her latest acquisition of purple gloves from Stratford.

'—has passed a papal bull for your ... for your death,' Cecil coughed into his hand.

'Do I care?' Elizabeth gave a wicked grin. 'No. But to keep you all happy I'll have Raleigh double the guard about me at all times. I find it curious he should give such an instruction for sin. Is he unaware of the Commandments?'

There was brief chuckle among the council.

'He says, and I quote,' Cecil watched The Queen as he spoke, 'this killing of the Protestant pretender to the true Catholic Throne would not be sin, for she is a heretic.'

A cold silence fell upon the room.

Elizabeth cleared her throat with a testy cough, the redness of her cheeks showing under the lead white of her makeup. 'Sir Walter. When you are at sea be sure to cut the throat of every Venetian you may happen upon.'

THE THEATRE

The carriage bumped along Bishops Gate Street heading north out of the crush of the city towards the more open reaches of Shoreditch. Riding in comparative comfort, the formidable legacy of London masters, Robert and his father William Cecil scrutinised the lands, they served to protect, in silence. One, an aged gent with a long grey beard was dressed in black breeches and crimson jacket topped with a conservative ruff covering the top of his velvet collar. His companion was in black with a shy white frill peeking from the cuffs.

The afternoon sun chased the last clouds from the sky bringing hope of warmth and better times ahead. The smell of the sewer ditch pervaded the air despite a cleansing rain. The carriage turned left on the last leg of its journey. Peasantry stepped aside to allow their betters to pass along the narrowing lane leading to The Theatre: no one wanted a beating for obstructing the passage of a lord, and nothing was going to keep them from their date with a king. Across the fields a windmill was being turned into the wind, its sails began to revolve with the reluctance of an arthritic limb.

The Theatre was near full when the carriage drew up outside. Cecil's driver stowed his whip and climbed down, and with a firm grasp opened the unmarked door.

'Here is something for you to enjoy the show.' Cecil dropped coins into the driver's open hand without so much as a glance his way. The driver doffed his cap, his eyes fixed somewhere on the distant skyline.

'We will be a while after the performance. Please ensure you are close to the door,' Robert Cecil dusted off his shoulders as he spoke before following his father into the building.

Inside was lit by ensconced torches, their oily smoke rose in slender quivering palls. The audience, with their packages of bread, nuts and berries, took their places before the empty stage. The Theatre soon took on the smell of bodies: dirt, sweat, and filth-encrusted shoes. Beer flowed as the curtain lifted. Voices rose in rowdy cheers as King Richard II walked onto the stage with flowing robes and a golden crown. Turning toward the audience he began, 'Old John of Gaunt, time-honour'd Lancaster ... '

The people fell silent as the king continued his speech. 'Against the Duke of Norfolk, Thomas Mowbray?'

'Ah, here come the messengers,' Cecil smiled as Mowbray and Bolingbroke took the stage to make their pleas before the king.

Shakespeare beckons. I shall make my way by the trough. I have all I need from this performance,' Cecil rose from his seat. 'The green room, after.'

Without waiting for a response Cecil made his way through the press of bodies to the side door where the piss trough beckoned. Wet earth squelched up around the edge of his boots marring their perfect shine.

A low ash fence blocked the view to the city where a few stragglers passed, muttering their complaints about the lack of food. 'Should the harvests fail again the riots shall swallow the Mercers,' The voice ebbed into the shadows of the alley.

'All yours, squire,' the gent glanced his way as coins brushed his palm.

Cecil stood at the trough and took aim. Resting his left hand against the plastered wall, Robert Cecil let his fingers explore inside a crack until they seized upon a leather thong. With a gentle tug he loosened the tiny parcel, slipping it into his sleeve. He fastened his trousers and returned to the theatre.

The play was in full flow as he skirted around the patrons baying for the king's blood. There was still plenty of time before the close of the final act and Will Kemp would give his song and dance.

'Excellent as always,' Cecil held the door open for Shakespeare to enter the green room, now devoid of players.

'Thank you, my lord,' Shakespeare closed the door, securing it with a latch. 'I shall come to the point and be brief. We shall be vacating these walls and sharing with The Rose.'

'Was Henry helpful?' Cecil poured himself a drink from a stone jar.

'Indeed, he was. He has been a most helpful—' Shakespeare paused, a smile tickled his lips, 'patron.' Cecil returned the smile. 'Word has come, riots are planned from Alders Gate to Billiter Lane. They hear of grain among the Jews.'

'I will ensure law is upheld within the city walls.' Cecil put the glass to his lips. 'Reeks of Essex. I so detest this sweetness. Have you nothing else?'

'I am sorry. We are favoured with it. Burbage is an admirer. I only partake of lighter ales. I have some if you wish it?' Shakespeare made to leave the room.

'There is no need, I can stomach this for now. Have you, by chance, met the Earl of Essex?'

'I have,' Shakespeare took a seat opposite Cecil offering his guest bread and meats from a platter. 'I do not trust him. There, I have said it.' Cecil raised an eyebrow, 'I think he only wants for himself. Though he is in high favour of her Majesty, he lusts for more. What more could a man in such position desire beyond what he has?'

'Keep an ear and do your best to garner his trust,' Cecil placed his glass on the table, swapping it for a plate of food. A muffled cheer from the audience filled the green room.

'The play is at an end. Will Kemp will begin his tomfoolery,' Shakespeare drew a testy breath. 'I think it is nigh time the theatre had a change. What say you? I am of mind for the play to be the only thing. Many are of such simple heart they forget the play and remember only the merry jape. Such pity, or is it only the wants of a bard?'

'No William, it is not. It is a fact close to the buffoons in parliament. They sit and discuss all manner of things privy to the country only to bury such concerns 'neath their own self-worth. Heaven forbid they care for any but themselves,' Cecil swallowed another roll of meat. 'Yet there am I among them with my nays, braying as an ass.'

There was a plaintive knock at the door, two tight wraps of a knuckle. Shakespeare rose from his chair opening the door to allow their visitors entry.

'Ah, Bolingbroke and Mowbray,' Cecil bade them to sit. 'My father will be joining us.'

'Well played, my good men. Were circumstances different I would offer you part in the Lord Chamberlain's Men,' Shakespeare returned to his seat. 'Do enjoy the meagre offerings,' he gestured to the food and wine on the table.

'Gentlemen, your visit will be brief. Thomas, this is for you,' Cecil pulled the parcel from his sleeve and passed it to Mowbray. You'll find all in order for your passage to Spain. From now on everything is to come in cypher, understood?'

'My lord,' Mowbray rose to his feet. 'You can trust in me. Have I Marie as my aide?'

'You have, she is skilled in cypher and moves with grace between court and common.' Robert Cecil cast a furtive eye at Bolingbroke. 'She has my complete trust. Now go, The Dawn Cutter leaves from Bylynges Gate for Cádiz on the morning tide. Be there.

'Bolingbroke, I want you to watch Ben Johnson and the admiral's men, report all you see and hear. This time, try not to inflame his temper,' Cecil paused, patting his stomach. 'Furthermore— '

A loud banging on the door interrupted the nest. 'Master Cecil,' Shakespeare dashed across the room, loosening the catch with a practised hand. 'Master Cecil, it is your father. He has taken ill.'

'God, man,' Robert Cecil bounded from his chair. 'Get him to my carriage.'

SLEIGHT OF HAND

Sweat and old ale, the smell of a good night's drinking. Musty breath and yellow smiles abounded as the games and gambling began. Cards and skittle, shove ha'penny, and as the eve wears dark, the men bet on goolie and cherry-pit for lusty favours. Smoky fires crackled with green wood, the sizzling sap a hissing adder amongst glowing faces. Merriment ensues, hands wander south of the naval, separating skirts and loosing purse strings. The night is young, and the people are foolish, there is still much to play for.

'Miss,' The Irishman's slender grasp on the edge of the bar gave way as his knees buckled beneath him, no longer able to sustain the weight of alcohol-laden fat. His plump face kissed the wooden plinth, once a deck board from a Spanish galleon, with all the finesse of a sledgehammer cracking eggs.

'With you in a minute sir,' the barmaid waved without turning from her task.

Laughter rocked the house as cruel pundits poured their scorn on the fat man trying to claw his way back to standing. No one noticed the door open, and the dark-robed gentleman scythe his way through the punters with the grace of an assassin. He stood beside the fat man, watching his struggle with the slipperiness of his own reality. Taking a pewter tankard from his pocket he used it to bang on the counter, his hope to rouse the attention of a serving wench. He was not to be disappointed.

'He with you?' The barmaid pointed at the hand groping along the bar in search of purchase.

'No,' he clubbed the fat man over the head with the base of his tankard. 'He is alone.'

'Let me see,' the barmaid stepped back, heaving her bosom back into her black leather bustier. 'Who must you be?' Tapping a finger to her lips, she eyed the visitor up and down. Leaning over the bar to espy his lower half she spoke with surety. 'Well, you've no shit on your shoes, so you came by carriage. You left your last place in a rush: still in your theatrics,' she circled her face with her index finger. 'It's sex at The Rose, violence at Crosskeys. Hm, you look kingly, so it's Bolingbroke, at The Theatre,' she winked, puckering her lips.

'At your service,' Bolingbroke bowed with a swirl of his cape.

'So, what's your pleasure to be, Bolingbroke?' The maid plucked a tooth from the counter and dropped it into a small tin. 'I'll keep it, case he wants it.'

'I'll be in the area for the time being at least, so room and ... ' Bolingbroke peered down her cleavage.

'Only the room, try anything else and you'll find yourself in the privy with your throat cut,' the barmaid feigned a smile.

'Now Marie.'

'Not here,' she growled. 'You may not make it to morning if you utter that name in these quarters.'

'Still not mastered the accent, I see,' Bolingbroke leaned in for a conspiratorial whisper, his pock-marked face brushed against her cheek.

Marie slipped one hand beneath the counter as she drew Bolingbroke to the edge of his balance, 'I'll cut a smile right across your throat.' Bolingbroke swallowed against the cold steel pressed to his flesh. 'There's a good boy. I've many a friend in here would turn a blind eye to your passing.'

'Understood,' Bolingbroke allowed himself a last glance down Marie's bustier. 'Room it is.'

'Six is free, has a door to the back,' Marie handed Bolingbroke a black key. 'I'm Nell, here. Now take him,' she pointed to where the fat man lay. 'Drop him in the privy.' Stepping out from behind the bar, she walked to the back of the room and opened the door leading to the stairs. 'Up and keep turning left.'

She watched Bolingbroke drag the fat man through the door by his black ponytail and crusted collar. Locking the door, she returned to the bar.

A cluster of sweating lushes anxious for their next golden fix rattled their tankards as Nell collected the cherry stones and goolie cup. Two empty crates were upturned, eager participants stepped up to show their skills.

'Gentlemen, gentlemen,' Nell handed one competitor the small box of cherry stones and around the other she tied a string from which was hung a small cup. 'Allow me to adjust your dress.' Nell slipped around the man, bending in front of him she cupped his manhood in her hand. 'Let's get the measure of you, good sir.' From her pocket she took a heavy wooden ball with a string through its centre. She threaded the loose end of the string through a hole in the bottom of the goolie cup, tying it off with a tug. 'Gentlemen. Your wagers and forfeits,' Nell took a crate from behind the bar, spilling the bread from it onto the floor. 'Jim has the cup and must use his supple hips to flip the ball into the cup. George must spit the stones into his beer. Jim needs only one ball in the cup but George, you need three stones. The winner gets a face-full of these beauties.' Nell grabbed her breasts, giving them a firm squeeze. The cheers could be heard across the Thames. 'But first, what secrets will they whisper in my ear?' She went to each competitor, in turn, listening for the promise of gossip. Nell ran the tip of her tongue across her lips, 'Some real juice on offer. Gentlemen, begin!'

Jim thrust his hips forward too hard, receiving a weighty ball in the groin for his efforts. More bread and beer changed hands in wager. George spat his third stone, this time finding the target. Jim thrust again; the ball rimmed the cup before bringing a tear to his eyes. He tried again, and again, his frustration the only thing getting larger. George landed his second stone, with a wink to Nell, who egged the pair of them on by running her fingers up and down her cleavage. Jim missed again. His frustration boiling over, he kicked George in the rear causing him to spit out his mouthful of cherry stones. Stones went everywhere, one into the cup.

'I win, the prize is all mine!' George lunged forward forgetting where he was standing. He tumbled, reached out, catching his hand in the front of Nell's bustier, exposing her charms to all. George clambered to his feet amid the jostling crowd, one tooth less than when he went down. 'I'm ready to receive,' he wiped the spittle from his lips with the back of his sleeve, smearing dirt across his cheek.

George stretched out his hands as he rushed forward only to be met with Nell's palm in his face. 'Just the face Georgie boy, no hands. You ain't got the class for that.'

George complied and went home a happy man. Jim nursed his losses in a fresh ale.

HEROES RETURN

The spring sun smiled upon the city. Gulls cried as they wheeled across the exposed mud, diving to pluck crabs scuttling among the detritus of London life. Dogs barked from the harbour wall, welcoming the Duc Repulse as it slid along the Thames on the incoming tide, passing the ever-watchful eyes in the Tower. Children ran along the sea wall kicking a tied bundle of rags, squealing with delight as they sent a stack of crates crashing to the ground. They stopped to wave at the sailors, every bit as worn and tattered as the children, grinning at their response.

Two heavy anchors splashed into the river, dragging their bills into the mud and pulling their flukes deep into British soil. They were home after more than six months at sea. The launch knocked against the pontoon jetty, its wooden hull creaking against the thick ropes bound around the Norman pillars. Essex was the first to disembark and settle his sea legs on the shores of the nation whose rulership he coveted. Southampton, as ever, was not far behind his friend and ally.

Bylynges Gate harbour was alive with traders exchanging barrels and ale for bolts of cloth, fish for meats; coins changed hands shaken in promise of more to come. A steady flow of merchants with loaded barrows heading for Leadenhall and Stocks Market along to Bowechurch where they could pay their tithes. Pony carts drawn by tired, thin horses clattered up alleys and down shadowed walks for as long as there was daylight to work by. With the theatres closed until Lent was done, the victualing houses enjoyed their peak season.

'Where are we headed?' Southampton stepped aside, avoiding a large pile of steaming horse dung.

'The Swan,' Essex pushed through the throng of people with gay abandon.

'Unusual choice.' A pail of dark yellow fluid splattered on the pavement from a third-story tenement adding to the ripe spring fragrance.

'We are the last to arrive back from the Azores. I saw one of Blount's men in the harbour, he passed me this,' Essex held a scrap of paper out for Southampton, who took it. After glancing at its contents, he handed it back. 'Charles will be at The Swan, we have much to catch up on. It's along Thames Street, beyond St. Magnus.' Southampton kept pace with Essex, sidling through the people, avoiding those his friend pushed aside, surprised at how the common people still saluted Essex and showered God's blessing upon him.

Crossing New Fleet Street, they glanced south toward London Bridge and its seething mass of life. Here societies funnelled into one another, converging in an equilibrium of souls coalescing into the lifeblood of the great city. London pulsed with wealth and poverty, each feeding off the other: the rich reliant upon the poor to meet their needs while the poor fought for scraps from the master's hand.

Minutes later they arrived at The Swan where a town crier gave the news. 'O yea, hear ye well. Spanish crushed in Cádiz and the Azores. The Earl of Essex leads successful rout of our sworn enemies.' Essex paused to hear of his latest triumph. 'Whole island and the cities captured, by the great Earl.'

'All appears to be in order,' Essex ducked into The Swan, taking his time to sift his way through the patrons to a table occupied by a gentleman in his late thirties sporting a fine moustache, waxed and trimmed; his dark brown hair brushed back, framing his youthful looks. Opposite him sat his mistress, Lady Penelope Rich. 'Charles.' Beckoning a waitress, 'Penelope,' he gave a sardonic smile. 'You made it back in one piece.'

Essex waited for Southampton to take a seat before he pulled his out into a more open view of the clientele. 'I got your message,' He slid the note across the table to Blount, 'Some halfwit passed it to me in open view. You should choose your spies with greater caution. It's a wonder the whole city is not aware of his actions.'

'I for one never saw it pass between you,' Southampton thanked the waitress, taking the tray from her as she reached over Essex to get to the table.

'You never see anything, Henry. Too much time reading bloody plays. What's the one you were lamenting over on the voyage? Richard, the idiot King, or something? We all know what a blathering nancy he was,' Essex chuckled into his wine.

'It was a huge success. Departed the city on tour. Should you find the chance to see Master Shakespeare's work I am sure you will find it most insightful,' Southampton sliced some bread to dip in his dripping jelly. 'Nothing we had on ship compares to the taste of this.'

'Pauper's food,' Essex scoffed.

'I too saw the play, Henry, it was clever in its guise. Cecil had it performed at his home in the Strand, prior to seeing it at The Theatre,' Lady Penelope smiled with contempt at her brother.

'Speaking of Cecil, his father passed away leaving him in charge of her Majesty's business. Parliament now sits at his behest. He is less tolerant of ministerial buffoons,' Charles dusted breadcrumbs from his silver doublet.

Penelope licked her lips, 'Better watch yourself on the Privy Council, brother.' Essex swept the comment aside with a flick of his wrist.

A man dressed in black jacket and brown shirt beneath a dark green, grease-stained velvet coat approached the table, his hair pulled back in a short ponytail.

'My Lords,' he gave a polite bow to Charles Blount, before recognising Essex and Southampton. As an afterthought, he doffed his cap to Lady Rich, 'Ma'am.'

'Bolingbroke,' Blount looked straight at him. 'News?'

'Yellow Ford,' Bolingbroke walked away, turning back toward the moorings on the Thames.

'He's the idiot I was referring to earlier,' Essex refilled his glass. 'You cannot trust such a dullard?'

'You still understand nothing of the common man, do you, Essex?' Blount put his glass on the table, twisting it ninety degrees as though he were looking for something in it. The waitress came and removed the glass, replacing it with another, filled with an amber liquid. 'You lack subtlety and self-control, your attitude will cost you dear one day,' Blount turned the glass again. The waitress returned, this time taking the food as well.

'How did she know I was finished? I may well have—' Essex turned toward the counter where the waitress had been.

'I told her to clear things away. Subtlety and subterfuge Robert, learn them both,' Blount chided. Southampton smiled at Penelope who shook her head, choosing to look out of the window at the beggars in the street rather than at her noble-blooded brother.

'I shall take a look at the travesty, no doubt it will entertain those of the street who have simpler minds,' Essex sipped his wine, hoping his glass hid his smile.

'Her Majesty is to hold a banquet in honour of your great and courageous efforts in Cádiz,' Lady Penelope told him, watching the dung merchant scrape and shovel his way along the street. 'I expect news of your return will reach her soon enough.'

'It will indeed. I shall go to her once I am bathed and cleansed,' Essex dusted crumbs from his jacket. 'I have worn the same few outfits for months; the sea does the silks no favours. Will you be joining us, Henry?'

'No,' Southampton met Lady Penelope's eye. 'I am no longer welcome at the palace. Since my infractions with her noble friends, I am off the guest list. You'll have to manage by yourself,' Henry pursed his lips as though contemplating his next move. 'Just make sure you leave the handmaids alone; they are not for your hands.'

'I will take what I want and do as I will with it,' Essex pressed himself back into his chair with his hands upon his heart. 'It is not my fault God made me so charming and irresistible.' All eyes turned toward him.

1599

Foundations and Plots

Another day dawned over London, washing the night away with splashes of red and yellow across a pale blue sky. Birds sang their dawn chorus, trilling for a mate as life burst out at every turn. The heavy spring rains had washed the upper streets of Southwark clean. Shakespeare walked over the patch of land waving his arms as he sprang from step to step. Richard Burbage followed close behind, his exuberance a match for his friend.

'We can have trap doors in the stage and rigging, so we'll fly Richard, like angels soaring from the heavens,' William danced around in the frozen earth. 'Canons and smoke,' he danced in merry circles stopping to point at his friend. 'Music.' raising his eyebrows. 'And above the grand entrance,' Shakespeare ran to the side of a muddy patch, 'here, totus mundus agit histrionem.'

'All the world's a playhouse,' Richard Burbage put an arm across Shakespeare's shoulders before he danced off again. 'We still need to get the materials. It's going to cost us everything to do it. Now the authorities have closed every theatre to the north, we have nowhere but noble houses to ply our trade.'

Shakespeare slipped beneath Richard's arm, took him by the hand and danced him out into the street. 'We may have lost the land upon which The Theatre stands but the construct remains ours,' He tugged a folded paper from inside his jacket. 'Look,' he cried, jabbing a finger at the page. 'The lease is quite explicit; it says that for twenty-one years we may have the land for our use. Anything we put upon it shall remain the property of the signatory.'

'Your point, William?' Burbage took the paper, following the text with his finger.

'The Theatre is ours. I say we take and use it to build this,' William threw his arms wide, exclaiming towards the bare plot of dirt, 'The Globe. Here, among the people, our patrons, on our doorstep.'

'Are you completely mad, Will?' Burbage laughed at Shakespeare's antics. Watching him dash to and fro, acting out all parts of an imagined scene.

'Assemble the Lord Chamberlain's Men: we are about to do the performance of our lives,' William spun around almost falling. 'Do you still know that magician fellow?'

'Dr John Dee? I do indeed. I shall enquire of him as to how we progress,' Burbage slung his arm around Shakespeare, steering him up the street. 'I propose a toast. To The Bishop's Cap we march.'

Bursting through the door of the tavern the two men, full of merriment, strode to the bar to place their order. Nell tugged a pair of tankards from their hooks and proceeded to fill them from a small keg sat perched on a rear shelf. Twisting the tap closed, she carried the ales over to her latest customers, sliding them across the counter into their eager hands.

'What brings two fine gentlemen such as yourselves into my hostelry at such an early hour?' Nell reached her hands behind her head, weaving her hair into a long plait. Her green smock pulled tight over her ample bosom.

'We are celebrating, madam,' Burbage scooped up his ale quaffing it as though it were his last.

'We are going to be neighbours, you and I,' Shakespeare gave a crooked wink. 'We are about to embark on an episode of utter madness,' Shakespeare clattered his full tankard against Burbage's empty one.

'To the Globe, and all those who frequent her,' Burbage laughed aloud.

'What's a Globe?' Nell wiped the spilled ale from the counter with minimal interest in her duty.

'A theatre,' Shakespeare's eyes widened. 'We are going to build a theatre here in Southwark. We have acquired a plot of land at the end of the street. We shall begin construction as soon as the ground has thawed.'

'And before the spring tides, or else we will be a foot under water. Timing will be crucial,' Burbage waved a hand at the joint of meat over the fire. 'Is it ready? All this excitement has me famished.'

'Only stew and bread, m'love.' Nell glanced back toward the kitchen where a huge black pot boiled on the plate.

'Then stew it is,' Burbage rubbed his hands together as though he were hoping to light a fire from them.

Nell went to the kitchen to retrieve a bowl of stew and suet dumplings.

'A new theatre?' Southampton rose from his seat near the fire. 'This is the most exciting thing to happen since Raleigh at Cádiz. Splendid!' Throwing a handful of coins across the bar he pointed to a large stone jar. 'If you please, Nell. Gentlemen, a proper toast. Spoils of war, Spanish brandy destined for the king himself.'

Nell poured all four of them a measure from the jar, the dark liquid drawing itself into a pool in each glass.

'May I ask if I can contribute to the setting up of ... the Globe?' Southampton drew up a stool beside them at the bar. 'I would be thrilled to ensure its success. How would a thousand pounds sound?'

Shakespeare coughed his brandy back into the glass. Burbage patted him between the shoulders. 'That is incredible, my Lord. I would thank thee greatly.'

Burbage stumbled over his own feet in his rush to stand and bow. 'I—I do not know how to thank you. Sir.'

Henry Wriothesley shook Burbage by the hand. He reached over to do the same to Shakespeare. Blushing, he asked, 'Could I ask an impertinent favour? I never did see Romeo and Juliet; would it be possible to open with the play?' Clearing his throat, he continued, 'While my bravery is at full mast may I also ask if I might have the best seat in the house for the performance.'

'Henry, my dearest friend,' Shakespeare rose from his stool, seizing hold of Southampton's hand he looked him in the eyes. 'Soft what light through yonder window breaks, the sun sets its light upon thee Henry and the moon is filled with jealousy. My dearest Earl, you shall go to the theatre where you shall sit as king with the whole stage before you.'

'You honour me more than I deserve,' Henry rose and returned the courtesy of a bow.

'Blimey, I've seen it all now,' Nell flicked her filthy dishcloth at the three men. 'Will I be going?' she quipped.

'Of course, Nell,' Southampton turned toward her. 'With Essex back on dry land your services will be needed elsewhere,' His tone was much quieter than before. 'There is to be a banquet at the palace in honour of the fleet's success in Cádiz. I shall arrange for you to attend as I am no longer welcomed in the presence of her Majesty.'

'Why ever not?' Nell mimed pulling a pistol from her pocket.

'Quite so,' Henry half-smiled. 'He's still alive. I do not see what all the fuss is about.'

'That and embarking on numerous quests with Essex abroad,' Nell removed her serving apron, revealing a black velvet skirt with pearl buttons around the waist.

'I must be going, Will. Dr John Dee is in town today at the Mercers Hall. I shall go and see if I can gain audience with him,' Burbage placed his empty stew bowl on the counter and left.

'That is indeed most fortunate,' Southampton waved Burbage farewell. 'It is rumoured you have come to the attention of Her Majesty, Queen Elizabeth. This is no small thing,' Shakespeare, eyes wide, blinked at Southampton. 'I expect, soon, you will receive an invitation to the palace. It is unlikely on your first visit, you will be asked to perform one of your plays. Like as not, The Queen will ask you to read to her.'

Henry clicked his fingers in William's face causing him to blink.

'Are you quite serious? How can I go before Queen Elizabeth? I, a lowly playwright,' Shakespeare began.

'And The Queen wears gloves made by your father. You are not just a playwright but a master of your craft. You will go to the palace and, without doubt you will come before Queen Elizabeth. I cannot go with you, but Nell can.'

'Nell?' Shakespeare peered at the barmaid, his brow rippling with questions. 'When did you change?' William held his hands in an open gesture.

'William Shakespeare, I would like to introduce you to The Queen's own lady, Marie.' Southampton rolled his wedding ring around his finger. 'Marie, I give you the great bard, William Shakespeare.'

'The honour is all mine, good sir,' Marie walked around to the front of the bar where she sat upon a stool gazing at William. 'I have long admired your work, from afar. Now I hope to become better acquainted with both it and yourself.'

'I must say, your speech has come on since you walked from there,' Shakespeare pointed to the vacant space behind the bar. 'What else can you do?'

Marie pulled a blackened flintlock pistol from her sleeve. It was small, inlaid with a silver pattern consisting of a circle with a vertical line through the centre on the handle. She kept the weapon half-cocked so all she had to do was fill the firing pan with powder and she was ready. 'I'm a good shot, Master Shakespeare.'

'I shall be sure to keep you on my side at all times,' William paused. 'I assume she is in Cecil's employ?'

'As are we all,' Southampton finished his brandy. 'Each of us has access to particular reaches of society. Only in this establishment is Marie known by the name of Nell, and from now on, no one has heard of her. I, with my extensive wealth and lands, am able to travel wherever is necessary. But you, Master Shakespeare, can do what no one else can. You can move people. You can speak both to their hearts and minds. You have access to people of influence in places where few are trusted. Watch yourself at court, beware of those who flaunt their power because they are nothing short of vipers.'

'I shall be sure to keep friends close,' Shakespeare drained his glass shuddering as the spirit coursed down his throat. 'I do not know why I drink; I do not enjoy it as it clouds the mind.'

'In court, there are no friends, only those looking for higher status. You will be a prize among the gathered. Most are charlatans trading on a family name. Others please The Queen. Many are just there to be seen,' Southampton straightened his cuffs as he orated. 'In answer to your next inquiry, I inherited my title when I was eight. With my father gone, my title meant I was taken in as ward of Lord Burghley. I was not raised, I was mentored. The Royal House of Tudor has eyes and ears throughout the known world, and we are but a few of them.'

'I see,' Shakespeare licked his lips, savouring the sting of the brandy upon them. 'I will keep my distance from the courtiers. I will be moving house from Shoreditch to Southwark.'

'There are good homes along The Bank, convenient for the ferrymen at any hour. Questions are never asked,' Southampton took a timepiece from his pocket. 'It is time,

Marie. You may use any of the houses, but I recommend Charring Cross since, should you need it, you will have access to the river.'

'Very well, I shall look for the theta house,' Marie curtsied, holding up the hem of her dress to keep it from dragging on the floor.

'Theta house?' Shakespeare asked after Marie as she reached the door. Without looking back, she tapped a finger to the upper corner of the door frame where a symbol matching her pistol was cut into the timber.

'I forget how new you are to our ways. I shall forward you a copy of the house cypher. Destroy it as soon as you have it committed to memory. Once learned, you will know which houses to enter and which to avoid.'

PREPARATIONS

The privy kitchen was not as grand as the main one. Dried fish hung, hooked at the gills on the end of hemp ropes, looped over small wooden pegs in a doweled rack. Pheasants hung in feathered braces beside chickens and coneys. Seasonal vegetables, piled in baskets and ink-stencilled crates, awaited their turn in the cook pot. A dusting of flour clung to every inch of the table: nothing escaped the wholemeal browning. Deft hands punched and rolled pastry until, at last, it had the pliability the cook desired.

In three strides she crossed the kitchen to the meat rack where she pondered the choice before her. With a finger to her red-painted lips she smiled. Taking a coney from a hook, she held its stiff carcass in one hand while she rifled through a crate of purple carrots and muddy turnips. Placing a turnip to her nose she drew a long breath. Satisfied it was good enough, she began rubbing the dirt from the vegetable off onto the rabbit. The cook rubbed an itch on her top lip with a knuckle. Tutting at the smeared face paint on her hand, she took her selection to the table.

With her hands on her hips, she studied the ingredients set before her. Turning on the spot the cook strode to the knives laid out upon the side, the bell of her dress dragged against the leg of the table. Taking a selection of knives, she turned again to retrieve a pot into which she poured the remains of a bottle of red wine and set it upon the stove beside the baking oven. Bending over she pulled the furnace door open and stoked the fire, the poker rattling on the iron grille.

'Miss Southwell?' The cook called for her assistant. There was long pregnant pause before any answer came.

'Ma'am,' A woman in house uniform: a plain blue-black outer skirt flowing from the shoulders, worn over a white inner garment that neither flattered nor revealed either form or fancy, her hair was tied in a tight plait coiled upon her head in a simple basket weave.

'Marie, why on earth?' The cook shook her head. Waving her hand toward the stove, 'Well, you can help all the same. I need more coals for the fire. I am going to make a sauce from the wine and some meat jelly, the stove needs priming.'

'I am told Miss Southwell has been taken lame, so Cecil has appointed me to your hand,' Marie grabbed the empty scuttle from beside the stove before heading out the rear door to where she hoped to find some fuel for the fire. Sunlight flooded through the open doorway snaring dust particles in its rays.

With a small knife in one hand the cook slid the rabbit across the table and cut across the inside of its rear leg. Stabbing the knife into the table, the cook snapped the leg at the cut and began to pull the skin back around the leg. Marie returned with the scuttle and rebuilt the fire before closing the small door on the hungry flames.

'There is beef dripping in the larder, could you get some and add it to the wine with a mote of flour and stir it 'til thick?' The cook wrapped her long slender fingers around the rabbit skin and pulled hard, grinning with satisfaction as it came away revealing the dark meat beneath.

'You are a dab hand in the kitchen, Your Majesty,' Marie stood one step behind Elizabeth, to her side.

'I have always enjoyed my time in the kitchens; hence I had this one built to suit my purposes,' Elizabeth cut through the neck of the rabbit with a crunch of bone. 'Could you get the salt and honey?'

Elizabeth quartered the rabbit and followed Marie around the table, tossing the meat into the boiling pot. Marie proffered the seasonings to Elizabeth who nodded toward the pot. The Queen took a wooden spoon and began to stir the mix.

'Now tell me about yourself,' She handed Marie the spoon and went to the table, snatching up a deep clay bowl. 'This will do,' she deposited the bowl on the table, took up the pastry ball and began to knead it out into a rough circle.

'I am unsure where to begin,' Marie sprinkled a pinch of flour into the pot. 'My apologies,' she cowered beneath Elizabeth's gaze.

'If I want something, I will tell you so,' Elizabeth brushed her hands down the front of her dress. 'You could start with where you are from. Do you have family in the city?'

'I am an only child, something of a disappointment to my father. He wanted a son, of course,' Marie continued to stir. 'I come from a town in Sussex. Horsham.'

'Near Chesworth House? We have something in common,' Elizabeth folded her arms loose across her chest.

'I am not of such noble stock, Your Majesty.'

'Then how did Cecil find you? I can only assume you work for him, so you must have a talent he spotted,' Elizabeth walked over to the stove and lifted the pan from the heat, taking it to the table.

'I was given unofficial tutelage by way of Collyer's School. The Master, James Allen, took pity on me when the plague claimed both my parents.' Marie stepped toward the rear door.

'There is no shame in being an orphan. But is the school not for boys?' Elizabeth finished spooning the rabbit and vegetables into the pie dish. She lifted the butter paddle from the table and rubbed her fingers along the blade. Having smeared the edge of the dish with the butter, she sealed the lid on the pie.

'There was an alms house; we were taught there, after school,' Marie took the pie and put it in the oven, pushing it into the centre with a wooden peel.

'Southampton came to the mercer in Horsham. When the market was in the Scarefax. I was chasing my friends round the stalls,' Marie allowed a smile to play across her lips. 'I always caught them.'

'And then you came to London?' Elizabeth tossed a cloth to Marie who caught it without looking and set about cleaning the kitchen.

'Not right away. I stayed at Cowdray Park before I moved near Mercers Hall and now Southwark,' Marie laid her cloth over a crate of vegetables.

'Southwark, in the stews?' Elizabeth mused aloud.

'Now I am here, as your handmaid.'

'I am sure you'll be much more than that,' Elizabeth picked at the hardening pastry on the table.

'I do hope so, Majesty,' Marie moved around the kitchen with familiar ease, wiping every surface in sweeping circles.

Elizabeth watched her, fascinated by her quick movements and dancing feet. 'You fence,' The Queen followed Marie's steps on the flour-dusted floor. 'Light turns, good weight. I'll wager Cecil has trained you well,' She continued the study of her handmaid. 'Have you used a bow?'

'Yes, Majesty, both long and crossbow,' Marie poured water into a bowl to rinse her hands. 'Thank you,' she took the proffered towel, 'though you should not.'

'Queen I may be, but as my Lord washed the feet of his disciples, I am sure I am permitted to pass a towel.'

The two ladies left the pie to bake while they stepped out into the cooling air.

The spring sun was waning in the sky. Grey-edged clouds moved in from the east in a celestial armada, trailing across a blood-streaked ocean of yellow and orange. Birdsong chorused from a nearby topiary giving the hedging a semblance of sentience. Narcissus bowed their pale crowns toward the early primroses while snowdrops swung their heads in the fading breaths of the day. The wagging tail of a small spaniel poked out of the border while its owner barked and clawed at the rain-softened earth. The ladies explored the private kitchen garden, discussing seasons for flower and vegetable.

Shadows shifted between the stems indicating the passage of a delightful afternoon.

'Leicester,' Elizabeth commanded, but the spaniel continued to throw up mud in its fervour. 'Heel,' she took a sharp breath. 'Dog.' The dirt-covered animal tucked its tail between its legs and hid beneath Elizabeth's skirts. 'Come, we must check on the pie before the crust becomes a black mass,' The Queen spun around leaving the spaniel by itself. Its tail shifted from one side to another until it was no longer able to resist the urge to dig.

A white silk spread embroidered with a golden sun covered the bed. Pillows lay in rolling hills of white and gold, the delicate stitching excited at the touch of candlelight. The gentle evening breeze breathed in through the open lead glass windows, inviting the candles to dance. The dark panelled walls, their details veiled in shadows from floor to ceiling, absorbed the gentle voices of The Queen and her maid.

Marie pulled the stool from under the dressing table, inviting Elizabeth to sit and be pampered. The Queen sat straight-backed, her hands in her lap as she watched Marie remove the decorations from the wig she had been wearing all day. Pinches of flour fell from the curls where Elizabeth had fingered her hair while preparing the special dish. Marie dropped the pearls into a polished clam shell, its mouth open for more.

'There, that is all of them. I shall have the candle master retouch the curls,' Marie remarked as she placed the wig onto its stand.

'Now I scratch my scalp,' Elizabeth raked her fingers through her short, fine hair where only the gentlest hint of red remained. She groaned with pleasure and satisfaction as she scarified her scalp. Once done, she reached for her wine glass, tossing its rich red syrup down her throat in one swift move. 'A few more and I shall be ready for the party.'

'I hear the good earl, Essex, is in rude health and full of swagger,' Marie drew back the door on the royal wardrobe, gasping at the plethora of golden gowns and velvet dresses. The wardrobe was deep and wide, larger than most commoners' houses, and every corner was occupied by a wooden mannequin bearing the finest garments.

'He should be, this ball is in his honour. He has tales to tell and wonders to express, as only Robert can,' Elizabeth looked back over her shoulder with a seductive smile. 'If only I were younger, I could have my pick of the finest stallions,' she giggled.

'Majesty!' Marie feigned surprise. 'What would you have me fetch?' she motioned toward the vestments.

'You choose,' Elizabeth lifted a lace veil from her mirror. 'Glorify me.'

Marie lifted a candle to light a lamp and stepped inside the trove. Tiny beads of light glittered on every gown, gold threads glowed with radiant energy, pearls pulsed with hidden pleasures while rubies bled. There were so many to choose from.

'Take your time,' Elizabeth called, watching the firefly flit among her finery.

The light stopped, hanging in silent wonder. Marie emerged with a white silk gown adorned with gold and silver emblems. A narrow ruff, a hand's breadth, the thickness of her finger, and a silver filigree surround hung with diamonds and pearls.

'I do not remember such a gown,' frowned Elizabeth as she rose from her stool and walked across the room, her eyes as wide as her smile.

'The emblems, ma'am? Are they not eyes and ears?' Marie lifted a sleeve for her Majesty to inspect. Elizabeth ran a hand along the fabric until she reached the puffed shoulders.

'Only one man could conceive such a design as this,' Elizabeth pulled the dress to her. 'How I miss you, Walsingham.'

She danced around the room in a ragged waltz, the dress as silent as her feet upon the Turkish rugs.

'I have not seen another like it anywhere,' Marie took the dress from Elizabeth and laid it face down upon the bed.

'Come on. Come on,' Elizabeth fussed at Marie's side. 'One is never too old to impress.'

Marie loosened the interwoven back of the dress, with the care of a mother holding her firstborn child she lowered the dress allowing Elizabeth to step into its silken womb. Elizabeth slid an arm into a sleeve, helping it along with her free hand. With a dip of her shoulder, she had her other arm in and the dress upon her back.

'He must have known you well, Majesty.' With gentle hands Marie pulled on the weave, watching in amazement as the fabric wrapped itself around The Queen in a loving embrace.

Elizabeth smoothed her hands down the bodice, allowing them to glide around her hips where she rested them. 'A wig I think.'

Marie returned to the wardrobe and came back with a shoulder-length cut, crowned with a nested plait, coiling down over one shoulder into a rattlesnake tail interwoven with gold. Marie darted over to the dressing table, her fingers picking through the wealth of diamonds, pearls and gems from around the globe.

'What are you doing, Marie? Dear Miss Southwell was never so daring.'

Marie smiled at her Queen as she adorned the plait with jewels, turning it into a resplendent crown.

'Shall I paint you. ma'am?' Marie admired the work in progress, unable to hide her joy and excitement.

'You may,' Elizabeth sat on the stool with her back to the mirror. 'Do I look as good as your face suggests?'

Marie continued her work, applying the lead-white paint to Elizabeth's face, neck and exposed chest.

'One more thing,' Marie espied a three-banded pearl necklace coiled upon a book of hours.

'My mother's,' Elizabeth sighed, and drew a deep breath as Marie fastened the pearls around her neck beneath the ruff.

'There,' Marie slipped the collar of the filigree surround over Elizabeth's shoulders and stepped back to admire her masterpiece.

The Queen rose to her feet, Majesty in motion. 'What is it? You are crying child,' Elizabeth took a kerchief from the dressing table and held it out to Marie.

'I am well, thank you,' Marie swallowed, 'You look beautiful, ma'am,' Marie took the kerchief and wiped her eyes on the delicate lace.

'Pull that rope,' Elizabeth instructed and motioned toward a heavy cord of twisted silks. Marie obeyed her

Queen, revealing a floor to ceiling mirror, behind the velvet curtains on the wall. Her Majesty gasped. 'Is this me? I look as one seated among the heavens. Marie, what have you created?'

Elizabeth swung her hips, and the dress moved in a flowing river of gold and white. Her jewelled hair glittered with the glory of heaven, a myriad of stars falling before The Queen.

BANQUET

Gentle melodies cascaded from the minstrel gallery over the Screen's Passage, serenading the throng of guests below. From the north stairs, the Black Earl and his wife, Lady Ormond, stepped through the parted halberds into the hall proper, where fire breathers spewed their coloured flames before the guests. Earls and lords from every corner of the realm strutted and displayed their immense wealth and status. Gowns of finest satin in green and gold brushed against Egyptian cotton and the tight-clad legs of pretentious lords. Mountjoy twisted wax into his perfect moustache as he debated with Tyrone O'Neil.

Servants passed among the guests, serving wine from crystal glasses and rich tidbits from stacked platters. Bread was broken and wine flowed as guests filled the great hall from one side to the other masking the tapestries hanging on the walls. Servants ran up and down the buttery stairs to the long corridor of kitchens and offices where food and drinks were prepped in readiness. As the tide ebbs and turns, the maids and menservants came and went as though mining provisions from the depths of beyond.

'You play a dangerous game, Tyrone. Vaunting yourself among the court of England's rose,' Mountjoy swapped his empty glass for full one, sipping from its rim as though he were afraid it might be poison.

'I am an invited guest,' Tyrone pointed out as he wiped his mouth with a knuckle, smearing grease into his beard. 'As such I am granted the freedoms afforded here.'

'Were the same niceties extended to the captured English at your last encounter?' Mountjoy held Tyrone's gaze, the young man unafraid of any challenge.

'As luck would have it, my courted friend has arrived.' Tyrone swung his hand toward the Screens Passage. Trumpets heralded the entrance of two Blackamoors wearing gold-braided uniforms bearing the heraldry of their lord and master. The Blackamoors walked in paused steps, each of them carrying a small chest in their white-gloved hands. The guests parted, allowing the two men to walk up to the raised dais where they knelt to place their gifts at the foot of the throne.

At the second trumpet blast, dancing girls swirled into the room scattering white petals from golden baskets; their red braids trailing down the back of emerald dresses. Behind them in silver and black, a resplendent Essex soaked up the moment.

'Essex,' Mountjoy swapped his cup for a plate piled with meats and pastries.

'My good lords and ladies,' Essex puffed out his chest. 'It is good for you to have me back. How you must have missed me,' he teased, winking at his sister as she spun beneath his outstretched arm. 'But I have now returned. Triumphant from Cádiz.' Cheers filled the room as Essex ran from lady to lady gathering praise and kisses galore. 'Let me regale you with tales of my courage and conquest.'

'Please do,' a voice chimed from the dais. Elizabeth took her seat upon the right-hand throne amid hushed gasps. Essex held his countenance, forcing his smile to broaden. 'Pray continue.' Marie handed The Queen her wine before placing Her Majesty's spaniel, Leicester on the empty throne to the left.

Essex bowed low before The Queen. 'Listen and listen well, for I have a most excellent tale to tell. It began in Plymouth from where we set out into the Channel to rendezvous with the Dutch. Four commanders: Duyvenvoorde, Sir Howard, my good self and some old pirate.' Essex jumped onto a table. 'Over one hundred and fifty ships set sail for Cádiz with sixteen thousand men. Cádiz would be ours; I knew it so. Biscay, however, caught us with a devil's storm. The fleet was broken and scattered.' Essex pranced about heedlessly, knocking glasses onto the floor and spilling food for his dogs beneath the table. 'I found Raleigh, the pirate, basking in the sun off the Azores. Charles Howard, a real commander, was pounding on the Spaniard's door. The Dutch held the line picking off stragglers and runners.

Another storm delayed our entry into the Bay of Cádiz, but we had them on the run. By noon we were on their heels hounding them into the tiny port of Puerto Real. I sent soldiers by the boatload to board the cornered Spaniards and take what was ours,' Essex snatched at the air as though catching a fly. 'Knowing the Spanish were trapped in their ships, I took a force ashore to rout the town and make my victory absolute.'

'And what of Raleigh?' Elizabeth sat tall in her throne. 'Did he do nothing?' The Queen raised an eyebrow.

'By the time the old pirate arrived there was nothing more to do than count the money and swab the decks,' Essex waved off the enquiry.

'It cannot have taken long to count, my sweet boy,' Elizabeth gestured to the two small chests. 'It must have been a tiny treasure ship.'

She could not help but chuckle. Essex drew his shoulders up.

'My most splendid Majesty.' Jumping down from the table he strolled toward The Queen, extolling her virtues. 'No treasure could match the wonder of you. No fleet is so grand, no army as strong and courageous as our Gloriana. Even the snow is not as pure or driven as thee,' Essex knelt before The Queen, his eyes locked on hers, his voice dropped to a whisper. 'Fools would say, just a woman, others know the lion within.'

Elizabeth slipped a ring from her finger as she leaned forward. 'For you, my proud son.' Essex closed his fist around the tiny jewel. 'I am sure you fought with all courage, some would say without fear, as you scaled the walls of the city.'

'How—'

Elizabeth placed a finger to his lips. 'What Walsingham began I have mustered into a mighty force,' Elizabeth sat back in her throne. 'The events of Cádiz are not unknown to me, my brave captain,' Elizabeth waved a gloved hand toward the room. 'Now go, the glow of your admirers grows dim.'

'You tease me so,' Essex stood proud, took three steps back before turning to delight and entertain his followers.

Music flowed once more, inviting the guests to dance and draw close. The men lined one side of the room, the women the other as the flute and drum played a three-step beat. At the end of the room, in front of the dais, each dancer bowed before The Queen, turned to join hands and step in time together to the far end of the room. A gentle pace for gentle souls.

Essex yawned and tossed dried fruits into his mouth. 'It's all I can do to stay awake.' Wiping his fingers in his beard he reached for a glass as a servant stopped before him.

'My lord,' the servant presented the pie. 'From the privy kitchen sir.'

Essex took the pie from the platter with a subtle nod toward Elizabeth. He sniffed at the crust, broke a piece off and tasted it. Blowing a kiss to The Queen he feigned his enjoyment and set the pie on the table.

'My Lord Tyrone, would you care for some coney?'

'Why not?' Tyrone drew a dagger, stabbing the crust multiple times. 'It's as hollow as its maker.'

'Indeed,' Essex turned his back toward the dais. 'I have something in mind that requires your assistance. Shall we get some air?'

'I'll be in London for the morrow. I'll come to your house on the Strand,' Tyrone stabbed a turnip in the pie. 'Thought it was her heart for a minute. Has more flavour though,' Tyrone searched for more.

'Very well, tomorrow it is,' Essex huffed.

'Who's that, doesn't look like your usual courtier?'

'I believe it is none other than William Shakespeare. Watch me have some sport with him,' Essex puffed out his chest and strutted across the room.

Tyrone watched Essex as he passed through the procession of dancers in pursuit of his quarry.

THE BARD

'From where do you herald?' Lady Penelope touched the glass to her lips.

'Stratford, not a great distance from Warwick,' Shakespeare gave an almost imperceptible nod to Penelope. 'I have a home there; I try to visit my family when possible.'

'You are married?' Lady Ormond joined the conversation.

'I apologise if it disappoints,' William kept his hands tucked behind his back.

'Why, if it is not the most talked-about man in London,' Essex thrust himself between the ladies. 'After me, of course.'

'William Shakespeare, meet my brother Robert Devereux, the Earl of Essex,' Lady Penelope stepped aside.

'Is that it?' Robert turned toward her. 'No mention of my daring heroism, dashing good looks and fabulous wit?'

'None, you are quite capable of promoting yourself,' Penelope waved her brother aside. 'Is there a purpose to your uninvited intrusion?'

'Of course,' Essex gave his sister a cynical sneer. 'My good friend Shakespeare must know of my poetic talent. I was wondering if he could demonstrate his great skill with a word or two.'

'My Lord, I am ill-prepared. I have no materials with which to write,' William stepped back taking in the full measure of his challenger.

'Allow me, good sir, to articulate a verse,' and without hesitation Essex projected himself above the music.

'Woe to the world, the sun is in a cloud,
And darksome mists do overrun the day;
In high conceit, is not content allowed;
Favour must die and fancies wear away.
O heavens, what hell! The bands of love are broken,
Nor must a thought of such a thing be spoken.'

Essex bowed with a flourish of his crimson-lined cape. Raising a hand to silence both Shakespeare and the minstrel gallery, he proclaimed, 'Now good sir, as you have accepted my duel of words, here are those you must use within your verse,' Essex drew a long breath. 'Brag, untrimmed, complexion,' he paused to smile, 'and lease. You may begin.'

'Might I have a moment to compose my thoughts,' William asked, stepping out into the middle of the dance floor. He paced from one side to the other tapping a finger to his lips. 'I have something … rather rushed. It may need polish, it may not.' Shakespeare cleared his throat and with a polite cough he began. 'Your Majesty. To what can you be compared?' He suspended a breath.

'Shall I compare thee to a summer's day?
Thou art more lovely and more temperate:
Rough winds do shake the darling buds of May,
And summer's lease hath all too short a date:
Sometime too hot the eye of heaven shines,

And often is his gold complexion dimm'd;
And every fair from fair sometime declines,
By chance or nature's changing course untrimm'd;
But thy eternal summer shall not fade
Nor lose possession of that fair thou owest;
Nor shall Death brag thou wander'st in his shade,
When in eternal lines to time thou growest:
So long as men can breathe or eyes can see,
So long lives this, and this gives life to thee.'

Shakespeare knelt before The Queen, his chest heaving as the guests cheered for more.

Elizabeth rose to her feet. 'I do believe Essex, he got them all,' Elizabeth looked down at the trembling bard. 'You must come and read to me. I am partial to poetry and plays too.'

'I would be most honoured, Your Majesty,' Shakespeare could not contain his joy.

LATE ENTRY

Round and around, over and over, the head of the pontiff rolled down the dance floor until it ran out of force and fell over beside the kneeling bard. Shakespeare picked up the coin bearing the image of Pope Clement VIII, turning it over in his palm. A second gold ducat rolled down the hall followed by a third. Two soldiers dressed in the black and gold of the Spanish hierarchy staggered into the hall with thick ropes over their shoulders. The ropes twitched with every step as they hauled the giant chest down the hall. Behind them two more soldiers fought a fanciful duel, their swords clashing beneath the crystal chandeliers. A swarm of fire-eaters blew flames of red, green, and gold forming a wall of flames. As the fire dissipated there stood Raleigh with his hat tucked beneath his arm and joy upon his face.

'Am I late?' Raleigh bowed low to the floor and threw his hat among a group of ladies, all of whom giggled with delight at such favour.

'Do approach,' Elizabeth stood tall with her arms open wide. 'Ladies and gentlemen, I give you, Sir Walter Raleigh.

Raleigh limped his way down the Great Hall waving and bowing to all those he knew. The scowling Essex could do nothing to dampen his joy.

'Majesty,' Raleigh swirled the golden cape from his shoulder before laying it at the feet of The Queen. 'A fitting rug for such a golden beauty. Many seas have I sailed and new worlds discovered, but none compare to thee.' Walter pointed his hand toward the ceiling and the minstrels began to play. 'A dance, Ma'am?'

'Why of course,' Elizabeth took Raleigh by the hand and led him out onto the floor. 'So great a gift deserves my personal gratitude.'

The two of them turned and spun, parted and rejoined as they danced and talked the night away. Others passed them on the floor, but Elizabeth saw them not.

'Excuse me,' Essex tapped Raleigh on the forearm.

'Not now, Robert, I am somewhat engaged,' Sir Walter turned The Queen aside, skirting a second suitor. The Queen laughed with delight, her thoughts harkening to lighter days before she bore the responsibility of the crown. Essex glared after the happy couple, watching every nuance of their interaction.

'Have you any idea who Essex has brought with him? His face is unfamiliar?' The Queen pointed by motion of the dance toward Essex.

'Hm, I do indeed,' Raleigh weighed his response. 'He, your Majesty, is none other than the Earl of Tyrone. 'Tis interesting company Essex keeps at such a time as this.'

Elizabeth gasped as Raleigh lifted her by her groin high into the air, made a half turn before he set her down and continued the dance. 'Essex failed to mention you were wounded,' Elizabeth tilted her head aside.

'An oversight, I am sure,' Raleigh pulled The Queen unto him, exhaling as they came together. 'The mission was fraught with danger, but we overcame our differences and conquered the enemy. Philip is still reeling from the sting.'

'Good. Perhaps he will think twice before he sends more ships against the Cornish coast.'

Elizabeth giggled with girlish glee as Raleigh leaned her back and blew gentle in her ear.

'I doubt. While in Cádiz report came to us of a new fleet being assembled. It is unfortunate, but it is under construction in many places. I suspect they are refitting merchant vessels.'

'Is the source reliable?' Elizabeth stumbled over Raleigh's foot.

'None other than Skeggs,' the smile faded from Raleigh's face. 'He was reported captured. A long journey through Flanders came to precious little.'

'That is, indeed, most grievous news,' Elizabeth let her hands fall to her sides and walked from the floor to her throne where her mood blackened.

ALLIANCES

AGENDAS

The Privy Council sat in silence as its members read the notices under discussion. Robert Cecil rose from his seat head bowed. He raised his gaze and addressed the gathered few. 'Majesty, Sir Walter, Essex.' Greeting each of the available officers in turn, he stepped out beneath the centre of the vaulted ceiling. 'Among the matters of concern is the trifling problem of enrichment. Since the introduction of Her Majesty's favours, it has come to our attention that price-fixing has become common place.'

'Oh please,' Essex sighed, waving his list of notes at Cecil. 'There are more pressing issues than the poor.'

'Robert!' Elizabeth wagged a finger at the Earl. 'Your flippancy is to be noted.'

'Really,' Essex put his feet up onto the back of a chair.

'The price-fixing has led to starvation in many parts of the country. People are no longer able to provide for their families. Money is scarce among the outer counties. London itself is not exempt. The Mercers' grain store has been attacked twice this month.'

'So? It's a few sacks of grain and some cloth,' Essex groaned. 'What of it?'

'You might recall, Essex, the Mercers' grain store is where your sweet wines are kept prior to distribution. It is unfortunate, for you at least, all one thousand bottles have gone astray,' Cecil cracked a smile. 'So, I guess, 'tis of no import to anyone.'

'A thousand bottles! I demand to be compensated!' Essex kicked a chair across the room. Jumping to his feet he cried, 'By all that is righteous, this behaviour must be quenched before it becomes rampant across the whole city.'

Raleigh looked at Essex with a curious glance. 'It is rampant across the city. Many are reduced to eating cats and dogs. Perhaps you should put your mutt on a leash.'

'Most amusing, Raleigh,' Essex dropped into his seat. 'Perhaps we can move along to the next matter?' Essex waved his papers again.

'Ireland?' Cecil peered down his nose at Essex. 'Would be one, or the report of Cádiz?'

'You choose,' Essex yawned.

'Cádiz,' Elizabeth steepled her fingers. 'I have two accounts. One has you, Robert, running rampant, climbing walls and securing the city.'

'All sounding credible,' Essex grinned, folding his arms over his chest.

Cecil folded his paper, 'If not untrue,' He tucked the document inside his favourite burgundy jacket.

'I have given my account and stand by it,' Essex took a moment to admire his fingernails.

'At what point did you take the town? Before you sent hundreds of brave soldiers to drown in their armour, or after you let Medina Sidonia ride away?' Raleigh stroked his beard.

'Poppycock!' Essex blurted.

'Others have also commented so,' Cecil brushed imaginary fluff from his jacket and straightened his perfect ruff.

'Who? Who would dare contradict the word of a lord?' Essex demanded. 'Would they call me a liar?'

'Well, I would. I was there,' Raleigh stood to face Essex. Leaning back against the wall he began his address. 'I have distinct memories of climbing aboard your vessel. I enquired as to why you might be sending boats filled with armoured troops to engage the vessels in the harbour. You had sixteen thousand men at your disposal with explicit royal orders to sack the town. You outnumbered the Spaniards three to one. The ships were of no concern. What you did, was give opportunity for the Spanish high command to instruct Sidonia to scuttle the entire bloody fleet and send twelve million ducats to the bottom of the ocean. 'Tis no wonder you only managed to bring back two ring boxes for the royal coffers.' Essex offered no explanation. 'Well?'

'Robert Devereux, you have been accused, do you offer no defence or decry the accusation levelled upon you?' Cecil held Essex's gaze.

'By all that is right!' Essex sprang to his feet. 'Is this how I am to be treated? I have nobler blood than either of you. And you Raleigh,' he sneered, 'are nothing more than an upstart commoner. There is not an ounce of nobility about you.'

'Be that as it may, he is a knight of the realm. He earned it,' Cecil raised his chin. 'Can the same be said of you?'

'How dare you insult me!' Essex stepped toward Cecil brandishing his sword.

'Essex!' The Queen bellowed. 'Keep your squabbling for the stews where it belongs,' Elizabeth stepped from her throne and snatched the sword from Essex. 'I will not have such a thing in my household. You are one step from treason,' She passed the sword to Raleigh, who turned it over in his hands admiring the craftsmanship.

'An interesting blade,' Raleigh rubbed the cluster of tiny rubies embedded in the hilt with his thumb. 'Might one ask how you came by it?'

Essex looked up at the ceiling clenching his fists. 'One may not. I do not answer to your kind.'

'But you will answer to me,' Cecil held out his hand to Raleigh. Sir Walter handed him the sword by its golden hilt. 'Interesting indeed,' Cecil lay the blade on a table by his side. 'Where did you get it?'

Essex turned aside, grabbing his cloak from his chair. 'I earned it,' He looked Raleigh up and down, 'Just like everything else I own,' He swung his black velvet cloak over his shoulder. 'Should you wish to see how, challenge me or give me Ireland and I will conquer it where all others have failed.'

Essex strode out of the room.

'Now, there is a possibility,' Cecil mused.

'Cecil,' Elizabeth snapped. 'What of the sword? Why so much interest?'

'Such swords first surfaced with the Armada in 1588. Sir Frances found them. He discovered more bound for these shores a few years later and again prior his death,' Cecil looked to Raleigh.

'I acquired this one,' Raleigh unsheathed the sword he had won in Cádiz, 'from a Venetian spy in Cádiz, posing as a Jesuit. Most intriguing, he was as English as you and I.'

'So, what are these?' Elizabeth took the sword examining it up close. 'It is exquisite.'

'They are called El Sagrada, blessed by His Holiness, who has issued a decree that should any man kill you, Your Highness, it would not be counted as a sin.'

Elizabeth's eyes widened, 'An interesting interpretation of the Holy Scriptures.'

'They consider you a heretic as you encourage desertion from Catholicism,' Cecil pulled a paper from his jacket together with a small, notched leather strip. 'Here, your Majesty,' he passed the items to Elizabeth. 'It is the message Raleigh spoke of from Skeggs.'

'Southampton, what did he have to say of Cádiz?' Elizabeth placed the leather strip over the letter, 'Bastards. Bloody garlic munching bastards. There will never be peace as long as I live,' Elizabeth thrust the cyphers into Cecil's chest.

'Southampton and Mountjoy both support Raleigh. Essex took command from the admiral and made a complete hash of things. As for letting the Spanish commander go free, only Essex knows why.'

'You must rein Essex in, ma'am. He assumes to be the next—'

Elizabeth raised a hand to Raleigh.

'I helped to raise him. He has been the nearest thing to a child to me. I thought, perhaps ...,' Elizabeth slumped into a chair.

'It is not your doing, Majesty. Do not punish yourself. There is so much at stake,' Cecil bit his lip. 'You must name a successor. Sign the deposition and be done with it. I fear for England should no one be named before the fateful day.'

'I know, I know,' Elizabeth held her face in her hands. 'If only. Always, if only. But alas, I found no one man suitable to bear the throne of my England. The same is true today,' Elizabeth wiped her eyes. 'Was there anything else?'

'Spain, Your Majesty.'

Elizabeth shook her head.

'If not now, when? Ireland seeks the hand of the Pope. He has ordered King Philip to act on his behalf. A new fleet is being assembled,' Raleigh placed a hand on Elizabeth's shoulder.

'Your strength is needed now more than ever,' she replied, and placing a hand over his she stood, turning to face him. 'I reinstate you as Master of my Royal Guard and The Tower.' She looked at Cecil, her eyes sad and reddened. 'Do whatever is necessary to protect this country and myself. I need some cheer; have Shakespeare come read to me. If he asks, something humorous would be best,' Elizabeth walked with a heavy heart from the chapel. 'I am retiring to Nonsuch Palace. Have preparations made.'

The sound of hammers and saws clattered and rasped over Southwark. Dark skies hung with threatening clouds. The hard ground, softened by an early high tide, was yielding to the builder's pick. The first of the two-ton timbers rose to point its finger at the brooding heavens. By late afternoon, the uprights were joined by crossbeams as the Globe took shape.

"'Tis a bold thing you do, Shakespeare, The Rose is but a spit away as are the baiting pits,' Dr John Dee examined the plans for the new theatre. 'To say nothing of the victualing houses and stews.'

'And none of it would have been possible without Peter Street. Without his knowledge we would have lost most of the timbers from The Theatre,' Shakespeare rubbed his hands with glee. 'It is inspiring, is it not?'

'It is indeed,' Southampton slung an arm around Shakespeare's shoulders. 'Do you have a play in mind for opening night?'

'I do indeed,' William slipped from Southampton's embrace. 'Soft! what light from yonder window breaks?'

'Oh, such a fine choice,' Southampton stood with his hands on his hips staring in wonder at the possibilities of the construction.

'Gentlemen,' Dr John Dee held the scrolled plans in one hand. He handed the scroll to Shakespeare, tied with a black ribbon. 'If you have no further need of me, I must depart from the city.'

'It has been an honour, John, I cannot thank you enough for being so expedient with the design,' Shakespeare held the scroll by its ends. 'A seat is yours at all times,' he bowed low.

'Most gracious of you,' Dr John Dee turned and vanished into the fading light.

'How does he do that?' Southampton laughed. 'It is of no wonder Her Majesty holds him in such high regard.'

Shakespeare wandered among the posts of the Globe, slapping each of the dark timbers as though he were vetting a horse.

'I heard you put on quite the show at the banquet. Is it true you now have the ear of The Queen?' Southampton watched a happy Shakespeare pacing out the measure of the stage.

'I met the challenge set by the Earl of Essex. I had heard his diatribe before. It is quite unbecoming of someone in such an office to behave in the manner of the gutter,' Shakespeare finished his pacing with a bow to an imaginary audience. 'It will be quite something. Ropes and pulleys to make the actors fly, trap doors for surprises and cannons to wage war on our competitors.'

'You are not lacking in ambition. Will,' Southampton steered the two of them toward The Bishop's Cap. 'Your older works, are they open to update or adaptation?'

'Always,' Shakespeare held the door to the tavern open for his patron, 'so long as there is a compensatory purse.'

Pushing their way through the heaving crowd they reached the bar to the welcoming grin of the new barmaid.

'Do you have a bevy of beauties at your disposal?' Will nudged Southampton's elbow.

The barmaid placed a jug of wine and two glasses on the counter, pouring a drink for both men.

'There are a number known to me, there has to be. I could not employ just anyone, now could I?' Southampton took his glass of wine over to a tabled booth adjacent to the rear exit. 'While in the company of Her Majesty, try to do nothing to raise her ire. Which is no mean feat.'

'I have heard tell of your exploits: fisticuffs, and duelling,' Shakespeare peered down his nose at Southampton, raising his eyebrows in mock surprise.

'One can be ... '

'Impetuous?' offered Shakespeare.

'Quite,' Southampton sipped his wine.

'Tell me, you have many dealings with Essex. How best should I handle the Earl?' Shakespeare slid his glass away from him. 'Too sweet for my palate, I prefer the whites of France or the abbot's tipple, nothing quite like a potent mead.'

'With regard to Essex, he is an impetuous oaf with a temper as quick as his wit. There is no way but his way. Play along with him until it upsets your moral compass.' Southampton offered.

'So, cruel a wit, were it not for your upbringing I would name thee a cad,' William ran a hand through his thinning hair. 'Alas poor hair, I knew it well.' The two of them laughed as they japed.

The night grew long and weary. The clientele grew louder with every ale passed among them. Some slept where they sat, others where they fell and more still slunk into the night with a whore in hand.

GOOD NEWS

The promise of summer, bright days and long nights beneath a blanket of stars, was but a dream. War ruled the people and scarred the land. A time of starvation and disease.

The Blackwater River coursed through the green lands dividing the two counties of Armagh and Tyrone. A lone horseman hurtled out of the woods across the dancing grasslands. His aim, the fort where O'Neil waited for word to come across the river from Dungannon. The portcullis rattled open. The rider ducked beneath the iron studded gate, his horse slipping on the wet stone. Carts loaded with fresh supplies of grain and vegetables were being unloaded into the deep storehouse. Muskets stood to attention along the length of the courtyard, each with a pouch of shot and a purse of powder.

The rider leapt from his horse with a grubby piece of parchment clenched in his hand.

'Where is my Lord Tyrone O'Neill?' The rider ran into the keep, sweat mingling with mud on his face.

'He is in the main hall, continue on through,' the guard waved the messenger on.

The main hall opened out from the narrow corridor giving it an illusion of grandeur. Narrow bench seats were pushed back against the wall behind tables covered in orange and blue banners, each with a golden harp embroidered in its centre. At the head of the hall a single table filled the entire width, and behind it stood Tyrone marking a map with a quill.

'Aidan,' Tyrone's frown blossomed into smile. 'There is news?'

'There is indeed,' Aidan handed the parchment to Tyrone.

'Fetch yourself a drink, lad. There's wine or ale on the table. I expect you're famished,' Tyrone beckoned a flame-haired serving girl to come forth. 'Fetch something hearty for my cousin Aidan, lass.' The servant curtsied and left the room. Tyrone scanned the handwritten note. Red Hugh promised full support,' Tyrone clenched his fist in triumph. 'We'll bloody those English bastards.'

'I saw the defences, that's some trench. And Hugh has men at the ready for a long stretch. The English will not get here unscathed,' Aidan took the tray from the servant, thanking her. 'Thank you, missy, it will be more than I need.' The girl returned to her post beneath the stuffed head of a stag mounted high on the west wall.

'Bagenal thinks he comes to re-supply the fort. He has no idea we have it,' Tyrone took an ale from the table, swirling it around. 'We'll be ready when he shows his smug face over the hill. We'll see to it he never sets eye upon this fort again.'

'Aye, the Redshanks are with us too. I suspect by the time the sun goes down there'll be a few more English among our number,' Aidan dipped a piece of bread into some beef dripping. 'I've not had such posh grub in a long while.'

'There'll be plenty more when we take the supplies bound for this fort,' Tyrone dragged some bread through the beef fat, 'Here's to victory.' The two men knocked their bread and dripping together before washing it down with fresh ale.

YELLOW FORD

The column of soldiers wound their way along the road deeper into the wooded hills. Soft light flickered through the trees casting mottled shadows over the men and horses. Four battalions surrounded the cavalry, followed by the artillery and two more units of soldiers to the rear. The path had become broken and sodden in places by the excess trampling of warriors through the heavy summer rains. It was only a matter of time before the inevitable happened.

'Pull, harder,' Henry Bagenal barked at the men. 'We need those guns to protect the fort. Use a horse if you must.' Bagenal trotted around the stuck cannon, cursing his luck. 'Leave the bloody thing, You men can follow on when they have it clear.' He rode off to the vanguard a soured man.

Without so much as a cursory glance back, the forces marched on, leaving the artillery men to dig out the cannon and haul their way through the deepening bogs.

'What is it now?' Bagenal demanded of the scout.

'The road ahead is cut off. There is a broad trench right across it, so we'll have to go around, sir,' The scout saluted. 'The ground is firm to the north-east.'

'It will take too long. You can be sure the Irish will have it covered. Curse this land, it will be the death of us all,' Bagenal stood in his stirrups as he surveyed the road ahead. 'We will follow the river,' he pointed to the broad valley down the long slope to the west. 'It will join the

Blackwater at some point. From there we can trace it up to the Fort.'

The column veered to the left, keeping the woodland in sight. The slope proved steeper than first imagined; much of its true form was hidden beneath the swaying grasses. The woodland erupted with a thousand screaming Irish Kern wielding axes and short swords. They hit the English forces at full pelt, hacking and slashing at anything living. Death came swift in a rain of blood and viscera. The Irish left as swift as they had arrived. In a fading heartbeat the woods were silent. The only sound to break the silence was the cry of the dying.

Henry Bagenal rode among the fallen, his countenance a flushed fury. His men had been caught unaware. They had marched across the whole country without incident and now this: a simple ambush. Before he could count the fallen, the hiss of arrows claimed more of his men. The rear of the column was under attack. His men were scattering into the woods and over the face of the hill. Undeterred, he pushed forward along the river leaving the rear-guard to do their duty.

Bagenal hung his head as he watched the second scout return. 'I hope you have better news,' he spat.

'My Lord, our enemy has built defences all along the hillsides and along the opposing bank. We are closed in at the rear.' The scout waited for orders.

'We press on, there is less than four miles between here and the objective,' Bagenal turned his horse aside. 'Sound the drums, we march.'

The drum beat a steady march as the column flowed down the hillside northward to the ford on the Blackwater River. The Irish challenged them at every turn. Muskets belched smoke into the late morning, the sun heralding another onslaught of cavalry and pike men.

The day was wearing as the fort peeked over a rise. The English lay in a gulf between the town of Armagh and the hoped-for sanctuary of the English fort. Bloodied and wounded they marched on, their optimism high.

Soft earth rumbled beneath their feet. The dark thunder of horses rose to fill the air as the horde of howling Irishmen poured from the hilltops around them. 'Charge! Let the land run with their blood,' Henry Bagenal commanded, wielding his sword high above his head.

The English cavalry broke from the ranks of the soldiers, lowering their pikes as they charged into the Irish wall. The pounding of hooves continued to rise as Red Hugh led his men through Yellow Ford straight into the vanguard of troops. The might of the English army stumbled, many fell, too many to be true.

The Irish cut through the English with ease. Veterans of Clonitibret and Carrickfergus, survivors through and through, felt their resolve buckle beneath the fury of Red Hugh. Henry Bagenal cut his way through the howling Irish and Scottish Redshanks leaving his mark on their flesh. Outflanked and outmanoeuvred, Bagenal was fast running out of options.

'To me, and to the ford.' Bagenal ploughed forward, spurring his horse through the iron thorns of pike and sword. His men, pressed from all sides, obeyed their unbeaten commander.

A lone cannon roared into life spitting iron teeth into the fields of battle. A spray of blood, and another Irishman went to an early grave. Death rained from the skies in a hail of arrows. Muskets spat hot vengeance at the invaders felling Englishmen by the score. A song of flesh and steel sang out over the fields of Armagh. Bagenal could see the light ahead. A break in the ranks of the Kern. Seizing the moment, he roared, a lion calling his pride to the kill. The English burst from the snare before it coiled around them. Tired and battered they ran after their master. Surging into the shallow ford. The jubilation of the English turned to woe.

Baying for blood, hot and sweet, Tyrone and Aidan crashed upon them and combining with Red Hugh's men they sealed the fate of the English. Outsmarted, the English fell in droves as the Kern drove their pikes deep into English hearts. Bagenal threw his short spear into the affray, striking Aidan in the thigh. The young man turned his horse from the battle venting his frustration in a guttural cry. Thrusting his hand into his saddle bag he drew out his pistol. Biting on the pain he poured black powder in the pan of his gun and cocked it at the ready. Turning once more he rode back into the writhing sea of steel took aim and fired.

Smoke coiled through the hiatus of reality as the world watched the passing of a life. The sword, once a symbol of proud leadership, rolled from fingers no longer capable of command. It toppled, a fallen banner, a surrendered soul. Henry Bagenal stared sightless at the blood red sky. He tried to blink but his eyelids could not cleanse his sanguine vision. A blanket of darkness wrapped its arms around him as he slipped to the ground, his life flowing from the black hole in his head.

'Bagenal is dead!' Tyrone bellowed in triumph, his joy overflowing as his enemy scattered before him. 'Let them run, all the way to the bed of their whore Queen.'

He turned toward his nephew, recumbent in the shallow wash of the ford, a dark stain consumed his thigh.

WILTING LAURELS

The afternoon sun glistened on the bloody grass. Crows feasted on the eyes of the deceased; their beaks dripped with crimson sauce. The Kern walked among the dying, cutting throats and piercing hearts with blades of woe. A thousand cries of the desperate and dying were silenced, as eventide cast a magic light upon the body strippers.

The grey walls of the fort offered no solace: cold and foreboding they had become nothing more than a curse. Iron clad hooves clacked beside the rattling wheels of wagons as the troops returned to their haven. Aidan lay upon a straw cot, his leg a sticky mass of old blood and black poultice.

'Is he anyone of import?' Essex peered at the stricken youth.

'Mind yer mouth, Englishman,' Tyrone sneered. 'The boy be kin. Any more of your contrite shite and you'll be next on a pyre.'

'Mind your temper, Tyrone,' Red Hugh stepped in front of Essex. 'I'd ask you to be more mindful of any casualty. These are our people. You may have no regard for those under your command, but we do.'

'I meant nothing,' Essex turned aside.

'Exactly.' Dipping a cloth into a pail of water Tyrone wrung it out and placed it over Aidan's brow. 'What brings you to Ireland, Essex? Not selling enough wine at home?'

'Tyrone, at least try to be courteous. His lordship is here at my request,' Red Hugh reminded Tyrone as he guided Essex from the infirmary. 'As for you Essex, I suggest you do nothing to rouse his ire. He is impetuous at best and as like to run you through. Tyrone and Aidan have been together since birth, nothing could separate them.'

They walked out of the candlelit gloom into the light of the inner bailey. Soldiers piled the spoils of war with their like: muskets, swords, shields, and armour gathered from the dead. The smell of roasting flesh carried on the breeze together with soft white ash. Essex dusted a few flakes from his shoulders until he realised the futility, instead he took shelter beneath a raised walkway. The sound of atrabilious voices dulled by the thick oak boardwalk drifted down as a dirge.

'Are they not rejoicing in victory?' Essex stared at the knotty timbers overhead as though they would provide any meaning.

'They'll celebrate when the cur has left the land,' Red Hugh gave a nod of affirmation to the passing men. 'I noticed something in London, at the banquet.' A young girl with flaming red hair came up with a tray of bread and wine. 'Do you commune?' Red Hugh furrowed his brow at Essex's lack of understanding. 'Do you partake of the blood and body of our Lord and Saviour?'

'We are not at church, this is not the Lord's day,' Essex fought back a smile. ''Tis a matter for clergy.'

''Tis a matter of faith. It is written to do this when in remembrance. The good Lord was dining with friends not conducting a service. Heaven forbid such a blessed thing should be reduced a meaningless ritual,' Red Hugh put some bread in his mouth, chewing it over as he watched his men wash the blood from their equipment. In silence, he drank from the simple horn cup and passed the tray back to the girl.

'You were speaking of London,' Essex took a cup of wine, swirling it around the horn he knocked it back in a single swallow.

'Such contempt. I would have thought one so learned would have deeper understanding of the Holy Scriptures,' Red Hugh coughed. 'I am an observer of people. I couldn't help but notice how Shakespeare managed to upstage you with nothing more than a handful of words.'

'The man is more practiced at it,' Essex began his defence.

'Is irrelevant. You were disarmed. It was your intent to belittle the man in front of the whole court. What you ended up with was a bloody nose. The man has a skill beyond the sword.'

'Your point being?' Essex snorted.

'If your plan is to succeed you will need every last peasant on your side. The Bard plays to a full house every day. The people flock to him. They hang on every word. Why not put your message in his hands?'

'A play?' Essex scoffed. 'You jest? I could write my own.'

'And who would come?' Red Hugh stroked his beard. 'But to Shakespeare, everyone comes. He also has the ear of The Queen, does he not?'

'Cecil too, most like. What of it?' Essex kicked at a loose stone sending it skittering across the cobbles.

'If that were true, then he has all the ears that matter, in all the world,' Red Hugh walked towards the keep. 'If you leave now you can return with news of this battle and deliver whichever version suits our joint venture. Be in haste, Essex, but not in a hurry. Plan well. We will need a sizable army here to lure the hand of King Philip into play.'

'You will write to him?' Essex followed Red Hugh into the keep, down along the narrow corridor into the hall.

'The messenger has been dispatched and I expect to hear from him in due course. I know he is anxious to form a foothold on English soil. What I offer is a back-door.'

TUDOR LIFE

NONSUCH

The summer wound down into autumn shades of gold and red; yellow fire lit the ash and oak leaf alike. The warm days caught evening chills, sending the court ladies scurrying for their shawls and cloaks.

Nonsuch Palace stood proud and tall in the heart of the Surrey countryside. Its cream-white walls, inlaid with a latticework of dark timbers, climbed toward an impossible blue sky. A light autumn breeze chased away the morning haze, leaving grass damp underfoot. The white marble fountain chuckled in the early sun as it threw a shower of glittering aqueous diamonds over bathing birds.

Peacocks strutted on manicured lawns while servants plucked rose petals for the royal baths. Elizabeth waited for her groom to finish saddling her horse. She checked her gloves, her crop, her hair tie, before rechecking them. Marie walked through the stables querying servants and grooms, rifling through saddlebags and checking tack. She folded blankets and stuck pitchforks in every pile of straw, the manure pile too. By the time the groom presented Elizabeth with her mount, Marie had finished her inspection and joined The Queen at the rear of the stables.

'Sir Walter.'

Raleigh walked over to Marie; she had never seen him looking so ordinary. There were no golden threads, no resplendent armour decorated with heraldry. He appeared to be nothing more than a squire, except perhaps for his sword and pistol.

'Can I be of assistance, Marie?' Raleigh adjusted his understated ruff, not quite the epitome of fashion.

'Why the servant clothing?' Marie flicked dust from Raleigh's shoulder.

'We are hunting, anything else would be cumbersome,' Walter held out his hand. 'Come, let me assist you,' He smiled at her protest. 'I know you do not need assistance, but would you refuse a gentleman the honour?'

Marie curtsied as she took the proffered hand and allowed herself to be led by Raleigh the few steps to her sleek black horse.

'I have taken the liberty of choosing your horse,' Elizabeth circled around them. 'Jasper may not be the best jumper but he has the heart of a bear. He will always go where you want him to. Raleigh, you can have Ginny,' Elizabeth pursed her lips unable to hide her smile.

'The feisty mare?' Raleigh shook his head in mock dismay. 'Must I always be foisted with the unruly women?'

'Ah Beth, at last. Now we can go before the deer are scattered.' Elizabeth gave a curt nod to Lady Ormond. 'There will be a Sabbath feast in honour of our guests, though in truth I wish there were not. The Spaniards are such a bore and I care not for the Saracen Ambassador. Whoever gets the best kill sits at my table,' Elizabeth peered down her long thin nose at Raleigh. 'Excluding you, Sir Walter. You will be there no matter.'

Elizabeth led the four riders around the back of the palace out into the forested Surrey hills. Dappled light lit the forest through the rustling canopy of gold and green. The recent dry spell had left the leaf litter crisp. They slowed to a gentle walk but still, the ground litter crackled the air.

Holding the reins in her right hand, Elizabeth swung her leg over the pommel of her side saddle. She sat for a moment before jumping from the back of her horse and making a quarter turn toward the animal's head.

'Very nimble, Your Majesty,' Raleigh swung down from his mount to take Elizabeth's horse. He fastened the reins to the wrist of a broken branch. Lady Ormond and Marie brought their mounts to Raleigh who fastened their reins to a nearby tree. 'Not to worry Beth, the trackers will collect them along with any kills we make. You have ribbon?'

Lady Ormond pulled an orange ribbon from her sleeve.

'Good, pass me your quiver,' Sir Walter took the quivers and slung them over one shoulder. 'You shoot, I'll keep you loaded.'

They walked deeper into the woods, being careful where they placed their feet should they step on a dry stick. The soft coo of a wood pigeon hovered among the foliage. Blackbirds sang a merry tune among the chirping trills of the woodland birds and the soft rustling breeze. The hunters stepped across a slender stream, the wet stones glistening in a brief kiss of sunlight. Their objective was now in range. Elizabeth shouldered the crossbow, held her breath and squeezed the trigger.

A soft wind rippled through the leaf canopy, flickering sunlight on the grazing hind. The deer raised her grey-brown head, her dark eyes staring deep into the forest. The bolt struck the deer in the neck, it staggered, its knees folded. The animal collapsed; strands of uneaten grass stuck to her motionless lips.

'Well shot, Your Highness,' Raleigh took the crossbow from The Queen and placed his foot in the cocking stirrup. Taking the string in both hands he pulled it back into the retaining latch and slipped a new bolt into the arrow track. 'The game is on,' he passed the crossbow back to Elizabeth, with a nod toward Lady Ormond as she sighted up a second hind.

'Blast!' Lady Ormond cussed as her bolt struck the neck of the deer. Before the animal could reach its stride a second bolt split its skull.

Marie had reset her crossbow before Raleigh could reach her. She unfastened her jacket, revealing a clutch of bolts sewn into the inside together with several throwing knives. 'One must always be prepared, do you not agree, Sir Walter?' Marie winked at the handsome knight.

'Indeed, but may one venture to ask where you acquired such implements?' Raleigh eyed the lining of her jacket with keen interest. 'I can see Her Majesty is well protected.'

'I have all my tools made by the smiths in Horsham,' Marie explained and slid a new bolt into her crossbow.

'The same as the Royal supplier.' Raleigh walked over to the latest kill, lowering each foot with care. He pulled a ribbon from his pocket and tied it to a branch above the dead deer. Kneeling beside the carcass he pulled both bolts from the neck and head. He ran his thumb around the tip of Marie's bolt, noting the small barbs where the metal overlapped the wooden shaft. Rising to his feet, he changed the ribbon for a bright blue one; there was no mistaking who this kill belonged to.

Marie followed behind Raleigh, signalling for Lady Ormond to get behind Elizabeth. The two parties stalked through the afternoon, keeping close to the shallow river. They wound their way north-east until they reached the edge of the woods and the limit of where the deer could be approached unseen. They skirted the edge of the woodland taking occasional rabbits by surprise. Raleigh gutted those shot by The Queen and Lady Ormond, but Marie was swift of foot and hand, always waiting, with her coney ready to string up.

The sun bled a crimson wash across the darkening sky as the hunters returned to feast.

St Paul's Exchange

Autumn leaves floated to the ground, weaving a tapestry of gold and green splashed with yellow and a smattering of amber. St Paul's Church, with its sunken roof and wayward spire, was still the grandest church in the city of London. Marie leaned against a pillar supporting herself from the breath of a drunken Poley.

'What I have, Marie, is worth more than the few coins from the master's purse. Cecil does not have what I desire,' Poley slapped one hand on the wooden pillar at Marie's shoulder, his knuckles whitening as he gripped the timber. Tapping his finger on the frill across her bosom, he wiped the spittle from his lips, 'You owe me it. I've done you favours no other man would for so little return.'

Marie tugged her jacket down at the waist, maximising her exposure. Poley opened his mouth in a mundungus tinged gape. His eyes widened as Marie ran her hand over his crotch. 'That's the girl,' Poley wiped the drool from his mouth moving in toward Marie's face.

Marie dodged the incoming vomit hole, whispering in his ear, 'Now tell me what you know, and I'll let you let keep your jewels.' Poley swallowed hard as the knife cut through his trousers, separating his testicles on its flat blade. 'In your own time, Poley.'

Poley raised his hands, 'There's no need.'

'There is every need when it comes to you,' Marie turned the blade through ninety degrees. 'Spill.'

'It's nothing,' Poley belched. 'Just Essex.'

'Just Essex?' Marie lifted the blade.

Poley standing on tiptoe lowered a hand, 'He, er, he has been in Ireland these past weeks.'

'Hands where I can see them,' Marie instructed and tapped the blade with her index finger as though tamping a pipe.

'Alright, take it easy.' Poley held his hands up in half-surrender. 'Essex boarded a ship in Bristol. He was seen leaving the Pale by some of Bagenal's men on their way over to Armagh. Our man on the inside at the fort sees his lordship in talks with Red Hugh.' Poley shifted his balance. 'No idea what transpired between them, but Essex came back in an awful hurry.'

'Just Essex? That's what you said … Just Essex,' Marie shoved Poley in the chest sending him backward over a pew. 'How many days?'

Poley rubbed the back of his head with a grimy hand. 'Week or two.'

'And you just thought to pass it along now?' Marie put a hand to her hip, waving her dagger at Poley. 'You feeding information to another?' She stepped closer. Poley backed up against the pew. 'Well?'

'None I swear, got a bit,' he mimed drinking, 'distracted.'

'I dare say Cecil will be none too pleased,' Marie dropped to Poley's side. Grabbing a handful of his thick hair she yanked his head back. 'I will pass this information up the chain. What happens to you is up to another. Me, I'd love to stick this knife in your festering guts and cut out your excuse for a heart.'

Marie stood sharp, leaving Poley to come to his senses. He watched her vanish into the shadows. With a deep sigh, he sagged into a sorrowful heap and poked a trembling finger through the hole in his trousers. Poley counted to two: all was well. He dragged himself to his feet and stumbled out of the church across Carter Lane towards the river.

THREE IN THE NEST

Marie slipped out of St. Paul's, turning right past the old oak tree where a thin nag gnawed at the paltry grass. She took the first right up Ave Maria Lane ducking inside the Mermaid Inn.

There was an unusual quiet to the inn. In a private booth a familiar face gave a welcoming smile. Marie walked over to the booth, sliding herself in beside Shakespeare. She flopped her palms on the table, noticing for the first time the smeared blood on her left hand.

'Anything we should know?' Henry Southampton wiped the blood from Marie's hand with a kerchief.

Marie rubbed her hands together, 'Poley. He thought he could make sport of me in St. Paul's beneath the gaze of the Lord.' Shakespeare sputtered his ale. 'Not to worry, Henry, I convinced him to talk.'

'And?' Southampton turned his cup between his hands.

'Essex has been in Ireland. In talks with Red Hugh. About what is not known,' Marie took some bread and meat from a platter a maid brought to the table.

'Explains his guest at the last banquet and his recent absence from court,' Southampton mused whilst watching the wine swirling around inside his cup before raising it to his pursed lips.

'The Earl has sent me a note,' Shakespeare passed the paper beneath the table to Southampton. 'It would appear he has a sudden interest in the theatre, in particular - mine.'

Southampton opened the parchment, keeping it beneath the table, 'Curious. I have seen this play on a number of turns. You keep your plays contemporary. So, they warrant regular viewing. But why Richard II?' Henry slipped the paper inside his yellow jacket.

'It is possible he wishes to become involved, though he mentions no patronage,' Shakespeare dragged his bread through the fat around the beef. 'I will converse with the Earl at leisure and find out what his intentions are with the piece. It is due an update; much has happened since its inception.'

'Thank you, William. Though I must caution care with Essex. He is in want of a lot for no return: he believes it his God-given right to have everything he wants, including the crown if he could,' Southampton drummed his fingers on the table. 'Madam Marie, might I suggest you wear your bust line a little higher. I know you are indeed single and wanting, but, in times such as these, I would ask you to be in the appearance of one taken with a suitor.'

Marie adjusted her bosom, pressing her ample charms down into her dress.

'Much better, thank you.'

'Are there any specific instructions for me for when I encounter Essex, as I surely must?' Marie brushed breadcrumbs from her attire.

'Try not to kill him,' Southampton swirled his glass again, raised it and put it back on the table, pushing it towards the discarded plates. 'I have no doubt he will pursue you as he did the previous maid, who is with child.

Should Her Majesty come to know of Miss Southwell's fate I am sure Essex would be scolded.'

'I will be sure to decline his advances,' Marie smiled and patted her side where her knives were secreted.

'I am to go to the Globe as Peter Street is finalising the stage entrances,' Shakespeare beamed as he ushered Marie from her seat. 'The theatre of dreams has become a reality. Tomorrow we take delivery of cannon and arms, lance and sword. Our performances will be the talk of the town,' Shakespeare gave a theatrical bow and took his leave.

'What do you suppose is Essex's purpose with Shakespeare's theatre?' Marie folded her hands in her lap.

'I cannot be sure, but I am long overdue time with him,' Southampton tossed a handful of coins on the table as he rose from his seat. 'If I should pour a few glasses of sweet wine down his neck I am sure his tongue will loosen.'

'Which way are you headed? I am to meet Lady Penelope and Lady Ormond at the New Gate for shopping. There is to be a ball at Nonsuch Palace, so I am instructed to acquire cloth and jewellery for the ladies, suitable for the Ambassador of Spain and the Saracen.' Marie waited for Southampton to open the door.

'I regret I must decline. Should Penelope espy us together outside of the court, we can be sure awkward questions will be asked,' Southampton took Marie by the hand. 'Take care, God's speed be with us all.'

He kissed her hand and left by Paternoster Row in the direction of Cheapside.

Shopping

New Gate wall clung to the sky, towering over the busy street where traders and shoppers jostled for position. Shadows stretched across the stalls darkening wares but not the mood of the excited ladies as they shopped for trinkets and treats. Traders bawled out their wares in a chipper trill, beckoning those with a purse to come and loosen its strings. Feral dogs and wild cats scavenged the streets for tidbits among the forests of dancing feet.

'Where have you been, we have so worried about you?' Lady Ormond fussed over Marie, planting a less than delicate kiss upon her cheek.

'We had best be quick if we are to be at the Mercers before the light fades, and the fabric all looks the same.' Penelope Rich fluttered her fan, shielding her eyes from the sun.

'Penelope, you do dramatise. There is yet time for tea and cake in Cheapside,' Lady Ormond placed her hand on the fan, stilling its beating wing. 'Tut tut, how could we not sup at the tea rooms and sample the latest perfumes?'

'Very well,' Penelope turned toward New Gate market preparing herself for the jostle of commoners. 'I still believe there should be a day for the better classes to shop apart from all these,' She pointed to a group of children rolling hoops to one another, their yarmulkes fastened to their heads. 'Should they be in the city after the Lopez trial?' She turned her nose in the air.

'I assume you refer to Dr Lopez?' Marie steered the ladies around the children. 'I for one remain unconvinced of his guilt.'

'You would doubt my brother?' Penelope gave Marie a sly glance. 'You walk among our number, and we count you as one of us, though you court no lord.'

'I do not think it proper to force allegiances, Penelope,' Lady Ormond stepped through their conversation, feigning interest in the bread stall.

'Spare a bite for a lady, mister?' The blonde woman wiped a dirt streaked hand across her cracked lips.

'What d'you have I might be interested in?' The baker eyed the woman from head to toe, his eye lingering on her bust-line.

Grasping a hand over her bosom she barked her response, 'A pox on you, filth monger.'

'Plenty more in the stews where you come from.' He raised the back of his hand toward the woman as she turned and ran east down Cheapside. 'What about you, my lady, finest in the whole city. You'll not get better bread anywhere,' the baker juggled two loaves taking care to give each one a squeeze. 'See how firm they are,' Lady Ormond smiled and moved along.

'How revolting,' Penelope hurried past the next string of stalls all selling grubby linens and used clothing. There were dirtier books for sale on the last stall, which neither of the ladies had any interest in. The lure of tea and cake along the road had captured their fascination. They skirted along St. Nicholas Shambles, passing the church of St. Michael le Querne, and sighted Cheapside Cross.

'Fear not, ladies, Goldsmiths Row is upon us. You'll not find another wretch between here and the Great Conduit,' Marie skipped a half-circle to face the ladies, walking backward on tiptoe as she dispensed her knowledge of the richer quadrant.

'You surprise me, Marie,' Lady Penelope stopped at the window of a goldsmith. 'Where did one such as yourself get such a wealth of knowledge.'

'I may have had humble beginnings, but I have not allowed it to influence my future. I am not defined by my past, or my family.'

'Well said, Marie,' Lady Ormond gasped at the display of neck chains and rings. 'I simply must have it.'

She disappeared into the shop to the sharp jangling of a bell. Moments later a gloved hand reached into the window to lift a simple locket.

The doorbell chimed again. 'Thomas will love this.' Taking the jewel from a tiny black leather pouch she laid it upon her palm for her friends to see.

'It is somewhat ordinary,' Penelope frowned and turned her attention to the next shop where naughty cakes stood to eager attention.

'I rather like it, it has genuine masculine qualities,' Marie pried the locket open. Leaning in close to Beth she whispered, 'Just like the Black Earl,' and winking, she closed the locket.

'If we are to take refreshment before the Mercers, now would be a prudent time.' Penelope thrust the door of the coffee house open and left it ajar for her friends to come in pursuit. 'I will have one of the cakes from the window if you would,' Lady Rich sat in full view of the street smiling at her two friends as they perused the wares through the window.

Marie lingered a while longer after Lady Ormond had taken her seat. She scanned the route back along the way they had come. East toward the Great Conduit and Mercers Hall she could see a dozen or more people milling about in the street. She ducked inside, taking her seat at the table with her associates.

WHITE RIOT

The afternoon waned toward eve as autumn days are wont to do. Crows alighted on the high stone walls, gargoyles to fend off demons, while gentry were ushered through the imposing oak doors of Mercers Hall. Recent troubles had brought the need for guards to be posted along Cheapside. The raiding of Essex's wine had left a nasty stain on the trusted name of the Mercers.

Tired wagons pulled by weary cage-ribbed nags trudged up Ironmonger Lane where the delivery gate stood in studded defiance of all who dared its strength. A filthy beggar girl with blonde hair, draped in tattered rags she called a dress, scuttled alongside the wagon yanking her grime-slicked shawl about her shoulders.

'Wagon ho!' The driver called in his broad Bristol drawl. A small window opened in the face of the gate, a cyclops' eye peering into the gloom of the waiting driver.

'What have yer with the Mercers this day?' gravel tones growled.

'We're collecting, five and twenty bales of linen and four sheets of sail for Queenhithe on turn of tide,' the driver shifted in his seat.

'There's nothing on the sheet for collection or delivery,' gravel tones begged to differ.

'We all know you can't read for shit, Bo'sun. Open the gate and we'll get loaded quick as ya like.' The driver spat black sputum onto the street.

'Aye,' Bo'sun slapped the window shut with a thick fingered hand. With grinding bolts, and rattling chains, the gate swung open. 'Enter Exton and pay yer dues to the master.'

'Will that,' Exton brushed his hand down the side of his thigh, folding his fingers around the heavy cudgel. He hefted it in his hand, dropping it over the side of the wagon into the hands of the beggar girl.

Bo'sun pulled on the chain easing the heavy gate from its rest. The cudgel cracked his skull, dropping him to the cobbles in an instant. The blonde girl wasted no time, her hands rifling through his pockets without disturbing his clothing. With a curious smirk, she watched the life drain from the back of his head.

'Jane, come on,' Exton growled. 'We've got work to do.'

Red, green and gold fabrics dripped dry from heavy clotheslines strung up across the yard. Horses tugged at hay in a makeshift stable to one side, while two women in leather aprons rolled dried cloth into bales. Three inner gates stood at the back of the yard, their red paint flaked and peeling. Black lettering of equal age and wear declared the bounty within.

'Crack it open,' Exton pulled back the cover of the wagon, revealing the hidden gang beneath the tarpaulin's folds. 'Get to it, and make sure his lordship's mark is left for all to see, or you'll be floating with the turds in the river.'

Five men sprang from the cart, their blades drawn ready. Jane slipped an iron bar up beneath the gate lock, splitting the timbers with a deft twist. The doors opened allowing the scourge to pillage at will.

Sacks of grain were hefted over broad shoulders, while barrels of wine rumbled over the cobbles to be loaded on the waiting cart. Exton pulled the tarpaulin back over the contraband with a serpentine hiss of canvas and sacking.

'Hang the message,' Exton threw a brown sack to the ground. The men all stared at the sack as though it would bite them.

'Aye,' a Hispanic voice cried out. 'What you do?' The merchant ran out into the yard as the men cut the sack open.

'Who are you?' Exton barked. 'A Lopez Jew?'

'What?' The merchant fell beneath a hail of fists. Clutching his hands to his head he cried aloud, 'Por el amor de Jesús.'

Blood poured from the split in his skull. His mouth opened and closed but no words came.

'Hang this and get going. Get to the docks as fast as you like,' Exton whipped the bony back of his horse spurring its tired limbs into life. The gang hoisted the message high over the door to the stripped warehouse, leaving it swinging in the deserted yard. Dirty Jane stopped in the gateway, turning toward the scene of bloody murder. A washing line fell to the ground, smothering the dead merchant in a death shroud. A dark stain seeped across the gold fabric, consuming it in a thirsty plague. She stared at the dead spaniel hung over the door of the emptied storeroom, the Latin note around its neck a mystery to her feeble mind. Licking her lips, she thought of how the dog might taste over an open brazier when shared with a few friends and some of the plundered sweet wine. Instead, she turned and fled, a cowing bitch, back to the gutter where she was spawned.

And Then There Were Three

Another palace, another banquet. Autumn golds faded to winter brown. The plush lawns were adorned with frost diamonds and the last petals had fallen from the rose garden.

Elizabeth and Marie walked side by side through the leaf-strewn gardens, amusing themselves as they watched the gardeners try in vain to gather the falling leaves. As fast as the rakes clawed and besoms swept, the bewitched leaves would hop and dance like faeries around a fungal crown. A sharp breeze cut across the lawns tugging at the loose curls of The Queen's hair. Elizabeth continued her discourse, unaware of the games her wig was playing. Marie tightened the braided bun at the back of her head pushing the pin in with a harsh twist. The early sun peered through its watering eye, unwilling to burn away the light frosting upon the earth.

Elizabeth tucked her hands into a white fur muff, 'Ireland is a legacy I could well do without. But there is no way to relinquish it without appearing weak.'

'Words do tell of growing alliances. Red Hugh is wooing the might of King Philip and the Venetians. Should he secure either, we will have a greater enemy knocking at our back door,' Marie stepped aside as The Queen's spaniel, Leicester, dove between them in pursuit of a leaf tugged by the wind.

'If that were so we would have to invade with our full might. But who would I send to quell the current revolt? Ireland has become the graveyard of all who plant a foot on its emerald gown,' Elizabeth gazed into the bluing sky.

'Why must my kingdom be so fraught? Is there no hope of peace in my lifetime?'

'Majesty, if one could be so bold as to suggest Mountjoy for the Irish charge, or perhaps your cousin Lord Ormond?' Marie knelt to take the stick Leicester had brought them.

'I should hate to lose either. Perhaps there is none up to the challenge? It would take the bravest of men to tackle Red Hugh alone; he was a man who served me well at one time. Now he has the young commander Tyrone at his heel, I fear we may not have a match for them,' Elizabeth took the stick and threw it. Leicester bounded away into a flower border where he began to dig with urgency.

'Could Essex not rise to the order?'

'My dear girl, I could not risk such a favoured son in a land of savages. Even if his cursed shadow Southampton and Sir Walter were with him, I could not subscribe to such a venture,' Elizabeth watched a rabbit cross the path. 'He is the closest thing I have to a son. I do not think this ageing heart could suffer such a blow and still beat.'

'You have the heart of lion; a kingly one. You have the strength to hunt and take down the most challenging game. Majesty, though such a loss would pain you dear, you would rise above it and thrash the next foe to raise their fool fist in your direction,' Marie put a hand to her mouth.

'Fear not, my child. We are alone, I shall not take offence at your word. Indeed, you have emboldened me. Lifted my spirits,' Elizabeth gave a polite nod. 'Cecil was indeed wise in choosing you for my protector. There are things a woman simply cannot discuss with a man. They should seek to lord it over in such times when my heart is troubled, and England threatened by persistent foe. No, I shall rise above all things in the strength of my God and my Saviour; I can do all things through his incomparable strength. I am assured it is He who has sent you to my side and not mortal man.'

'Majesty,' Marie curtsied. 'You honour me beyond my worth.' Leicester returned with a mauled rat in his mouth. 'He too seeks only your affections.'

The gravel crunched beneath their feet as they made their way back to the palace where they were greeted by Lady Ormond and Lady Penelope, both of whom came bearing gifts. Leicester placed his muddy paws on Lady Penelope's green dress, signing his sodden signature before running off into the palace, his claws clicking across the stone floor.

'Oh, my new dress!' Lady Penelope attempted to bat the dirt from her skirts to no avail.

'Be careful, my lady, Leicester is more a member of this family than others would pretend to be,' Elizabeth forced a smile to her face as she walked past the two ladies into the palace. 'I shall be a moment. Please, do wait in the drawing room. There are documents to be revealed.' Turning to Lady Ormond she took her hand from her muff; in it she held a fine leather grille. 'I trust you have the latest dispatch from Thomas?'

'I do, Your Majesty,' Lady Ormond pushed her fingers up her sleeve removing a slender parchment.

'Good,' Elizabeth lifted her skirts revealing the toes of her worn leather boots. 'To the drawing room with you. I will be as brief as I can.'

By the time Elizabeth had made a quick change of gown the ladies were on their second glass of wine and their mood was lighter. Penelope was reclining on a chaise longue, running her fingertips over the silver and gold threads, her ears attentive to the conversation. Marie had settled into a high-backed chair looking far more elegant than her upbringing, while Lady Ormond set a glass to her lips, and in the other she clutched the parchment.

The conversation flowed between Marie and Lady Ormond through a veil of idioms and metaphors, many of which were lost on Penelope. Lady Rich smiled her way through the talk, fishing for tidbits among the mystery.

'Ladies,' Elizabeth strode into the room draped in regal gold and purple robes. Removing her gloves, she took the parchment from Lady Ormond. 'The contents of this paper are not for public ears. Should anything contained within it leak out, it will be treason. Understood?' Elizabeth swept the glasses aside and unrolled the paper on the table. 'This bears the mark of the Black Earl,' Elizabeth indicated a motif of a harp and crown. 'It is therefore imperative it fits the correct grille. Only then will I accept it as genuine correspondence,' Elizabeth eyed each lady in turn. 'No matter what the messenger may claim. All members of the Walsingham pact have a motif and grille unique to them. Do you have yours?' The ladies all nodded. 'On you?' Lady Penelope pulled her grille from a sleeve, presenting it to The Queen. 'Do not be so foolish as to carry the one thing connecting you directly to the nest. It pays to keep it safe, but not at hand. Lose it in the wrong house and your head will follow.'

Penelope flushed scarlet, 'Majesty, I—'

'Do not interrupt me, Lady Rich, there is little time to act upon what I see,' Elizabeth placed a fine leather grille over the letter revealing the message hidden within. 'We have been routed in Ireland. Armagh is in the hands of the savages, Bagenal dead, over one thousand souls lost, many deserted. A new strategy required. Ends.'

'Majesty,' Lady Ormond placed a hand to her quivering lip. 'I have not the words.'

'You must take your leave and go to your husband at once. My carriage is at your disposal,' Elizabeth placed a hand on Beth's shoulder. 'Go at once, before my heart breaks beyond repair. Instruct Thomas to do everything necessary. I shall come to Ireland when I can.'

'Who now can lead England against the Irish? They are proving too strong in the field for us. Is there not a noble who could rally the troops beyond the call of duty?' Lady Penelope glanced aside.

'Is there one you might suggest?' Elizabeth turned toward Penelope. 'I can think of none whom I would send into the jaws of such a beast. Raleigh is needed at home to ward off assassins. Sir Clifford, my champion, is not a man familiar with the terrors of war. Who would you propose to send to such certain death?'

Penelope lifted her head, blinking the moisture from her eyes.

'You cannot be serious. You would send your own brother?'

'Majesty I ... the people would ... ' words tumbled into one another as Penelope fought to control her wayward tongue.

'I would rather sever a limb than send my beloved Robert to that hell-hole,' Elizabeth pushed Lady Penelope aside as she stormed from the room wiping her tears on a glove.

Marie snatched up the grille and cypher and ran after The Queen, leaving Lady Rich to ponder her thoughts alone.

Rewrite

In the upper reaches of the Globe, Shakespeare sat poised with his fingers to his lips listening to the drama unfold on the stage. The sun had arced its way into the afternoon. It was always a trial breaking in new performers, but this one was beyond reproach. He was glad it was the closed season, and they still had time for the real actors to rehearse for the grand opening.

'Whilst it is a noble effort, I find the character of Bolingbroke tiresome. He lacks humour,' the actor called unto the heavens.

'My dearest lord,' Shakespeare rose to his feet, leaning forward on the handrail, he glared down at the actor clad head to toe in silver and black silk. 'As I have previously explained, it is not about you but about Bolingbroke. You are merely chosen to portray the would be king.'

'I am not one of your half-wit troop that I fail to grasp the base mechanics of your so-called craft, but ... '

'Essex, play your part and stop being such an arse,' Shakespeare pushed himself back from the rail.

'Why is everyone so bloody precious! I am sure I could come up with better speeches than this diatribe,' Essex scoffed, flicking through the pages as though wafting a stench from his nose.

'My dear Earl,' Poley stepped forward. 'It is of no matter what you think; here, it is Shakespeare and his fellows the punters come to see and hear. Here, you are but a pawn.'

Essex rolled the script tight in his hand, his other rested upon the golden hilt of his sword. 'I should watch your tongue Poley.'

'Or,' Poley brushed the script aside.

'Come now my trusted fellows, let us save the angst for the performance,' William walked out on the stage, every inch the commander. 'We are a long way from performing Richard II. We have a more pressing demand to open with Romeo and Juliet. So ... ' Shakespeare gestured for Essex to leave the stage. 'Gentlemen, enough for today. Ideas have come to me for the rewrite. I shall have new scripts to you by summer. But now we must focus on finalising the theatre and familiarising ourselves with its new features. Never has theatre been so exciting,' Shakespeare snatched the script from Essex. Brandishing it as a sword, he chased the actors from the stage keeping a wary eye on the fuming Earl.

'Be mindful how you tread with him William,' Southampton stepped from the rear of the stage. 'In company he will always play safe, but never let him catch you alone.'

'I am thankful, as always for your advice. Such company I am not used to,' Shakespeare gave a polite bow.

'There is no need for such formal courtesies with me Will,' Southampton lifted Shakespeare's hand. 'You stole my heart and admiration the moment you first put ink on paper.'

Shakespeare tucked the script beneath his arm and covered Southampton's hand with his own. 'My dearest friend, in this city you are alone in your care for me. Only in the arms of my beloved Ann do I feel such warmth as your heart conveys.'

'William, you are more than the sum of your words. Because of your request to Cecil, the world will never know of the depth of your valour.' Taking a kerchief from his breast pocket Southampton wiped his eyes.

'I am sure you did not come here to discuss friendship alone. What troubles you my friend?' William put an arm across Southampton's shoulders and led him from the stage through the rear door of the Globe.

The afternoon was cooling fast. Their breath began to hold in the late winter air. The Thames flowed beneath an ice crust where commoners jousted on bone skates beneath the expanse of the fading sky. Their wooden shields and armour clattered against the rock-hard ice. Undeterred, the would-be knights rose again laughing off the pain as they wiped blood from their brows. The fun would continue as long as the light remained.

'I love it here,' Shakespeare waved at the passing buildings. 'The stews, victualling houses, the filthy street. Everywhere you look there is life. Never has a place inspired me so.'

'From the same place you find inspiration, many find only death. There have been defeats in Ireland. Her Majesty flounders for an answer. The Spanish prepare for invasion and assassins stalk the streets looking for a way to spill the royal blood.

Moreover, Essex is known to be courting the Irish Lords. To what purpose one can only guess,'

Southampton paused to watch a cloaked figure in a doorway. 'Interesting.'

'The man or his manner?' Shakespeare half-turned toward the Thames, pointing at some distant object.

'Both. You do not see many Jesuits this side of town,' Southampton's gaze followed where Shakespeare pointed, laughing perhaps a little too raucously.

'He is a brute too,' William turned Southampton back toward the Bishop's Cap.

'And strangely familiar,' Southampton dared a last glance. The figure ducked into an alley. 'Let us get back and see who is in. If he is still there, Poley can go see what becomes of him.'

'He is a good man, Poley,' Shakespeare held the door of the Inn open for Southampton.

'He would cut your throat if the price was right,' Southampton quipped. 'But fear not, he knows the price of tampering out of his remit. Speaking of the devil,' Southampton invited Poley to join them in a private booth.

'Is it work?' Poley loitered by the seat.

'It is,' Southampton turned to face him. 'There was a Jesuit, around Grope Alley.'

'Tall,' Poley nodded, 'big bastard.'

'That's the one,' Shakespeare interjected, summoning ales.

'See where he goes,' Southampton slid some silver across the table. 'Take care Poley. There is more to him than we know.' Poley pulled a woollen cap over his head and vanished through the back door.

'He wasted no time,' Shakespeare noted the shadow flit past the window.

'He fears nothing. Poley has faced many demons and survived them all. I shall have to speak with Marie and have her warn her Majesty,' Southampton dropped a copper coin on the maid's tray.

'Take heart, Henry, I am to read to The Queen this eve,' Shakespeare raised a hand. 'Fear not; I shall speak to Marie, not to her Majesty, directly.'

'You learn fast Will. You are an asset, as was Marlowe,' Southampton sighed. 'But you, we still have you,' Henry pursed his lips. 'Has Essex mentioned, at all, why he wants this play? Richard II.'

'Not outright, he has not,' Shakespeare took another mouthful of ale. 'It is as though he believes himself to be Bolingbroke.'

'The one who becomes King,' Southampton raised an eyebrow.

'I think we may have stumbled upon his intent,' Shakespeare put his tankard on the table. 'All at once my ale has soured my mouth.

LATE ARRIVAL

Everything was ready. The banquet hall was an ocean of gold and white except for the Queen's table. The ash floor had been polished to a liquid sun finish. Every table was draped in a fine golden silk inlaid with a tapestry of pure gold depicting the Monarch in her youth. Golden candlesticks stood at the centre of every table, each one burning twelve candles of purest white. Mirrors lined the walls, angled to amplify the light to the ceiling where chandeliers glittered with diamonds.

Minstrels played Greensleeves, while choristers harmonised to a single voice. The Queen's table was in dark contrast, pulling the eye, demanding everyone's attention. A black velvet cloth carrying the weight of the world in a web of pearls hung over the table, tumbling down the two shallow steps to the dance floor. Three huge candelabras lit the table with a golden light, radiating the hue of Queen Elizabeth's gown. Her red hair flowed about her shoulders as a shoal of shimmering fish turning in a moonlit ocean. Raleigh sat to her left, his gold and black outfit a perfect match for Elizabeth. To her right, having won her place on the hunt, Marie, dressed to kill in a low-cut gold dress of woven silk scarves each fastened with a diamond brooch. Her blonde hair was a coiled plait pinned through with her favourite knives.

Guests from across the globe were announced and led to their seats by jesters, fire breathers and jugglers. Acrobats tumbled across the floor passing trays of drinks between them. In three corners of the room a lion sat tall and proud tethered with a heavy chain. Once seated the food arrived on gold and silver platters. Roast hogs stuffed with apples were lifted onto tables followed by a hind of dear and flanks of beef. Meats of every kind smothered the tables. Elizabeth rose to her feet followed by a scraping of chairs as the guests turned to bow and curtsy. 'Let the feast begin,' Elizabeth flung out her arms to a fanfare of trumpets and a herald from the choristers. Meats were carved, bread ripped open as the chatter and clatter of rich dining began. The minstrels continued to play as Essex entered the room heading straight for The Queen's table.

'Majesty,' Essex bowed, his long beard almost touching his knees.

'Late,' Elizabeth did not look up. 'Fashion or rudeness, I can barely tell the difference anymore.'

'I was held up, unforeseeable,' Essex gave a polite cough.

'Go on,' Elizabeth waved a hand at Essex. 'How was the whore saved?' She contemplated him, her mouth a sliver of flesh.

'I ... ' Essex floundered, his eye met with Raleigh grinning. 'I have been working on something at the theatre,' He brushed his beard against his chest.

'Yet William is here,' Elizabeth pointed to Shakespeare at the next table. 'If you are staying, there are seats by the door. If not, leave,' Her words were cold.

'Majesty, it would not be right for me to sit ... such.'

'Why not? You flaunt my favour as though it were nothing. Your mother rides in my carriage as though she were Queen, and you permit the she-wolf. Is there anything you are not telling us?' Elizabeth placed her cutlery beside her plate.

Essex glanced at Marie and his sister sat beside the smirking Raleigh, 'It would appear my seat is already taken,' His gaze bore into Marie.

'She earned it,' Elizabeth entwined her fingers. 'Now sit among the Blackmoors, or leave,' The Queen unfolded her hand, stretching out her arm as a swan reaches to its mate, she pointed to the door.

'Very well, if that is where I am to be,' Essex enunciated every word before turning to take up his seat.

'Another time Sir Walter, try not to grin like a fool,' Elizabeth picked up her fork, prodding at the food on her plate. 'I have an idea. A chance for Essex to redeem himself,' Elizabeth sunk her fork into some venison and lifted it to her lips. 'A tournament. Arundel, in the spring. Something to look forward to. Among all the usual revelry we will have three challenges. Archery, the sword and a joust,' Elizabeth surveyed Raleigh as she popped the meat into her mouth. 'What say you?'

'If I must, for your honour I would lay waste to the Venetian Empire,' Raleigh raised his cup to The Queen.

'Try not to groan next time,' Elizabeth beckoned a serving girl. 'Fetch me a plate of sugared almonds and marzipan. I am in need of sweetening,' She turned to Marie, 'Have you tried marzipan my dear?'

'I have not your Majesty,' it is not found on the streets where I grew up.'

'Quite. My apologies, I forget your humble childhood,' Elizabeth leaned in to whisper. 'You wear your disguise well, at all times,' Elizabeth sat up smiling. Marie returned the smile with a polite nod. 'I need entertainment,' Elizabeth called out, 'where are my midgets?'

A troop of dwarves ran into the room to be greeted by rapturous laughter and equal applause. Soon they were wrestling one another while the guests wagered on a winner. Essex slipped from the room; his ardour rankled beyond repair. 'I fear the boy may lose his head if he does not learn to control it,' Raleigh jabbed a fork in the direction of the departing guest.

'Impudent, but adorable nonetheless,' Elizabeth selected a pink almond from a tray.

1599

Riled

Spring was upon the city. A gelid Thames slurred its way through London, the ice slurry scouring dirt from the stone embankments. Tortured souls hung blue and naked from chains rusted and coarse, the cost of theft. Tall ships, merchants from France and beyond, slipped into moorings. Ropes were slung and tied off on ancient pillars as old as the city itself. Barrels laden with wine rumbled down the gangways into hands eager to whisk them into storage. Sacks of grain were hidden beneath bolts of cloth, a treasure more valuable than Spanish gold.

A tired sun, obscured by a grey wash, cut a sliver from the clouds to peer down on London. A wily feline groomed itself in the temporary spotlight, soaking up the tepid warmth. Gulls wailed at the paltry scraps, their anguished cries falling on dispassionate ears. Should they venture close enough they would add meat to any broth.

Amid the clatter and chaos Essex strutted with Southampton at his side, a barnacle stuck to a stalwart hull.

'Why are we here?' Southampton ran his hand over a plump sack.

'Too many eyes in the palaces and too many tongues in the victualling houses. Here I can see my enemies approaching,' Essex stood with his hands on his hips counting the assembled cargo. 'I no longer have the direct ear of The Queen. It would appear some harlot has my seat at her table.'

'You refer to Marie?' Southampton stifled a yawn. 'The young girl from Sussex. A beauty if ever there was one,' his mind elsewhere.

'Harlot, hanger on,' Essex bit back. He turned to Southampton placing a firm hand on his shoulder. 'Only you, can I trust, Henry. Raleigh is naught but a jumped-up commoner. Cecil disgusts me. As for Penelope,' Essex shook his head. 'Strumpet!'

'Does she not do your bidding in chamber matters?' Essex waved Southampton's question aside. 'Has she not succeeded in alluring Blount? Is he not rallied to your cause?'

'Blount would no doubt be allured by you if you wore a dress,' Essex snorted.

'I am glad to see your wit has made a full recovery from the ball. Alas the rest of you remains in a dire sulk,' Southampton walked to the edge of the Thames where he watched the detritus flow by on the tide. 'I do hope they have the foundations of the Globe dug; this tide is keen to breach the banks of Southwark.'

'Fine, it can wash all the shit from the city,' Essex held his kerchief to his nose. 'You can smell the commoners from here. The whole place reeks of filthy whores and cheap ale. Why on earth anyone would build a theatre in the midst of such scum is beyond me,' Essex spat in the river. 'The cleanest thing they've seen in years.'

'Shakespeare has tremendous vision for his theatre. It is to be three stories high with a thatched roof open at the centre to light the stage and lengthen the time of performance. You'll like it there. One level is for the better classes, you'll be able to enter and watch without brushing shoulders with the common folk.'

'You almost make them sound human,' Essex drew a breath. 'They make my flesh crawl. They remind me of The Queen. When will the old hag step aside and allow me to do my duty.'

'Cecil pushes for James to have the throne as he is of Royal descent.'

'Descent, pah. I am of Boleyn blood. My mother was sister to Elizabeth's. I have a blood-born right to the throne of England. I have supporters at the ready to back me in my claim,' Essex cast a glance to Southampton. 'I trust on your favour Henry. You'll be at my side when the shout goes up,' Essex stated with a cold heart. 'I'll wear the crown; you can be sure. All I need are the people behind me and the nobles at my side and the crown is mine. I'll sign the bloody Ascension Act in Elizabeth's own blood if I have to.'

'You'll need help to win the commoners to your cause. Your immense charm will not make them put their necks out for you Robert. What you need is a skilled craftsman, one who knows how to stir the hearts of men,' His gaze stretched across the river to Southwark. 'There is such a one.'

'The balding imbecile, Shakespeare! How pray tell could he be of any worth to capture the crown? You think he would wield a sword against the royal house? I doubt he could lift his cock to piss in the wind without making a scene of it,' Essex sneered. 'It is odd though. Red Hugh counselled along the same path. He too thinks the bard persuasive. It is well, I have sown a seed and have the fool labouring with a play.'

'It is you he speaks of when he talks of Bolingbroke and the crown,' Southampton smiled. 'Cunning indeed. It will veil you when the play is submitted for approval to the Master of Revels.'

'I need no veil. I will ensure the play is read and approved by favourable eyes.

But this is all bye the bye. Can I trust your tongue is loyal to me, Henry?'

'You have my heart and soul to call upon,' Southampton grasped Essex by the hand. 'Have I not proven this both home and abroad?'

'Indeed, you have. What I have to say, Cecil does not know. I have heard in Ireland they have made a pact with Spain. They are to host the Spanish with aim to open a back door into England. The Papacy has issued an edict declaring The Queen a heretic. There is a price on her head. It is only a matter of time before the Armada lands in Ireland.'

Southampton's hand fell to his side.

Raise the Roof

A sky as grey as the Tower hung over London threatening hail upon the frozen earth. The cold air amplified the clatter of hooves and rattling carts through the Southwark streets. A dusting of reeds filtered down around the lower walls of the Globe, settling as golden threads on the deep frost.

The spring tide had washed all manner of filth down the streets in its haste to reach the lower marshes. The plummeting cold of the night froze the tail of the tide, covering the earth in a biscuit of ice.

Southampton stepped back to admire the work, 'It's looking good, Will.'

'That it is,' Shakespeare hugged Southampton with the affection of a brother. 'Not seen you for a while. Have you been out of town?'

'You could say, I have been on a jolly to Cádiz with Essex and a few fellows of The Queen's navy,' Southampton smiled. 'You are looking well, my friend.'

'Indeed, I am in rude health,' Shakespeare walked across the street into the Globe, where he stood in the centre of the pit. 'Can you imagine how it will be on opening night?' Southampton gazed up at the thatchers pinning down the bundles, carpenters cutting patterns with fret saws while others laboured to complete the walls and build the framework for the stage.

'What are those for?' Southampton pointed at pulleys mounted above the stage area.'

'So men might fly,' Shakespeare leapt into the stage area, prancing from one spot to another as he explained the hidden details of his latest masterpiece.

'Trap doors, cannons and flying men!' Southampton chortled. 'The greatest show on earth.'

'The whole world is a theatre, this is but one glorious instrument in its symphony,' William bowed.

'Will you open with Richard II?' Southampton asked in a subdued tone.

'Alas not. I think something more popular. Romeo and Juliet is the order of the day. This place was birthed from my love of the theatrical, so love it must be. Richard II needs much adjusting to reflect the mood of the city. The lead is seldom available, so it will have to wait for its appointed time.'

'I'm famished, let's eat and celebrate my sound investment. The Chamberlains Men will go from glory to glory,' Southampton entwined his arm with Shakespeare's and practically dragged him from the theatre.

The Bishop's Cap was quiet. The two men walked over to their preferred booth and took their seats. Southampton slid a curtain across the window closing out the granite sky. Darkness would soon descend upon the city in a chilling grasp. Drinks were served in silence, Southampton poured out a crimson wine from a black bottle while Shakespeare quaffed his ale. They ate and drank in silence until at last, the food was finished but their drinks refilled.

'And now our thirsts are slaked, and our bellies filled, it is high time we talked of court and city streets,' Southampton thumped the stopper back in the bottle.

'There have been numerous sightings of the mysterious gent,' Shakespeare began, pausing to sup his ale. 'Poley has seen him both at the Tower and down the Strand as far as Westminster. It is well Elizabeth has retired to the country. I think only ill can come from such as he.'

'Cecil is of the same mind. He has spoken to Raleigh who believes it to be the same man he fought in Cádiz.'

'A spy, perchance?' Shakespeare mused.

'Quite. A dangerous one too. I have mentioned him to Essex in private, but he has no recollection of the fellow,' Southampton brushed crumbs from his jacket. 'Will,' he leaned closer, 'Essex has designs on the crown. Be careful not to get ensnared. If caught he will take all those around him to the Tower.'

Shakespeare pressed himself back into his seat, 'I had such thoughts when he asked for changes to the script of Richard. Is he losing his grip with this?'

'His grasp was slender at best. Beware, this is all I can offer at this time,' Southampton appeared to deflate. 'I love the man, I genuinely do. But I see nothing but bloodshed in his current course.'

Shakespeare rubbed a hand through his thinning hair, sighing as another strand came away in his fingers.

As evening drew in, the tables began to fill. Laughter and cussing blued the air. There were squeals from the handmaids, as uninvited hands explored their clothing.

Fists flew as tables tumbled, spilling cards and ale upon the floor. The fighting patrons were ushered out as keenly as rats from a grain store, but it did not deter any from taking bets on the outcome of the brawl.

'Never a dull moment,' Southampton rose from his seat. 'I am off now. I have other ears to rend before retiring. Take care and let me know when the opening night is to be.'

'It will be as soon as the winter closure is over. It may not appear so, but the Globe is quite near completion. I cannot tell you how excited I am,' Shakespeare straightened 'Until the next time.' Southampton bowed and made his way through the rear exit.

William sat pondering his tankard. He lifted it from the table, it felt disappointingly light. His eye wandered to the bar and the mistress of the house, he smiled as she laughed and jested with the patrons. They may not be the highest of society, but they were certainly the greatest. Here among the dung strewn streets walked the people who were the heartbeat of London. They carried the grain to feed the world and the wine it lapped up in greater quantities than water. It was their backs that bore the burden of city life. The rich barked out their orders and the people fought for crumbs from their master's table. In return for the servitude of the downtrodden, the masters would beat and deride them. Nothing had changed in Southwark since the Romans built the first settlement on the bank of the Thames.

Shakespeare put his tankard back on the table twisting it a half turn. The waitress came with a plate of bread and meat, together with a fresh ale. The bread was black and hard as it should be, the meat sat as an island surrounded by jelly and dripping. William took the bread and broke it. He scooped the bread through the jelly and dripping; pushing it into his mouth, he closed his eyes and soaked up the flavours.

When he opened his eyes, he was no longer alone.

GUIDO

The air in Bishop's Cap drew in around their table. Shakespeare pushed himself back in his seat pulling his ale close to him. Opposite him sat a tall gentleman with a waxed anchor beard, the wax turned his dark auburn hair almost to black. The man's hair was thick with waves, tied back in a braid. Dressed entirely in black, his outfit was priestly yet menacing. He placed his hat upon the table next to a wooden crucifix, which he turned until its long end pointed at William.

'I am a priest, Guido, I represent his holiness the Pope in England. You have become of interest to me,' his accent was Italian with hints of something closer. 'You work for Essex, no?' Shakespeare nodded his affirmation, keeping one eye on the bar.

'The maid will not be of any assistance to you. I only wish to talk,' Guido smiled revealing perfect teeth. 'For now, at least.'

'May one inquire what you wish to discuss?' William sipped from his ale. He placed his drink carefully on the table holding it between his hands.

'I need to contact the Earl,' Guido cast a glance toward the door where a couple were engaged in a lively haggle of the price of pleasures. 'It disgusts me.'

'They are people, not saints,' Shakespeare drew a breath, settling the unease in his heart. 'The Earl has a house on the Strand, you can locate him there or leave a message with a servant.'

'I wish it were so simple. His Holiness forbids open contact with such sinful men,' Guido reached inside his robes, retrieving a gold handled dagger with a ruby set in the pummel. He set the dagger down on top of his wooden cross. 'Others have failed before you to relay messages. I trust you are not full of folly?'

'Marlowe?' Shakespeare stared at the dagger. 'A dagger, the fang of the serpent?'

'I am no serpent. I am a mere messenger to the hand of God.' Guido ran his finger down the length of dagger's blade.

'Tell me more of this message,' William wagged a finger at the dagger. 'Am I too, to receive this in a dark alley, or have you a more public plan?' Shakespeare swirled the ale in his tankard before downing it in a single swallow.

'You will drink no more of this cup in my presence. Your mind must be clear as to my intent. My time is limited. Tell the Earl to be at Armagh by the week's end,' Guido spread his hands on the table, drumming his fingers on the scarred wood.

'How am I supposed to do that? I have no appointment with him, and he will need three days to make the journey.'

'Neither of which are my concern,' Guido pushed himself up out of his seat, leaning in close to Shakespeare. 'You have your orders,' He gathered up his belongings and left, scything his way through the patrons. William pushed his tankard across the table. The barmaid ran to the rear door, reappearing moments later with Poley.

'Master Shakespeare, is everything alright?' Poley placed a hand on William's shoulder. 'You tremble like a cornered animal.'

'He was here, the Jesuit. He left a moment ago,' Shakespeare nodded towards the door. 'Something stiffer than ale is required if you please, miss.'

Poley ran for the door vanishing into the darkened streets he knew better than any man.

'Take a seat sir, I'll fetch his lordship,' The maid passed the brandy to Shakespeare.

'I'll go myself. Thank you for the medication,' he returned the empty glass.

'As you wish, sir,' the barmaid returned to her duties.

William rubbed his brow, straightened himself up and headed for the rear door. The sound of the inn dulled as he closed the door behind him. His boots clunked along the wooden floor as he wound his way to Southampton's private rooms. Shakespeare paused at the door, the sound of muffled voices from within pricked his interest.

'Knock man,' Shakespeare reproved himself. "Tis a matter of state,' He gave two sharp knocks on the door with his knuckle.

'Enter at your peril,' the familiar tone of Southampton's voice called. William grasped the handle and gave it a firm twist. He pushed the door open and entered the room.

'William, William, my loyal friend, how pleasing it is to see you. Please, have a seat.' Shakespeare took up a seat at the card table, next a dark-haired lady of elegant dress and hazel eyes, around her pale neck hung tears of pearl.

'It is a pleasure to meet you at last master playwright. Henry speaks of you often,' The lady's soft tone danced upon Shakespeare's ear.

'William, may I introduce you to my lady and wife, Elizabeth Vernon. Up on a rare visit to the city,' Southampton gestured toward his wife before joining them at the table. 'What is it that brings you to my chambers, Will?'

'A matter of state I fear,' Shakespeare glanced at Elizabeth.

'Elizabeth is a fine confidant. Her ears only work when needs must,' he smiled at his spouse.

'I shall delay no longer. After you left the booth, I was joined by another. The Jesuit.' Southampton's face drained of colour. 'He calls himself Guido and has the most appalling of Latin accents, I believe him to be of English descent,' Shakespeare reached for the decanter on the table, taking a hefty swig. 'My apologies, but the thought of the man unnerves me. Poley has gone after him as we speak.'

'What was he after?' Southampton poured a glass of wine for each of them.

'He wanted me to pass a message to Essex. He is to be at Armagh by the week's end. I explained it was not possible for me to approach the Earl, to wit he produced a dagger identical to that which killed dear Marlowe.'

'Heavens,' Southampton gasped. 'It is no wonder you are so unnerved. Fear not William, your message will reach the Earl. I am to see him in the morning after Elizabeth has departed for Cowdray House. Perhaps you should attend. That way if ... Guido, was it?' He asked William who was downing his third glass of wine. 'If he is watching he will observe you with Essex, assuring your safety.'

'I do hope so Henry, be sure I do.'

ESSEX

Rain dripped from the ceiling forming muddy puddles on the floor of the Privy Council chambers. Essex drummed his fingers on the underside of the long table as he listened to issues of state. Unrest in Kent and Sussex darkened The Queen's mood.

'Whilst the home counties may be squabbling over grain, we have far more pressing issues in Ireland.' Robert Cecil stood to address The Queen.

'What has that dog Tyrone done now?' Essex straightened in his chair. 'Has he taken more weapons from your secret stocks, Robert?'

Cecil glowered. 'You know much for a pompous upstart.'

'Gentlemen, please,' Sir Walter Raleigh suppressed a smile. 'The Irish revolt needs to be contained.'

'The Irish must be crushed,' Elizabeth snapped. 'Everyone who has gone to Ireland has failed to bring them to heel. Is there none worthy of me to go?' The Queen drew her lips tight. 'Thought so.'

'I'll go. Give me the men and I'll have them routed in a month. They are nothing but savages. A sound thrashing is all they need to learn their place,' Essex examined his fingernails. 'I can leave as soon as the men are mustered,' He turned to look at Elizabeth.

'Bravo,' Cecil all but cheered, catching the lure in Raleigh's eye. 'We have ten thousand at the ready. I can send word to have men mustered across the entire realm. We can be ready by the end of the spring tides.'

'It would need one as brave as you to take on the Irish commanders. You may avail yourselves of my lands in Munster if you wish.' Offered Raleigh.

'Are you all quite mad? Essex will not go to Ireland as long as I am its Queen,' Elizabeth's voice trembled. 'Essex is the nearest thing I have to family. I cannot risk his blood in such a way. There must be another who can go in his stead.' She glanced at the faces of her council; all were of one accord.

'Your Majesty,' Essex rose from his chair, bowed. 'As much as I share your blood, I also share your passion for unification. I know those who lead the rebellion, Tyrone and Red Hugh will be no match for us. They still use the same strategies as they have for centuries. A massed force will crush them in a moment. I know where their forces train and where their supply routes are,' Essex bowed again. 'I too can think of no other man to bring peace to the realm.'

'Essex,' Elizabeth ran from the room, a hand to her eye.

'I'll give orders to muster the nation,' Cecil perused papers on the table. 'You will have your men and all the arms you need. Set a date and it will be so.'

'May God go with you Essex, you'll need it,' Raleigh offered his hand. Essex considered it and gave it a light shake.

'I believe her Majesty is to have a spring tournament at Arundel. I shall leave after,' Essex tightened his grip. 'You have a firm grasp Sir Walter, you'll need it to keep your sword in hand when we meet on the field of valour,' Essex turned and left the room whistling a jaunty tune.

The rain had eased to a cold drizzle. Essex walked out of Westminster heading for the Strand. A shaft of sunlight broke through the blanket of clouds turning the moisture on his cloak into a waterfall of diamonds.

'God bless you Lord Essex,' the commoners called as they passed him by. Essex met them with a smile or a nod, lifting their spirits if only for a moment.

The Strand was quiet for the time of day, there were few cattle or carts bearing wares from the western farmsteads and Smithfield. From there it was but a short hop to the markets at Newgate and Cheapside within the old Roman city walls. Carts loaded with barrels rumbled along the streets, their drivers wary of all passers-by. The city teetered on the brink of revolt; with the right encouragement the whole world would erupt.

When Essex arrived at his house, he found Southampton, leaning on the mantle in his study, swirling his wine around a delicate glass. 'How fares thee, my friend,' his voice gentle and kind.

'Couldn't be finer, my dear fellow. I have this moment taken hold of a marvellous opportunity to show my worth as regent. You, Southampton are looking at the commander of her Majesty's forces to Ireland,' Essex replied, bowing to the knee. 'Probably the last time I shall bow to any man.'

'Ireland!' Southampton set the glass on the mantle over the fire. 'The graveyard of lords. Are you quite out of your mind?'

'No, never been better, or felt more sure of myself,' Essex took the spurned wine from the mantle, downed it, and threw the glass into the fire. 'I have made many visits to the green isle. I know the lands as well as I know London. With a fresh force of more than ten thousand men I shall march up to Tyrone and Red Hugh and take all that is theirs for my own. I shall take Munster and use it as a footstool. I will accomplish all Raleigh and those other halfwits have failed to do,' Essex spun around snatching up a decanter. 'I shall be King of Ireland. Elizabeth will have to sign the Ascension Act or be removed with force,' He grinned.

'Careful my friend, the city is full of ears,' Southampton straightened his back. 'Let not the hope of power cloud your judgment. London is on the brink of revolt. Foreign spies roam the streets, Southwark too is not safe from the eye of the Vatican.'

Essex batted the comment aside, 'Southampton, my most loyal and trusted friend. 'Let them hear. I do not fear the wrath of The Queen, she would not pen my execution order. She will scream and shout with the fury of hell but take my life she will not.'

'I wish I were as confident as you,' Southampton mused. 'I will accompany you as always.'

'The hag will forbid it,' Essex spat the words.

'Has that ever stopped us?'

'No,' Essex clapped a hand on Southampton's shoulder. 'Nothing will change that. A mere woman will never break our friendship. Henry, my friend we have much to prepare and blood to spill. I feel a visit to a den of iniquity is in order. I can catch up with the playwright while I am at it. I have some ideas for the royal play.'

'How do I look? Will it suit?' Essex stood in white tights and blue jacket, his shirt ballooning with frills. 'Well?'

'Are you wishing to blend in, or stand out?' Southampton swallowed. 'Southwark is something of an enigma to you is it not, Robert? You are going from house to house, and whore to whore, not a strut about the royal courts. Have you not something a little more ... ' Southampton swirled his finger about in the air. 'Crass.'

'Crass!' Essex coughed into his wine. 'I think it is the first time you have used the word? Perhaps you would have me dress in my servant's clothes.'

'An excellent idea, call the man and have it done.'

'What!'

'Your servant will have the ideal garments. I can change when I arrive, I have quarters at the Bishop's Cap. You, however, do not. You will stand out like the dandy you are in those tights. Are you wearing undergarments?' Henry attempted to lift the tail of Essex's jacket.

'One does not lift a gentleman's shirt to inspect his derriere?' Essex playfully boxed Southampton about the ears.

'You brute, Robert. How can I be seen in public with reddened lobes?' Southampton feigned a terrible hurt.

'Come Henry, if we spend much more time in tomfoolery all the best strumpet will be spoiled. I'll not pay for second sittings; the thought alone makes me nauseous.'

'Go change while I ready a carriage. We'll ride as far as Church Lane. I have a ferryman there who will take us across without question.'

'I'll be back in a jiffy, old boy, for tonight we hunt only the fairest of maidens,' Essex called over his shoulder as he left the drawing room. 'Failing that, whatever is left so long as it's clean.'

GREEN SICKNESS

The carriage was a simple two-seater with a sole driver up front. The dappled mare pawed at the ground, impatient to get going. The afternoon was already beginning to fade. A cold breath of winter hung in the air, forming soft eddies of warmth before chill bitten faces.

Essex climbed into the back seat pulling the rough woollen collar of his borrowed coat about his neck. Southampton tapped the driver on the shoulder falling prematurely into his seat as the horse lurched forward.

'York Lane, quick as you like,' Southampton smiled at Essex.

'York Lane,' Essex cried. 'We could have walked, 'tis but a stone's throw.'

'When will you learn the art of subterfuge. Is there no subtlety in you Essex?' Southampton held his face in his hands.

Essex pondered the question, 'None. Alas I have no need for it. Should I give the word, heads will roll. Dear old Lopez would attest: if he could.'

The carriage came to an abrupt halt. Sounds of merriment drifted up from the river, half-echoed laughter amid the clattering of iron and the dull thud of wood. Southampton led them down to the edge of the Thames where the ice was at its thickest.

'Completely frozen,' Essex pressed his foot against the ice. 'Are we to walk across?'

'Unless you wish to go to the bridge and be seen by those who know you,' Southampton gave a nod to the east. 'That way if you will. This way is not for the faint hearted.'

The two friends walked out upon the frozen Thames; the ice groaned beneath their feet. Southampton stopped to watch the peasantry ice joust with bone skates and homemade armour. Their wooden shields, held together with old rags and lengths of twine, did little to protect them from the enquiring lances.

'They put on quite a show,' Essex remarked.

'And for no more reward than the cheers of a friend,' Southampton replied almost falling over a vanquished competitor sent sprawling on the ice.

'Come on Henry, before all the best whores are taken,' Essex made purposefully for the south bank and the safety of dry land muttering to himself. Southampton lifted the fallen warrior from the ice, dusting him down with much encouragement. His eyes wandered to the bank where Essex was already on the towpath. With much reluctance Southampton followed his friend, climbing up the frozen bank with effort. Essex was a little way ahead waving his arms as though in full flow of conversation with himself. Southampton increased his step until he was back at his friend's side, where he caught the spur of Essex's conversation.

'What say you Henry,' Essex clapped a hand to his shoulder. 'Once I have sorted the rabble in Ireland, we come back to these shores and stir the hearts of the people to order her Majesty to pronounce me heir apparent. Could the common man have a better choice!

King Robert Devereux. It certainly has the royal sound to it,' Essex practiced the name, 'King Robert.'

'First there is the small matter of Ireland. You'll not get Tyrone and Red Hugh handing it to you on a platter,' Southampton steered them past the closed bear baiting pit down toward the Bishop's Cap. The last light of day vanished beyond the clouds. It was a fair night wrapped in a frosty blanket. Candles glowed with a warm light of hospitality in the windows of the inn. A few doors down, veiled in shadows, the Globe awaited its first audience.

Essex opened the door with his usual aplomb, hoping perhaps to gain an admiring audience. Instead, there was a drunken scowl and a loud belch to announce the would be king. He strode to the bar, finding himself among common fools and harlots by the score. Southampton walked to the back corner, his secluded booth. He smiled briefly to himself before he removed his cloak and took up his seat. Essex appeared with a young girl on his arm, not yet a woman, the green sickness was still a blessing to her.

'Jess,' Southampton addressed the young girl directly. 'Is it not?' The girl replied with an affirming nod. 'My friend will take utmost care of you. Won't you?'

'Indeed, I shall,' Essex kissed Jess light upon her brow. 'The delights of a real man shall be all hers,' Essex grinned. 'And she has yet to bleed, so no bastard surprises,' He raised an eyebrow at his friend.

'So sophisticated, it offends my senses. I feel quite ill.' Southampton brushed a hand across his brow.

'Toodle-do!' Essex waved a cheery goodbye and led the young girl to the upstairs rooms.

'Has he finally left?' a familiar voice enquired. 'I do not trust the man.'

'And neither should you William. He would as quickly sell you down the river as he will bed that child,' Southampton pointed to the empty seat, 'Join me, please.'

The inn was getting busy, early drunks were swept aside by a fresh batch of bodies. Gentlemen, with escorts on their arms, were swept among the dregs of ferrymen and drunken sailors. The tide would not turn until morning, so there was plenty of time for fooling around and brawling. Songs rang from hearty throats; the approach of spring was in every heart. The winter ban on the theatres would be lifted and the Globe would open its doors to the public for the first time.

The ales arrived with plates of food. A warm, flickering oil lamp smoked silently on the table. Shakespeare tore at the bread, smearing it with beef dripping. He licked the excess fat and meat jelly from his fingers. Southampton sliced at a ham, separating the fat from the pink meat. 'Where are the hounds when you need them?' he dropped the fat beneath the table. A wiry black mongrel appeared clearing the master's scraps.

'What am I to do with Essex. What he proposes for the play is nigh treason. It will be my head on the block if I were to stage such,' Shakespeare dropped a glob of fatted bread into the eager maw of the mongrel, who proceeded to sweep the floor with its tail. He pushed himself back in his chair pressed his face to his hands and blew out his cheeks.

'Much like that hound, he will keep pushing until he gets what he wants. Placate him. We know his overall aim, it is the method we have to expose, and the threat can be dealt with,' Southampton caught the hand of passing girl. 'Are you working?'

'I am sir, what is your desire?' The girl curtsied, pushing out her chest.

'I would like you to go and assist the young maiden with my friend up in chambers. Here, take this coin, I trust it to be sufficient.'

The girl's face became a broad smile. 'I shall do whatever the gentleman desires,' She left at a quick step for the stair door.

'It should keep him occupied for a while longer. If only his sister was here,' Southampton mumbled through a mouthful of meat and ale.

'I'll do all I can to keep the earl happy. If he lets any secrets out you shall be the first to know, Henry,' Shakespeare wiped the grease from his lips with a cuff saying, 'I will go now before Essex's appetite is satiated. I do not wish to spend a moment with the man when he reeks of fornication. His cologne can be offensive enough, what was the last one, horse piss?' Southampton waved him adieu chuckling to himself. He watched Shakespeare engage with the commoners with admiration, never had a man such a rare talent as to be able to allure the rich and poor alike. All too soon his friend was gone, leaving Southampton in the company of Essex and a night of going from 'ouse to 'ouse and 'ore to 'ore. The end to all this could not come soon enough.

GATHERING STORMS

The morning sun opened its languid eye upon the steaming city. A pale-yellow light pushed its way through the clouds, casting long icy shadows along the streets. Cattle wandered in through New Gate, driven by a weary herder accompanied by an equally tired maid bearing a yoke of empty pales. Heavy hooves clonked on the hard cobbles as the bovine convoy headed toward slaughter.

Market stalls began to appear as rickety poles were thrust into holes to stake out their reserved pitches. The lingering odour of excrement mingled with the yeast of fresh risen bread. Bakers, butchers, clothiers bawled their wares upon the streets, crying out the chorus of another day of commerce.

All at once, London was awake, the beast had stirred and was out on the prowl. A figure clad in the robes of a Jesuit danced and parried his way through the growing crowds and the cattle down Warwick Lane. Passing the Mermaid Inn with haste, Guido flitted across the junction, vanishing down Ave Maria Lane where he turned east into the brightening sun before cutting beneath the sainted oak of St Paul's Church. Once inside he availed himself of the rich shadows, avoiding the light of the east window upon the dawn altar where morning song was in progress.

Down among the shadows, in the darkness between the pews, Guido knelt in prayer. 'Hear me, Mary Mother of God. I confess my sins to you directly as the priests here have given their hearts to heresy.'

'Very noble indeed,' Essex perched beside the kneeling Jesuit. 'The time will come when the true faith will rule again.' Guido nodded his head in agreement while maintaining his penitent stance. 'My allegiance,' Essex held the hilt of his golden sword out for Guido to assess.

'May the blessings of his Holiness guide your sword into the hearts of all heretics,' Guido touched the hilt of the sword with the handle of his dagger. 'We are brothers in arms and faith.' Keeping his head bowed he got up and sat beside Essex, his eyes fixed on the only undefiled image of The Blessed Mother, Mary. 'You have spoken to the playwright?'

'I have his message,' Essex snapped. 'You can inform your men I will be in Ireland after the spring thaw. I have secured the backing of the Privy Council to take a force to Ireland to liberate it.'

'Why wait,' Guido turned his head toward Essex. 'The Armada needs only a few days to sail to Ireland. We will land at Dublin. The ships will sail with a full complement of people ready to establish Spanish rule with the blessings of The Holy Father. A warrant has already been issued for the execution of the witch Queen. He has declared it no sin to kill a heretic.'

'I see,' Essex drummed his fingers on his sword. 'Am I at liberty to spread this word among the keepers of the Sagrada?'

'You may, and you are free to recruit among your noble friends,' Guido spoke with an air of self-assured confidence. 'Any who wish to keep their heads will declare allegiance. We are going to keep the Sagrada at your home in the Strand.'

'What!' Essex turned in his seat, to be greeted by the grinning face of Guido. Essex stared at the dagger nestled in his groin.

'To refuse the command of Venice is to refuse God.'

'Essex swallowed his pride, 'Such an honour, and surprise. I would be only too glad to have the blessed articles in my home.'

'I thought as much,' Guido flicked the blade, cutting through Essex's breeches, before slipping the dagger back inside his jacket. 'Do not cross me again. I understand your fetid blood ties to the royal whore, for that you have my sympathies. But if you refuse to obey the papacy, I will gut you and leave you flopping about on the quayside. Your unique position puts you in the best place to cut the bitch's throat. See you do not waste such a divine appointment,' Guido placed a heavy hand upon Essex's shoulder as he rose to his feet. 'God is *always* watching,' he emphasised 'always' with a hiss before sliding into the shadows.

Essex stared up at the image of Mary, a slight quiver upon his lips. 'Am I to be Judas? Is it all I have become?' Drawing a sharp breath, he forced himself to stand. With his head bowed he signed himself with the cross, muttering, 'Steady my heart and hand for what I am about to do.'

Essex walked out of the church as one going to the gallows. His steps were heavy, his mood sombre, the wind whipped his hair about his face, but he cared not. The spring sun did nothing to raise his spirits. Essex wandered the streets of London, his ears deaf to the cry of the common man calling out his name. Across Knight Ryder

Lane and down Paul's Chase until he stood at the water's edge where the mighty Thames beckoned him come. Essex drew his sword weighing it in his hands. He smiled as the sun caught the ruby in the hilt. The gold handle glittered, as alluring as any siren at sea. 'Are you a blessing or a curse?' He turned the sword over in his hand. Grasping it by its hilt he held it up to his face, kissing the blade. 'Or a means to an inevitable end,' He thrust the sword back into its scabbard as the Royal Barge passed by, its oarsmen working as one to conquer the seaward tide.

'One day, your highness all that is yours will be mine,' Essex spun on his heels, 'You there,' he called to a ferryman. 'Can you take me to Arundel Place?'

'Aye sir, the wind is with us. It will take but a moment even against the tide. The ice has broke. Them 'as lucky they never fell through last night.' The ferryman loosened the ropes from the capstan. Essex boarded the vessel, taking up a seat to the stern. He watched the ferryman push the boat out with an oar, hoist the small sail and trim it to the wind. The muddied Thames lapped eagerly at the hull as London passed them on either side. Paris Garden on the Southwark shore swarmed with tiny vessels crossing between there and Black Friars. Ants upon the water, carrying their contraband back to their nest while their Queen passed by, oblivious to the world.

'Keep us to the starboard side of the Royal Barge,' Essex hunkered down behind the sail.

'I'll keep us close to the shore as can be sir,' the ferryman moved to block Essex from prying eyes. The sharp twang of the lyre and harpsichord plucked at their ears as they sailed past the barge. 'Prefer a shanty m'self.'

The small ship cut through the murky water, carving through flotillas of excrement and rats until they bumped up against the small jetty at Yorke Place. Essex took a small coin purse from his sleeve dropping it into the ferryman's hand, 'You never saw me,' Essex lowered his gaze, 'Understand?'

'Never saw who sir?' the ferryman fastened the ropes to the jetty. 'I see so many I never notice faces,' He added, whistling the music from the royal barge. Essex tugged his collar up about his ears, striding up the short jetty toward the rear of his home. Out of sight of all but the sun.

The sun had reached its full height, its warmth pleasing to the soul. A simple black cart pulled by a single black horse stopped outside Yorke House. Its driver jumped down and banged on the door with the ball of his fist. The door opened and the driver walked in.

'What the bloody hell are you doing here Exton? You know we cannot be seen together,' Essex fumed.

'Delivery,' Exton thumbed over his shoulder. 'The Jesuit says you're expecting them.' He turned and walked out to the carriage with Essex at his heels.

'It's broad daylight man. People will see, you fool!' Essex tried to stop Exton pulling the covers from the cart.

'See what? A battered old market box,' Exton shoved Essex aside. 'Your fussin' will get more attention,' Exton growled beneath his breath. 'I'll need help to move it.' He sat on the wooden box. 'Whatever's in it is mighty heavy.'

'I'll get some servants. That bloody Jesuit, Guido, has not heard the last of this,' Essex strode into his house bellowing orders. Exton waited for the help to arrive, keeping his face obscured by his tattered hood to avoid catching the eye of the wealthy pedestrians.

'His lordship requests we put the box in the library.' It took all three footman and Exton together to carry the box before Exton waited alone with the delivery.

Essex appeared, swilling wine around a glass. His cloak gone, his ruff in his other hand and his shirt hanging open at the collar. He stood by the box tapping it with his foot. He held out the empty glass and ruff toward Exton who stared at them. 'Oh, for pity's sake man. Do you not know your station among gentry?' Essex tossed the ruff on a chair and put the glass on the mantel over the fire. He paused for a moment to add more wood to the fire and raked through the ashes. With a short sigh he returned to the box. 'Open it,' He ordered.

Exton pulled a key from his pocket and unlocked the box. Essex put a foot on the lid as Exton was about to open the chest. 'That will be all. Here's something for your trouble,' Essex dropped a small purse in Exton's hand.

'Your lordship,' Exton bowed and left, closing the front door behind him with a sharp tug.

Essex closed the library door, shutting himself in with Guido's box. He lifted the lid, smiling broadly as the treasure was revealed. The box was filled with golden swords, each one had a ruby fixed in its hilt. Essex took one out, feeling its weight and balance. He took out his own sword, comparing them against each other, 'Who would know,' He swapped the swords and strapped his new command to his side.

STRATFORD

Sunlight played down upon the tall grass growing on either side of the hardened dirt track, Sweet violets trembled in the breeze as though conversing with their stout, neighbourly primroses. The scent of meadows filled the warm air, lengthening the days as summer peered over the horizon.

Far from the bustle and crowds of London the village straddling the banks of the Avon had grown slowly to house more than fifteen hundred residents, Stratford was no longer a humble village. William rode into town as any other man, quiet, unnoticed; here he was the son of the alderman and glover, John Shakespeare.

William turned his horse up the High Street as far as the Atwood, a well-established inn frequented by many of the villagers. A young boy offered to take his horse to the stables and see it rested and fed, for a nominal fee of course. Shakespeare tousled the boy's hair, sending him on his way with a copper coin held tight in his hand.

The Atwood bustled with patrons, though nothing could compare to the Bishop's Cap. Having availed himself of victuals, William took up a seat by the front window where he could watch the world go by. Ting-ting sang a stick on a barrel ring, as children chased by the window in a melody of laughter. A farmer driving his handful of cattle out to pasture and the beaming smiles of two teenage girls staring back at him through the window.

William leapt to his feet and ran to the door where he was embraced by his two daughters, Susanna and Judith.

A tint of sadness coloured his heart as he thought of Hamnet, his beloved son, no longer upon the stage of life.

'My sweet girls,' Shakespeare embraced his children kissing them repeatedly. 'My beautiful, beautiful girls. How have you been keeping?'

'We have all been well but missing you sorely. Mother will be pleased to see you, she reads us everything you send,' Susanna, the elder of the two girls replied. 'Can we shop? Mother has sent us out for meat and provisions for supper. Grandfather is coming with Grandmother; we are to have a celebration.' The girls pulled their father out into the sunshine where a warm breeze carried the prospect of joyful times to come.

'What are you celebrating? There is no birthday,' William pulled his daughters unto him. 'Or has one of you a suitor?'

'Oh yuck!' the girls grimaced.

'The very thought,' Judith, a mere fourteen years, shuddered.

'Come now, think of the family, you are my hope of grandchildren,' William teased, resisting the pull of his children. 'Go ahead, and get whatever your hearts' desire, be it meat, or vegetables.'

'Vegetables,' Susanna turned about, thrust her hands to her hips, 'are for the poor. Really father, I thought you would know that!' She chided.

'I am so sorry,' William fell to his knees with his hands held in supplication. 'Could you ever forgive me?' Susanna huffed and withdrew to the market stalls. Judith shook her head in disbelief and went after her sister clutching a purse of coins. William rose to his feet, dusted down his clothes and went in pursuit of his children.

The market was busy, not unlike New Gate, the exception being the lack of diversity among the people. Here there were only the working classes and no foreigners. Stratford was far from any city influence. Sheep outnumbered the people, with wool being the epitome of fashion. William pushed his way through a flock being driven up Bridge Street to the High Cross, at the heart of the Market, where the Justice of the Peace waved him over.

'I trust you have your papers William?' The alderman asked.

'Richard Quyney, how fares thee,' William fetched a folded paper from inside his doublet. 'Did it go well in London?'

'As could be expected, better if truth be told. The Queen took pity on us due to the savagery of the fires and the plague. We've been granted a break from taxes and levy. Though we have no true justice, just us aldermen keeping an eye over things.

One thing though, The Queen did give mention to your family, she gave her well wishes and greetings to your mother, Mary. It appears after all these years she does remember her visit to your mother's all them years back.'

Shakespeare took the papers from his friend, 'Tell me Richard, is Wallace the stone mason still here?'

'He is indeed, you'll find him over back yonder,' Richard pointed toward the far end of the market. 'Keeps a spot by the river, carries most of his stone by water. Why, what's you thinkin'?'

'Clopton Bridge is in need of repair, I thought I'd make a contribution. The town needs the bridge, without it all will suffer,' William placed a hand on Richard's shoulder. 'It's been a pleasure speaking to you. But now I have business to attend to and two daughters to find.'

'Fare thee well, William, and do pass on what I said from her Majesty,' Richard waved to his friend as he went on his way.

The market quickly thinned out into more regular housing, some of them fronting businesses. One such house was the Stone Mason, a brown sign depicting a hammer, chisel and a rock hung over the door of the home of Wallace Hart. The oak timbered house stood out from its neighbours; the three-storey building was the only one of its kind to have survived the devastating fire which had devoured most of the street. Wallace himself was down by the river vetting a pile of stone.

'Wallace?'

'William!' Wallace, straightened up from his work. 'What brings you to my home?'

'I have a proposition for you. Clopton Bridge,' William gestured toward the bridge spanning the Avon. 'If I leave funds, could it be fixed? I should hate to see my hometown impoverished by its demise.'

'It would be my honour, sir. Would you partake of an ale while we sort the detail?' Wallace waved to his spouse indicating his requirements. Shortly after she reappeared with ales and bread.

'Thank you ma'am,' Shakespeare took the tray from the woman and sat on a boulder close to the water's edge. 'I will leave the monies with you to get started and further sums with my father, John, who I shall see this eve.'

'Why, that is most generous of you. Obviously, London life suits you.'

'Indeed, fortune has favoured me. Soon I shall be opening my own theatre on the south bank of the Thames,' Shakespeare wiped the drips of ale from his chin.

'Incredible. Who'd a thought it, Master Shakespeare, lord of London. You'll be at The Queen's knee next!' Wallace guffawed. Shakespeare found himself unable to resist the infectious laughter of the old stone mason.

'Thank you kindly for your hospitality,' Shakespeare downed the rest of his ale as he rose, brushing crumbs from his clothing. 'I must venture forth and round up my lambs. I sent the girls shopping for supper.'

'All the best, William. May the blessing of heaven be upon you.'

Shakespeare paused, 'And upon you,' He walked along the riverbank, watching the swans glide on the mirrored water. When he reached the bridge he sighed. The once strong structure was crumbling with neglect, though he did like the way the ivy hung over its sides, the vines dragging in the water. Perturbed, he turned up Bridge Street back into the market. It was not long before he found his children, struggling under the weight of the lamb they had chosen for supper.

'Here, allow me,' William lifted the dead animal over his shoulder. 'Did you fetch a goose?'

'The butcher is bringing it later with the quail and beef. We could only manage the lamb,' Susanna sighed, glad to be relieved of her burden.

'Go ahead and warn your mother of the delivery,' William shooed his children in the direction of the High Street. With a glance over toward Henley Street, the place of his birth and adolescence, he ambled along greeting all who passed him by. He stopped to take in a sight he had once wished to lose from memory; the old slaughterhouse, the place where he would go as a child with his father to collect hides for gloves and horse piss for tanning. Some things never change. Shakespeare put his hand to his mouth and nose and passed by as swift as he could. Now he wished he had built New House further down the High Street, if the wind came from the north-east the odour of the slaughterhouse would be at their door, he shuddered at the mere thought.

NEW HOUSE

Standing at the door to his home he paused to smile and take in the street. Stratford was pleasant, a comely village, full of charm and approachable people. He adjusted the lamb upon his shoulder and knocked thrice upon the door. At the sound of familiar footsteps on the other side of the door William adjusted his doublet and stood tall.

'William,' Anne, his wife, threw her arms about William's neck kissing him deep. 'I wasn't sure, at first, whether to kiss you or your lamb,' she took the animal from his shoulder. 'How was London? Is the city as busy as they say? Have you met The Queen yet?'

'Please, Anne I am barely across the threshold and I am assailed with questions. First, pray tell, how is everyone?' William chortled, as he followed Anne through to the rear kitchen where she laid the lamb upon the table and gave her shoulder a deft rub. 'London is as London will ever be; a seething mass of humanity in a simmering cauldron of ethnic diversity, a world-renowned city of sin.'

'You obviously like it there, and it suits you,' Anne positioned an iron spit over the fire.

'You don't sound entirely happy with it all,' William opened a drawer beneath the table taking out a small curved bladed knife set in a stag horn handle. 'I'll skin this while you prepare the fire.'

'I notice our daughters are nowhere to be seen,' Anne snatched up an apron tossing it to William. 'You won't want to get your doublet filthy.'

'I almost forgot,' he put the knife down and set about unfastening his doublet. Anne watched him from across the table where she began to knead dough in a trough. 'The girls told me my parents will be coming for supper?' William twisted the embroidered buttons one by one carefully releasing their hold on the embroidered fabric.

'Take care my love,' Anne squeezed the dough through her fingers. 'You'll get that blessed animal's wool all over your breeches. Which, I must add, fit in a manly manner,' She blushed.

'Then I shall remove them also,' William popped the cufflinks on his sleeves and slipped the doublet from his shoulders. Without taking his eyes from Anne he stepped over to the door, hung up his doublet and dropped the latch.

'Why sir, I have no means of escape, what if ... ' Anne's words were cut off by William's tender kiss.

'I should not want you to,' he kissed her, tasting her mouth as he pulled her tight to him.

The fire cracked, hissed, and spat as the flames licked up the sap from the green wood.

'Welcome home, my love,' Anne rested her head against him, breathing in time with the rise and fall of his chest.

William kissed her light upon her brow holding her in the loop of his arms. 'Perhaps when the Globe is built the family could come and see a play. I can hire a sloop and we can cruise the Thames from Southwark to Richmond, to the Tower and back again.'

'How wonderful, I would like that,' Anne slipped from William's embrace. 'But for now, we have a meal to fix before the lamb decides to get up and return to its mother.'

William adjusted his dress and returned to his skinning duties. He spun the knife in his hand contemplating the first cut. 'Where to begin.' He tapped the blade upon the lamb's chest. 'But, soft! methinks I do digress too much,' he slipped the knife into the chest cavity slicing all the way up to the throat where he cut around the neck. 'I would prefer to have done this while the kill was fresh. But alas, it is not to be so,' William inserted the knife under the skin sliding up the leg to the hoof. Humming softly to himself he proceeded to open the other legs and peel back the skin, slicing away the fat layer keeping as much as possible of the meat.

'You're making a fine job of that animal, my dear,' Anne separated the dough into smaller loaves. 'Quite the skilled man with your hands,' she bit her lip.

'What could I compare to thee,' William let the words flow softly from his lips. 'For though I travel to the corners of this great nation where I illume the stage with my craft. There is no other place I would rather be than in your arms,' William walked around the table. He took Anne in his arms, lifting her chin, he kissed away her tears and held her close. 'Never, shall I be seen in the embrace of another woman. Though men may accuse me, I will be yours unto my dying breath. For none have known me as you. You are mine and I am yours, my soul weeps when we are apart. Every time I return to London it gets harder to leave you. Though I have many friends among the rich and poor alike, none hold my heart as you do.'

'William,' she wept, not of sadness but of unconditional love.

'Mother?' the girls were at the kitchen door rattling the latch. 'Is everything well?'

'Your father locked me in,' Anne lifted the latch allowing the two girls into kitchen. 'You know how he likes to jape.'

'Indeed, we do, he suggested we eat vegetables!' Judith stressed, throwing her arms around her mother's neck. 'Could you imagine such a thing?'

'Vegetables aren't so bad, my dears,' Anne stifled her laughter. 'With enough meat on your plates, you would not know they were there.' With a huff the girls turned and left the kitchen, leaving William and Anne to laugh away the afternoon.

By the time the rest of the family arrived, the dining room table was already set. Susanne and Judith, had worked hard, polishing the silverware and folding napkins. The house was filled with smells of cooked meats and buttered pastry. John Shakespeare, now quite elderly, checked the table together with Mary, his wife, before taking up his seat.

'I s'pose I must doff my hat to my son as he is master of this 'ouse,' John groaned taking his seat. Mary stoked the fire before taking a seat beside her husband, where they waited as the Shakespeare sisters began ferrying food to the table.

William followed Anne into the room, carrying the goose on a platter. He waited for everyone to be seated before placing the bird in the centre of table. He took up his seat at its head and led them in the grace of the Lord.

'Mind if I carve?' John was already out of his seat with a carving knife in his hand.

'Please do,' William gestured with an open hand to his father who proceeded to carve the goose with precision. As he was serving his own portion there was a loud knock at the door. 'I'll see to it,' He waved William back to his seat. 'You enjoy yourself,' John walked out of the dining room closing the oak panelled door after him.

'Evening squire,' the gentleman at the door spoke with a learned Yorkshire accent with a hint of Latin. 'The master at the inn said I might find you here.'

'John,' John Shakespeare shook the offered hand. 'John Johnson, how might you be?'

'I am well,' John Johnson stepped back with his arms spread. 'As you can see. Travelling the world has been kind to me.' a wooden crucifix swung about his neck.

'Thought you'd gone to enlist? Here you are, man 'o God. Good fortune suites you,' John Shakespeare appraised his visitor. 'What brings you out this way in these plagued times?'

'I have an order for muster from London, do you have any reprobates who would benefit from a sojourn in Ireland?' John Johnson offered the scroll with a flourish.

'Oh, I'm not the sheriff anymore, but I'm still an alderman. I'll pass this on to Quyney in the mornin' he'll get it sorted. There's a couple of rough lads in holdin', they'll be a start.

Where are my manners. We're sitting to supper; would you care to join us. My son is up from London, I'm sure you two would have much to talk about.'

'Er, you must excuse me, I need to get to my father's estate. I still have a long night ahead of me,' John Johnson doffed his hat revealing his auburn locks.

'Quite the picture you are, young Johnson. You get on your way now and Quyney'll get the muster started first thing,' John waved his visitor a fond farewell. He closed the door fastening the latch for the night.

'Who was it father?' William asked, his mouth bulging with food.

'John Johnson, on his way to see his family in York. Dropped this off from London, got a fancy seal on it for muster papers.'

'Let me see, I might know from whom it came,' William washed his food down with a slug of ale. He wiped his hands on a napkin and took the scroll from his father. 'I know this without any doubt. This is from the hand of Essex. Why would a commoner be carrying such papers, and be allowed to travel through plagued lands? There is more to this man than meets the eye. Tell me of him,' William returned the scroll to his father.

'Oh, he's a big fellow, strappin'. Over six feet tall, got a fine beard and a mass of auburn hair.'

'Wears a wooden cross,' William held his hands close together. 'About this size.'

'You know him? It's a wonder he didn't want come and have some supper,' John Shakespeare cut himself some more meat from the platters, which he smothered in thick sauce.

'I don't know him as John Johnson,' William wiped his mouth. 'I know him only as Guido.'

BACK IN THE NEST

Sunlight streaked through dappled clouds on the first morning without a frost. Spring could not come soon enough. Vapours snorted from the horse's nostrils as it ground at the bit. Foaming spit drooled from its lips adding to the dark stain on the rider's chaps as he rode along the Uxbridge Way toward St Giles in the Field to the west of London. Pulling the reins hard to the right the rider steered the horse south towards Westminster.

The city was in sight now, the easterly breeze carried its scent upon its breath. The fields of Covent Garden stretched out to the left. Prior to the Church of St. Martin in the Fields church; the rider slowed his horse to a walk and crept into the church ground where he alighted, allowing himself to catch his breath.

A high stone wall ran around the church to a dark gate whose iron bonds had rusted deep into the weathered wood frame. The rider drew himself together and banged three times upon the door, twice more in a lighter rap. He waited for the answering knock, the short silence before it came was deafening. A woodpecker's drumming, at the bark of a gnarled oak chipped at his nerves. He could feel the heave of his chest rise and fall, a wave pulling at the sand.

'Lord or Master?' a voice croaked from beyond the door.

'Neither is king,' the rider replied. The heavy door swung open. The rider led his horse through the gate releasing its reigns. The horse wandered over to a stone trough where it drank deep from the cold water.

'Master Shakespeare, what has you in such a quandary?' the gatekeeper latched the gate with sleight of hand.

'Am I pleased to see you, Robert. To trust what I have to tell, to any other, be a most difficult thing,' William puffed, one hand upon his chest. 'If only my heart would calm.'

'Walk with me, William,' Robert Cecil spoke softly, his words a reassuring balm. He placed a gentle hand in the middle of Shakespeare's back guiding him along the path toward the house. 'Much has happened, much is to come.'

'And much from those close to home and within the circle of the crown,' Shakespeare stepped over the threshold into Burghley House.

'Do fetch our guest a drink and some meat,' Cecil waved a servant off to do his bidding. 'In here William,' he guided Shakespeare through to the study. 'Your arrival could not have come at a more fortuitous moment.' Shakespeare slumped into a chair, allowing the high back to give him strength and to take courage from those gathered around him.

'Why, my man, you are positively rattled,' Sir Walter Raleigh took a kerchief from his pocket and gave it to Shakespeare.

'Thank you, Walter,' William wiped the fine linen about his brow and neck.

These men before you have all come here today in preparation for the tournament at Arundel. Her Majesty has seen fit to prepare Essex for his war on Ireland with a trial of combat against Sir Walter,' Cecil began to explain the meeting of spies, Raleigh shook his head with dismay.

'There will be ambassadors from many corners of realm: Ireland,' He waved a hand at the Black Earl and Mountjoy. 'A delegate from the Moorish lands, France and Spain will be represented. We must have all eyes and ears open. Assassins are everywhere, the Catholics will stop at nothing to put one of their own on the throne of England.'

'I, for one, am glad I do not get invited to such events,' Shakespeare sipped at his drink, pushing himself back into the embrace of the chair.

'Sorry old boy,' Raleigh feigned sorrow as best he could, but nothing could keep the smile from his face for long.

'Gads,' Shakespeare stared at the seal on the letter in Cecil's hand.

'Her Majesty insists,' Cecil chuckled. 'She would also like a private reading of Romeo and Juliet before the tournament.

'Can my heart take any more fright without bursting within my humble frame?' William steadied his hand as he broke the royal seal.

'Now,' Cecil tucked his hands behind his back. 'What is your news?'

'O, where to start,' Shakespeare skimmed through the invite one more time. 'I was at my home, in Stratford, visiting my family before the new theatre season begins in earnest. We were about to carve the goose when there came a knock upon my door. My father went to see who should be calling at our abode at such an hour. He chatted with the visitor for a while, inviting him to sup with us.

By good fortune he declined, but he did give my father a letter, a muster order in fact. When my father returned to the table, he showed me the papers,' Shakespeare read the face of each man in turn. 'The seal was of Essex.'

'What! The indignant brat.' Raleigh tossed his drink into the fire. The flames billowed with the breath of a dragon as the brandy ignited. 'I have seen no such orders, have you Cecil?'

'None,' Cecil steepled his fingers, pondering. 'There is more, I sense,' his brow furrowed as his eyes fell upon William.

Shakespeare swallowed hard as Cecil's gaze bore into him. 'It was delivered by Guido.'

'My, my,' Mountjoy and the Black Earl chimed together.

"Tis as we feared,' Raleigh stepped toward Cecil. 'He is courting the Catholics and Spain.'

'He has alliances in Ireland too. Tyrone speaks well of him as does Red Hugh,' the Black Earl ground through tight lips. 'He cannot be trusted. We must all maintain our guard and not let slip anything is awry. He is soon to venture for Ireland. I will ensure our eyes are alert in every province.'

'Do this,' Cecil instructed with the calm of an executioner. 'Thank you, William. You may return to your home. I will inform Southampton personally. You need not concern yourself any further. I would suggest you focus all your energies on your performance before her Majesty, she is a most attentive listener.'

IT IS FINISHED!

Standing proud over its lowly neighbours with its golden crown shining in the bright spring sun, the Globe Theatre waited for the first curtain call. Winter was at an end and spring had burst upon the bustle of London to the cheerful tune of the lark. Shakespeare stood at the door to his theatre, one hand upon his heart the other upon the oak frame.

'As the phoenix rises from the ashes, so you have risen from the ruin of another. Such wonders have I in mind for all those who cross your threshold,' William opened the door and stepped inside his dream. The sound of mocking laughter and the clash of steel turned his joy to sorrow. He ran in full fury across the yard, 'What in the love of God is going on here? Have you gentlemen no respect?'

The duellist stopped, turned toward the enquirer and bit his thumb toward him, 'For you, a mere yokel?' Essex glowered, sneering, 'None.'

'Of course, you have not, you have no respect for yourself,' William retorted, holding his ground as Essex jumped down from the stage pointing his sword at William's chest.

'Care to try and upstage me now scribe?' Essex spat. 'Who will applaud your fine words now?' He pushed the sword into Shakespeare's chest, piercing his tunic. 'You have no one to protect you now. I doubt her Majesty will come riding to your aide.'

'Robert,' Mountjoy leapt from stage knocking Essex's sword aside. 'He has been called to the palace; it would not be fit if he were to arrive scarred. Control yourself and act like the gentleman you purport to be,' Mountjoy put himself between the two men, easing Essex back.

'I see whose side your coin falls Charles. I thought you were loyal?' Essex shifted his stance to a more defensive position.

'Essex, stop this tomfoolery!' Southampton strode into the yard. 'What has he done to you. Would it not be better for you to journey to Arundel and set the field in your heart?'

'Oh, I had almost forgotten the bloody tournament,' Essex thrust his sword into its sheath, the sunlight catching the ruby in its hilt. Shakespeare cast a glance at the sword then to Mountjoy who gestured him to calm. William stepped back, pulled himself up onto the stage. He walked its length and breadth trying to erase the scuff marks.

Mountjoy reached out to Essex, 'Robert,' Essex shrugged off the hand of his friend. 'Oh please, not another tantrum.'

Essex whirled around pulling a dagger to Mountjoy's throat, 'It will be more than a tantrum. I'll be glad to paint the town red with your traitor blood.'

Mountjoy raised his hands, 'Robert, think of what you are doing?' he eased the blade aside.

'I think it's time we all left for the countryside,' Southampton ushered them all toward the door. 'Did anyone see where William went?' They all glanced around the theatre, but Shakespeare was nowhere to be seen. "'Tis of no import. Come gentlemen, let us make haste to Sussex and the company of friends.'

'If they are as trustworthy as you two, I had better take a second suit of armour,' Essex snorted. Pushing his way through them he strode out of the door with his nose in the air.

At the sound of the closing door a hatch opened at the rear of the stage. Shakespeare crawled out smiling to himself as he stood proud. 'Such fun we are going to have within these walls,' he chuckled, closing the hatch. Whistling a merry ditty, he walked back around the stage, and headed for the exit.

ARUNDEL

The bright morning sun shone with the intensity of summer. Small clouds dusted the otherwise clear blue sky, though the chill of spring held the heat within its grasp. The tilt yard was almost ready, the central tilt with its golden rails and posts was being strung with bunting in the favoured colours of The Queen: black and white, to match her gown and robe. The counter tilt was simple, golden rope suspended between black posts along either side of the tilt. The grass was scythed to within an inch of the ground.

Quintains stood to attention on either side of the tilt in anticipation of the first strike. The target dummies were weighted with heavy shields, one with black and gold the other a more princely silver and black. The Yard Master barked his commands to the ground crew, who scurried about at every order scrutinising every buckle, shield and lance.

At either end of the yard a cluster of small tents was being erected in matching colours to the quintains. This was to be a royal tournament, there would be no tenan and venan here today.

A stable boy appeared, leading a white stallion out to the tilt. The horse paused at the quintain, pawed at the ground and snorted. The boy tugged at the reigns, 'S'only a dummy, boy, later it'll be Raleigh. You'll get to piss on 'im if master Essex has his way.' The horse whinnied and snorted all the way down the tilt and back again, over and over, until it walked and trotted the path to glory without fear or distraction.

A blacksmith's hammer chimed with the resonance of a church bell calling the faithful to heel, only this time they came for swords and shields. Hot sparks showered from the glowing metal as the hammer forged another shoe for waiting horses. Steam rose with an angry hiss as the blue iron was thrust into a bucket of cold well water. 'Lets 'av yer,' the blacksmith lifted the horse's hoof between his legs, twisting the black shoe against the animal's hoof until he was happy with what remained to be done. 'Little more and you'll be ready to dance all over that struttin' ponce,' the blacksmith gave a nod to the far side of the yard where Essex was strolling up the tilt accompanied by a young woman. 'Don't trust that'n, never 'av, never will,' he spat into his forge as he thrust the horseshoe back into the heat and pulled on the billow's cord.

'My dear girl,' Essex cooed, 'you simply must visit my quarters after the tournament. In fact, I insist,' The earl stepped in front of the young woman only for her to sidestep away.

'Essex, I will not be seen anywhere near you in private,' Marie retorted. 'I have her Majesty to attend to. It was not you I came out to meet. You flatter yourself and fool no one,' Marie feigned a move to the left before stepping to the right and vaulting the central tilt.

'Astonishing!' I can only wonder how one such as you moves in the sheets,' Essex's smile slid across his face.

'You'll never know,' Marie turned about and walked in the opposite direction.

Essex watched her, while he adjusted his dress, before strolling off toward his pavilion end. The morning was passing at a steady trot. Essex perused the arena in which he was to display his valour before his cousin who sat on the coveted throne.

He thought of life and what he had achieved. The memories of glorious victories filled his mind: the thrill of the Armada, the battlefields of Flanders, where he gained his first golden sword, and there was Cádiz, spoiled by the jealous Raleigh.

Essex knew he would one day rule England. Elizabeth would pass the mantle across and he would reign supreme in her stead. Raleigh would soon find himself in the Tower, waiting for the one o'clock bell. He could wait, it was only a few years at most before Elizabeth would die of some festering pox. He smiled to himself as he greeted passers-by, those working on the Yard and those setting up stalls. Today, lesser mortals would try to entertain the crowds gathering at the castle gate. Tomorrow, the heroes of war would take to the field of valour - only one would walk away with the laurels.

Piece by piece, the outer yard began to fill. To one side, a set of stepped seating backed by standing positions for the less than noble. All of which flanked the Royal Pavilion, where a heavy oak throne was being pulled into position by a tired old shire, more interested in its nosebag than its work. Carpenters chiselled at the rails and supports, cutting last minute designs into the structure. Royal haberdashers and seamstresses worked together in a symphony of thread and fabric, decorating the royal throne with cushions of lush velvet and pearls.

As the light began to fade, braziers were lit, and torches ensconced at every post, pillar and tent. Only the owls remained to hoot and cheer at the night.

Night Owls

Their warm breath hung in the air as the three men met beneath the gaze of a lurid moon. Moonlight played upon the river as it bid the tide to rise at its command.

Cloaked in darkness, the three stood in a single silhouette against the lunar light. One tall and broad, an ox of a man, pointed an anxious finger at his comrades. 'There is no time for error on your part. You must rally your forces and cross to Ireland with all haste.'

'If only it were so simple,' Essex huffed. 'The nation is in muster. Men are being gathered from every jail cell and alehouse in the land. Cecil has promised more than ten thousand men to be at my disposal.'

'An army fit for a king,' Red Hugh whistled through his teeth. 'But how many will be true soldiers?'

'Precious few, which is fortunate for you,' Essex smirked, enjoying the moment. 'It has been a while since I stood on the fields of valour. 'Tis the reason The Queen had this whole debacle organised.'

'You think this all about you?' the tall man shook his head. 'Is there no limit to your vanity?'

'Guido, my grand fellow. I am the future of this nation. The throne is mine by right. Whatever the dried-up hag thinks, I'll have the throne one way or another. It will not be long before Cecil has the accension order signed and delivered to the rightful heir,' Essex stared at the imposing walls of the castle.

'James,' Guido's face was granite in the half-light. 'The Catholic option. The Holy Father's first choice,' His tone was cold, flat, not to be argued with.

Red Hugh drew a long breath, counting off the heartbeats before Essex closed his mouth and answered. 'My good man, James may be the Catholic choice, but he is not the peoples.'

'You will write to him offering your support when you challenge the crown,' Guido considered Essex. 'The peasants may call your name in the streets, but you are no king. You could not command the might of Venice. You are nothing more than a whore's bitch.'

'Now listen to me,' Essex began. The cold steel of Guido's dagger rested against his cheek.

'I am done listening. I know of the muster. If you care to remember, I delivered your letters to Stafford, York and every plague-ridden filth hole in between. I think perhaps your sickly-sweet wines have addled your tiny brain,' Guido poked Essex in the middle of his forehead. 'Now you listen and obey like a good pup. You will contact James and tell him you have the support of both Ireland and Spain. You may inform him you intend to challenge for the crown to ease him into his rightful place.

Any deviances on your part will result in an unpleasant death,' Guido slipped the dagger back inside his robe. 'I am done here. The next time we meet it will be to discuss terms of accession for his future highness,' Guido loomed over Essex.

'James,' Essex swallowed hard. 'I will do everything possible to ensure a smooth transition back to

Catholicism,' Essex stepped back, finding the cold stone of the castle at his back.

'Good. I should hate to waste the blood of a brother,' Guido gave a nod to Red Hugh before he turned and was absorbed in the shadows.

'If that Spaniard thinks I'm going to win the crown and hand it over, he is more stupid than he appears,' Essex wiped a hand across his throat.

'He is no more Spaniard than I am. I've met enough consuls and ambassadors from the courts of Phillip than I care to mention, and he does not fit,' Red Hugh stared off into the darkness where the River Arun washed the horizon. 'He's more English than your Queen, I'd bet my life on it.'

'Be that as it may,' Essex stepped out of the shadows to relieve himself in the river. 'I will write to James and make the pretence of an offer to secure his accession. I had best go along with the papacy for the time being. As for Spanish gold, well, who can live without it?'

'Not I,' Red Hugh led the way along the outer perimeter of the castle until they reached the front entrance where the guards let them by without so much as a nod. 'The Holy Father is determined to secure a backdoor into England. He promises a pot of gold at the end of every rainbow. Though we've yet to see a single coin in our purse.'

'That will all change soon enough,' Essex strode through the gates of Arundel Castle with all the pomp of a reigning monarch. 'Once I am in Ireland, I will ensure enough gold comes through to meet my purpose. I'll put

food on every table as I drain the coffers of England dry.'
The two men laughed their way to their chambers, as they
bade each other pleasant dreams.

Essex paused at his door; his spirits too high to end
the night so soon. Lifting a torch from its bracket, he
wandered the halls toward the darker wings of the castle
where noble eyes never roamed. The flickering light of the
torch lit only a few feet of darkness, long stretches of the
passageways remained under the blanket of night.

The soft light of a candle peaked beneath a door,
spreading its glowing fingers in the dark. Essex pressed
his ear to the door. His eyes closed as he pictured the
scene inside. He closed his hand around the handle.
Twisted it. There was no resistance. It was unlocked. He
smiled at his fortune and entered the room.

A small candle burned in front of a mirror on a
dressing table. A simple green gown was slung over the
back of a chair, together with undergarments. Essex
examined the plain knickers, dropping them back on the
chair. He sat the torch in a sconce beside the dying fire,
his attention turned toward the bedchamber.

Walking on the balls of his feet, he stepped across the
bare wooden floor testing each board for creaks and
groans. The chamber door was ajar. Essex pushed the
door with the back of his hand until it could go no further.
A dull light from the other room cast lingering shadows
over the empty bed. 'Blast,' Essex cursed beneath his
breath. With a reluctant sigh, he withdrew from the room.

Taking up his torch he left without closing the doors
behind him. Striding through the near darkness, he fled
before any guards might witness his trespass.

Warrior's Field

It could have been summer were it not for the morning chill. Spring may be in full swing but breath still hung in the air. The soft chatter of birdsong was audible at the edge of the yard where a narrow band of trees fenced off the view to the Sussex coast. The yard was a frenzy of souls.

Armour bearers polished steel with zealous hands. Grooms brushed down their horses over and over until every last hair was in line. Carts of ale and foods of all kinds trundled over the packed earth.

The resolute call of the bell tolled the hour. 'For whom the bell tolls,' chanted the unwashed peasantry as the first warriors took to the field of valour beneath the noon day sun. One sported a sigil of a red rose in a golden hand, the other a white rose on a gold background.

To either side of the tilt stood a rack of hand swords, broadswords, and poniards together with knucklers, bucklers, round and tall shields. Halberds and javelins stood tall and proud, beside axes and long hammers. There were weapons to suit every taste and class of fighter.

The two warriors went out together in silence, save for the clank of ill fitted armour. They walked to the back of the tilt where they parted ways, each of them turning toward their own field end. They rounded the tilt, grasping a weapon from the racks as they passed by. Neither man spent time to select their arms, took whatever came to hand. The last few paces brought them before Queen Elizabeth and her entourage, seated on the raised platform.

The flag of St George hung limp over the black velvet canopy, the wind no more than a shallow breath. Elizabeth sat in a golden gown strung with ribbons of pearls. Her hair flowed over her shoulders in a tumble of red curls, topped with a glittering ruby diadem.

'Ma'am,' the warriors bowed.

'First to the field,' Elizabeth clapped her hands together. 'Let the games begin.'

The two warriors raised their weapons and stepping back they turned to face each other. A roar rose from the crowd as pike and sword clashed and sparked, a blacksmith's hammer on hot steel. The white rose swung his sword down to block the sweep of the pike, which he followed with an uppercut to the face of the red warrior. Blood oozed from the red warrior's nose into his mouth, which he spat at his foe. Blinded by spittle, the white rose wiped his eyes in time to see the iron clad fist swing into his jaw.

The white rose staggered backward, loosening his grip on his sword. Red stepped forward, pulling a rondel from his side, he brought the short blade to bare at the throat of his enemy. White blocked the blade with a timely gauntlet, grasping the blade in his chain-mailed hand. The two men exchanged blows, striking the small target grids mounted on the front of their shoulders.

Red pushed forward using his height to leer over the white rose. White Rose swung his free hand low grasping the bottom of Red's chest plate. He leaned backward pulling Red down. As they fell, White Rose put his foot into Red's groin, kicking out as they rolled together on the grass. Red tumbled through the air, landing with a clank of steel and a snap of bone.

'Yield! I Yield,' Blood oozed from the knee joint of Red's armour. White Rose thrust his sword in the air claiming the victory. Elizabeth dropped a small kerchief to the ground. White Rose left his foe on the battlefield to receive the favour of his Queen. Red's screams could be heard all the way across the tilt.

A second bell tolled, 'For whom the bell tolls,' chimed the peasantry as a new White Rose rode out to the list to take a name.

'I Robert of Canterbury, call Ernst of Surrey to the tilt,' the knight stood tall and upright with his eyes fixed on his monarch.

'I am Ernst of Surrey; I am ready to joust.' Ernst bowed before his Queen.

Elizabeth rose to her feet, all those about her rose too. Leaning forward she grasped the hand rail, 'Have at him,' she growled.

The two knights strode to their tents, where their mounts pawed at the ground. Ernst swung himself up into his saddle. Taking his lance, he slipped the handle through the arret until the grapper was snugged against it. Ernst folded his arm over the lance, pinning it to his side. He leaned forward, checking the fit of the chamfron over his horse's face. 'Easy boy,' He stroked the animal between its ears before sitting tall in the saddle. Ernst made a point of checking the fastness of the ecranche fitted to his left shoulder. Satisfied he urged his mount out toward the list.

The two knights waited at opposing ends of the list each with a lance held tight beneath his right arm. 'Joust!' commanded her Majesty. The two men urged their horses into a canter, their lances coming into line with their target. The poles scraped along each other until Ernst struck the ecranche on Robert's shoulder, scoring a point. With lances raised they turned at the end of the list to face each other again.

Hooves pounded on the spring grass, amid the snort of horses and the jeering of the crowd, as the lances clattered together. Once more the knights turned at the end of the list and came at one another. Ernst pulled his lance in as tight as he could and waited until the coronet of his lance passed the head of Robert's horse. With a sudden lift, he brought the lance up, striking Robert of Canterbury full in the chest. The lance shattered, three points to Ernst. None could hear Robert cuss and spit as he turned for another charge.

Ernst seated his new lance and signalled his readiness. Keeping his lance ready, Ernst began his charge. Once again, he waited for Robert to make his move. White fumbled, his lance drifted to the outfield leaving him open. Ernst thrust forward. He lifted his lance striking Robert to his right breast. Robert spun from the saddle, landing full force on his face; his foot twisted in the stirrup. Ernst turned at the end of the list, where he raised his visor to watch Robert of Canterbury be dragged off the tilt, face down in the dirt.

Money and foods exchanged hands as wagers were met. Ale flowed from cask to pot, whetting the whistle of many a thirsty throat. Hogs roasting over open fires were turned with grimy hands. Oils were splashed over the blackened flesh and spread by gloved hands. Smoke rose from the pyre carrying the aroma of roasted pork over the battlefield, a summons to come and feast from the hand of their monarch.

'Feast and be full. Elizabeth, the blessed virgin Queen, wishes you well,' a court crier called over the clamour.

The castle bell rang forth the hour. The yard cleared revealing the empty list. Silence fell upon the ale gladdened crowd as Elizabeth stood with her arms spread.

'My good and noble people,' her voice carried the authority of one used to being obeyed. 'Today is a spring celebration. Today you common men have been invited to tread the same soil as the noble lords who rule over you. Those sworn to protect these lands and indeed my person.

It is with the greatest pride; I am today able to have two of our greatest warriors do battle for my pleasure and yours. I call to the field, The Earl of Essex and Sir Walter Raleigh.'

The crowd roared their delight as the two knights rode into the arena for the first time. Essex on his white stallion, a gift from Spain, and Raleigh on a black stallion commanding the eye of the entire field. The two rode to the fore until their mounts were nose to nose. They turned first to bow to Elizabeth then to the crowd whose cheers rose to new heights.

'I give our Master of Horse, Commander of armies and conqueror of Spain in both France and Flanders. My personal favourite: Essex,' Elizabeth gestured for the crowd to be more vocal.

'And does my hero on my other side need to be introduced? Guardian of the Empire, founder of new worlds, master of the seas, and plunderer of Spanish gold: Sir Walter,' Elizabeth clapped her gloved hands with fervour. 'Raleigh.' The crowd cheered. Essex inspected his gloves, as though he expected to discover some fault since the last time he checked as Elizabeth had begun speaking.

'My people I give you, the battle of champions,' Elizabeth admired her two loyal subjects, one a hero, one an heir to the throne. 'Let it be a clean fight,' she leaned in closer. 'But do make it entertaining.' Elizabeth returned to her seat. 'To your ends, gentlemen, and come out fighting.'

'For whom the bell tolls,' the semi-inebriated peasantry slurred and spat, as the bell tolled one. The late spring sun shone in the clear blue sky. The lush green lawn spread around the old mound and its round fort in a verdant moat.

Essex waved at the people, tossing the occasional coin into the crowd. Fists flew in drunken flurries and flailing arms, with all the skill of courting ducks. Essex laughed as the fighting intensified with every extra coin.

Raleigh hung his head in shame, to treat your fellow man in such a manner was as debased an act as whoring before your betrothed.

He trotted over to his tent where he beckoned a squire to fetch provisions from his table. 'Have them dispersed among the people,' He turned his mount back toward the list and waited with his lance at the ready.

Essex continued to throw coins into the crowd until his last penny was spent and his amusement had run its course. He rode his horse over to Raleigh, in a high stepping stride in cadence with its master's whistle.

'Very pretty,' Raleigh scoffed.

'Why thank you, good sir,' Essex smiled with all the allure of a drunkard.

'I meant the horse, though in truth there is little to choose between you,' Raleigh chuckled as he directed Essex toward his end of the list.

'I'll take that smile and beat the man out of you for it,' Essex trotted down the gaming field pulling his mount around the turn. The two men faced each other. Essex pointed to the ecranche: a bright red shield with its five fusils conjoined in a bent argent fixed to Raleigh's shoulder. Raleigh glanced back behind him as though Essex were pointing to some mote of interest.

'Gentlemen,' Sir George Clifford, The Queen's Champion, interrupted the proceedings. 'At arms. There shall be one point for a shield strike, three for a clean lance break and five for an unseating. May the best man win.

'Your Majesty, the field is yours,' George Clifford bowed and returned to his station at The Queen's side.

Elizabeth rose to her feet, a broad smile spread across her face. The warmth of the afternoon sun lit her countenance bathing her in a soft halo of golden light. She raised a small white lace kerchief above her head. 'Let the games begin,' she dropped her hand as though she were striking a foe. There was a breathless pause as both knights leaned into their saddles and urged their charges toward the other.

Never had one hundred and forty feet felt so far. The rhythm of the canter, the stifled breath of the knight the suspended animation of the crowd, all waiting. Stride after stride, the quivering lance held in anticipation of impact. The scything of wood on wood, as the lances scraped along their lengths until the final lift and, 'One point, Sir Walter,' Elizabeth pointed to her left where Sir Walter was mid turn. 'Turn two. Ride!'

Essex surged from the start; his lance held tight to his side. Keeping forward in the saddle he brought his lance about early, striking Raleigh across his chest. 'My dear Essex, the rules are there for everyone,' Elizabeth chided. The crowd roared with delight.

'I'll wager my lunch Essex dethrones Raleigh in five turns,' a peasant slurred, waving his tankard high above his head. Beer spattered those around him. 'Come on pretty boy, show us what ya got.'

This time Essex waited a heartbeat longer, he took a moment more to level his lance and stabbed it right into Raleigh's shoulder. The lance exploded at the breakpoint. 'Four points to Essex,' Elizabeth cheered louder than all her consort. 'Turn three. No delay.'

As a drum beats the walk-to-run, four quick beats of the hoof beneath the sun, the knights began their charge. Thump-thump, thump-thump the cantering hearts, one hundred and forty feet to lance. The clash of steel, the out-swung shield, unseated, both knights clattered to the field.

The air hung in silent awe only to be sundered by the drunken cries of.

'Finish the fight.'

"Ave 'im Sir Walter.'

'Essex for King.'

Essex was the first to his feet, yanking his lance from his mount, he threw it aside, 'Sword!' he yelled as he flexed his shield arm.

Raleigh got to his feet, adjusted his shield and raised his visor, 'That was fun, shall we dance or parlay?' his smile stretched across his face.

'Sword!' Essex bellowed, scanning the field for his squire.

'Not the parlay type?' Sir Walter waved to The Queen and gave Shakespeare a half-salute. 'Not to worry, I'll fetch us both one,' Raleigh ran across the short distance to the tents where he enquired after weapons. He returned a while later with two swords tucked beneath his arm.

Essex was still fuming when Raleigh returned and offered the gold handle end of his sword, the encrusted ruby glittered in the bright sunlight.

He snatched the weapon from Raleigh's hand and stepped back. 'En guard,' Essex thrust forward, catching Raleigh off guard. Essex thrust forward again, advancing half a step with every point. Raleigh countered each blow with his shield until he had a firm grasp on his sword.

'Must you always seek to cheat your way through life?' Raleigh swept the next attack aside and struck Essex in the chest with his shield.

'I'm just quicker witted, that's all. You, however, are getting long in the tooth and that limp of yours will cost you dear,' Essex taunted as he cut and thrust his way across the tilt.

Raleigh leaned first left, then right, before catching the base of Essex's shield with his own and thrusting it into his face. Essex wiped the blood from his chin. 'You cad,' Essex swung his sword upward from left to right, but Raleigh was already out of the way.

With a slash of Raleigh's blade, the end of Essex's beard floated on the breeze, 'You've lost some of your stuffing, dear boy. Never mind some little tit will use it for nesting no doubt.'

'Bastard,' Essex ran at Raleigh, his shield raised. Raleigh stepped aside, kicking Essex in the rear as he did so.

'Perhaps your sister could teach you how to shave?' Raleigh readied himself for the next attack.

'You'll pay for that too!' Essex stalked toward Raleigh; his sword gripped tight in his hand. 'Does The Queen know about your wife?'

'Does she yours,' Raleigh retorted. 'And what of the maid you knocked up?' Raleigh blocked the downward cut with his shield and kicked Essex's knee aside. Essex dropped to the floor, his sword tumbling from his hand.

Raleigh stepped on the fallen Sagrada, 'Yield?' Raleigh held his sword to Essex's throat. Essex puffed and spat blood on Raleigh. 'You look about ready for the block. Do you yield?' Raleigh moved his sword and pushed the point into Essex's shoulder.

'Halt,' Elizabeth commanded. The event fell into utter silence. 'I declare Raleigh the winner of the melee.'

Essex shrugged off Raleigh's offered hand and stomped across the field of valour to his tent. While Sir Walter went to receive his prize, 'Would you consider an archery contest with Essex?' The Queen tilted her head in enquiry.

'I would, ma'am,' Raleigh accepted the small kerchief from her hand.

'Tell me Sir Walter,' Elizabeth half-turned toward Shakespeare. 'What do you make of William?'

'In what way?' Sir Walter accepted a seat beside Elizabeth from where he could see Essex inside his tent, throwing his armour at his serf.

'Can he be trusted with higher things than mere performance?' Elizabeth gestured for the games to recommence. An ensemble of soldiers took position on the field in mock battle, re-enacting the sacking of Cádiz.

'I find him to be an honest man, passionate in all he undertakes, yet vulnerable.'

'Indeed so,' Elizabeth laughed as a soldier in Spanish armour was kicked in the backside by a clown dressed as Essex. 'He is skilled in his craft, one fit for the subtle services of Cecil.

Oh, come on, have at him, he's a bloody Dago!' Elizabeth yelled at the affray. She turned back to Raleigh, 'I do love a good scrap.

See to it he is protected at all times. I should hate to see any harm come to him,' Elizabeth placed her hand on Raleigh's. 'There are those who would seek to use him for their own gain.'

'Consider it so, ma'am. I shall have eyes and ears about the city put on watch,' Sir Walter rose from his seat.

'I should like Marie to be ... close to him. She has skills and makes for a fine wench,' Elizabeth waved him adieu.

'Come on, smack him properly!' Elizabeth returned to the matter at hand.

To Ireland

It was time for the theatre to open after an extended lent. Spring was at a close, and the last frost had faded with the haze of summer's approach. The day was bright and warm, yet the city was quiet.

London was not unaccustomed to the muster. Neither was it unfamiliar with war. But what it had never witnessed was vacant seats at the first play of the season. Romeo was about to court Juliet on the stage of the Globe, but so few were queuing it was likely to remain closed. The brothels too had empty beds, and the inns had spaces at the bar.

It was to be the opening show, a once only chance to make an impact and declare the new Globe Theatre open to the masses. The theatre was now a place where the poor and working men could rub shoulders with the aristocracy. But on such a clement afternoon there was not a soul to be seen in the whole of Southwark. Everyone had taken to the Thames for a ferry, or hitched a ride upon a cart, or joined the throng to march across London Bridge and make the journey to the Tower on foot.

The sound could be heard over half of the city. A clamour of men and horses. Voices barking orders to an untrained assemblage of thieves, robbers, crooks, and a smattering of soldiers. All jostling with one another to grab a musket, sword, pike, or shield: no one got them all, not even the trained troops among them. The biggest muster England had ever witnessed was preparing to move out. Dinner of meat and bread had been served, it was now time to serve country and Queen and take the fight to the Irish on their home turf.

'Shakespeare has certainly taught the little upstart how to hold a crowd. Quite the actor,' Sir Walter Raleigh waved his kerchief in the air.

'Let us hope he can keep his men so enthralled once they cross the Irish Sea,' Robert Cecil mused. 'As much as I loathe the man and would hate to see him ascend the throne, one does have to admire his pluck.'

'I would not have rushed into the jaws of death with such bravado,' Raleigh steered his horse out of the crowd with Cecil close on his tail. 'Ireland is the graveyard of many a brave lord. Essex is not one of those. I have had the dubious pleasure of fighting at his side and was never sure whose sword I should fear most.'

'I understand your reticence, Sir Walter. There is much about the young earl which leaves a bad taste in the mouth. I can only assume her Majesty feels the same,' Cecil pushed his horse out into the empty street from where they turned to watch the spectacle unfold.

'How so?'

'She still refuses to sign the accession. If she dies now we have no direct heir to the throne. The bloodline will have to rout back to James and return the nation to Catholicism and the rule of the Papacy. And none of us want that. Do you Walter? I doubt you'll keep your head on your shoulders should a Catholic sit on the throne of England once again.'

'I fear you may be right Robert,' Sir Walter put a hand to his throat. 'King Philip would indeed like something back for all the borrowed gold. My head may well cover the entire cost.'

'We should go and make the most of the time this event gives us,' Cecil turned his horse toward the city. 'I should like to get out of these peasant rags and get into something more suited to my office.'

'Oh, I don't know Robert, that tired old smock, and worn trousers give you quite an earthy appeal,' Cecil harrumphed as he rode off, leaving Essex to strut and fuss over his army.

Essex rode to the front of the column where he raised his gold handled sword high in the air for all to see. With a flourish he pointed forward and led his army out of London. People lined the streets, two deep on both sides of the road for four miles, many of them hailing Essex as the new king. Prayers were offered and sung in churches, as the army marched by on the long road to conquest. A rabble mustered to fight a war they did not want; against a people they did not know. Ahead of them lay a week of solid marching before they would reach the fleet to take them across the Irish Sea and far from home.

BEFORE THE PALE

The sun saw them only as far as the first afternoon, before cloud and cold chilled the sky. With each day the meals grew more scant, insufficient for the hardiest of men. Morale waned and numbers thinned. By the time they reached the Menai Strait, two thousand had fled with whatever arms they carried. More would be gone before they reached Beaumaris.

Five warships waited to ferry the men across the Irish Sea to the Pale, a pitiful strip of land bought with the blood from centuries of war. Smaller merchant vessels buoyed the rough seas among the warships, carrying the lower ranks, mules and munitions: the less important things. The inviting lush green fields around the castle were where the army spread its camp around the moated bailey, only the lords would rest in the safe haven of the thick stone of the inner walls.

Essex and his friends rode across the narrow wooden bridge leading to the south entrance of the castle. The clump of the horse's hooves masked the grinding of the small mill to their right.

'Well, at least there's no blasted fog as there was in Helbry. I had feared we may never get across the River Dee,' Essex groaned as he dismounted his horse at the stables.

'I fear I shall never get the feeling back in my arse,' Southampton rubbed his aching rump.

'Oh, come on Henry,' Mountjoy chortled. 'I am sure you have had rougher rides in Southwark.'

'They do not last as long as this one has,' Southampton straightened his back with a loud click. 'I need a drink.' The three men headed for the hall and what they hoped would be a time of rest. They walked across the west wall where the main hall stretched along its length.

Inside, the floor was littered with buckets and basins positioned to catch rainwater. The stone floor was unremarkable, functional, nothing more. The cold Welsh air blew in from every corner, swirling dust.

'What have I done so wrong to deserve this?' Essex gave a weary sigh.

'Well,' Southampton cast an eye around the room. 'At least you have us.'

'I reiterate, what have I done so wrong to deserve this?'

'It appears Southampton, today we have two arses,' Mountjoy put his arm across Henry's shoulders. 'But only one of them is full of shit.'

'Where are the maids? I need a bath,' Essex called.

'Absent. I expect they have better things to attend to,' Mountjoy went in search of help, returning with a squire and two maidservants. 'Here you go, Robert.'

Essex examined the three servants, 'I suppose they will suffice,' He walked round the servants as though inspecting troops. 'Where are our rooms?'

'Rooms sire?' the squire flinched. 'There are none, my lord. The castle is in need of much repair. The Constable is in town seeing to urgent matters. We were not expecting you for a couple of days, sire. Nothing has been prepared.'

'Such incompetence will not be tolerated. I demand to see the Constable at once!' Essex stamped his foot, rattling his spurs.

'I — I regret to …' the squire began.

'Regret, I regret ever taking on this bloody task. I have a war to wage man. And you regret,' Robert thrust his hands to his hips. 'I too regret,' he leaned forward until he was face to face with the squire, 'ever coming to this God forsaken land. Now, get me a room — at once,' Essex roared, his face red with rage.

The squire swallowed, 'I regret … '

'What is this?' A tall gentleman, his black hair tied in a ponytail, strode into the room and stepped between Essex and the squire. 'I assume you are Essex?' The man pushed the squire aside as he studied Essex. 'Your rooms are at the inn along the street. We had been informed you had been held up at Penmaen Mawr?'

'I was, but chose to make my own passage across as no ships were coming for me,' Essex took a half step back. 'And you are?'

'I am Rhobin Bulkeley, Constable of Beaumaris and the castle. While you are with us, I suggest you keep your temper to yourself.'

'How dare you speak to me as a commoner,' Essex placed a hand on his hilt.

'Robert!' Mountjoy pulled him away from the Constable. 'Excuse us; it has been a most arduous and unpleasant journey.'

'This whole debacle has been conducted in the worst manner and in the extremist wet I have yet endured.'

'And you have yet to reach Ireland,' Rhobin Bulkeley passed them by. 'This way, gentlemen, if you please,' he checked to see if they were following.

Outside a light drizzle had turned everything dark. The grey stone now shone, if it had been a more clement day the castle would have been more hospitable. Essex watched as the squire and maids returned to the stable to attend to their horses. As they left the castle, back across the wooden bridge, the drizzle turned to rain, which a fresh steady wind drove into their faces.

The inn was close to the castle. Its interior a warm welcome from the wet outside. A bright fire burned in the hearth; a pot of stew simmered over the flames. The aroma of hot food brought a growl to the English bellies, all thoughts of hostility were soon forgotten.

'Your host, Cafell, gentlemen,' Bulkeley turned aside. 'Your ships will be ready in two days; the tide will be at its highest. You'll not get a better opportunity to leave.' Rhobin pulled the door shut behind him and returned to his duties.

'One gets the feeling we are unwelcome,' Essex snorted as he turned his attention to Cafell.

'If you'd care to follow me, I'll show you to your rooms,' Cafell's voice was a song of words and motion with the strength of the mountains she called home. Her red hair was a ripple of flame coursing over her shoulders.

'Are you local?' Essex watched her dress sway with the rhythm of her step. Her shoulders relaxed as she turned to face him, her green eyes burning in the light of the candle in her hand.

'Why do you ask?' Cafell met the Earl's gaze.

'Just making conversation,' Essex perused her bust line.

'So why stare at my bosom? Conversation will be minimal as will the service be,' Cafell eyed Essex up and down. 'I prefer men,' Cafell turned the handle in the nearest door. 'This is yours. Baths will be drawn in the next hour, food is when you want it. You two gentlemen have the adjacent rooms to the right and left. They are all much the same. 'Tis a humble inn.' She left the three of them speechless as she returned to her duties.

'I am going to eat first and then retire. This has been a long wet journey,' Southampton opened the door to his room, tossed his cape inside and closed the door. 'I'm ready to feast.' Southampton pulled a thin leather binding from inside his jacket.

'What is that?' Essex made a grab for the binding.

'Did you not bring yours? This is the first draft of Richard II, with all your rewrites,' Southampton grinned.

'Ah,' Essex held out his hand.

'I'm afraid not. Master Shakespeare delivered yours in person to Essex House, did you not receive it?' Southampton clutched the binding to his chest. 'I could not betray such a skilled master. My love for the theatre and the written word is stronger than for my betrothed'

'Now who's being an arse?' Essex pouted.

'Still you,' Mountjoy retorted, giving Essex a hearty slap on the shoulder as he followed Southampton towards the dining area. Essex bit his lip and drew in a testy breath, before straightening his jacket and following the others in search of victuals.

CAMP LIFE

The rattle of pans and pots fought with the crackle and hiss of wet timbers around the campfires. From the wall of the Friary to the north of the castle, around to the east and all along the southern boundary wall, the starving English army were like locusts devouring the land. Light rain hung in the air, a grey curtain holding back the sun.

Cooks stirred the broth with less zest than a sloth, while others broke stale bread into small pieces. Fifteen thousand men queued at the various victualing stations to receive their daily ration. The meat had run out and the vegetables were nothing more than weevil-infested memories.

The grass beneath their feet had churned to mud. Wagons cut deep through the long spring grass, ploughing up the fertile soil beneath. 'Whatever happened to the promise of regular food?' one soldier remarked, knocking his piece of bread against the side of his bowl. 'It'll take half the Irish Sea to soften this crust.'

'You could always piss on it,' another guffawed.

'Might add some flavour to the stew while you're at it,' the laughter was brief but well meant.

It had been eight days since the procession left London. There were no cheers, or last hurrahs, only rain and abject misery. The endless damp, and wet feet, brought more than a few to blows. Others were developing coughs: with so many souls in close proximity, disease would not be far away.

Men huddled around meagre fires, shivering in thin clothing not suited to the outdoor life. Soldiers walked among the mustered, checking arms and training the unschooled in the martial arts of combat. A short conflict would remedy all ails. A quick scrap and back home across the sea.

The day passed with little change in the light or weather, the light rain persisted until sunset when it chose to pelt down upon the earth. Many sat huddled in makeshift shelters of stick and straw, clutching their bellies, while their captains basked in the warmth of candlelit tents. The groans of the sick rose and fell with the tide of their pain. Many parts of the camp had become latrines, where dysentery infected soldiers could no longer make the walk across the encampment. The wet and cold was taking its toll, and not a single soul had yet faced the enemy.

The enlisted soldiers had separated themselves from the mustered men. Though their rations were better, they had been served with the same hands. By morning, the death toll had risen to the hundreds.

A shy sun peeped through the thick clouds blurring the narrow seas from Ireland. Gruel simmered in pots, as uninviting as an elderly whore. The horse feed was more appealing to the hungry stable squires. The army would march on barley and weevils, washed down with watered ale, while their captains feasted on meat and wine.

The camp scrambled to life. Orders were barked and tents were collapsed and loaded onto wagons. Wagons were hitched to horses shivering in the cold breath of the late spring morning. Lines of men and munitions formed at the docks to the south of Beaumaris Castle. The enlisted troops were filtered out and loaded on to the five galleons of Royal service. The rest, the mustered criminals and less than willing volunteers, were herded toward the lower end of the dock.

A flotilla of small merchant vessels and chartered fishing boats bobbed on the uneasy sea. 'Call your charge as you pass to receive your transit orders,' a thick set man ordered, a long tobacco pipe hung from his mouth.

'Theft of livestock,' the man kept his eyes down.

'Fishin',' the master pointed to a ramp leading off to the left. 'Got a coin?' The man shook his head. 'White sails.' The line moved on.

'Poaching,' the next one stared the master in the eye, his coin at the ready.'

'Dark sails,' the master whispered, soft as a courting prince. And so, the day wore on, merchant and fisherman alike carried the dark and white sails.

By mid-afternoon, the ships were full, not a soul remained on land. The fields surrounding the castle were nothing but mud and debris. The galleons unfurled their sails. Ropes creaked through iron pulleys as the sails were turned to catch the wind. The canvas snapped taut as the ships followed the tide along the Menai Strait. No one came to see them off, no cheering crowds, no cries of acclamation: just the screech of gulls diving into the sea to feast on ejected breakfasts.

Behind the galleons, the white-sailed merchants and fishermen trailed at a distance. Keeping up the rear, the dark sailed vessels loitered in the foaming wake of the fleet. The evening was fast approaching and with it the veil of night. But for now, at least, it was forward to the unknown land beyond the Pale.

IRELAND

Wild waves lashed the ships with their salty whips. Grey skies had turned to black, transforming the sea into pitching tar. Rain pelted the ocean in a war of water and waves. Nothing Essex had ever experienced in the Bay of Biscay could have prepared him for the ferocity of the Irish Sea. Locked in his cabin, perusing a map of the approaching lands, he plotted out his victory course. Candlelight guttered in the draught whistling through cracks in the cabin. The galleon tossed in the sea, not much more than driftwood towing a sea anchor.

Outside the men fought the elements to secure the cargo and keep the powder dry, as the ocean rushed through the ship to fill the hull. Lamps swung to and fro, casting flickering light over the men, up to their calves in water. Bucket after bucket was taken up top and tossed overboard only to be swept back on the next wave.

The smaller vessels were scattered among the foaming waves, their sails straining against the assault of the wind. Not all would make the six-hour journey, this would be the last night for many. By the time they reached the shelter of Dublin Harbour, they were two hundred men adrift. Essex strode from his ship, every inch the commander in chief. 'Get me the Archbishop,' he barked at the harbourmaster.

'He'll be in the church, always is when the weather is bad,' the harbourmaster continued to check his manifests. 'You'll have to find him yourself, my day is full enough,' he turned away, finding a stack of crates to count and weigh.

'Blasted land. Do they not know who I am?' Essex stropped off to the city to find the elusive Archbishop.

The first white sails appeared at the harbour mouth. As the morning wore one, the harbour began to fill with the English army. White sailed boats tugged at their anchor chains, keen to return home. Not a dark sail was to be seen anywhere.

Southampton walked over to the harbour master who was now ticking things off his manifest, 'Has the boy gone?'

'Gone to find the Archbishop,' the Harbour Master straightened up with a smile.

'Get this back to England as fast as possible,' Southampton held out his hand. The Harbour Master took the leather strip from Southampton without looking at it.

''Tis done, the Dark Sails will be returning this eve, the storm will be all blown over.'

Southampton dropped a small red purse in the man's hand, 'There will be more like this. I have no idea how long we will be out here. Is our man in the north still the same?'

'No, sir. Due to a neighbourly dispute, our man is fled. The replacement be none other than the Black Earl.'

'Good tidings indeed. The best thing since London,' Southampton gave an almost imperceptible nod to the Harbour Master and went on his way. 'Well, Mountjoy, things are looking up for us. Let us hope we do not have to spend an inordinate amount of time traipsing about these savage lands.

'Essex will not be pleased when he sees how many deserters he has before they even loaded a musket. It must be three thousand, or more since we left London. I was surprised by how many bought passage on the dark sails. I cannot blame them, poor wretches,' Mountjoy and Southampton made their way along the docks to an inn, where they paid for board and rest for a few days in advance.

'There is no way I am sleeping under canvas until I absolutely must,' Mountjoy kicked off his boots and stretched out his feet, wriggling his toes. 'I look forward to a well-drawn bath — after we've eaten of course.'

'Pity you could not talk Penelope into accompanying you,' Southampton's eyes sparkled over his glass.

'Make sure never to mention her in front of Essex. I can only imagine his rage,' Mountjoy laughed. 'Gives me every reason to go home.'

'Quite.' The two men raised a glass to one another.

She lay there motionless before a startled crowd. The young girl with a dagger in her breast and poison upon her lips. How silent. How tragic. Such triumph. The audience roared and clapped. Such merriment no theatre had ever seen. After the first day they packed the Globe time after time. In awe at the spectacle of the stage filled with trapdoors and hidden secrets. Shakespeare was a triumph; the whole city was queuing to get through the doors. And yet he was nowhere to be found.

'Let not my cold words here accuse my zeal: 'Tis not the trial of a woman's war,' Elizabeth mused. 'My dear William, one might think this to be a more contemporary plot. Am I not a woman at war? And doeses my foe not plot my demise at every opportunity?'

'Ma'am, there is none with insight such as yours,' Shakespeare in modest tones. 'But, such as it is, my hand is oft pushed by others whose motives one cannot tell,' William sat upright on his stool. 'I have often dreamed of moments such as this; to read to one such as you.'

'You flatter me, William,' Elizabeth leaned forward, her hands upon her knees. 'But, does the rat not succeed in getting all the meat he does desire? Would such a rat who steers the quill desire a station higher than his blood would reach?'

'Those rats of which you speak, do think their wealth, and social stance entitles them to greater things. Things which are in themselves, much greater than the one who seeks them.' Shakespeare licked his dry lips. 'Ma'am, is there not a little wine I might use to whet my whistle?'

Elizabeth waved for a servant, 'Fetch Master Shakespeare the fine wine, not the sweet liquor Essex solicits.

Did they not sometimes cry, 'all hail!' to me? So, Judas did to Christ: but he, in twelve, Found truth in all but one: I, in twelve thousand, none.' Elizabeth paused. 'We have known each other but a few short weeks, and yet you see the cry of my heart and the despair which darkens my pillow at night. How is that so?'

'Ma'am, I ... ,' William glanced out of the window where the Thames flowed by. ''Tis but the words of a man on a page, sought to express the loneliness of royal reign. Where one supposed a common man, such as I, in truth though you be surrounded by lords and a thousand serfs. Yet, you sit alone with the world upon such slender shoulders. It is hard enough to bear family strife, but to balance the powers of the world: such as Spain and Venice, who seek to shed thine mortal blood. With such a burden to carry. 'Tis a wonder you have a moment's peace from your thoughts.'

'If I were a younger woman and not of this,' Elizabeth gestured to all about her. 'Then, good sir, I should embrace you, for such a mind to think of me in my solitude. No man, not even Leicester, ever saw the state of my heart. A heart which fluttered for some, and desired others, but not once was given in haste or love to any but my Kingdom,' The Queen dabbed the rare jewel from her eye and gazed at it on her gloved hand. 'Such riches, William, sit upon your father's work. Such fine stitching and, see how this rare treasure sits. My tears have been shed for so few. My beloved friend Walsingham and my dearest Leicester. I shed no tears for Mary, though she were my kin,' Elizabeth sighed and rubbed the tear with her thumb until all trace of it had gone.

'Ma'am,' William held the play in his lap. 'Perhaps we should break? I can return when at last it is done.'

'It read just fine. Be sure not to perform the deposition while the crown is upon my brow. It would be treasonous to do such a thing,' I hope, in the future, your company may come here and perform it for me in person.'

'It would be an honour Ma'am,' William bowed his head.

'I should ask that you take your leave. One tear is quite enough for the day,' Elizabeth rose from her seat. 'Would you accept an offer of the royal barge to take you back to London?'

William hesitated, 'It would be a delight. Though there would be no need to stop at Southwark wharf.'

'If my barge were to stop there, I doubt it should have any gold on it by the time it returned. It shall take you to Westminster. Marie will accompany you; she has been assigned as your escort.'

'I have seen Marie about town in recent days. I shall, without doubt, enjoy her company,' William remained bowed as he stepped back from The Queen.

'Come with me William,' Marie appeared at his side.

As they left the room together, Cecil stepped out of the antechamber, his dark hair brushed and oiled back. 'My dear Pygmy,' Elizabeth said by way of greeting.

Cecil almost smiled at the jibe, 'Ma'am,' he stood to one side with his back to the window. 'I have the latest report from Ireland.'

'Is it won?' Elizabeth popped a sugared almond into her mouth from a tray of sweets.

'No Ma'am, quite the contrary. Our eyes have it Essex was three thousand men light by the time they rallied in Dublin. He did, however, get time to be sworn into office and hold a parade in honour of St. George.'

'Did we not do the same here?' Elizabeth sifted through the almonds.

'We did, but not to the same extent. Essex has also been unsuccessful in the south and has lost the support of the Naval vessels. It is feared the Spanish are sending an armada as we speak.'

'How many ships must they have? To send fleet upon fleet to our shores?' She crunched down on the almond with a gleeful smile.

'It has also come to my note, Essex has suffered an injury to his rear,' Cecil chortled.

'How so?'

'While showing off to Arthur Chichester. He charged at the pikemen who failed to see the funny side and held their ground. Poor old Robert was forced to about turn and got a prick up his rear!' The pair laughed aloud.

'There is good news, Essex has captured some local fortifications but at the cost of some men in skirmishes in Leinster. Five hundred, and a few officers. But it is the

White Knight who is of concern. It would appear he has turned traitor to aid O'Neil. This does not bode well.'

'What is the cost of all this?'

'Essex runs us a ruinous £10,000 per day,' Cecil swallowed, clearing his throat he added, 'He is fighting on many fronts. The army is in at least three places with heavy battles through Leinster and Munster and more in the north.'

'Is he a complete idiot? Who fights so scattered? He was supposed to secure the Pale and move across with support from those already there,' Elizabeth sought another sweet.

'Many of our advocates were lost, some before his arrival. He is, in my opinion, not the leader he believes himself to be,' Cecil clasped his papers behind his back as he held Elizabeth's glare. 'Which leads me to the matter of accession.'

Elizabeth picked up a handful of sugar frosted almonds, weighed them in her hand, 'Go on. But consider your words with care, there is much you can lose,' She stared at Cecil, unflinching, as she crushed the nuts in her hand and sprinkled them on the floor for the dogs to scrap over.

'Ma'am, a decision must be made. With so many threats to your life. Need you be reminded of the seven assassination attempts. England must have a worthy successor to further the work you have done since succeeding your father. You cannot leave the throne open to Essex; he would ruin us within a year.'

'Essex is my sister's son and therefore the nearest by blood,' Elizabeth removed her gloves as she rose from her seat. 'Would you rather James?' Cecil stared back; his face devoid of emotional betrayal. 'You do, do you not? Pah, it is worthless to try to question the grand inquisitor,' Elizabeth flicked her hand at Cecil, 'I will sign when I am ready to sign, and not a moment before. Not so long as I still draw breath,' Elizabeth walked from the room with her head high, humming Greensleeves. Cecil watched her go, a smile daring to tickle his lip.

FAMILIAR PLACES

Summer was breaking everywhere. The warm sun drove the morning mist from the cattle fields to the west of London, where meat for the morning markets was being prepared. William Shakespeare walked with an air of confidence hitherto unknown in his stride. The success of the city was his to enjoy. Night after night the people queued to be entertained by the Chamberlain's Men. How different his world now was. No longer did he seek the counsel of friends in the corners of dingy inns and victualing houses, where the rats were tastier than the meats on offer. Now the people sought him. Shakespeare was the theatrical force to be reckoned with.

All this notoriety did not come without a cost. Envied by those who considered him to be The Queen's lapdog, William's fame all but excluded him from the up and coming writers of the day. There would always be contenders as sure as there were pretenders. William no longer cared. He could afford to pick and choose his friends. Enemies, however, were a growing concern. The wayward stews of Southwark were not safe for any man, especially one who courted lords and royalty.

'William, have you access to Cecil House?' Marie let her gaze wander the early morning streets. Traders were setting up their stalls as the walked through the throng towards Cheapside.

'Are we to partake of cake and tea?' William replied, skirting the subject as best he could.

'Cecil House was my question, but yes, the cake also,' Marie looped her arm through William's, pulling him to her side. 'We have work to do while we shop.'

'Shopping? How tedious. But Cecil House, I have been there but once,' William pulled Marie aside as the contents of a chamber pot splattered on the ground. 'The weather in London is absolute shit!'

'You are such a wit William,' Marie shook her head. 'There is something I need to see further down. They walked past the goldsmiths with their glittering displays, through the deepening crowds of the well-to-do down to the coffee shop beside Mercers Hall.

'Is this the yard where Essex keeps his wines?' Shakespeare peered around the corner, along a back alley where silhouetted figures unloaded long boxes from a wagon. Too long for wines and too shallow for anything but fish. 'What else is traded here?'

'We shall soon see, but first the cake is calling me,' Marie her voice trailed to a whisper as she began to peruse the display of sugary treats. Marie ushered William into the coffee shop where the aroma was as intoxicating as the smell of tobacco in London's best smoking parlours. 'There William, the seat by the pillar. We can watch London pass by as we converse.'

William swept the table and dusted the crumbs onto the floor for the rats to pick over later. He watched Marie haggle over the prices as though she had any want of coin. Her dark hair was pulled up beneath a blond wig to better match her painted face. Though not a lover of the lead paint, she did not wish to offend her Majesty. The Queen had eyes on everyone including those who acted on her behalf.

Light from the window was masked as a wagon rattled out from the alley, pausing outside. The driver, a large man, wrapped in a cape, climbed from his seat onto the back of the wagon where he brought a short club down on the tarpaulin. Glancing in through the window, he swung the club a second time before poking at the covers. Satisfied, he returned to his seat and rolled on by. Sunlight streamed through the window as God's light came in search of sin.

'Is it me, or do you see Guido everywhere?' Shakespeare steadied his hand, so as not to spill his drink.

'I have yet to make his acquaintance,' Marie pulled the purple gloves from her hands and slapped them on the table. 'I do hope to,' She reached over and closed William's gaping mouth, patting his cheek she added, 'Together with Sir Walter and George Clifford, I am sworn to protect my Queen. No other ruler has ever lifted people from among the commoners such as she. Were it not for the intervention of Cecil, I would likely as not wound up a prostitute, or worse.'

William reached up and took hold of Marie's hand. He turned it over and back again, tracing the veins on the back of her hand with his forefinger. Together they watched the people pass by the window: some would stop and see the cakes; others would see those within and gasp with excitement. William would always acknowledge those who bade him well and oft as not those who bit their thumb and ran away.

'Does it not upset you at all William, when such as they chide you so?'

'My dear sweet girl, I was once such as they. Though my mother came from some rich stock and her family once entertained The Queen at their home, I was raised in more humble surrounds. My father was a glover. One of my duties would be to fetch hides from the slaughterhouse a mere spit from our home. I would gather up chamber pots and tip the piss into buckets: tanning was not a pleasant task. Our home did not smell of the flowers of spring,' Shakespeare sipped at his drink.

'Which is worse, the smell of old piss or the reek of death?' Marie placed her cup beside Shakespeare's. 'I would rather smell of chamber pot than corpse.'

'You must remind me, who taught you such charm?' William rose from the table offering his arm to Marie. 'Then I might give them space to pass.' Marie took the proffered arm, and they left the coffee shop and went to explore the delights of the Mercers' yard.

The morning had all but departed as they wandered into the open yard. Purple cloth hung on every line and wall; the cobbled yard ran with its dye. An old wagon lay broken in a corner, where a worn-out nag gnawed at a half bale of hay. Open sacks of grain lay pillaged in sagging heaps, the best of their contents long gone, while rats picked over the remains. The gate to Essex's stockpile hung ajar, its doors fastened with odd lengths of rope waxed together, and an old rotting dog's carcass slung against them to prevent the wind from prying it open.

Even so, there was space enough to see the stack of long boxes etched with the image of a cross. Bottles of wine lay where they were discarded, some still half-filled with the sweet wine of Essex's fortune.

'Keep a watch,' Marie slipped a dagger from her sleeve and cut the rope securing the gate.

'Marie, they will know for sure someone has been here.

'I doubt they care,' Marie slipped through the gates making straight for the long crates. 'From the writing on the side, I would say these were Papal. This marking, the cross with the jewel.' Marie pushed her dagger beneath the lid and levered it open.

'What is it?' William afforded himself a cursory glance into the stockpile.

'Swords, of many kinds,' she lifted one out appraising it.

'Sagrada. The same as the one carried by Guido. Bring one, we'll get it to Cecil right away.'

Marie slipped back through the gate leaving it to swing pendulously in the growing breeze. Shakespeare ran after Marie, as they crossed the yard, weaving their way through the drying fabric. Out into the alley, they retraced their route up Cheapside back toward the Strand and the nest at Cecil House.

The city was in full swing. People wove their way among merchant carts and Noble's carriages. The wealthy shopped while the poor scavenged among the scraps tossed from tables. Rats scurried amongst the ankle-deep mat of horse dung, and human excrement, left where it landed. A young man halted at the roadside, pawing at his trouser fastening in desperation to relieve himself against the wall of a tenement in Friday Street, afterward he continued his discourse with his female consort.

'Dare we stop to rest my aching limbs?' Shakespeare waved a flagging hand at the Mermaid Inn.

'Master Shakespeare, however do you finish anything if you must rest at the first sign of exertion?'

'Writing is far less stressful than maintaining this brisk pace. I fear I was not destined to compete on the field with athletes,' Shakespeare wiped the sweat from his brow.

Without breaking pace, they ducked many a drenching from chamber pot and pail as they sped along Fleet Street, keeping to the side of the old Gatehouse. All the while people called to Shakespeare, 'There goes Romeo with his Juliet,' and every time William would wave and smile with joy, though his heart beat against his ribs and fire seared his lungs.

Never had London felt so vast or the Strand so long. The splendour of Cecil House came into view as they passed Somerset Place. 'Wait,' Marie grasped Shakespeare by the arm. 'There... by York Place. Is that not the same wagon?'

They crossed over to the north side of the street, keeping their stolen sword tucked out of sight. Shrouded in the cloak of eddying shadows they spied the cart with its tarpaulin thrown back. Deep gouges lined the cargo space striped with a dark stain.

'What do you suppose they have done with the poor soul?' Shakespeare said in prayerful tones.

'We can learn nothing more from here. Come, William, before we are seen,' Marie spun Shakespeare around, kissing him firm upon his mouth. Holding on for longer than she ought.

'Marie, what has come over you?' William gasped.

'I fear we were seen,' she led him along the alley toward a hidden gate which she opened with a key. 'It was my first thought, I am sorry. I meant no offence. I needed to hide us both.'

'No offence taken,' William smiled, whistling to himself as he closed the gate behind them.

Marie took another key from her bodice and used it to open a dark door studded with iron. She pushed the heavy door open and stepped inside where the cold air of the servants' quarters caressed her with its soft breath.

'The master is waiting in the library,' the footman said.

'Thank you. Please lead the way,' Shakespeare waved the man on.

'Sir.'

They followed the footman out of the serving area, down a long hallway with polished floorboards. Family portraits hung from every wall. It was impossible to avoid the gaze of the Cecil's, and Walsingham too, whose piercing eyes traced their every step.

They entered the library, where Robert Cecil stood by the window in a purple gown with a small white ruff about his throat. A black cap covered his crown, and his face gave no secrets away. It was not possible to read the countenance of the spymaster. 'My dearest friends, please,' Cecil pulled a chair from the table. 'Be seated.'

'Thank you, Robert,' Marie placed her house keys on the table. William offered the sword.

'Where did you get this?' Cecil stepped forward and lifted the sword from the table taking its weight in his hand. 'These are appearing in all quarters of the city.'

'It came from the Mercers' yard. From Essex's stockpile. There are crates full of them. Delivered by that wagon,' Shakespeare pointed out of the window to the cart turning in the road outside, its tarpaulin fastened over a fresh delivery.

'That is the home of Essex,' Cecil gestured without looking up. 'The wagon has been busy of late as have his frequent guests.'

'A tall gentleman, often dressed as a Jesuit Priest,' Marie stated.

'Guido,' William shuddered. 'The thought of the man chills me.'

'The same man who called at your father's home, and who has been seen courting the nobility of the land. I do not like the feel of this at all,' Cecil tapped a finger to his lips. 'Do you have any knowledge or insight into what he might want?'

'When we met, he wanted me to speak to Essex. I can only conclude he is, in some devious way, hoping perhaps to put Essex on the throne,' William's voice trailed to a whisper. 'To hear it from my own mouth is a frightening concept indeed. I see now what Essex wants with the play.'

'Enlighten me?' Cecil pressed.

William stared straight into Cecil's gaze, 'A rallying cry.'

PARLIAMENT

A dull sky brooded over the sullen city. News from Ireland did nothing to lift the mood. The Privy Council sat in quiet confer, muttering and shuffling their feet in discontent. Cecil rose to take the stand, while her Majesty sat in the High Chair, drumming her fingers on its arm.

Cecil, gripping the lapels of his black coat, drew a long breath as he rose to his feet. The room fell into a hush as all eyes watched the Secretary of State stroll to the middle of the chamber. With a polite bow to The Queen, he began his discourse.

'Your Majesty, my lords. It has come to my attention, the war in Ireland is nothing short of chaos. There has been no coherent strategy to the campaigns in the south, nor the north. To whit, they are being fought on two fronts by a divided army. Forces are scattered with insurmountable losses. Essex has now drawn together all the remnants to face Hugh O'Neill in a showdown at Bellaclinthe on the river Glyde,' Cecil spoke in measured tones, keeping his emotions under control at all times. The Privy Council erupted in cries for Essex's deposition and a real commander to be put in his stead.

'This is a frivolous misuse of power. Can Essex be trusted to bring his friends to heel?' Voices called in outrage.

'Have you any proof, Cecil,' Elizabeth's words went unheard among the cacophony.

'This ... peacock struts his way about Ireland, without a care for his men or country. Deserters have appeared in droves at ports across England,' Voices, but no faces to back the claims, shouted all the louder.

'Silence!' Elizabeth bellowed. 'I hear nothing but bickering children. If you cannot back your claims, keep silent. At least then you will appear wise.

Now, Sir Robert. Your report.'

'Ma'am,' Cecil raised an eyebrow. 'We have lost, through combat or other means,' Cecil scanned the council, acknowledging their concerns. 'More than five thousand troops. I would remind you, the campaign is costing the crown in the region of £10,000 per day.'

'What!' Elizabeth leapt to her feet. 'A soldier's wage is but two-pence a day!'

'Ma'am. The Lord Commander of Ireland, Essex, has now knighted over one hundred men amongst his number. It has been reported from the Irish, he only draws his sword to make knights,' Cecil paused for her Majesty's comment. Silence. 'I am further advised, Essex has sought entreaty with Red Hugh.'

'Out, all of you — out!' Elizabeth stormed from her chair to the centre of the chamber, driving out the entire privy council. 'Not you Robert. We have matters to discuss.'

As the clopping of heals on bare boards faded beyond hearing, Elizabeth turned her full fury on Cecil, 'Do tell, Robert, what has the bone of my bone done now to weaken the stance of the crown beyond the Pale?' Elizabeth plucked the glove from her hand and inspected her nails.

'Your Majesty,' Cecil removed his woollen cap. 'The soldiers are deserting at an alarming rate. Tyrone has made passage possible through his lands. It is a simple matter for any soldier to cross the fields of battle unscathed and catch a vessel home to Poole for a pittance.'

'Are they not fed? Why then are they so disloyal?'

'Ma'am. The commissioning officers are known to divert the supplies to their own supporters, those loyal to Essex. They are well victualed indeed. As for the men, they eek out an existence from the land. A land we have scorched and slaughtered. The few acres of greenery we may have missed have been set upon and rendered worthless by the Irish savages,' Cecil tucked his hands behind his back awaiting the Royal response.

'So, the men desert because they starve? Issue a decree commanding the officers to feed the men. Or be brought home to justice.' Elizabeth waved the matter aside.

'They do not believe threats from London have any strength. They are protected by the Lord Commander of Ireland. He has sworn to protect their blood with his own. Essex has curried the favour of all. He is more popular there than anywhere,' Cecil took a paper from inside his jacket.

'What is this?' Elizabeth glared at the parchment.

'Perhaps you should read it for yourself, the hand it is written in is most familiar,' Cecil held the paper out for Elizabeth who took it with care from his hand.

'Is he serious? The treacherous bastard!' Elizabeth screwed the paper in her fist. 'I sent him there with one instruction. All I wanted was for him to subdue the bloody savages, not jump in bed with them. Must he do everything with such utter disrespect? The pompous, jumped up arse!' Elizabeth made toward the door, stooped and looking back over her shoulder.

'I am returning to Nonsuch, where I shall remain. Parliament is at your mercy. Unless there is a matter of execution, see to it I am not disturbed,' Elizabeth ranted, slamming the chamber door. Cecil smiled with every crash and clatter as Elizabeth left Westminster for the last time.

The sun pierced the grey cloud, its golden fingers played upon the water. Red Hugh rode his horse into the centre of the river Glyde until the water lapped at its belly. Behind him, the Irish army waited to wade in after their King.

High on a hill, Essex sat on his mount, watching Red Hugh make himself vulnerable to attack. Mountjoy watched the scene from his post at the head of the British forces, waiting for Essex to give his command.

Essex urged his horse forward into a gentle walk. The clouds rolled back their blanket to let the sun illuminate the battlefield. Essex reached the edge of the river and halted.

Commander and King eyed each other, assessing, 'Will you not meet me half-way my good Earl?' Red Hugh lowered his reins to the saddle and raised his hands in an open gesture. 'I hide nothing from you. My sword is with my men. Come parlay with me, the water is divine.'

'I am sure it is,' Essex leaned forward in his saddle. 'I have come not for war, but to seek cessation of hostilities.'

'Bold for an invader,' Red Hugh laughed. 'Show me. Come into the water, and we'll talk of truce. Stay where it is dry, and this war will never end.'

Essex walked his horse into the water, sinking up to his knees. 'Are all your horses so small?'

'They are, but they are wary and they are strong,' Red Hugh lowered his tone. 'Does anyone else know of this?'

'None,' Essex smiled. 'Not even Mountjoy and Southampton, and they have been at my side at every step.'

'That is grand. We are safe to continue. We shall have a truce. Without you, we could never have had this war. Without the guns and powder, we acquired from the Pale a lifetime ago, none of this would have been possible.' Red Hugh straightened in his saddle.

You sir, have been more dependable than the Holy Father himself. Little have we seen from Venice other than the Jesuit.'

'They dare not risk open conflict with England without assurance of inside help. I have letters from King James affirming his support for our final action,' Essex held out his hand.

'To peace on our terms, and no other,' Red Hugh grasped Essex by the hand. 'Do not betray our trust. I have sent my demands for peace to your Queen. I doubt she will accommodate much of it. But you I trust.'

'Believe me Red, when I say, I have our best interests at heart. The crown cannot continue as it is,' Essex and Red Hugh turned back to face their men, both with a broad smile.

Essex rode up out of the river and trotted across to Mountjoy, 'Charles! Charles, it is great news. Red Hugh has agreed to my terms for a truce. The war is done. We can return home as conquerors. I have done what no one before me was able to accomplish, not even Raleigh. I have beaten the Irish.'

Mountjoy sat agape as Essex rode on by to address his men. 'What in God's name man!? You had him, right there.'

'We have peace, war is over,' Essex cleared his throat. 'My men. You have followed me, and you have fought for me and by my side. It is because of your heroism we stand here now at peace. Our enemy has left the field of battle, the war is over,' Essex stood in his stirrups. 'The war no man could win. They sent me here, to the graveyard of Earls, to join those who have fallen before. But I, Robert Devereux, Earl of Essex, Lord Commander of Ireland, have the victory no one could attain. Prepare yourselves to feast and celebrate like never before.'

The sky filled with cheer, as a roar of victory tore across the land on both sides of the river. Essex rode through the ranks of battle-hardened soldiers, soaking up their praise. Mountjoy turned in silence and rode back up the hill. He watched the Irish army disperse, their song fading as they marched back to their camp.

Mountjoy faced the cacophony of the British and their championing of the all-conquering Essex. He turned again and skirted around the cheering crowd, passing the whole ensemble, until he arrived at a small wagon where a flame-haired lass sat upon a bridled horse.

'I have a message for you Missy,' Mountjoy addressed the girl with the respect due to a courtier.

'What is it, my Lord?' Missy turned her horse toward the Pale.

'Tell Southampton, the arse has joined the head,' Mountjoy drew a long breath letting it out in a testy blast.

'Are you serious my Lord?' Missy searched Mountjoy's face for signs he might be jesting.

'Aye,' Mountjoy sighed again. 'Now go girl, and may God go with you.' Missy dug her heels into her horse and fled, her long hair trailing behind her. 'God's speed, girl. Who knows what Essex will do next.'

Dark clouds rolled in from the west, carried by the cold breath of the Atlantic; soon the sun would be shrouded from view. Crows feasted on the fallen, strewn across the land: tomorrow's fertiliser spread beneath a tear-filled sky. The kiss of the rain aroused Mountjoy from his stupor. No matter how he felt in his heart, he had a show to put on.

BREAKFAST AND PARLAY

Castle Derg was in a party mood. From one end of the town to the other, celebrations could be heard. Never had so many throats sung in such a stupefied symphony. The cool touch of September hung over into late morning. Some revellers were still slurring their songs, while others slept - clutching their ale in one hand and half-gnawed bread in the other.

Essex picked his way through the sleeping men like a strutting peacock with no one to impress. Irish or English, no one could tell one side from the other in this uneasy unification. The floor of the great hall was littered with sleeping soldiers still partying in their dreams. Essex walked out through the unguarded front gate, up the road to a lone hill overlooking the town, where Red Hugh sat on a make-shift throne outside a red tent. The flags of Ireland and England rippled in the wind, whispering threats of wars to come.

'Will you break your fast at my table Robert?' Red Hugh set a goblet of wine next to a steaming bowl of oats. 'It may not be your usual fare, but it is the best we have to offer. I am sure things will improve in days to come.'

'I do not have long, as I must return to London under warrant. As Lord Lieutenant of these lands, I must hasten to inform her Majesty in person of the treaty between our nations,' Essex lifted a spoon of oats to his mouth.

'To a successful journey,' Red Hugh raised his glass and toasted Essex. 'Were it anyone else these fields would be bathed in blood.'

'I could not have achieved it without your help, Hugh. I am quite sure Tyrone would not have been so accommodating.' They both gave a small laugh.

'Aye, he still holds his captivity at her Majesty's behest as a debt due. He's a hothead, but an Irishman right through. There is none like him: a leader and a warrior. A man I would be glad to pass my crown to,' Red Hugh stirred his porridge with a slow hand, his eye cocked toward Essex.

'Fierce in all he does,' Essex wiped the corner of his mouth with the tip of his finger. 'Now to business,' Essex pushed himself back in his chair, trying to find a comfortable position. 'Who was this thing built for?' He squirmed a little longer.

'Tyrone,' Red Hugh's smile was lost in the tangle of his beard. 'The chair was made for a future king.' Essex straightened up and drank his wine. 'So, my friend, what will you tell Elizabeth on your return?'

'I shall explain, in simple terms, how the treaty will benefit both sides. England will be at peace with its nearest neighbour, acting as a defensive barrier against Spain,' Essex watched Red Hugh for signs of betrayal, he knew how deep the Catholic bonds to both Spain and Venice ran. 'Add to that the revenues from all the lost trade which will return to our shores. You, of course, will prosper from this, while I broaden my reach back at home.'

'Is that all you seek?' Red Hugh offered to refill Essex's glass. 'Should not the throne be yours?'

'I will deal with the accession in due course. Though, considering the how aged the hag is, time is not on my side,' Essex snorted. 'It will not be long before I make my play. Now I have subdued your kingdom for her, it can only be a matter of weeks before Cecil is forced to draw up the document. Though I believe he would rather instate James over me,' Essex mused.

Red Hugh cleared his throat and reached for his wine. 'When will you sail?'

'On the morrow. It should take no more than four days for me to reach London. I shall make use of Cecil's horses. At least this time they will carry something other than love letters from James to London.'

'You think Cecil is courting James in Scotland?'

'We all use Scots, you have the gallowglasses after all,' Essex's eyes were drawn to movement on the horizon. 'It is time for me to depart. I believe you are about to have a visitor,' He pointed to the figures in the distance.'

'That would be the Latins. You had best be gone,' Red Hugh pushed himself up out of his throne, standing between Essex and the Latin contingent. 'They will run you through without question.'

'Then I must bid you adieu,' Essex bolted from his chair, leapt onto his horse and was gone before anyone could miss him.

The morning slipped by, unnoticed by the masses as the noon sun fought with the grey sky, and summer threatened to make an appearance. Essex closed the door to his room and slumped into a chair. He sat for a while pondering the few clothes he had dragged over from

England and which now lay strewn across the room. Who he had entertained in his room he could not remember. Neither did he care, strumpet existed for that very purpose. He smiled as he poured himself a measure of wine from a crystal decanter, 'Here is to me and all that will be mine,' He threw the claret down his throat and set the empty glass back on the small table. With a weary sigh, he dragged himself out of the chair and commenced packing his clothes.

With a shirt in one hand and a short black formal jacket in the other, he weighed up which he cared about more. He tossed both onto the bed and left the room snatching up the decanter on his way out.

'Soldier?' Essex barked at the bleary trooper.

'My Lord,' the soldier swayed to attention.

'Is the Black Earl at hand? Lord Ormonde?' Essex thrust his hands to his hips.

'He's in the yard sir, checking his tack. He has said he intends to return to home,' the soldier wilted under Essex's scowl.

'Does he now?' Essex strode out of the hall, pushing aside anyone who got in his path.

The yard was bathed in a halo of golden light where the sun cut through the heart of the clouds. 'Ormonde?' Essex shouted. The Black Earl continued with his preparations. 'Did you not hear me?'

'We all did,' the Black Earl retorted with a fleeting glance.

'Then why did you not answer your commander?' Essex puffed out his chest.

'Because she is not here,' the Black Earl dropped the straw he had been using to brush his horse. Essex bit his lip, his green eyes flashing with rage. 'Are we done?'

'Done!' Essex opened and closed his mouth. 'I might be, having singlehandedly brought the Irish dogs to heel, but you are far from done.' The Black Earl brushed Essex's wagging finger from his face. 'You will remain here, in charge of my army, I shall be returning to London under general warrant of the Great Seal. I intend to inform her Majesty myself, of the terms of the Irish peace agreement. Do not destroy what I have accomplished with your personal feuds.'

'As you wish,' the Black Earl took a blanket from a pile and put it on his horse's back.

'What are you doing now?' Essex attempted to snatch the blanket from the horse.

'Do you expect me to walk everywhere? I shall finish preparing the animal before I commence a tour of the camp. Now if you have somewhere more important to be, I suggest you go and leave the command of the men to me. Perhaps you would like me to return the decanter to save you some valuable time?' the Black Earl took the vessel from Essex and waved him on.'

'You have not heard the last of this insubordination?' Essex backed away, his hand resting upon the jewelled hilt of his sword.

'Do not,' the Black Earl held fast. 'think my cousin would let it go unpunished. Have you not heard the jest among the men? They say Essex only draws his sword to knight his friends.'

'You arse,' Essex sneered. 'When I am done in London, I shall return and have you executed. You will learn who is the Commander, and who is his servant.'

'Until then,' the Black Earl turned his back and straightened the horse blanket. 'Fare thee well Robert.' Essex kicked at a straw bale before leaving the yard. 'Fare thee well,' The Black Earl removed the horse blanket, folded it and placed it back on the pile.

MESSENGER

The early sun embraced the fields of Ireland in a lover's caress. Flowers waved among the tall grass, their heads turned to woo the wind. The last of the clouds had been swept aside as Missy thundered across the landscape. She leaned into the neck of her horse, her long auburn hair trailing behind her. She had to reach the Pale and get the message to Southampton, God willing, the news could be home before Essex. Missy rode throughout the day stopping only to water the horse and refill her flask.

A day had almost gone by the time Missy passed through the gatehouse in the south wall. 'I have a message for Master Southampton,' She stated to the thick-set gatekeeper.

The gatekeeper reached behind her and slid a heavy iron bolt across the door, 'This way missy.' Lifting a lamp from the wall, he walked out of the small room closing the door behind them both. 'His lordship is over yonder,' He held the lamp out in front of him, its dull yellow glow lighting no more than three feet ahead. 'Luck is with you lass. I was about to go off duty, and there's no one after me on the door until first light.'

''Tis about time fortune smiled my way,' Missy ducked beneath the gate keeper's arm, through a narrow door into the side room of a large house.

'I'll knock at the front and let him know where you are,' the gatekeeper closed the door, locking it with a key.

Missy sat by a table where a solitary candle danced in the dark. It was not long before a knuckle rapped on the door. 'Just a word, no company,' Missy fixed her eyes on the direction of the knocking. The door opened; Southampton entered carrying a menorah.

'Are you well?' Southampton placed the candle stand on the table and fetched drinks from a nearby cabinet. 'I must apologise for the poor stock. This room is seldom used,' He put two glasses on the table and poured a glass of wine for them both. Missy eyed him, noting the glasses. 'Do you not?'

'No sir, I only serve,' Missy hid her face for a moment.

'Then what can I get you?'

'I have water sir,' she showed him the flask. 'I have an urgent message from Lord Mountjoy. He says to tell you the ... ' Missy paused. 'The arse has joined the head. Sir,' she blushed.

'Oh,' Southampton sipped from his glass. 'I must relay the message at once. As fortune has it, there is a ship sailing within the hour. I'll have someone show you to a room. You must rest tonight and tell of the events as you saw them.' He put his empty glass on the table and left the room. Missy took her flask from her belt and drank from it, wiping her mouth with her sleeve. She glanced at her lap, and mud-spattered trousers, before loosening the tie of her riding cloak.

'Miss?' A young girl of no more than twelve years stood at the door to the room. 'The Master has sent me to show you to your room.' Missy rose from her seat and walked around the table, before deciding to take the menorah for extra light. She followed the maid down a corridor lined with painted portraits of the most miserable looking family she had ever seen.

Missy followed the maid around a corner and up an uneven flight of stairs to a two-step landing. The maid opened the door to the left-hand room and let Missy enter first. 'The master has asked you join him downstairs at your earliest convenience,' she pointed to a door at the back of the room. The maid locked the door they had entered through and left via the rear one.

Missy searched through the drawers of the nearest dresser rifling through the array of underwear, shirts and a few simple dresses. It was evident Southampton had frequent visitors of both sexes and many sizes, as all wardrobes and cupboards were stocked for every occasion. She chose a simple drawstring shirt and work trousers. She was not one to fuss and preferred a more versatile attire. She poured some water from a jug into a shallow bowl and refreshed her face in the cold water. Taking a cloth from a pile beside the water bowl, Missy dried her face and returned it, in a crumpled heap, to the stack. She retrieved her candlestick and headed downstairs for what she hoped would be a pleasant evening.

Southampton got up from his chair by the fire to greet her and show her to the table. She was used to waiting on others and found Southampton's grace toward her disarming. The only men to treat her like this were, well … no-one. The table could seat eight but had only been laid for two. 'Are there no others?' She asked, checking the room for exits.

'No, it is just us. You can eat alone if you wish,' Southampton waited by a chair.

'No, my lord, it's ... it's ... '

'Too much? We can go to the victualing house, or the inn if you would prefer?' He stepped back from the chair. 'The choice is yours,' He walked around to the other side of the table.

'This will be fine, thank you, sir,' Missy pulled out her chair and sat.

'Tara?' Southampton called as he took up his seat. The maid appeared, carrying a decanter of spirit and a jug, together with a pitcher and two glasses. She placed them on the table and left the room.

'The decanter is a provincial Italian wine, and the other is your local dark ale,' Southampton poured himself a glass of wine and held it under his nose, 'Quite fragrant.'

Missy took the pitcher and filled it from the jug. The black liquid clung to the ceramic jug like a receding tide. She held the drink to her nose, 'Smells like a wet dog,' she took a long draft, and was half-way through wiping her mouth on her sleeve when she remembered her company. Southampton waved the moment aside with a slight smile. Tara reappeared with trays of meat, bread, and vegetables: purple carrots, parsnips, and summer greens.

'I was unsure as to what you may prefer. I know field rations have been dire, to say the least.' Missy licked her lips as Tara brought more trays of sweet delicacies. 'Now, to business,' Southampton stabbed a carving fork into a side of beef and proceeded to cut it into portions with a silver dagger. 'Tell me what you know of the truce.'

Missy took a handful of the cut meat and a hunk of bread, together with a bowl of dripping, 'I've seen Essex on occasion since the battle at Yellow Ford. I served at the victory banquet where he was a guest,' She stuffed meat into her mouth like a starved child, her cheeks bulged. 'I heard they were planning something for London. Red Hugh was to go over as an honoured guest to the palace at Westminster. Since then, letters have been frequent. There's also the Jesuit. I don't like him,' Missy reached for more ale.

'Tall gentleman with a poor Spanish accent and unruly auburn hair?' Southampton asked, stifling a belch.

'That would be him. He's been at the Ford and the Derg. He travels under a warrant signed by Essex. He is exempt from all plague restrictions. Did you know?'

'Interesting. I do know he was in both Stratford and York. One wonders why he gets such freedom,' Southampton held the fork to his mouth, lost in a moment.

'Do only the Privy Council have such power?' Missy wiped a drop of ale from her chin. 'Would Cecil give such rights?'

'Indeed even I do not possess such things,' Southampton pouted. 'This you may not know, but how did the battle go?'

'I was made field medic. Injuries were few. When we got to the river at Derg, my people were way off. Essex went forward alone. I was no longer required, so I got sent to the rear. Odd given my job and all.'

'This has been a long time coming. And from what I've read, I believe this is only the beginning. Essex is planning something. Something huge. You have done well Missy, stay the night and rest. You can leave on the morrow at your leisure. I suspect Essex will be through here any day,' Southampton pushed his plate aside. 'All of a sudden my palate tastes of dirt.'

'Sir?' Missy leaned toward Southampton. 'Would it be best if I bore the message to London?'

'My dear girl, have you any idea of the peril such an undertaking would present?' Southampton clutched his hands together beneath the table considering her proposal.

'Would it be worse than running through the battlefield with but a bandage?'

'No,' Southampton smiled. 'Nothing like it,' He got up from his chair and opened a small drawer in a writing desk. 'Take this note. Go direct to the address on the front. Speak to no one about your purpose until you meet face to face with Robert Cecil. Show the seal to any of Robert's mail boys at any Inn with a stable, and they will give you a fresh horse, or carriage, if one is available.' Missy took the letter and headed straight for the door.

TWO HORSE RACE

A tired moon cast its weary light upon a darkened sea. The wind snatched the top of the waves as the ship rode the sea with ease. The wind blew out the sail, driving the ship across the Irish Sea to England and the start of a two hundred and fifty mile journey to London for a date with Cecil.

Missy climbed into a hammock and let the sea rock her to sleep.

It was still dark when the ship's mate woke Missy from sleep. She climbed out of the hammock and made her way up to the top deck before she disembarked in the shadow of Beaumaris Castle. A tall gentleman with a tricorn hat greeted everyone leaving the ship, most passengers were military, injured beyond fight.

'Who might you be, Miss?' the gentleman indicated for her to move to one side. Missy showed the letter to the constable. 'My name is Rhobin Bulkeley. I am the law in these parts. Follow me. I'll get you what you need.' The last soldier limped from the vessel. 'Follow me,' Bulkeley led them out of the castle dock, down the short walk to a jetty which reached out into deeper water. 'Jones, get this lady across the Strait and make sure she has the best horse available.' The man showed Missy to the boat and began to bark out orders to his scant crew.

The chain rattled over the mount as the anchor was pulled up. Pulleys squeaked, and ropes snapped taut as the sails dropped into the wind. The small boat cut along the

Menai Strait towards England as far as Deganwy. A short while later Missy was disembarking to the Welsh mainland.

'This way,' Missy struggled to keep pace with Jones' long gait as he strode to the nearest stabled inn. 'Mick, horse and supplies for London,' Jones ordered a younger man with military authority. 'I assume you can ride?'

'I can. I can shoot too,' Missy patted the pistol on her hip. 'I've spent my life at war sir. I can do more than bandage.'

'Good,' Jones turned toward the stable where a horse was being led out. 'You'll like as not need it.

'This is a fine animal, should do you a solid day. Follow the coast road until you see a painted rock, turn right there. That'll set you on the road to London. You'll find frequent villages; most have a pony at the ready. Ride well, Miss,' Jones stepped back to let the horse pass. Missy grabbed the reins and swung herself up into the saddle.

'Thank you kindly, sir,' Missy dug in her heels and set off, rising to a gallop along the mud streets.

The late morning sun shone upon a glistening sea, as calm as a sheltered pool. Fishermen sorted the catch under the watchful gaze of gulls. A gentle song drifted from an old salt playing a wheezy squeeze box, accompanied by a tired hurdy-gurdy. The droning melody draped itself over the gravel voices, adding velvet to chains.

Southampton held out his hand, inspecting his fingernails, while half-listening to the whine coming from Essex.

'Now, how am I supposed to get home and tell The Queen the wondrous news of the truce. No more bloodshed. I have secured peace between our two nations,' Essex puffed out his chest.

'What exactly did you broker?' Southampton asked, his attention rested on the fishermen.

'Restitution of lands, self-ruling,' Essex waved his hand about in the air as though swatting a fly. 'Be known as Catholics, something and some other,' He thrust his hands behind his back and began to stroll along the harbour walk.

'Some — thing and some other,' Southampton mused. 'Her Majesty will be most impressed, I'm sure.'

'Oh, bugger off, Henry,' Essex spat back. 'I have yet to see you get involved in the fighting, let alone the sophistication of diplomacy. Try not to be a toad. We only need one Cecil. It will all change once I am charge.'

'Are still hoping for Elizabeth to sign the accession?' Southampton held his ground as Essex spun him around.

'Face me Southampton, and say it to my face,' Essex grasped Southampton by the collar.

'You — have yet — to be named — the successor,' Southampton stared into Essex's green eyes. 'Clear enough for you?' He gripped Essex's hands and yanked them from his jacket. 'I have fought and killed more than you. Who was fighting the Spaniards in Cádiz while you climbed the bloody castle walls? Who shielded you in

Flanders? Who, if not I, has dragged you from whorehouses where you wanted to fight every man that was 'bigger' than you? How many knives have I kept from your back, Robert?'

'I ... I,' Essex stammered.

'Yes, you. The only one you ever think of,' Southampton turned and walked away. 'The next ship sails tonight. Be on it.'

'You dare threaten me?' Essex yelled. 'I am of royal blood. The blue blood of the Boleyn's runs through me. What are you, but common dirt,' Essex strode two paces forward, his finger wagging. Southampton raised his hand as a sign to end the matter and walked away to his lodgings, his hands in his pockets and a tight smile upon his face.

Essex spun on his heels and sought solace in the fishermen's inn where the melancholic melodies deepened his mood to the depths of the abyss.

'Still here,' Southampton sighed as he lifted Essex's arm over his shoulder and helped him to stand. 'Your ship is about to sail. I will accompany you back to London. We can ride in my carriage all the way, while you prepare yourself to meet The Queen. You might be a total arse, Essex, but you are still a friend and an heir to the throne.

Can someone help me get the future king to his ship, there's coin for willing hands.' Two burly men stepped up and lifted Essex by his arms and legs and carried him out to the ship. Southampton put coins into the men's hands as he thanked them for their service. Southampton left

Essex groaning into a pail while he went to catch a breath of air.

A light wind tugged at his hair as he came on deck. Hopeful gulls wheeled around the ship in search of scraps; there would be no comfort for them on this voyage, its only passengers would not be dining.

'We should be in Anglesey after midnight, Sire,' the captain reported. 'I should take this opportunity to get some rest. Your young lady got away; the constable saw her off himself. Your carriage is ready on the mainland. We'll be docking there to save a bit of time.'

'Thank you, captain. Thank you,' Southampton nodded toward the door. Two minutes later he had walked the deck and seen enough of the sea to know there would be no excitement on this leg of the journey. He watched the skies darken over the seas as Anglesey broke the horizon. The near-perfect black of the landscape rose from the waters as a barricade to dissuade visitors. A pale notch, in the otherwise unbroken line, marked the entrance to the Menai Strait. The ship pointed its prow to the gap and sailed the gentle breeze home to dock in Deganwy.

Southampton was woken by a gentle hand upon his shoulder, 'Ah, Jones, are we here so soon?'

'Sir, the lady was away two days now,' Jones said in hushed tones. 'Shall I ready your carriage, and will you be breaking your fast with us?'

Southampton glowered at the recumbent Essex, 'I should think so. He'll want a bath, or at least I want him to. The man reeks.'

'I'll get it seen to, sir,' Jones left the room as quiet as he had entered. Southampton swung his feet around from his bed and got up. He walked over to the dressing table and scooped a jug of water from a barrel. Pouring some of the contents into a bowl, he invigorated himself with a brisk wash before shoving Essex with his foot.

'Gad, what is it?' Essex covered his face with his hands.

'We have arrived in Deganwy. I have arranged food and a bath for you,' Southampton put a kerchief to his mouth, 'You stink,' He screwed up his face. 'I shall leave you now and see you at the Inn. When we are ready, we shall take a carriage. Refresh the horses as often as we can. We can make London in four days.'

'I'd prefer three,' Essex thrust himself to his feet and staggered into Southampton. 'Sorry, legs are bit stiff. Head not yet functioning,' Essex straightened up. 'Do we have any wine? Mouth's a bit dry.'

'No, we do not,' Southampton held Essex at arm's length examining his boyish face. 'Are you ready to be king?'

'Aye captain,' Essex flashed a smile as he fell back onto the bed, having knocked himself over with his zealous salute. 'Are you not going to help me up, Henry?'

'No,' Southampton closed the door behind him as he left.

BACK HOME

CECIL HOUSE

Foul rain darkened the world, blurring the lines between the city and its encompassing lands. Grey figures walked pallid streets where the downpour melted the manure in an effluent tide.

Missy trotted over Charring Cross onto the Strand, where opulent houses loomed on either side. Some were as grand as castles, some were larger than the forts where she had tended the wounded from the Battle of Yellow Ford. She thought it impossible anyone could need such a dwelling; how many families lived within? She dismounted her horse and led it through the rain, taking a moment at each door to read the names from their brass plates.

A dung cart stopped ahead of her; its driver hidden by a long cape dragging the ground. He took a shovel from the rear of the cart and began to clear the road. Excrement splattered into the cart, sliding into every crack. The dark effluent dripped through the rough boarded floor, back onto the filthy streets of London. Missy led her horse across the street to a large imposing three storey building large enough to house the population of her village. The brass plate declared 'Cecil House'. She knocked once on the black door and waited.

The rain continued its deluge, running off the rooftop to add to the torrents on the ground and running from her clothing. Her horse whinnied and tugged at its rein. 'Easy girl,' Missy's soft brogue was lost in the rain.

The door swung open revealing a gentleman in a bright red jacket and black trousers. 'Yes, can I be of assistance.' the servant stated.

'I seek Robert Cecil, I have word from Southampton,' Missy looked up at the servant.

'Send her to the rear garden.' a stern voice commanded. 'She can leave the animal in the stable.'

'Around to the right, at the Cross. You'll come to the Church of St. Martin. Follow the narrow path to an iron gate, knock thrice and enter,' the servant closed the door with a final clunk.

The dark finger of the cross pointed the way through the veil of rain. She walked with a short gait; every step measured against the long ride from Wales. She could feel the ache set in, her legs heavy, her arms void of strength and she doubted she could sit for a long while. It had been the longest three days she could ever remember. She turned right toward St. Martin's church where she found the iron gate beneath the welcoming arms of an old oak. She knocked three times, and the door swung open. The same morose servant was there to greet her.

'The animal goes over there, beneath the shelter. You enter over there,' Missy followed his outstretched arm to where it pointed. A dark portal appeared to have been cut into the wall of the grandiose house. Missy led her horse over to the stable and removed the saddle, hanging it over the divider between two stalls. She filled a pail with oats and refreshed the straw before ensuring there was enough water. Satisfied her horse was catered for she walked over to the entrance and knocked. The door ground open on heavy hinges. The servant, still dripping from his excursion in the garden, closed the door behind her and led her through the house in silence to the library where Cecil sat waiting in a high-backed chair with his fingers pressed together in his lap.

'My dear girl, please take a seat,' Cecil pointed to the chair opposite him. 'Is there anything you need?'

'Some sunshine if you have it. If not, I'd settle for a drink and a bite to eat,' Missy dragged the her cape from her shoulders, handing it to the servant with a polite nod.

'See it done,' Cecil ordered his servant who disappeared without a sound. 'Now, you have word from Southampton, I believe?' He held out his hand. Missy took the note from inside her blouse and handed it over. Cecil broke the seal and read the note.

Once he was done, he beheld Missy as though measuring her worth. 'Southampton trusts you. Enough to send you the length of the country with such important information. Which I must add, you have not attempted to read, for which I commend you.

'He says you were at the battle when Essex made the accord with the Irish.'

'I was also at the feast for the victory at Yellow Ford, attended by Essex.'

'Hmm,' Cecil glanced out of the window. 'Ah, just the man.' There was a knock at the front door. 'Show them in,' Cecil called.

'Robert,' Sir Walter cast a glance at the visitor.

'Ah, William, how goes it? The play?' Cecil folded his hands in his lap.

'Marvellous! Things are coming together well,' Shakespeare beamed. 'Would you like a copy, Robert?'

'No thank you, I'll wait for the show. I would not want to spoil any surprises. I enjoyed the last version. I shall look forward to your view on current politics and power,'

Cecil caught Missy's eye. 'Where are my manners. Gentlemen this is Missy. She has some rather grave news from Ireland. Essex has signed a peace treaty with the Irish. Sir Walter I would ask you to accompany me to Nonsuch, so I may avail her Majesty of the news.'

'Rather you than me, Robert,' Raleigh smiled.

'And you William, can take care of Missy. Southampton's nest in Southwark should be ideal lodgings.'

'Missy, you may be with us for some time. I do not think it prudent to send you back to Ireland,' Cecil insisted.

'Thank you, sir,' Missy half-laughed. 'I've no home to return to.' She looked down at the water-stained floor.

'You are most welcome to spend some time at the Bishop's Cap,' William enthused. 'The greatest alehouse in London, certainly among the stews.' Missy stared at him; her brow furrowed.

'The stews, my dear,' Raleigh paused to allow the servant to place two trays of food and drinks on the table. Raleigh took a finger of meat from the platter. 'Are a hive life, mostly low-life. A world of fun and frolic.'

'Not to mention dangerous,' Cecil injected. 'Am I wrong?'

'Danger is all part of the fun Robert, why not come down yourself and partake of an ale,' Raleigh licked his lips, fighting back his mirth.

'Pah! How much fun would they have in the presence of the grand inquisitor? I should doubt the patron's tongues would wag so wild in my presence as they do yours,' Cecil raised an eyebrow.

'O let us not argue or berate one another about class and standing. We have food, we have wine,' Shakespeare put on his best stage voice. 'We have company,' he held out the platter of food and a glass of wine for Missy. 'Take, eat, drink, and enjoy. Regale us with tales of your home and the perils of your journey.'

Missy took the goblet and food and worked her through it all as she recounted the Battle of Yellow Ford and the more recent campaign, right up to the moment her legs almost gave out at the door to Cecil House.

'Do you have a carriage. Raleigh?' Cecil rose from his seat, his bent back creaking with scoliosis. Cecil sighed, 'As if being so short were not bad enough, I am now hunched and toady,' He glanced at each of his companions in turn, and saw he was lacking in sympathisers. 'Alas, such a wretch am I.'

'Do not be so hard on yourself, Robert. That's what we are here for,' Raleigh quipped.

'O joy,' Cecil shook his head dismayed. 'What have I done to deserve such friends as these? Come Raleigh, let us go and cheer The Queen.'

NONSUCH PALACE

Surrey basked in a well of golden light, a warm summer sun played upon the lush lawn of Nonsuch Palace. Elizabeth walked through the garden, stopping to inhale the scent of flowers planted throughout the gardens. Precision cut topiary edged every pathway, creating a labyrinth of colour and wonder. Sparkling ponds glittered in the light of a thousand fairy wings dancing around the lilies. Willows wept over petal strewn seats, where spent roses had cast their crowns.

The Queen watched the black carriage enter through the wrought iron gate and come to a halt at the steps of the house. She recognised at once the hunched figure of Robert Cecil and the bold stance of Sir Walter as they disembarked. Elizabeth took a small white ivory fan from her purse and opened it with a flutter. She held out her hand for her lady in waiting to take her purse. 'We have guests, Marie; Master Shakespeare shall have a larger audience than he was expecting. How Joyous for us all, I do so love the company of Raleigh. Cecil, however, can be so tiresome. Let us go and see our guests.'

Marie followed one step behind with George Clifford, The Queen's champion, one step in front. They ambled along the pathways, taking in the flowers and chatting about the hedgerows and wonder of the palace. Raleigh and Cecil both waited by the carriage for Elizabeth to join them. 'It does men good to wait, do you not agree Marie,' Elizabeth covered her mouth with her fan.

'That would all depend on the man and the occasion, Majesty,' Marie replied. 'Every man should wait for their Queen, but not all would wait for me.'

'That is true,' Elizabeth took a step back. 'But is there no man who waits for you, at all?' a smile teased on her lips. 'Does the Bard not keep you entertained?'

'Majesty!' Marie gasped. 'I have had no such relations with him, or any other. I would not be fit to serve you if I had, and I value you above any man.'

'You are so sweet,' Elizabeth smiled. 'But beauty such as you possess is a rare thing. I know courtiers who have enquired about you.'

'Others have tried to help themselves too,' Marie stared straight ahead. 'All were met with firm refusal.'

'Have none raised any interest?'

'None,' Marie replied.

'Not Essex?' Elizabeth teased.

'None.' came the curt response. 'Though that does not always dissuade him.'

'I am surprised.'

'I would not wish to go the way of your former handmaid,' Marie covered her mouth. 'Forgive me Majesty, for I have spoken about that which I ought not.'

'Indeed,' Elizabeth stepped forward, closing the matter.

Raleigh greeted his Queen with a bow worthy of any knight. Cecil crooked a smile. They followed Elizabeth into Nonsuch Palace, keeping a respectful distance until they were offered a seat in the room where a temporary throne had been erected on a black velvet platform with four posts supporting a silver silk canopy.

Elizabeth took up her seat on the throne, where she sat with her faithful spaniel, Leicester, on her lap, 'Pray, do tell Robert, what has you looking so fierce. One might be forgiven for thinking all is lost abroad,' she stroked the spaniel behind its ear.

'I shall not prevaricate, your Majesty, it is the actions of Essex that bring us here,' Cecil watched Elizabeth's smile turn to a thin line. 'He has bartered a truce in Ireland.'

'What!' Leicester ran for the door. 'I told him to subdue and conquer,' Elizabeth hissed as she clenched the arms of her throne.

'Yes Ma'am,' Cecil straightened up. 'It has been but three days since the agreement. Essex is now travelling back with Southampton. Doubtless, he will be here any day.'

'Is the boy a complete imbecile?' Elizabeth ground out her words through gritted teeth. 'All he had to do was kill Red Hugh and Tyrone, and all would be done. Did you not give him sufficient men?'

'Seventeen thousand men and three thousand horse. He had the best officers and the most experienced soldiers,' Cecil began.

'And yet he failed,' Elizabeth sighed. 'This whole Ireland issue wearies me. I will deal with Essex whence he returns, until then ... Until then I need to eat. The boy can wait.

Marie, go find William and have him join us, he can read to us over our meal. Something light, I do not want that lover's spat.'

'Romeo and Juliet?' Raleigh offered.

'Yes, that!' Elizabeth waved a hand. 'Something light, some sonnets perhaps.'

'I will see to it, your Majesty,' Marie left the room in search of the Bard.

'What are we to do about Essex, Ma'am? He runs amok making a mockery of your authority. He must be reined in,' Cecil's countenance fixed in a blank stare.

'I will deal with Essex when he returns and not before. 'Tis nothing more than a minor disciplinary matter,' Elizabeth retrieved her spaniel from his hiding place behind the door.

'Majesty,' Raleigh weighed in. 'It is treason to disobey a command from the highest level and assert his own authority as commander.'

'He is the High Commander of Ireland. I am sure that should give him the right to choose. Should it not?' Elizabeth snapped.

'No Ma'am, it does not,' Cecil objected. 'He is still subject to the absolute rule of the crown. This is nothing less than a direct challenge to your position. You can be assured he will, in no doubt, request you sign the accession order. More so now, as he will claim to have brought peace between England and Ireland.'

Elizabeth's eyes narrowed to slits, 'You dare to tell me who should sit upon the throne after me?'

'No, your Majesty. I am simply stating Essex will once again push for a signature. If no name is put forward, we will as like, face a worthy challenge from Scotland,' Cecil met The Queen's stare with a cold heart.

'James! Do you suppose to have James readied for the throne? A Stuart?' Elizabeth placed the spaniel on the floor and stormed toward Cecil. Raleigh stepped aside as Elizabeth swept by. Her lead-white face reddened by rage. 'Whose bloody interests do you have Cecil? Mine or yours? Whose agenda do you follow?' She pressed her face to Cecil's.

'The nation's your Majesty,' Cecil remained calm, his face granite. 'Always the nation. Do you think Essex worthy to be king?'

'That is not for you to decide,' Elizabeth hissed, her eyes bore into Cecil. 'Blood determines worthiness.'

'He would still not be the first in line,' Cecil replied, as calm as a frozen pool.

'Do not push me, Robert. Perhaps you would like some time in the Tower yourself?' Elizabeth looked him up and down and turned away. 'Damn you, Cecil. Get out of my Palace, I'll not speak another word of this, this day.' Cecil turned and left the room, guiding Raleigh toward the door as they went.

Elizabeth stood by a window watching the garden: how the smaller birds were pushed aside by the larger one, though this did not stop them from daring to dart back in for a tiny morsel. 'Do you suppose this is how they think of my kingdom?' she asked of the room.

'Majesty?' George Clifford turned to face his Queen.

'Oh, I was wondering if those around me are like the birds pecking one another for the better crumbs. Will they pick over my corpse with such relish?'

'Such things are not for me to ponder, your Majesty. I live to serve you. A future monarch I would not serve. For, to me, there is none like you,' Clifford swallowed hard and lowered his head.

Elizabeth softened, the tightness left her countenance, 'Thank you,' she croaked, through a tightening throat. 'Such kindness is a rarity. If it were possible, I would store such precious jewels, so I might see them again in darker times. My closest friends have never fared me so well. I am honoured to have you in my service.'

'Thank you, your Majesty,' Clifford stood tall and proud. The sound of footsteps on the bare oak floor broke the enchantment over them. Clifford stepped back into his rightful position as Marie and Shakespeare approached The Queen.

'Ah, my favourite bard,' Elizabeth forced herself back into her sovereign mould. 'I was going to ask you, William, to read to myself and my guests. Unfortunately, they have had to leave,' she made a play of dusting her hands together. 'Nevertheless, I should like to hear you read for me. The day is quite clement; what do you say to some fresh air. We can all go to the canopy in the arboretum, the roses are quite astounding.'

'That would perfect, your Majesty. Marie tells me you do not want a play, but would rather partake of lighter works,' Shakespeare flexed the leather-bound pages in his hand. 'I shall be only too happy to oblige.'

'Let us delay no further,' Clifford could you call a servant and have them bring suitable refreshment to the arboretum, then join us there?' Elizabeth smiled. 'Let us go before the best of the day is done.'

MORNING

A watery sun peered through the window catching dust particles in its pale light. A morning mist covered the gardens in a cataract of haze. Elizabeth sat at her dressing table her eyes closed as she soaked up the imagined heat of the sun. Marie wrung out a cloth in a bowl of hot water and began to melt away the lead-white make up from The Queen's face. With gentle but firm strokes she revealed the small-pox scarred skin and pale lips. With a kind hand, she swept aside the few strands of hair and massaged The Queens's scalp.

Marie worked in silence, allowing The Queen a moment of near solitude when no voices bayed for her attention and she could focus on the small still voice calling to her spirit. This was the one time she could heed the voice of God without distraction, or the need to hide in the chapel. Marie understood The Queen and allowed her every indulgence in this time of preparation for her day.

Once she was done, Marie took a step back, curtsied and left the room without a word.

Elizabeth lowered her head, sighing as she rubbed her neck with both hands. To her left sat a rare glass mirror pitted with as many flaws as her own skin. She chose instead, the one of polished bronze as it gave the illusion of a glowing complexion, a picture of health. Mornings were not a joyous time for a woman of sixty-seven who had endured a life of illness and the immeasurable stress of endless wars. Life had its pleasures, but they were beginning to wane, except for the love of hunting and the thrill of the ride. And what of love? Her country was her one true love. Denied the embrace of the Earl of Leicester, she had chosen chastity over carnality. Her country was all she needed, but her country needed a successor, and she had none.

Footsteps beyond the bedchamber door. Elizabeth inclined her head toward the sound; they were not the steps of a woman. The door burst open and there in his favourite silver silk and black attire stood Essex. Proud as a peacock he strutted across the room. 'I have done it!' he declared tossing down a document sealed with a royal stamp. 'The war with Ireland is over. *I* have secured the victory.'

'Elizabeth snatched up a gown, clutching it to her bosom. 'How dare you! How dare you burst into my chamber while I am in a state of undress! What kind of man are you? Have you no respect at all! Get out! Get out!' Elizabeth rounded on Essex. 'I no longer recognise the boy I raised.'

'I have known you all my life, we are family. What son waits at his mother's door?' Essex laughed. 'Read the paper. Red Hugh has capitulated. We are at peace. Are you not pleased?'

'And I told you to kill him!' Elizabeth still held the gown to her as she jumped to her feet, her chair clattered to the floor. 'Get — out!' she surged towards Essex who stepped back into Marie, knocking the tray of food from her hand. Silver plates and goblets bounced across the floor in a splatter of crimson wine. Marie, not yet in The Queen's bedchamber, bent to gather them. 'Get out, get out, get out,' her face red, Elizabeth shoved Essex from her room and slammed the door.

'I thought you would be better pleased,' Essex huffed at the closed door. He spun around knocking Marie aside. 'This is your doing, harlot,' he spat and stormed from the palace.

It was some time before The Queen was ready to recommence her toilette. The rising sun had burned away the mist, and the truth beyond the veil became visible. Elizabeth beheld the lawn, the hedgerows, the flowers, and then all the gilt, everything had lost its lustre.

Marie reappeared with a fresh tray of provisions and placed it beside the bed where The Queen had chosen and laid out her own outfit. They ate in silence, Marie testing all the food she had prepared before passing it to The Queen.

Elizabeth walked over to her bed and stared down at the simple gold outfit and single string of pearls, a modest wig with a simple coiled plait and a pair of purple gloves. Marie lifted the nightgown over The Queen's head and wrapped a bone corset around her slim frame. Criss-crossing the lace, she fastened the girdle with a tight knot and allowed the ends to hang. She placed the inner skirt of silk and lace on the floor for Elizabeth to step into. Lifting it up, she cinched it about The Queen's waist and smoothed it down with her hands. Elizabeth signalled for the dress. Marie undid the back and opened the fastenings, hidden within the many folds of the skirt. She lifted the dress up and held it open so Elizabeth could slip her arms into the sleeves and step in amongst the skirts.

Marie walked around The Queen pulling the sides of the bodice section into place so the skirt would flow around her.

When at last, all the fastenings were secured, and the bodice laced, the joins vanished within the delicate stitching. Elizabeth adjusted the sleeves to her own comfort and patted down her skirts until they flowed about in eddies of lace and cotton. Marie hung pearls around The Queen's neck before painting her face afresh with the lead oxide make-up. Her lips she reddened with cochineal. With the wig seated upon her head, she was ready to begin the day in Parliament.

The two women walked out of the bedchamber, down to the waiting carriage to take them to London. George Clifford waited at the foot of the steps in his silver and black dress armour. 'Ride ahead and have the Earl of Essex summoned to the Privy Council at once.' Clifford ran around the house to the stables where he mounted up and galloped out of the palatial grounds to London.

A Change of Fortune.

They had left the sun in Surrey. London huddled beneath a monotone grey sky, waiting for the light to find a way through to its heart. Streets filled with people going about their daily business, piling carts with barrels and bales, squelching through the filth. Market traders bawled out their wares, declaring their bread, cheese, or ale to be the finest fare in the land. Someone was lying.

The golden carriage turned right through Charring Cross, down into Westminster. Another came in the opposite direction from the Strand with an accompanying knight in armour. The Palace guard opened the gate to allow the golden carriage into the courtyard. The second carriage came to a sudden halt as halberds and pikes were angled toward it.

'Who goes there?' a brusque voice hailed the driver of the carriage.

'George Clifford, The Queen's champion with the Earl of Essex under escort,' the knight replied.

The guards raised their weapons and allowed the escorted carriage through. When they reached the steps to Westminster Palace, the golden carriage had been removed. 'With me,' Clifford commanded Essex who stood to adjust his doublet and the frills of his shirt.

'In time,' Essex smirked. 'One cannot rush one's entrance into the Palace. He adjusted his sword belt, so the ruby hilt was visible when his hand was at rest. 'Yes, I think I am ready now. It would do a man such as yourself a lot of good if you were to observe how a gentleman such as I conducts his life.'

'Really,' Clifford pointed towards the entrance. 'Her Majesty awaits.'

'You speak as if we have not met before,' Essex examined Clifford. 'You sire, lack class. How did you get the job again? Was it on the fields of valour, did you lay siege to Cádiz, or battle the Armada? A mere joust?'

'They are waiting, sir,' Clifford levelled his gaze upon Essex, his right hand lowered to his sword.

'Think you could best me?' Essex scoffed.

'Sir,' Clifford curled his fingers around the handle of his sword. 'I would not keep The Queen waiting any longer than is acceptable, sir,' he nodded towards the door. Essex hesitated, opened his mouth to speak but thought better of it. Clifford followed him inside, keeping his hand on his sword. The rest of the walk to the Council Chamber was in silence. Essex could think of nothing to amuse him. 'Wait here,' Clifford knocked on the door with a clenched fist. The door opened enough to let him in.

For such a small gathering, the noise within the council chamber was nigh to riot. The arrival of Clifford did little to quell the disquiet.

'Order,' Elizabeth's first call went unheeded. 'Order! Gentlemen!' she stamped her feet, her voice shrill. 'Are you children that I need to shout to be heard by my own council?' her knuckles whitened as she gripped the arms of her throne. 'I have not the patience for this behaviour. Act like the gentlemen you are supposed to be. Now,' bringing her voice under control, she stared those gathered in the eye. 'we are here to discuss with Essex, his recent actions in Ireland.'

'He must be punished, your Majesty, for his failure to follow orders. How many more times will he be let off?' Raleigh bit his tongue.

'Punished, Sir Walter? Was he not successful in any way?' Elizabeth objected. The door opened, Essex walked in and took his seat at the table. All eyes fell upon him, including Elizabeth's.

'Oh, do not mind me, carry on,' Essex picked up a copy of the list of items for discussion. He put it back on the table with quiet discomfort. Upon it, one word: Essex.

'My dear Earl,' Elizabeth peered down at him, her face taut. 'I do not recall asking you to join us. This meeting is about you, not for you.'

'You may well have pushed Her Majesty a little too far,' Cecil uttered beneath his breath.

'Here boy,' Elizabeth pointed to space at the end of the table in front of her throne. Essex rose from his seat, tugged his doublet down and walked as slow as he might. Elizabeth got up and stood before him. 'As if your failure to follow a simple order were not enough, your intrusion into my private chamber was beyond contempt.' Without warning, Elizabeth slapped Essex across the face. 'Dear boy, it is indeed time to clip your wings,' She slapped him again, then boxed him about his ears. Essex stepped back. The room fell silent. 'I told you to kill Red Hugh and bring the savages to order. Ah,' she raised her hand signalling Essex to be silent. 'I will be listened to this time, make no mistake. You had over seventeen thousand men. More than your enemies, under your command. We have lost some of our finest commanders. Yet you return, unscathed. I knew of your truce days ago. Within three days of it being signed, I had word of it.' Essex dared a glance at Cecil who stared back, his gaze cold.

'Can you not pay attention for one moment,' Elizabeth raised her hands. 'I can see no option open to me, other than to remove your sweet wine monopoly,' she sat back on her throne.

'What! Are you out of your mind? I'll be ruined. Humiliated,' Essex spun around, turning his back on The Queen. In an instant his hand was around his sword. He could feel the ruby pulse in his palm. George Clifford drew his blade as he stepped forward. Essex turned again waving his sword at The Queen. Clifford brought his sword up, thrust forward, as Raleigh leapt from his seat, sword at the ready. Clifford slipped the tip of his sword through the guard of Essex's Sagrada and flicked it across the room, disarming the Earl. Clifford put his blade to Essex's throat as Raleigh seized him from behind.

'Get this recreant traitor from my sight!' Elizabeth bellowed. 'He is to be held under house arrest in his home in the Strand until I decide what is to be done with him.'

'Elizabeth,' Essex implored, finding a blade pressed against his spine he raised his hands to shoulder height.

'Get out!' Elizabeth pushed herself into her seat, her head held high. Everybody watched as Essex was marched out of Parliament.

A Turn of Tides

The scent of autumn bonfires filled the tavern as patrons filed in from the misty night outside. A waft of smoke drifted in every time the door was open. Candles burned in every corner, chasing out the shadows. Bolingbroke was doing his best at goolie but missed the cup more than he caught it. Shakespeare, ale in hand, tossed coins against the wall trying to knock down a playing card: the Jack of Hearts.

'To The Queen!' came a cheer from the bar as another reveller fell off his seat. 'As we remember her accession, God bless her!' Ale sloshed across the floor adding to the swirl of swill and sawdust.

'Eat, drink, for tomorrow we die!' Shakespeare cried, triumphant as the Jack of Hearts toppled face first into the dust. 'Someone steady this ship; I fear we have been set adrift.'

'William, I think perhaps this should be your last ale,' Marie reached out a hand to Shakespeare as he staggered backwards.

'What? Ever?' he cradled the ale to his chest. 'Alas, my love it would appear there are those who wish us part,' he attempted to lick the ale from the tankard.

'King, and clown, of the stage,' Southampton saluted as he passed through the crowded inn. 'Once more unto the breach, William,' Southampton planted a fresh ale into Shakespeare's hands.

'Ah, my fine beauty, you have a twin sister,' William quaffed the ale with vigour.

'Henry!' Marie protested, unable to restrain her mirth as Shakespeare peered into the empty tankard, disappointment drawn on his face.

'My dear girl, he has much to celebrate. With Essex still confined to his house, the play is done. We can celebrate from succession to epiphany,' Southampton grasped Marie by the waist and swung her around.

'Are we dancing?' Shakespeare grasped Bolingbroke's hand and began to jig until he fell on his arse to guffaws from all those present.

'A genius with words, a wonder to witness perform, but a terrible dancer,' Southampton offered a hand to his fallen comrade. 'Up my friend and know your limitations.'

'What is man that he should be so mighty, and yet be brought so low by a mere drink,' Shakespeare lamented the dregs of his ale. 'O dark bodied beauty, how I mourn thee. For what can one compare to thee. One touch upon the lips and my cares begin to melt away. For though art more lovely than a maiden, far simpler and yet, without responsibility for all that follows your consumption.'

''Tis but a drink William,' Marie turned the bleary-eyed bard to face her. 'Would you lament a maiden so?'

With a hand on his heart, Shakespeare replied, 'No. I should mourn and carry a broken and contrite heart to my grave. For never in the wonders of this world was a more complex and wonderful thing made. To have the love,' William slipped from her hands, 'of a woman, who is true and noble of heart, is to have found a treasure more precious than rubies. Love outshines all things; it remembers no wrongs and covers every fault with the gentleness of a lamb.'

'You, my friend,' Southampton applauded. 'Are beyond drunk. And yet words flow from you like a fount of honey. I would give up all wealth to have such a gift. For with such a tongue one could tame any enemy and gather all the kings of the earth in one room and have them vie for your attention alone.'

'You flatter me, Henry,' Shakespeare slumped into a chair. 'Alas, my dark mistress has the better of me.' There was a dull thud as William's face collided with the table.

Dark clouds gathered in York House. Essex stared out of his window across the Thames, where bonfires raged at the night, their brilliant flames dancing in the dark. Peasants spun and sang at the top of their voices as they cavorted with one another in celebration of the accension of Elizabeth. The yellow flames of the fires rippled over the water with an inviting allure. The earl swirled the wine around the glass until it was as warm as his hand. He set the glass down on the windowsill and walked away from the festivities.

With a yawn he wandered into his study where a parchment lay pinned open with a dagger, its ruby pommel glinting in the candlelight. He reread the words, smirking at how The Queen would react to the Irish Lord's requests under the treaty. With each read through his mirth increased, until a raucous laugh ripped from his lungs, filling the house with its happy sound.

'What has you in such spirits?' Penelope sidled up beside him.

'Ah, my harlot sister. And how is Mountjoy? Still strong in the saddle? Hmm,' Essex's laughter roared in his sister's ears.

'And you are still an arse,' Penelope scanned the letter on the table.

'Not for your slutty eyes,' he snatched the paper from the desk and threw it in the fireplace where it was consumed by yellow flames. 'Stick to love letters and luncheon invites with hags and half-breeds.'

'The same hags and half-breeds that used to keep you warm of a winter's night?' Penelope blocked the slap aimed at her face. 'Not so, brother. You are in a precarious position, one shrill scream and the guards come running.'

Essex grasped her by the throat, 'Scream now harlot,' He squeezed a little harder. Penelope grabbed the dagger from the table and stuck it in her brother's hand. 'You bitch!' this time the back of his found its mark. 'Scream all you want. I'll kill you before they get through the door.'

With a hand to her cheek, she spat at her brother, 'I hope they take your head,' Penelope strode from the room her boots thudding on the bare boards as she slammed the door behind her, rattling the cross swords on the wall. The sound of Essex's laughter followed her up the street as she ran for her carriage.

'Is this serious? Do they suppose I would agree to any of this preposterous nonsense?' Elizabeth handed the letter back to Cecil. 'As much as we may have prospered

341

from the truce, I am in no way inclined to give heed to any of it!' she waved an idle hand at the letter.

'Ma'am, it is most likely the truce will collapse and the feud recommence,' Cecil sighed with a tired air.

'They are always looking for an excuse for a fight. Let us string this along until after the Christmas festivities. I should hate for anything to sour such a sweet time,' Elizabeth bit down on a sugared almond.

'It would be a frightful thing to run out of marzipan and almonds at Christmas, Majesty,' Cecil winced as Elizabeth crushed two of the sugared treats with a gavel. 'I so hate that.'

'I know,' Elizabeth crushed another nut. 'I mean, do they, in truth, expect me to capitulate to self-governing Ireland with restitution of confiscated lands and churches, freedom of movement and a strong Roman Catholic identity. In respect of Irish sovereignty, he now accepts English overlordship! But requests the viceroy be at least an earl, and of the Privy Council of England,' Elizabeth raised an eyebrow to Cecil. 'The man is a complete idiot.'

'On the face of it. If, however, we assume there are other plans afoot then this is a fine stalling play. Red Hugh will have all the time required to recoup his forces and strengthen his position throughout the land. We know the Spanish are amassing a new Armada and are in talks with the Irish lords. It is only a matter of time before they sail and settle in Ireland where they will have a backdoor into England.'

'They would not dare,' Elizabeth growled.

'They dare, indeed,' was Cecil's flat reply. 'I believe it has been their intent for many years now.'

'Walsingham did once try to forewarn me the threat would come from Ireland, but I never thought of a collusion.'

'Let us not forget they are all puppets of Venice. The Holy Father has put a price upon your head. Killing you would not be a sin as you are, in their eyes, a heretic, Ma'am.'

Elizabeth cleared her throat, 'Is it wrong to doubt his parentage? I think at this moment, they were not married?'

Cecil smiled back at her, 'Ma'am.'

'So, what now?' Elizabeth snatched a part filled goblet of wine from the table and downed its contents.

'We wait,' Cecil refilled the glass, 'Until one of the sides makes a positive play, we have no way of telling on which front they will strike. I believe there to be several options open to them right now. The Irish, who are becoming more numerous on the city streets as we speak, may launch an all-out attack against us in the Pale and the adjacent lands. The Spanish will sail under the Vatican flag and attempt to colonise Ireland, then attack as a combined force. Or —' Cecil poured himself a drink.

'Or?' Elizabeth pressed, swirling the claret around in her goblet with one eye on Cecil.

'Or Essex will do something utterly stupid.'

'Robert,' Elizabeth groaned. 'When will you let the boy alone? I do not think for a moment he would do anything that would risk either his life — or my own,' She raised a hand to the inevitable protest, 'Despite his antics in the Privy Council, he remains blood.'

'Has that ever stopped anyone from taking the crown before? Should the opportunity present itself, I would not rule it out,' Cecil held his glass in both hands, warming the wine. He watched the crimson liquid cling to the sides where imperfections in the glass gave it purchase.

'Must I always keep one eye over my shoulder and a hand on my sword?'

'Yes,' Cecil stated. 'It will always be that way. A man will lust after power more than wine and women combined.'

'I think that sums you up completely, my dear toad,' Elizabeth put her empty glass on the table and gave Cecil a delicate peck on the cheek. 'But do not fear, I will always love you, Robert.'

'Really, Ma'am?' Cecil moved his head to one side, his eyes slightly narrowed.

Elizabeth regarded him, 'No.'

'Ah, I thought not.'

1600

CHRISTMAS

ESSEX HOUSE

The fire crackled and spat, sparks chased one another up the chimney in an ascending dance of fairy dust and glitter. Smoke capped flames roared in the hearth, driving back the bite of winter to bring a mote of Christmas cheer to the gloom. A candelabra sat on a small table casting long shadows about the room. Essex held a glass of rum to his mouth. His warm breath hung in the glass as he stared into the flames, a parchment held loose in one hand.

'What is to be, my dear Penelope, when kings are made to sit in the dark and celebrate the season of goodwill alone, with only their sister for company?' he pouted into his glass, inhaling the warm aroma of spiced rum.

'Drop the melancholy act, will you Robert, perhaps a brace of whores would warm your mood — or your wife?' Penelope hid her smile in the shimmering shadows.

'And yet here I sit, mocked by my sibling, as my mind rots in this infernal cell,' Essex sloshed his rum into the fire. The flames burst, gorging themselves on the incandescent liquid. 'The wine is gone, the riches dwindle, and the bastard Queen sits upon a throne she is unfit to mount. In truth, she is unfit to be mounted, let alone the throne; more of an elaborate piss pot than a seat of power.'

'You must rein in your words, that is treasonous talk. Should any of your staff mutter in the wind and Cecil catch its ear, you, my fine dandy, will finish your days on Tower Hill,' Penelope refilled Essex's glass from a decanter. 'There are those in parliament who are baying for your blood. One wrong step and, rest assured, your neck will be stretched before the commoners.'

Essex sighed, his chest heaved with the effort, 'Shut up. You know nothing of what keeps me alive. I will have what is due to me. Elizabeth will not last much longer; she is tired and old. The strain of keeping the nation afloat is wearing her down. It will not be long before some disease, or other, feasts on her scrawny frame and kills her. Then, my dear sister, I will be king.'

'What of James? He has first rights, does he not?' Penelope licked her lips, savouring the kiss of rum on her tongue.

'I have communicated with James, explaining my stratagem for taking the throne, which, I may add, is but a few short weeks from now. I have convinced him to send his mercenaries to help take the city. He believes he will be crowned king. I have promised him as much as I could without stating it. — What?' Essex watched his sister circle the room until she stood between him and the life-giving warmth of the fire.

'Have you lost all sense of reality. James would take the crown from you in a heartbeat. It is Cecil you must woo. He is the ever-present threat. There is no place you can hide from his eyes; they are everywhere,' Penelope dropped to her knees before Essex. 'You must desist from this course of action. You cannot take the city with a few wild Scotsmen. The guard has been doubled throughout the palace. Tripled in some quarters. How do you suppose to rally support? You will need an army, not a drunken mob! Do not do this,' She searched his bloodshot eyes for signs of normality. 'I implore you.'

'Implore all you like,' Essex pushed her aside and stood in front of the fire. 'This is what I have planned all along. London will burn. The people will come to the call of their true king. Even the mighty Shakespeare has no idea he is to be my messenger, the evangelist of my cause.' From the mantle over the fire, Essex took a leather-bound manuscript and waved it in his sister's face. 'This is my clarion call to rouse the commoner from their imbecilic depths of thought, to rise and conquer at my side. The people will be my army.'

'You are quite insane! Left alone with your thoughts you have allowed yourself to believe your drunken ramblings. The commoners will not put their necks in a noose for anybody. It is quite obvious you have spent no time among them. They are not, as you suppose, idiots. It is the commoner who runs the nation, not the rich. If they choose to turn the other cheek, you will be stranded.'

'Get out. Go to your common friends and show them your skirts, I'm sure they would pay a halfpenny for a flash of sagging flesh. Lord knows, most of the Lords have,' Essex pointed to the door. 'Out!'

'You fool. You arrogant cock-sure fool. You will die in ignorance and shame,' Penelope threw her glass into the fire where it shattered in a fireball of rage.

'No, my dear harlot of a sister. It is you who are ignorant of the masses. They love me. I am the hero of the people. It is my name they shout in the streets. It is I they follow behind as I march to war, and they will do the same come the day.'

'Truly you are deluded beyond salvation,' Penelope walked past Essex. In the blinking of an eye, her brother swept his arm up from his side and across her face and sent her sprawling into the door.

'Get out,' Essex turned back toward the fire. He took a poker from the stand and thrust it into the flames. 'If you do not leave, I shall be forced to brand you the whore you are.' Penelope scrambled to her feet, reaching for the door handle as the hot poker swung toward her face. She screamed. Essex froze, his ear tuned to the corridor beyond the door. 'Be careful of the attention you seek,' Essex hissed as he held out the poker. Penelope recoiled from the hot iron. 'Last chance to leave.'

'Do not worry, Essex, I am going. Going as far from you as I can,' she yanked the door open and stepped out into the cold air of the corridor where a guard's dark eyes peered from 'neath a furrowed brow. 'I am fine,' She straightened her dress. 'It is my brother who ails,' Penelope saw herself out. The snow swirled around, enveloping her in its silent shroud.

STRATFORD

Ducks slid across the frozen surface of the River Avon as they landed on the crystal-clear ice. Children threw stones in the hope of breaking the thick shield, but to no avail. The river refused to yield to anyone's demands. Snow lay in a thick blanket on the ground, hiding the frozen earth for the second week. A bright sun lit the blue sky in a cold yellow glow. Gloves, scarves and thick hide coats were the order of the day.

The Shakespeares walked together, chatting and laughing as they threw snowballs at one another. Snowmen stood like sentries at every corner, their stick arms pointing at awkward angles, while their charcoal smiles remained locked in a frozen gasp.

William scooped up a handful of snow, rolling it into a rough ball he hurled it at Susanne. Judith squealed with shock and delight as the missile, intended for her sister, found its mark on the back of her own head. William ducked a clumsy throw from Anne, as he moved in close, losing his footing he tumbled into his wife landing in a soft crunch of snow. They fell into each other's arms, filling the air with raucous laughter. Their eyes met. They kissed long.

'Ew,' the two girls screwed up their faces. 'We were playing in that snow. Now it's just ... Ew.'

The happy couple laughed all the more and kissed again and again, until the girls begged them to cease. 'You'll understand when you are betrothed,' William teased.

'I do not think they will,' Anne reached out for William's hand. 'I have yet to see them so much as smile at a boy.'

'Oh, please father, make her stop. She always teases us about boys and grandchildren. Could you imagine anything quite so horrible?' Judith protested, kicking snow at her mother.

'All this activity has given me an appetite. What do you say to rushing home and tucking into the goose?' William made a run toward the nearest house. Judith and Susanne shot past him without looking back.

'Wallace has made a fine job of the bridge,' Anne pointed to the river.

'He has indeed,' William looped his arm through Anne's as they walked through the snow. When they arrived at the house, the girls were dancing from foot to foot, huddled together. William unlocked the door and they all rushed inside.

They ran about the house, piling fresh logs onto the fires before they burned out. Soon the house was warm enough to remove coats and scarves. The table was laid in haste, with everyone taking bites from the meat and bread, as they piled the remains of Christmas dinner on the table. William poured himself ale from a cask, and wine for Anne and each of the two girls.

'You must return with me to London once the festivities are over. We have a fine house in the city, not far from the theatre. You can come and see a play at the Globe!' William enthused.

'And which would it be? Something tragic? A comedy?' the girls chirped in turn.

'History?' Anne smooched closer, 'I would prefer something with a bit of bite,' She nibbled at William's ear, while keeping an eye on the children.

'Oh, please,' Judith squawked. 'It's just not right!'

'It is, however, how you came to be,' William laughed.

'To be or not to be, 'tis disgusting, and should be confined to dark places,' Susanne grimaced. 'I for one would love to see the city. We could visit the Palace!'

'And have tea with The Queen,' Judith squealed.

'Who knows what excitement the city holds for you. It is filled with knights and villains. Peasants rub shoulders with lords among the masses in the markets. Horses, cattle, cats, and dogs all are free in the city,' William flung his arms around, as though he were addressing the groundling at the Globe.

'What? They cost not a penny?' Judith asked, her brow furrowed deep for such a whelp.

'No, my dear, they are merely not prisoners. Cattle are driven through the streets by herders, cats, and dogs weave their way through the legs of all who walk the streets.'

'Then it is decided,' Anne scooped up her girls in her arms, kissing each in turn. 'To London, we shall go.'

RICHMOND

Heavy snow drifted over the fields, masking all traces of life. There would be no hunt today. Elizabeth frowned at the frozen world, as though a fierce scowl would force the weather to submit to her will. She spun around, handing the saddle to the stable boy, hitched up her skirts, and crunched her way back to the palace, trailing her entourage behind her.

'Ma'am,' Raleigh called after her to no avail. Elizabeth had other things on her mind. 'She's impossible!'

'She will not be happy without a ride,' Clifford winked to Raleigh.

'I know how she feels,' the two men snorted. 'You had best be after her Clifford, she is fast escaping in this blizzard.' Clifford quickened his pace vanishing out of sight as the snow swirled around them.

The sharp twang of a harpsichord resounded around the music room as Elizabeth stabbed at the keys. There was nothing melodic or symphonious in the music she was playing, and, as such, this just served to aggravate The Queen further. Greensleeves was slaughtered, along with other tunes, as Elizabeth pouted and played. Her faithful spaniel, Leicester, was keeping out of reach of her feet and hands.

'Ma'am,' Raleigh waved a small silver plate piled with marzipan treats beneath her nose.

'Walter, are you trying to tempt me with an almond delight,' Elizabeth licked her blackened teeth. Raleigh withdrew the offering. 'I did not say I could not be tempted. Return them at once, or I'll have you locked in the tower.'

'Ma'am,' he proffered the dish once more. Elizabeth took the whole pile, stuffing the delicate fancies into her mouth two at a time until they had all gone. 'Wine?' Raleigh held out a glass and decanter. Elizabeth nodded, then shook her head but took the decanter. She poured herself a drink and drank it straight down.

She waggled the glass over her head, 'I have found what I want — something to stifle my misery. More wine,' she waggled the glass again.

'You have the decanter Ma'am,' Raleigh pointed to her other hand.

'So I do,' she gave Raleigh a rueful grin. 'So, help me with it and tell me tales of the high seas. Speak to me of treasure and sinking the Spaniards.'

'Where is Clifford?' Raleigh refilled The Queen's glass.

'Off on an errand,' Elizabeth sighed. 'Hunting us all some game for supper I think.'

'Elizabeth, tell me you have not sent him out to catch some game?'

'No, I have sent him to amuse himself with something gamey in the Liberties,' Elizabeth roared with laughter as she drank another glass of wine. 'Somebody fetch more wine and bring me something to soak it up. I do not wish Sir Walter passing out on me.'

'Oh, it is going to be one of those drinks is it,' Raleigh loosened his ruff and collar as he downed his drink in one. 'Eat, drink, and be merry for tomorrow we die.'

'Well said, sir, but you are still two glasses behind me.'

The hours passed swift as the night bled into day. Candles were lit, and music played as Raleigh re-enacted his journeys to the new lands. He told of Virginia and the endless coast of America. Raleigh sang of the Azores and the struggle of Cádiz, Flanders and Ireland. As he did so, he lamented upon lost friends and forgotten heroes. He quoted Shakespeare, Marlowe, and spun a few poems of his own into the mix. Elizabeth laughed and clapped as they ate and drank into the small hours. When at last satisfied, Raleigh took Elizabeth by the arm and escorted her to her chambers where Marie waited to put her Majesty to bed.

1601

JANUARY

Grey skies obscured the sun, drawing all its heat away from the frozen earth. Lonely snowflakes drifted in pendulous rhythm as they fell, languid from the sky. Frost clung to the windows despite the warmth inside, and perhaps too the velvet drapes were doing their part to keep life within the rooms of Essex House.

'And this is your plan? A play?' Guido shook his head dismayed. 'What! You expect everyone to prance along to the theatre and take up arms?' He scratched his head.

'You are an uncultured swine who has no understanding of the importance of the theatre. Everyone goes to the theatre: the old and young, the rich and poor. They go, not to be entertained alone, but to be informed,' Essex threw his arms around in a theatrical display.

'You think it enough to call men to arms? The Holy Father was reluctant for you to be the first choice to replace the ageing hag. Now I understand why,' Guido sipped from his glass.

'There will be more than enough on the streets by the time we reach our goal,' Red Hugh took a hunk of bread from a platter and smeared it with dripping. 'The Earl is the most popular man in the country, and he commands more attention than Elizabeth herself. He will make good on his promise. You, sir, are addressing the future king of England. I should watch how you speak to him, tomorrow he may be signing your death warrant,' Red Hugh walked around the room, his boots scuffing on the bare boards. He turned and stood at Essex's side. 'I have fought both for and against his lordship, and I am certain I stand beside royalty this very day.'

'You may think so, but I do not,' Guido ran a finger along the edge of his dagger. 'I also, have fought against him: in Flanders and Cádiz. Though it was the far nobler Raleigh who bested me that day,' Guido leaned forward in his chair. 'I remember a young upstart trying to train the troops at Tilbury,' He paused to drink some wine. 'Still a boy, yet given such a command.'

'Preposterous! You cannot have been at Tilbury on the eve of the Armada, you were not old enough. And no Spaniard would have been allowed within a mile of her Majesty,' Essex spat.

'Indeed,' Guido raised an eyebrow. 'I have not always been a Spaniard, or a Venetian. No, my noble friend, I am a man of York. My name is Johnson, John Johnson.'

'I remember you, a huge nest of unruly auburn hair. Quite useless with a sword if I remember rightly,' Essex leaned in to meet the gaze of Guido.

'My first day in training,' Guido smiled a ghost of a smile. 'Should you care to try me today, I would be only too glad to gut you and watch you flop like a fish on the floor.'

Essex eased himself back in his chair as he reached for his wine to soothe his parched mouth. He sat tapping his forefinger on the rim of his glass, his eyes fixed on the smiling Guido. A man who had known him for more than thirteen years, and yet he knew nothing of him. Can a man be so invisible and yet so public? Essex pondered in the silence of the room as Guido emptied and filled his glass, unaffected, as he drank the best of Essex's cellar.

'Tell me, Guido,' Red Hugh spoke in hushed tones. 'What are the plans for Ireland? Are we to bow and kiss the papal arse like the English?'

'No, my friend,' the smile slipped from Guido's face as a knife cuts a throat. 'A new armada is readying as we speak, larger than any before it. Not only soldiers but a whole community. Farmers, families, holy men to bless the land, and the greatest warriors who walk the hills of Spain. Don Juan Del Aguila, the Eagle, will fly to Ireland and lead it to victory. Thousands of soldiers at his command, the English will soon learn the taste of defeat. A doorway will be open to us to walk through and conquer this blighted land, and whosoever may be king will bow their knee to Spain and to Catholic rule,' Guido spoke with a cold heart in which there was no bargaining or clemency.

'Amen, may it be so,' Red Hugh doffed his cap. 'You can rely on our full support when the moment comes. We will be only too glad to drive the invaders from our shores.'

'I am glad to hear it,' Guido turned his attention back to Essex. 'And where do you stand, your highness?'

'With my trusted friend,' he glanced up at Red Hugh.

'Time will tell. Time will always tell,' Guido rose from his chair. 'Is there a date for the play?'

'The first week of February, we will pay the Globe to stage the revised version with the deposition. We shall take the Privy Council by surprise, and force Cecil to make The Queen sign the accension order.'

'Complicated,' Guido took his cape from the back of a chair. 'If you are so convinced your plan will succeed, why not kill them both and take the throne?' He swung his cape over his broad shoulders and fastened it to his collar. 'You will need greater strength than this if you are to rule for long. She has done more than forty years, do you imagine to do the same?

I only want to hear from you when you have the royal sceptre in your hands. Until such time, I will be waiting,' Guido left by the front door in a blast of icy wind.

'We will show that idiot how things are done in England. He may have been born here but his heart is in the papal lap,' Essex snorted.

'He is a dangerous man,' Red Hugh sighed. 'We cannot be sure whose back he has, only that he will put a knife in it.

I will gather all those I can for the 6th. I know the perfect man to get the Lord Chamberlain's Men to agree to stage the play.'

'Who?'

'Southampton.' They laughed, long and hard into the night.

Back in the Nest

The wind whipped through the stews stirring up the soft snow in a flurry of blinding white cold. Candles flickered and guttered in the windows. Wintery fingers probed at every crack, forming iced veins over the inside. Booted feet crunched through the snow, leaving an easy to follow the trail all the way to the Bishop's Cap.

Warm air ran from the cold north wind as the door to the inn was opened. The smell of food, hot meats and winter pickles, stirred the tastebuds of Shakespeare and Marie as they hurried to their usual spot near the crackling fire. Shakespeare shuddered as he huffed into his cupped hands. 'How can it be so cold? We only came from the theatre, and yet I am chilled to the bone.'

'This is by far the coldest I have been since I ran the streets as a child,' Marie hunched herself into a ball, rubbing her upper arms. 'The play is looking good Master Shakespeare. I think this is quite the best performance of Romeo I have seen yet. The new theatrics are amazing to behold,' Marie accepted a steaming mug of spiced wine. 'This is what I need the most,' She let the vapour rise into her face, eyes closed as she breathed in nutmeg, cinnamon, and pepper.

'Thank you, Marie, your words are most generous,' Shakespeare cradled a steaming jug of his own as he watched the waitress load the table with leftover seasonal fayre. 'I'm famished,' Shakespeare grabbed at everything, filling his mouth with as much as he could, grunting between mouthfuls.

Marie pulled at some bread, tearing herself a huge piece. She pulled out the soft centre from the end crust and stuffed it with cold meat and jelly. She sat admiring her masterpiece before burying her face in her delicious creation. Amid their grunts and satisfied groans, there was the occasional slurp of cooling wine.

The door at the rear of the tavern opened, and a miserable Southampton dragged his feet into the room. With a groan he dropped into the seat beside Marie and cut himself a portion from the meat on the table. He poked at the ham and prodded at the beef, before picking at the goose as though it were diseased. 'Southampton? What ails?' Shakespeare asked, setting his plate aside.

'Oh, 'tis nothing,' Southampton's chest heaved with the effort of his sigh. 'In Truth ... '

'Evidently, not so. Come, partake of the spiced wine, it is well mulled. More spice than Marie,' Shakespeare swirled his tankard under Southampton's nose while dodging a kick to the shins from Marie.

'Nothing could compare to a maiden such as thee. Especially not a glass of mere plonk,' Southampton snatched the tankard from Shakespeare's hands, downing the contents in one. 'It is fair, but not the palest of imitation to you.'

'I am flattered, but that does not change the matter of your melancholy,' Marie slipped an arm around Southampton, giving him a firm but gentle squeeze. 'We are your friends, more than that, we are a family.'

'Essex,' Southampton growled. 'And his Irish comrades are making their moves,' He admired each of them in turn. Shakespeare wiped his mouth on his sleeve stifling a belch, while Marie placed her glass back on the table. 'They have demanded you, The Chamberlain's Men, perform the new edition of Richard II in February at the Globe. Once Romeo and Juliet has run its course,' Southampton dropped a red leather coin purse on the table the contents clunked on the scarred wood.

'What is this? A bribe?' Shakespeare weighed the purse in his palm. 'Four pounds I should wager, not a penny more.' Southampton tilted his head in query. 'I am right!' Shakespeare clapped his hands. 'From your demeanour, I would guess there is more.'

'With the deposition.'

'Is he mad? That is treasonous! To write it is one matter, but to perform such a thing in public is to invite the noose,' Shakespeare sank back in his seat.

'Nevertheless, that is the demand. Essex has also demanded half the tickets for his guests — the other half we are free to sell to the peasants. His words, not mine,' Southampton turned the tankard a half turn. The waitress appeared with a full decanter of brandy, a jug of mead, and wine.

'I see,' Shakespeare mused.

'Were you not going to invite your family to the city for the Winterval?' Marie questioned, biting her lip.

'You cannot act as though you suspect anything. To act otherwise would draw the wrong kind of attention. If it were not bad enough that Red Hugh flaunts himself about the streets, Guido is still out there. Both were seen at Essex House, and we can only assume some form of conspiracy abounds.'

'The charlatan, has he no shame?' Shakespeare banged his fist on the table.

'No,' Marie bit her lip as she snatched her glass from the table. 'He thinks of none but himself.'

'What does he hope to gain from such alliances?' Shakespeare stared across the table as though blind.

'For the longest time he has been trying to force The Queen to sign the succession order so he can seamlessly take the throne upon her death,' a grim smile snuck across Southampton's lips as he thought upon the situation. 'It is unfortunate, the paper is controlled by Cecil.' Marie chuckled into her wine, almost choking on the crimson nectar. 'I do not know all Cecil does, neither would I claim to do so. What I do know is, after the campaign in Ireland, Essex met with Red Hugh, who sent his initial demands home with Essex. From prior visits, I know Essex is close to Red Hugh, not so with Tyrone. The younger man has little love for our Earl. I also know of the connections between Red Hugh and Spain; that is my greatest concern. Like my protector I fear the Irish may collude with the Spanish.'

'Could we defeat Spain if they embed themselves so close to our shores?' Marie swirled the last dregs of her drink around before slugging it down her throat.

'I do not know. Spain is a powerful foe. They have resources we do not. They also have the backing of the papacy,' Southampton placed his hands upon the table. 'I am sorry for dragging you into this sordid affair. When I signed as your patron, I never imagined you would be put into such a tenuous position.'

'Me neither,' Shakespeare picked at the meat on the platter. 'I cannot pretend I have any idea where this will all end. At least one of them will go to the Tower, and perhaps others to the gallows. Either way, it will not be fun,' he scratched at his nose. 'Marie, my dear girl, can you forgive me for dragging you so deep into the gutter. Southwark is a dirty place at the best of times. This, however, beats them all into a goolie cup,' He raised an eyebrow.

'We have precious time to prepare, can you get the play in shape?' Southampton pushed himself up from the table.

'The Lord Chamberlain's Men are the most accomplished crew I have ever been party to. You can rest assured; Richard II will be ready on time with all guns blazing.' Southampton smiled at Shakespeare, a smile he meant from the depth of his soul.

February

Under House Arrest

Heavy curtains blocked out the sun, no light from the outside world penetrated the room. Wine flowed from decanter to glass and gullet, and talk turned from travel to conquest and bloodshed.

'The rehearsals have begun,' Southampton sipped from his glass. His eyes drawn to the dancing flames in the hearth. 'They have completed the first run. Quite remarkable considering.'

'Considering what exactly,' Essex snorted. 'They are mere actors. It is all they are capable of. What say you, Red, do you suppose an actor could rule?'

'I suppose a skilled one might,' Red Hugh watched Essex's smile fade. 'A good leader has to put on a believable act, or no one will follow him, no matter who he thinks he may be.'

'Well said,' Mountjoy raised his glass to Red Hugh, much to Essex's displeasure.

'Are you so bloody stupid! A man is bred to rule. The simple do as he says, or they forfeit themselves. A ruler rules with power, not an act of it. Pah! How did I end up in the company of such buffoons,' Essex drained his glass and reached for the decanter.

'So, what is the plan?' Red Hugh sat his glass on the mantle over the fire. 'You have yet to convince me you have anything more than a parade in mind.'

'I have told you all in detail, but if I must entertain you as simpletons, I shall. My people are procuring the message bearers for tomorrow. The word to be ready will hang from every street. The whole city shall be aware. When the day comes for the final hurrah, the people will be in such high spirits they will run from their homes, as they always have, and follow us to victory.

We will ride through the city, en masse, your people and mine, and we shall take what is rightfully mine.'

'You think it that simple?' Mountjoy challenged. 'The common man will rise and follow you to death?'

'What nobler purpose is there than to join with one's King?' Essex sat back in his chair with a fresh glass of wine. 'The witless Shakespeare has written the call to arms. He is unaware his play will be performed in every available venue across the city. Word will spread among the masses, and they shall rise to the call. I have no doubt.'

'We are with you all the way, have no fear. This is no small gesture we make,' Red Hugh offered his hand. 'I bear no threat. I carry no sword. My hand is yours as always.'

Essex took Red's hand and held it in a firm grasp. 'What of you two? Now is not the time to be faint of heart.'

'I'm in,' Mountjoy added his hand to the union. 'Southampton?'

'I have stood by your every decision in battles far and near. I have not always agreed with your methods, or choices, but I have always been there with you wherever we were. That does not change now,' Southampton pledged his honour to the agreement.

'Then we are in life and in death, wherever it may lead us, let it be glorious,' Essex raised his glass. 'To glory and the crown.'

'To glory and the crown,' they all cheered as one, downing their drinks and throwing their glasses into the fire.

'I suggest you all go and prepare; the time is nigh upon us. Cecil watches the place like a hawk but is unaware of all the exits. Leave by the jetty. I wish you well gentlemen. The morrow will be a dawn like no other. Elizabeth refuses to allow me access to the court of England, so I shall take action and remove that toad Cecil once and for all. We'll see if he likes the bloody tower so much when he is on the inside wearing the shackles. I wonder what secrets we'll learn when we turn the screws on him?'

'There are a few things I'd like to ask him myself,' Red Hugh fastened his coat about his waist. 'Why he's such an arse, for one?' They looked at each other and laughed long and loud as they filtered out into the late afternoon sun.

Extra candles burned in every corner, but no light could lift the gloom of the Privy Council. Shadows flickered over angry faces as Cecil listened to the growing demands for justice. The hard wooden chairs grated across the bare floor as Raleigh rose from his seat.

'I have delivered your request to Essex House in person. At which point I was assured his Lordship was indisposed and could not be disturbed. I could hear sounds of merriment coming from the drawing room. He did indeed have guests, one of whom I am certain was Red Hugh. The man is not worth another word,' and with that Raleigh sat.

'The eyes have it that Guido has also frequented Essex House along with a few other notable reprobates,' Cecil folded his hands together on the table. 'We will send the High Sheriff to bring him in the day after tomorrow. To give him one more day to respond is more than fair in the current circumstances.'

'Another day, another week, the man will not change,' Raleigh sighed.

'We can only hope that is so,' Cecil almost smiled.

A Change of Plans

The sound of smashing glass could be heard out on the Strand, together with all manner of blasphemous language. Furniture crashed against walls as Essex rampaged around his home. 'Fortify the doors. Have the irons brought up from the cellar and fix them over every window,' Essex screwed up the note left by Raleigh, tossing it in the fire where the flames devoured it in a rush of heat.

Send a messenger at once to all the theatres, Richard II is going to be performed tomorrow, and further delay could cost our lives.' The door to the garden slammed shut.

'What has you in such a state? We have days before we ride.' Southampton placed his hands on Essex's shoulders as he gazed deep into the eyes of his friend. 'Such torment I have never seen upon your brow, not on the fields of Flanders, or the walls of Cádiz. Why are you so vexed?'

'That crusty turd of nature,' Essex huffed out the name, 'Cecil.'

Southampton pointed to the ashes in the fire, 'The letter?'

'It was a demand to attend the Privy Council, they wish to know of the visitors to my house and why I have flouted the restriction upon my travel,' Essex twisted out of the embrace. 'They are sending the High Sheriff to take me in,' Essex stabbed the logs in the fire with a poker. 'Southampton, you are the only one I can trust. Get Red Hugh to gather the men at the Globe tomorrow. We will party like never before. We will rally the city behind us and force Elizabeth to sign the succession order. Before the cock crows on the third day, I will have either the order signed or her head in my hands.' The flames raged higher with every stab of the poker.

THE GLOBE

Crowds milled along the frozen bank of the Thames under a bright winter sky. The bear baiting ring on the hardened mudflats by the river was emptying as the time of the performance drew near. Marketeers and merchants removed their wares, knowing for the next three hours the only people they would see were those coming to relieve themselves in the river before darting back to the play to see what they had missed. More still were crossing the Thames on foot, part-skating over the ice to avoid the prying eyes of the guards and crowds over the bridge.

Among the growing throng, the sing-song lilt of the Irish could be heard, their cheerfulness blending with their coarse banter. 'I hear it's a special performance tonight. Bit of royalty comin' to the south side,' one patron remarked.

'Bloody snobs, not worth another word. I would rather cast my lot among thieves. At least you know they're out to rob ya,' another sneered. 'Balls to 'em, I say. They have their palaces, and they can bloody stay there. The libertines belong to delightful souls, such as we.' Throwing his arm around his friend's shoulder, he punched the air and cheered. Those around them did the same, filling the air with joy and laughter. His friend slipped away to rouse another to his cause.

The fresh painted goat-hair plaster walls of the Globe reflected the sun upon the crowds, as they swarmed through the double iron-studded doors. Some paid their coin to ascend the stairs to watch the world from the seat of the gods. While the masses flocked forward to stand among the groundlings and bathe in the spatter of blood and whatever else may be flung from the stage.

Three thousand souls, packed to capacity, in the small theatre, gazed upon the decorative splendour of the heavens with its royal blue sky with golden stars and sun. The Roman pillars held its sculpted mass high above the stage were painted to appear imperial, giving the illusion of a grand palace from a bygone Roman age. From every level, the braying crowd would heckle and call out their views. Some would mock the few words they could hear above the cacophonous din of the common rabble. Even the nobles, who sat perched around the edge of the hallowed stage itself, often struggled to listen to the words expressed from the mouths of the actors. Some came to watch, and others came to partake. Some had paid all they had to spare, while others dipped a finger into their wealth, or abused their privileged rank to get in free.

Anne Hathaway and her two daughters sat at the front of the stage watching in wide-eyed wonder as Bolingbroke fights for all he believes in, while a weak and weary King does little for his people. Armies march to Ireland where they are lost and left to defect. Knights fought across the boards, and blood was spilt in more significant measure than ought to be. The crowds cheered and booed as the King was usurped.

And thus, a new king would strut the boards as the actors were changed without notice to the bard. Richard II limped forth, a broken man, his hair transformed from black to red and pearls strung about his neck as the clustered tears of a fallen kingdom. But fear not for Bolingbroke, the new king enters stage right.

The crowd is filled with mirth as Richard adjusts the crown upon his tatty wig. He attempts to curtsey, 'How to lament the cause. I'll beg one boon, and then be gone and trouble you no more. Shall I obtain it?'

Bolingbroke joined those seated around the stage, as Essex strutted out in his most elegant black and silver royal robes, his ruffed collar cutting a line across his throat, keeping his head tall and proud, 'Name it, fair cousin.' The crowd is in uproar as chants for Essex to be king come from all quarters. The actors continue unabated though no-one could hear a word being spoken

'Then give me leave to go,' Richard begs almost tripping over his words.

'Go wither?' Essex directs the crowd to cry out.

'To the Tower, to the Tower,' the baying crowd calls.

'Go, someone convey him to the Tower,' Essex swings a boot at the departing king. He stands triumphant, with one hand on his hip, as he waves to the adoring masses. 'On tomorrow's dawn, we solemnly set down our coronation. Friends, lords, everyone,' Essex rested his hands upon Shakespeare's daughters as he leaned over the audience. 'Prepare yourselves!' He surveyed the cheering crowd, three thousand voices calling his name. 'Unstop the barrels and have your fill. Celebrate my friends, for the night belongs to such as thee. But on the morrow, rise and come out upon the streets for we ride to Westminster where you will have a new king!'

The doors to the theatre swung open, barrels of ale were rolled in among the groundlings, as revelry overshadowed the play. Song broke out in every corner, singing out the exploits of Essex throughout his youth, from the Spanish Armada to the conquering of Ireland. Essex took his ale from the many offered to him. Drawing his golden sword, he raised it heavenward and gave a toast unto himself. Golden swords glittered throughout the theatre in victorious salute. A figure slipped through the crowds, bent over to hide his true stature. A giant among Elizabethans, Guido made his way to the stage where Essex was drooling over Judith and Susanne.

'I would suggest you lock them up with their father,' Guido glared at Essex. 'Now is not the time for your lust.'

Essex spun around, 'Put them in hell,' he ordered Southampton. 'I'll get their pleb father,' He walked out through the left stage door. 'William, William where for art though William?' Essex sloshed his drink around, with theatrical aplomb.

'Essex?' Shakespeare appeared around a corner coming to a sudden stop on the tip of Essex's sword. 'A place is reserved for you in hell. Do not fret, your family is already on their way. Now move. Your purpose is served,' Essex pointed the way with his sword. Shakespeare walked back to the stage, leaving Essex behind. He hesitated by the door to untie a small rope before he walked out onto the stage.

The whole theatre was in an intoxicated uproar. Wherever Shakespeare set his eyes there was fighting, feasting, and fornicating. No-one noticed him. All the wealthy nobles had fled the stage, leaving it bereft save for Southampton who stood with the door to hell open in the platform. 'Please William. For your own sake.'

'Tell me this is all a dream?' Shakespeare lowered himself into the hatch. Southampton's pitiful gaze followed him.

'Oh, do not waste another word on him, Southampton. The man is a mere fortune teller. A needy, hollow-eyed, sharp-looking wretch, A living dead man,' Essex grasped the edge of the hatch door. 'Here, for your relief.' The bucket clattered on the hard floor.

'Essex,' Shakespeare called. 'I do desire that we may be better strangers.' Essex opened his mouth, closed it, and slammed the hatch down. 'At last, we are all together,' William pulled his family unto him. 'Fear not, for this hell is not our final resting place.

The sounds of drunken revelry filled the night, as did the stench of vomit and urine, as the front of the stage became the favoured latrine. 'They will sleep soon, and the masters have all left for more comfortable quarters. Soon the ale will run out,' Shakespeare placed one hand on the shoulders of his daughters. 'We only have to wait until dawn to make our egress.'

The late afternoon drank its way into the oblivion of night. William shuffled over to the rear portion of the stage only to discover the rope to the door had been refastened.

The Shakespeare family held each other in a shivering bundle of humanity. The only light came from a guttering candle, left on the stage when its owner passed out while attempting to relieve themselves. It was to be a long, cramped night. Try as they might they could not resist the pull of sleep upon their eyes.

THE COUP

All too soon morning was upon the city. The cries of traders broke the crisp breath of winter. A familiar pompous tone called out to its loyal followers. 'My fellow men,' Essex puffed out his chest. 'Arm yourselves with the best of the Vatican.' Many chests were broken open among the groundlings. 'Take what you need. We have a city to stir, and a throne to capture.'

Gold handled swords were passed among the rebels, their Papal blades the finest any of them had ever laid their filthy hands on.

'William?' A hushed voice called through the rear exit of the stage. 'I have loosened the stage door. You can come out.'

'Marie? Is that you?'

'It is. I told you I would never be far away. Essex fastened the rope you untied. Now no one will fasten it.' There was a dull thud followed by the sound of something heavy being dragged across the floor.

'Marie! Marie!' William crawled across to the rear of the stage. Pressing his face against the panels, he tried to see what was happening.

'I am well, William, less can be said for the guards,' Marie opened the small door allowing the yellow light of her lamp to invade the gloom under the stage. 'Now hurry and be quiet.'

The Shakespeares crawled out of their temporary prison, allowing themselves a moment to straighten up.

'There is a clear route to the nearest door. We can be gone before anyone notices,' Marie hurried ahead while William followed with his family close to him, signalling them to remain silent. They walked past a guard who lay in a pool of his own blood, while another sat propped against the wall with an ugly swelling on his forehead. 'Marie is most effective,' he ushered his family past the recumbent guards out into the freezing morn.

'We must not delay. Essex will make his way to London Bridge as soon as they are all able to stand,' Marie ran ahead, pausing to tap three times on the door of the Bishop's Cap. The door opened but a hand's breadth. Marie's breath hung in the cold air as she conversed at the door. Shakespeare held his family as close as he could, as they ran down the shallow bank of the Thames and along the frozen mudflats towards Westminster.

'What do you mean gone!' Essex roared at the unfortunate messenger, as his fist slammed into the youth's face. 'You three, when you have finished playing with one another, get after them,' Essex wiped the spittle from his chin. 'Everybody out! We have no time to waste. Should that damn hack beat us to the prize, everything shall have been for nought,' His voice rang out into the streets. 'As if it was not misfortune enough to have the Lord Keeper and his men locked in my cellar, I must have this,' he hissed under his breath. The rabble ran out of the building, keen to escape.

With a sword in one hand, while trying to finish dressing with the other. Red Hugh waited on his horse; arms folded across his chest. He leaned down toward his squire, 'Tell every one of our men to keep behind me.' The squire gave an almost imperceptible nod and went about his task.

Essex strode out the theatre, kicking the door shut behind him. In a few strides he was at his horse, a breath later he was in the saddle with his Sagrada held high. 'For your King and country.' He pointed the sword forward and urged his horse on. The mob moved out, shouting and hollering for all to come and support the new king as he rode for Westminster. 'Join us and be the first to see Essex as King. Come out, come out. Essex for King,' They banged on doors and rattled windows in a bid to rouse the city.

By the time they had reached London Bridge, with its tall houses and narrow streets, they had more than two hundred men. Essex at the front, still waving his sword, and soaking up the adulation of the masses. They crossed the bridge and followed the bank side, marching through the fishermen and merchants, grabbing every loose and idle soul they put a sword in their hand, and a coin in their purse. The ranks of the ignorant pushed their number to beyond three hundred and the time had come to push on to the seat of power.

Westminster Palace loomed on the distant bank of the river; its bare stone walls a cracked reflection upon the frozen Thames. Children on bone skates wove among the growing number of market stalls and traders setting up shop on the ice. Crows swooped down to catch morsels, only to fall victim to a fowlers snare.

'Ready William? How's your balance?' Marie pushed Shakespeare onto the ice. 'Go, with haste.'

'Hold, you servant of a whore!' A deep voice commanded.

'Guido,' Marie glanced at Shakespeare. 'Run!' William slid and slipped his way through the market, begging the pardon of those with whom he collided. Marie drew her sword and dagger. 'Ready?' She twirled the small blade in her fingers.

'Pray Mary is merciful as you descend,' Guido drew his sword from its sheath taking a moment to admire the craftsmanship. He strode toward Marie with his Sagrada pressed to his lips.

Marie stepped aside, avoiding a vicious thrust. Guido swung around, overreaching with a clenched fist. His foot slipped on the frozen earth. 'Careful of your footing,' she teased, lunging at his side, her sword cut through his cape. She danced around the iced pools, dodging every attempt on her life. Twice more she cut through his clothing, once deep enough to find the flesh beneath.

'Stand and fight,' Guido raged, as he flung himself forward.

'I think not,' Marie ran for the frozen river, Guido lunged again, catching her shoulder with the tip of his blade. Blood oozed from a small cut. 'I've bled worse on my curses.'

'You disgusting whore. Ending your life will bring honour to God,' Guido stepped onto the ice.

'Your view of the divine is twisted. You are more wicked than the devil himself,' Marie continued to back away toward the far shore, the sound of traders barking out their wares rang in her ears.

'You will find no shelter among those filthy wretches. Your stench could be followed anywhere,' Guido frowned as he saw Shakespeare being helped up from the ice onto the Westminster jetty. 'You have kept me long enough.' He thrust forward. Marie dove for the ground sliding beneath his blade and through his legs. She stuck her dagger upward into Guido's groin. The big man crumpled to the ice dropping his sword. Marie scrambled to her feet snatching up Guido's sword.

'You're not the big man you appear to be, I missed everything,' Marie glanced over to the Palace, Shakespeare was nowhere to be seen. 'I'm not the killer you are. I hope you die slowly,' she stabbed his sword through his boot, Guido screamed as the bones in his foot moved to accommodate the blade.

'You will burn in hell for this,' Guido spat.

'Must be going,' Marie left Guido to vent his vexation and followed Shakespeare's egress.

A bright sun shone on the Strand, and the Essex rebellion passed Temple Bar. 'Come join the new King!' The cheering mob cried as they advanced on their quarry.

'I am surprised he has so many willing to follow him,' Red Hugh eased up to allow another group of would-be warriors to join the ranks. 'But I have yet to see any who appear as though they could handle a sword.'

'And yet they conquer the known world with such as these. Essex is well loved, more than his cousin, The Queen.' Southampton rode forward, cheering with the troops as he went.

'How fairs the crew?' Essex asked, as Southampton fell in step at his side.

'The mood is right, and the spirits are high,' Southampton rode with a satisfied smile.

'A man is easily bought, the mere promise of something better is sufficient to persuade most fools,' Essex pointed to the road ahead, where everyone was fleeing the street. 'What is that?'

'I shall go and see,' Southampton urged his horse into a gallop, its hooves clattered and splattered on the muck strewn streets. 'You there,' he called to the man with a clanging bell in his hand. 'What is the urgency?'

'Sire,' the man paused in his task. 'I have been ordered by Lord Cecil to proclaim, the Earl of Essex traitor. 'Is that him? I must alert his lordship at once.' The man turned, ringing his bell with all his might as he ran for his master. Southampton turned about and charged back to Essex.

'Well? Spit it out man,' Essex demanded.

'Cecil has declared you a traitor. It is now or never Essex,' Southampton puffed.

'Oh, traitor am I,' Essex turned in his saddle. 'The time is now men. We charge on Westminster,' Essex reared his horse and led the charge toward Charing Cross.

The clatter of rebel hooves on cold swept stone stomped toward the Court Gate of Westminster, from where the soldiers spilt out. Essex swung out of the Strand, arcing into the broad square, his bloodthirsty warriors hot on his trail. Charring Cross filled, as his three hundred rebels spread out to meet the forces of the Royal Guard. Red Hugh kept his men to the rear of the square, where more guards were emerging from St Martin in the Field and the old Reading way. Soldiers closed in on all sides.

Essex rushed toward a small palisade strewn with haste across the gateway where a familiar figure stood waiting. 'Come, boy, 'tis time you learnt what it means to fight like a man,' Raleigh drew his sword as he walked through the barricade.

'Is this all she has to defend her? Old men?' Essex tossed his head back and laughed. Soldiers surged out around the barricade, lowering their pikes into the affray. Swords clashed, and bones snapped, as steel struck home. Southampton parried a half-hearted lunge aside as he turned his horse about. The animal kicked out at anything close enough, friend and foe went clattering to the floor.

A drunken rebel rushed at Raleigh, in a swift cut ale spewed from his gut to the street. Raleigh pressed forward, calling his men at arms to his side, he made for Essex. The sound of musket balls chimed across the courtyard, ricocheting off armour and brick. The peasants fell to the might of The Queen's men. A pretty blade no match against a skilled hand.

Essex reared his horse, attempting to crush Raleigh, but the old warrior was too smart for such an elaborate move. He side-stepped the horse and threw his weight against its flank, sending the animal into the crowd. Essex pulled hard on his reins, turning his horse for a quick kick at his assailant. Raleigh was not there. 'Boy!' Essex turned toward the voice, as a gauntleted fist punched his calf. Essex yelped, as the pain shot up his leg. A second blow spurred him into action, and he lashed at his fleet-footed assailant, his sword glancing off Raleigh's shield. Hands pulled at his stirrup. Essex swung again, this time he succeeded in sending Raleigh to the floor. He glanced over the melee. The army was pressing in. Red Hugh and his men were retreating up the Strand. He kicked his horse into action and charged through the battle with mad abandon. By the time he reached the Cross, the fight was done. The fire had left their bellies. His men scattered as ashes in the wind.

Essex, sensing defeat, rode hard to his home. Jumping from his mount, he ran inside and bolted the door. Moving from room to room, he closed the shutters, and sealed them with iron bars. In the silence of his home, he stood; waiting. His heart pounded in his chest, demanding release from captivity. Sweat poured from him, though his house was cold and near dark. A solitary candle flickered in the draft coming through the cracks in the doorframe, where reinforcements had been made in haste. He swallowed against the rising bile in his throat, his tongue sticking to the roof of his mouth.

Dust motes drifted in the candlelight as Essex watched the door. It felt as though the whole house was dying. A fury of voices outside, amid the clump of hooves. The hinges rattled with the force of blows. A deep angry roar of something ancient stirring from its slumber. Something inevitable as night called his name, 'Essex, open up in the name of The Queen. There is no escape, we have your home surrounded,' Raleigh commanded.

Essex took a half-step back. He licked at his lips, but there was nothing to wet them. 'I demand a fair trial. I fear my intentions may have been misunderstood.' The door handle rattled in his grasp.

'You are under arrest for high treason,' a new voice, older, emotionless. 'You will be tried by the highest court in the land.'

'I might have guessed you would be here to gloat, toad,' Essex rested his head against the door as he slid the bolts back. The fading light caused him to squint as he opened the door, allowing his captors to take him.

'Take him to the Tower,' Cecil stepped aside to allow the guards to take Essex. 'I will question him myself.' Essex glared at his captors; his mouth drawn into a tight line. 'Fear not, I shall go gentle,' Cecil smiled. 'At first.'

'Move,' Raleigh shoved Essex in the middle of his back. 'Traitor coming through!'

'Enjoy it while you can, Raleigh,' Essex tried to wrestle free from the guard's grasp. With a deep groan, he collapsed to the floor beneath the weight of the guard.

'Try it again, and I will break your arms,' the guard pressed his knee into Essex's back. 'Do you understand?'

'Yes,' Essex cried out, nodding his head. The guard stood, ensuring Essex felt every move he made.

'Now move,' the guard shoved Essex toward his horse, where he tied one end of a rope to the pommel, and the other he fastened around Essex's wrists. 'My Lord,' he passed the reigns to Raleigh.

'This saddens me,' Raleigh mounted Essex's horse and urged it forward pulling the failed king behind him.

SIGN YOUR NAME

Elizabeth stared at the parchment on her desk. No amount of sunshine streaming through the window could make it pleasant. The document detailed all Essex had to say. 'Why would he do this?' She asked more of herself than Cecil, who waited at her side. 'How tight were the manacles to make him confess to this?'

'There were none,' Cecil offered, both surprised and disappointed. 'Reverend Abdy Ashton led him to confession. He simply sat and gave up every one of his associates. He has a particular dislike for his sister Penelope. It would appear she was passed around as a favour to all who took interest.'

'Do you believe it to be so?' Elizabeth held the quill between her fingers as though she might break it.

'What I believe is of no importance concerning Lady Penelope. It is the number of high lords that is of interest to me. Most of them I knew about: Mountjoy, Davies, Cuffe, Southampton of course, though Meyrick and Danvers are something new.'

'Must I sign? He is all that remains of my blood,' Elizabeth put the quill aside. Balling her fists, she banged the table. 'I will not do it! I cannot send my last relative to the gallows,' she turned to face Cecil, her eyes red, her breath short and sharp.

'Then he will rot in a traitors' jail and the people,' Cecil paused, 'the people will see you as weak. Had he been a common man —'

'But he is not a common man. He should not be treated as such.' Elizabeth injected.

'Was Mary a commoner? Or your mother?'

'How dare you!' Elizabeth snatched the parchment from the desk, thrusting it into Cecil's chest. 'My mother was unwanted, my father, he ... ' Elizabeth drew herself up. 'He was wrong. Mary was plotting my death.'

Now Cecil cut in, 'As was Essex, he is also guilty of kidnapping and imprisonment. How many more times will he be allowed to mock the crown? With the backing of Ireland and Spain,' Cecil halted. He took a handkerchief from his pocket and dabbed The Queen's tears.

'I know,' Elizabeth returned to her desk and smoothed out the parchment. 'A war is coming like no other. Spain has a new armada, and old foe has been brought to the helm to command it. It is only a matter of time,' She dipped the quill into the inkwell and watched the dark liquid bleed from its nib.

'Indeed, Majesty.'

'He always did want my signature,' she held the quill with a firm grip. 'Now, at last, he has it,' Elizabeth blotted the ink and passed the paper to Cecil. 'To think he who would betray me has sat at my table all along. Take it and do what you must.' Cecil took the paper and backed from the presence of The Queen.

THE TOWER

Cold wind sliced through the cell, dividing marrow from bone. Essex shuddered in the gloom as he picked at the remnants of his last meal. He watched his breath dissipate in the candle's light. Soon the sun would rise, and light would shine upon him from the small window. He would enjoy a moment of warmth until his hour came.

There was the stiff squeak of steel as the inspection window opened in his cell door.

'Get yourself in order. Your time will be at one of the clock. Be ready,' the Yeoman sniffed. 'Your pretty face didn't help yer this time. Like the young girl your grandfather held in this cell,' He slid the tiny window shut and walked away. A sliver of light from the winter's morn cut into the gloom, lighting nothing more than the sorrow on Essex's face.

'Yea, though I walk through the valley of the shadow of death,' the Earl watched his breath rise to the heavens, carrying his hopes to the Mercy Seat itself. 'I shall fear no evil.' A smile played at the corner of his mouth. 'For if you are with me,' He rose from his mattress of straw, teased his beard between his finger and thumb and stood tall. 'Then ... ' He cleared his throat and pronounced every word with increasing aplomb, 'who can stand against ME,' He laughed to himself. The cold stone tower took his voice and it stirred with cries of ancient blood. The distant wail from a Scavenger's Daughter wracked across his mind. 'At least I am to be spared such ruin,' Essex dusted the cell detritus from his sleeves as he walked toward the light, piercing the darkness through the slit in the wall. He watched the sun claw its way across the sky and strike upon the scaffold where he would climb the stair and bare his neck.

'Brave words indeed,' Sir Walter tried to resist gloating. 'I should like to introduce you to an old acquaintance of yours,' Raleigh beckoned the lean figure to come forward.

'I didn't hear you knock, Sir Walter,' Essex folded his arms across his chest. 'But you always were a sneak. They'll catch you one day. Your luck will run out sure enough.'

'That as it may, today is all about you. But then isn't every day?'

'So, who is this?' Essex straightened up, placing one hand on his hip. 'Not the kind of person I would be seen dead with.'

'The name's Thomas Derrick, sir,' the man met Essex's glaring eyes. 'You gave me this job,' he added with a half-smile.

'Never met a Derrick in my entire life, I'm sure of it,' Essex threw back his head and laughed.

'You caught him raping a girl in Westminster, sent him here as executioner. Ironic really,' Raleigh twisted the ends of his moustache into tight points. He took a small red pouch from his belt, holding it out to Derrick. 'Here you are, my good man. Do a thorough job,' Raleigh reached out for the door handle. 'As much as it grieves me, you deserve this Essex. Oh, and should you see your friend Guido, or Guy Fawkes, whichever name he should appear under, send him my regards,' He closed the door, leaving Essex him to contemplate his end.

Essex listened to the roar of the lions as the jungle cats of the menagerie called for meat. The bright noon sun peered in through the window, its scant heat could not drive out the winter chill. Essex shuddered in the cold embrace of his cage.

Footsteps broke the silence. Heavy, purposeful steps, ''Tis time.' the key clunked in the lock. 'Your hour approaches,' the constable of the tower swung the heavy iron-bound oak door open, its weary hinges groaned their lament at the passing of another soul. 'Your attire ... sir,' he tossed the bundle into the cell and folded his hands behind his back while he waited for Essex to dress.

'Is there no privacy! I am the Earl of Essex ... '

'Guilty as charged. You'll get the same axe as the lumber they used to build your scaffold,' the constable stepped aside to allow Essex to pass. 'Follow the guard. Keep your eyes to the ground. In here your position is always low. Now move,' He shoved Essex in the back, urging him along the dark corridor. The flickering torch guttered as winter's breath attempted to snatch the flame at every turn. The soft scuff of leather across the stone floor interspersed with the thump of the guard's boots as they led the Earl to the parade ground. The smell of death stirred memories of his days of glory against the Dutch, but the moment soured in his mouth as the reek of excreta and rotting flesh turned into a foreboding incense.

The bright winter light burst through the open door temporarily blinding Essex as he stepped from the gloom into the purifying February afternoon. He walked along with two pairs of Yeoman Warders. Their velvet cloaks shrouded their armour, this was to be no formal affair. The entourage walked west from the White Tower. Turned sharp north where the halberdiers flowed around an oak platform: four feet high, three yards across, railed around with small poles.

Essex drew a deep breath, watching its warmth evaporate. A hiatus of life before it passed into memory. He placed his hand upon the rail, sliding it up toward the platform five steps away. The wood felt warm to his touch despite the winter chill upon it. Glistening on the ebony plumage of a raven picking through the straw-strewn platform, the bright sun shone from the pale blue sky.

As he climbed the steps, the panorama of the parade ground opened before him. He scrutinised the handpicked audience: The Earl of Ormond and his Lady wife, his sister Lady Rich, Sir Francis Bacon, Lord Munro with Shakespeare, and Raleigh, the last to take up his seat, scuttling in from who knew where. He turned his head to the north where his gaze rested upon the Devereux Tower, 'Oh grandfather,' he breathed, 'what shame have I brought upon our blood?' A gentle hand on his back pressed him forward to the platform where the block waited to grasp his throat. He turned his head toward the crowd once more, at least he had been spared the public humiliation of Tower Hill. A priest stood to his left with a small vellum-bound book of common prayer.

'Are you in need of absolution? Have you cleansed your soul of all sin?' The priest spoke in a solemn tone, his head inclined toward Essex.

'I am absolved. I stand ready to pass from this life into the open arms of M ... ' Essex paused, 'My God.' He raised his hand to his collar releasing the clasp on his black cloak. With a flourish, he swirled the cloak over the Priest's hands closing the prayer book. 'You may take your leave,' he waved the priest from the platform.

His scarlet satin waistcoat brought sighs from the ladies gathered, handsome and debonair to the last. Robert Devereux, 2nd Earl of Essex, stood with his feet apart, his hands on his hips, he raised his head and smiled. 'I desire you my Lords here present, to see my just punishment,' He paused to drink in this moment 'The number of my sins are more than the hairs on my head,' He bowed his head, before lifting it higher, 'I pray you all pray with me that when you see my arms outstretched, my neck,' he made a sweeping gesture toward his feet, 'upon the block and the strike to be given, it may please God to send down his angels and lift my soul to His mercy's seat.'

Essex grasped the handrail with one hand, while performing a small bow to Raleigh seated opposite. A thud to his right drew his attention. Clad in black, his face covered by a leather mask, as dark as night, the executioner waited. The scarred steel axe was held in his right hand with the end of the handle resting on his worn leather boot.

'It is time,' the executioner pointed to the floor.

Essex walked the few steps around the platform and knelt, the golden straw was smooth against his palms as he lowered his neck to the block. He closed his eyes, the scent of the straw took him back to autumn days spent riding through the countryside of his beloved England with Elizabeth at his side When he opened his eyes,

Raleigh was goading on the executioner but it was not for him to choose when the axe would fall.

The bell tolled one.

'Executioner,' Essex thrust his arms out, 'strike home.'

There was silence and a soft thud. Lady Rich shrieked, Essex's eyes widened, he could feel a tugging at the back of his neck and heat as his blood flowed upon the straw.

Another short hiatus and the axe fell again. Raleigh clenched the purse in his hand chuckling. Essex's head tipped forward; his hands grasped at the straw. Pain-wracked through his body. It was a bright day, why was his world turning dark? Again, something tugged at his neck, a little grinding of bone on steel. One more time the axe was raised. One more time it sunk into the Earl's pale flesh. This time his head rolled free.

The executioner stooped to retrieve the severed head, holding it aloft by its hair he proclaimed aloud, 'Long live The Queen.'

'The Jack of Hearts has fallen. His friends will no doubt be after you too Shakespeare. Those chains might be for show now,' Lord Munro tapped a finger on the manacles around Shakespeare's wrists. 'But the heart of her Majesty is fickle. You should not have let him,' Munro waved a hand toward the scaffold, 'have that play. And all for a few pounds!' Shakespeare lifted his gaze from the ground, his face ashen, his brow laden with regret.

ALAS

The late summer sun faded with the afternoon as its warm caress turned a cold shoulder. The table had been set for a select audience, among them Raleigh and Cecil sat in a snug corner with their Queen. Elizabeth, captivated by the master storyteller as he wound up the angst of the last lament of Henry Bolingbroke,

'I'll make a voyage to the Holy Land
To wash this blood off from my guilty hand:
March sadly after; grace my mournings here;
In weeping after this untimely bier.'

Shakespeare bowed before The Queen of England.

'Bravo,' Master Shakespeare, 'Bravo,' Elizabeth stripped the gloves from her hands and applauded with all her might. 'Never has one put it so bold as you. I salute your bravery on all sides,' She beckoned Shakespeare to stand before her. 'In truth you were trapped in a difficult space. Had you remained at the Globe you would have been guilty by association, and likely as not been killed by Essex. But you chose the greater risk: to come before the throne and warn your Queen of the imminent threat. Such courage is a rare thing. What can I do to thank you? Name it, and it shall be yours.'

'Ma'am, to stand before you and see you in such rude health is reward in itself. There is however one small thing I would request of you,' Shakespeare took a long breath.

'Which is?' Elizabeth smiled.

'To be struck from the record. I wish only to be remembered for my words. I am no hero. I am not a warrior, or a knight. I have not the skills of Cecil, or Raleigh. I am but a bard, that is all I wish to be.'

Elizabeth studied Raleigh and Cecil, her lips pursed with a plethora of questions, 'Can it be done?'

'It can, as far as I have influence,' Cecil stated, with the slightest tilt of his head.

'Then let it be so,' Elizabeth stood. 'William Shakespeare of Stratford, I hereby decree all record of your involvement in anything beyond stage and curtain be removed from all records both past and future.'

'Thank you, ma'am,' Shakespeare bowed again. 'It has been the greatest honour to serve your Majesty.'

'This, however, does not mean your time at the Palace is over. I should very much like The Lord Chamberlain's Men to perform before me here. Furthermore, it would delight me to have you read your works to me in private.'

'As you wish, your Majesty.'

'Is there anything else on the agenda?' Elizabeth turned a questioning eye on Cecil.

'The Irish await the Spanish fleet,' Cecil sighed.

Elizabeth slumped into her seat, 'What did that boy unleash upon us?'

Thanks for reading.

I hope you enjoyed this story. I would appreciate your feedback, please consider leaving a review.

Printed in Great Britain
by Amazon